CHASING HER FIRE

A SMALL-TOWN ROMANCE

BAILEY BROTHERS
BOOK 5

CLAIRE KINGSLEY

Always Have LLC

ISBN: 9798506588559

Published by Always Have, LLC

Edited by Susan Gottfried

Cover Design: Lori Jackson

www.clairekingsleybooks.com

❀ Created with Vellum

For everyone who's wanted to see Logan and Cara hate sex since book two.
You're welcome.

ABOUT THIS BOOK

Sexy firefighter Logan Bailey is an expert at putting the wet stuff on the hot stuff—on and off duty. But he just did the unthinkable, and it wasn't trading in his tube socks. He slept with his nemesis. His mortal enemy. The crazy redhead he loves to hate. Cara Goulding.

And no matter how much he wants to lie to himself, he has to admit, it was mind-blowing.

Cara will not be tempted by the one night she spent with prince dickhead—even if her traitorous body remembers every earth-shattering moment. It was a mistake and she's stronger than that. She'll just keep avoiding him and pretend it didn't happen.

But the feuding small town of Tilikum might not be big enough for the both of them. Avoiding each other isn't working. And with every moment they're forced to spend together, the sparks get hotter, the flames grow brighter, and the tension borders on unbearable.

Until they both reach their breaking point and their fiery relationship explodes.

PROLOGUE: LOGAN

This prologue also appears as the epilogue at the end of Rushing In: Bailey Brothers Book 4.

My head swam and the walls spun in a dizzying circle. I was so fucking drunk I could barely stand. But I really didn't care. All that mattered was getting my fucking pants off.

Why was that so hard?

Too much alcohol. That was why.

She grabbed my shirt and yanked me toward her. Our mouths crashed together, tongues darting out. She tasted like bourbon. So fucking delicious.

I kept fumbling with my pants and finally got the button open. Zipper down. Good. Get them off. Gotta get naked. Was she naked? Didn't know. Couldn't see. Probably because my eyes were closed.

Her hand wrapped around my dick and I grunted hard.

Apparently my pants were down around my ankles. Had I blacked out for a second? Maybe.

Fuck it. I didn't care. Felt too good.

We stumbled a few steps and tipped over. I couldn't quite remember where I was, but I was sure glad there was a bed here to catch me. I rolled over, pinning her on her back, and crawled on top of her.

I thrust between her legs, but my erection hit fabric. Damn it, what was in my way? I needed to fuck her, and I needed to do it now.

Bracing myself with one arm, I reached down between us. Panties. I hooked my finger beneath them and groaned. Silky wetness waited for me in there. I slid my finger up and down a few times.

She ripped them down her legs and kicked them off, then grabbed my shirt and hauled me closer. Suddenly her tongue was in my mouth and her pussy was hot and ready for me.

I shifted my weight, trying to line up my cock with her opening, but I lost my balance and toppled over. Damn it. I couldn't be too drunk to fuck her. I was hard as steel. If the room would just stop spinning for a fucking second, I could get this done.

She whimpered something that sounded like *fuck me now*. I sat up and manhandled her, rolling her onto her stomach. Then I grabbed her hips and lifted her ass in the air. Kneeling behind her, I drove my cock in.

The rush of sensation almost knocked me over again. She was so hot. So wet. So tight around me. I held her hips and thrust into her, slamming my cock into her pussy.

So fucking good.

She arched her back and I reached up to grab a handful

of her hair. Oh yeah. Now I had her right where I wanted her.

I plunged into her, yanking on her hair, my dick sliding through her wetness. She cried out a steady stream of yeses while I fucked her as hard as I could. I was an animal—grunting, muscles flexing. I couldn't remember where I was or how I'd gotten here. I just knew that this was fucking awesome.

Her pussy clenched around my cock and I grunted again. She arched harder, moaning, and her inner muscles pulsed. I slowed down, thrusting with her rhythm while she came all over my dick.

Hell yes. Not too drunk to make her come.

The room tilted, and I closed my eyes to keep from falling over. The tension in my groin skyrocketed, heat and pressure building. My back stiffened and I drove into her again, sinking my cock in deep.

I exploded inside her, coming so hard my consciousness faded. I just kept thrusting, plunging in and out of her while my cock throbbed. The hot pulses of my orgasm kicked the breath from my lungs and by the time it was over, I wasn't sure if I could take any more.

Fuck.

I slid out of her and she slumped onto the bed, like she couldn't hold herself up anymore. I certainly couldn't. My sense of balance was gone, and I fell onto the mattress next to her, my vision going black.

I WOKE up in a dark room. Where the fuck was I?

Still too drunk. Couldn't think.

Shirt was on. No pants. Where were my pants? Groaning

at the way my head swam, I rolled over. Somehow got to my feet. My pants were on the floor, so I grabbed them and tugged them on. Took a few tries.

Too fucking drunk.

Wait, had I fucked someone tonight?

Blinking, I looked around. The room was empty. Bed made, although the covers were rumpled. No one was in here, so I probably hadn't.

Confused, I grabbed my dick through my pants. It really felt like I'd fucked someone. And why had my pants been off?

But maybe it had been a dream.

A really good dream. But still a dream.

And I took my pants off all the time. That wasn't weird.

I was too drunk to know for sure, or to figure out why I was in someone's bedroom in the first place. I had a vague memory of Levi telling me I should go lie down. Maybe I had.

Whatever. I needed to find my phone.

It was hard to keep my eyes open as I stumbled out of the room. Where was my phone?

I just needed to call Levi for a ride.

1

LOGAN

Groaning, I sank my cock deep inside her. Fuck, that felt good. I held her hips, hauling her against me as I pounded her from behind. Slam. Slam. Slam. I was going to come any second, but it didn't matter because she was already coming all over me.

Hell yes.

A few more hard thrusts and I was done for. I growled like an animal while I came deep inside her, my cock pulsing with my release. With my hands still gripping her hips, she looked back at me over her shoulder and—

"Logan!"

Sucking in a breath, I jerked awake. What the fuck?

Levi banged on my bedroom door. "Are you up yet?"

I grumbled something my brother couldn't hear. It was our day off. Why was he in such a hurry? The least he could do was let a guy sleep in.

And I'd been having a good fucking dream.

Except she was—

No. She was nobody. Just an amalgam of past pussy. Not real.

I started to roll out of bed but stopped. My sheets felt... wet. I lifted the navy-blue bedding and looked.

Oh, for fuck's sake. Again?

I groaned in frustration. Something was wrong with me. Maybe I needed to see a doctor. I'd had more wet dreams in the past few weeks than I'd ever had as a teenager. That couldn't be normal.

And now I had to find a way to wash my sheets without my brothers noticing. If those assholes caught me doing laundry again, they'd never let me hear the end of it.

Maybe I needed to start sleeping on a towel.

I hauled my ass out of bed, squinting at the light streaming through the broken blinds, and narrowly missed hitting my shin on a plastic laundry basket. My station wear —the clothes I wore while on duty—were hung up in my closet, but I usually tossed the rest of my clean clothes in the basket.

Bending over, I dug out a pair of gummy bear boxer briefs and dragged them on. I had to wear something. Gavin lived here, which meant his fiancée Skylar was here so much, she basically lived here, too. That was fine—Skylar was a cool chick—except I couldn't walk around naked, and my room shared a wall with theirs.

Earplugs came in handy. I didn't want to think about the fact that my little brother was getting laid much more often than me.

Because, Jesus, I hadn't gotten laid in a long time.

Except—

No. No thinking about that.

I scrubbed my hands over my face and went to take a shower. I had to wash the fucking jizz off.

∼

AFTER MY SHOWER, I dropped the towel on my bed and grabbed the first set of clothes I could find that smelled clean. My t-shirt had a hole in it, but whatever. I threw a flannel on over it and tugged on some socks and a pair of jeans, then went out to find my brother.

Levi tossed a video game controller onto the cluttered coffee table, narrowly missing a soda can, and raised his eyebrows. We were identical twins, but seriously, he looked nothing like me. We had the same dark hair, same brown eyes, sharp cheekbones, and square jaws. Okay, so we had the same face, but I still maintained we didn't look alike. I figured it was because Levi hated to have fun, but I lived for it.

"What?" I asked.

"Are you done putting on your makeup?"

"Why are you in such a hurry? Yesterday Gram said to come over *sometime tomorrow*. That doesn't mean we have to be at her house at eight."

"Which is good because it's ten-fifteen."

I ignored him. Gavin's black and white cat, Princess Squeaker, jumped off the couch and rubbed against my leg. I picked her up and snuggled her against my chest.

"There's my girl."

She meowed at me, which sounded more like a squeak, hence her name.

I rubbed her head. "Are you hungry?"

"I already fed her."

"Then I guess you need a treat." I kept her tucked against my chest and took her to the kitchen.

"Don't give her too many," Levi called from the other room.

"Okay, Mom." I rooted around the cupboards until I

found the cat treats, then set Princess down and gave her a handful. "Why is he always trying to ruin our fun, huh?"

"Can we go?" Levi asked.

I gave Princess one last stroke down her back. "Yeah. I'll drive."

Levi didn't argue. I shoved my feet in a pair of shoes— they were probably mine—and we went out to my car.

"Hey baby." I ran my hand over the front fender of my 1970 Chevelle. She was black with a double white stripe on the hood. A fucking classic. She was still in rough shape—she needed a lot of work to get her back to her former glory—but lately she'd been running. That was progress.

Evan, our second oldest brother, was the car guy in the family. He'd made a career out of restoring cars like this. Muscle cars weren't my living—I was a firefighter for the Tilikum Fire Department—but I'd wanted a Chevelle ever since I got a Hot Wheels replica in my Christmas stocking when I was nine. I'd scored this one quite a few years ago, although she'd spent more time in my garage than on the road.

Soon that was going to change. I'd been saving so I could afford to hire Evan to do a full restoration. I had the money. Now it was just a matter of Evan having time in his schedule.

The driver's side door was heavy and tended to stick, so I yanked it open and climbed in. Levi got in the passenger side. It took him three tries to get the door closed.

My baby needed work, but she was going to be hot when she was done.

I turned the key and the engine revved but didn't turn over. "Come on, Betty."

"We can take mine."

"She'll be fine." I held the steering wheel in a gentle grip and gave her a second. Then tried again.

Her engine gave a satisfying rumble, the vibration moving through the whole car.

"That's my Betty. Good girl."

"You know it's weird that your girlfriend is a car, right?"

I laughed, stroking the steering wheel. "She's the love of my life."

"You could fall in love with worse," he mumbled under his breath.

"What?"

"Nothing. Let's go."

I pulled out of the driveway and headed down the street toward Gram's. It was the beginning of February, so Tilikum was still covered in a thick blanket of snow. We wouldn't see the ground until March, most likely. But it hadn't snowed in a few days, so the roads were mostly clear. I had to admit, owning a muscle car when you lived in the mountains had its disadvantages. Betty drove like shit when there was snow on the road. But I loved her too much to care.

"Speaking of girls, we should go out tonight," I said.

Levi made a noncommittal noise in his throat.

"Come on, man. I need to get laid. So do you, I might add."

"Shut up."

"I'm not taking no for an answer. Fucking Gav is engaged, so he won't go out with me. Most of the idiots at work are married. You're the only wingman I have left."

It was weird, but over the last few years, most of the friends I used to party with had either gotten married or left Tilikum. Or both. My crew had dwindled to the point that I had to beg my grumpy-ass twin to go out if I didn't want to hit the bars alone.

"What else do you have going on tonight?"

He opened his mouth like he was going to say no, then paused. "Fine. Whatever. But I'm driving separately."

"Sounds good, brodentical, because I don't plan on going home alone."

Gram only lived a mile or so away from us, in the house where we'd grown up. Our parents had died when we were kids, so Gram and Grandad Bailey had taken us in. The old farmhouse had a big porch and a yellow front door. Gram's gardens kept her busy, as did her chickens. Every time she referred to them as her peckers, it made me laugh like a twelve-year-old kid.

Granted, I probably had the sense of humor of a twelve-year-old.

I eased Betty into the driveway next to Grace's car. I didn't think much about why my sister-in-law would be here. Gram's house was a second home to all of us. Plus, Grace was pregnant and Gram was the best cook in Tilikum. She probably made up reasons to come over just to see what Gram was baking.

Hell, I did that all the time and I was only eating for one.

We got out, our shoes crunching in the snow. It was cold as shit out here. I was glad Gram had asked us to come help her move some furniture around, rather than do something outside.

The smell of fresh-baked bread wafted out as soon as Levi opened the front door. I knew she'd have something baking. If we were lucky, there'd be cookies too.

We found Gram in the kitchen, sitting at the big farm-house table our grandad had built. The whitewashed cupboards had more than a few dents, and light filtered past the blue checkered curtain in the window.

Gram looked up from her tea. Her hair was more silver

than black now, but she still wore it in a long braid down her back. Lines creased her dark skin, especially around her eyes, and they deepened with her smile.

Grace sat with her at the table with a steaming cup of tea. Her blond hair was cut in a short bob and she'd tucked it behind her ears. We'd grown up next door to Grace, and she'd married my oldest brother Asher. Now she was pregnant with Gram's first great-grandchild.

"Ladies," I said, pretending to tip a hat. "Bailey twins at your service. What can we do for you?"

"Jack and Elijah built me some new bookshelves," Gram said. Jack was Grace's stepdad and Elijah was her younger brother. Once I'd have called him her *little* brother, but he wasn't so little anymore. The kid was growing up fast. "I need to make some space in the front room, so I thought we could move things around in there."

"Sounds good. Just tell us where you want everything."

I whirled around, ready to get to work, and almost had a fucking heart attack.

It was *her*.

Cara stood a few feet in front of me—way too close for comfort—her red hair loose around her face. I had a sudden vision of her flipping that hair over her bare shoulder. But not standing, like she was now. Bent over in front of me, naked, all that flaming red hair cascading over her pale skin.

Fuck.

I'd successfully avoided her for the last few weeks, and I did not like being in close quarters with her now.

"What the fu—" I stopped myself from saying *fuck* just in time. No matter how old we got, Gram still didn't tolerate swearing in her house. "What are you doing here?"

Her green eyes narrowed and she lifted her chin,

drawing my gaze to the slope of her throat. I wanted to run my tongue up—

Nope. No I didn't.

The hard-on I was suddenly sporting might have suggested otherwise. But come on, that was just my dick. Everyone knows you can't trust a man's junk.

Especially when it comes to crazy redheads.

She opened her mouth to speak and I braced for impact, knowing whatever she said was going to piss me off. In fact, the simple act of her lips parting was already pissing me off.

But her eyes flicked to Gram and Grace behind me, and I could practically see the bitchy comment die on her lips. "I'm having tea with Gram and my boo."

The fact that she was behaving herself in front of Gram kind of made me want to do the opposite. To pick a fight with her in Gram's kitchen, just because I didn't want her to be right. Ever. But I decided it was probably best if I didn't. Because quite honestly, I wasn't sure if I could trust my mouth any more than I could trust my dick around her right now.

"Whatever," I grumbled and moved past her, giving her a wide berth.

A few weeks ago, before the night of Skylar's book launch party, I would have fired off a smart-ass comment. But now? I was worried if we started going at each other, like we usually did, I'd say something that would give me away.

I'd been drunk as fuck, but I knew what had happened. Every time I saw her, even at a distance, my body reminded me. I'd done the unthinkable.

I'd fucked Cara Goulding.

2

CARA

"What are you doing here?"

The asshole's eyes were on me and I couldn't tell if the look on his face meant he wanted to fuck or fight. Not that I was going to give him the satisfaction of doing either. I darted a quick glance at the table. Grace looked worried, like she was calculating whether she could get her adorably pregnant self out of her seat quickly enough to stop me from murdering her brother-in-law.

Gram just looked mildly amused.

They didn't need to worry. I wasn't fighting with Logan, especially because it looked like he wanted to. As for fucking, that was a *hell no, not in his dirtiest dreams*.

"I'm having tea with Gram and my boo."

His jaw hitched and for a second, I thought he'd still say something shitty. He usually did. To be fair, so did I. We'd been at each other's throats for years.

While he hesitated, I searched his face. Did he remember? I hadn't been this close to him since—

"Whatever," he grumbled and swept past me. He practically dragged his shoulder against the opposite wall, like he was trying to stay as far away from me as possible.

It wasn't far enough. The scent of him washed over me, doing maddening things to my lady parts. It was a stupidly unfair trick of the universe that Logan Bailey smelled so good—warm and woodsy, but clean like a fresh glacial spring. If someone could bottle that, they'd be a millionaire.

And why was I suddenly noticing the way Logan Bailey smelled? I'd never given a shit about what he smelled like before.

Before.

Oh yes, before. In those wonderful, carefree days when my vagina had not been acquainted with prince dickhead's, well, dick.

New topic, Cara. Let it go. It wasn't like he even remembered. We'd both been drunk off our asses—obviously, that was the only way I would have let Logan anywhere near my sacred lady temple—but I remembered it all too well. That fucker had the audacity to give me a spectacular orgasm. One I could still feel when I closed my eyes at night.

God, I hated him.

None of my thoughts touched my face as I swept over to the table and took my seat. For the first time in my entire friendship with Grace, I was keeping something from her. She didn't know that I'd slept with Logan after Skylar's book launch party. Granted, I wouldn't lie to her if she asked me about it. But she had no reason to suspect anything, hence no reason to ask probing questions.

Gram got up to supervise Levi and Logan while they moved furniture in the front room. I casually sipped my tea. I wasn't sure why I hadn't told Grace. I had nothing to be ashamed of and Grace wouldn't judge me. It was one of the reasons I loved her so much. Grace was the one and only person in my life who loved me for who I was, despite the fact that I was a certifiable mess.

No, I wasn't worried about Grace's reaction. I simply didn't want to talk about it. Much better to pretend it hadn't happened and move on. It wasn't like it had meant anything. We'd been horny and too drunk to know better.

So drunk. As much as I hated Logan, I could admit I was impressed that he'd been able to get hard after all the whiskey he'd been drinking.

But I still hated him.

I clung to that, second-guessing my choice to not pick a fight with him. Because if I didn't hate Logan, I might do something worse than sleeping with him while drunk.

Especially with the way his scent lit up my body like a fireworks display.

I definitely had a date with Mr. Bigshot tonight.

Mr. Bigshot had batteries. He wasn't as good as the real thing, but he kept his fucking mouth shut, and that was more than I could say for most men.

A little smile stole over Grace's face and her hand strayed to her belly.

"Baby B kicking again?" I asked.

She nodded. "A lot today. I wonder if it's something I ate."

The icy cold organ in my chest that passed for my heart warmed a degree or two at the happiness shining in my best friend's eyes. She was finally living the life she'd always wanted—the life she'd been so patient to get. Back before she'd been *my* Grace, her then-fiancé Asher had stopped a guy from raping her outside a bar. He'd killed the guy with his bare hands—as he fucking should have, if you asked me —but he had gone to prison for it.

I'd met Grace not long after and watched as she

remained steadfastly loyal to him for seven long years. At the time, I'd teased her about the lack of dick in her life, but in reality, I was awed by her. She loved him so much, she hadn't let anything sway her. Not even when he'd come home a bigger fucked-up mess than I was—and that was saying something.

Her gentle stubbornness had seen him through the worst of his transition back into the world. And lucky for him, he'd gotten his head out of his ass in time to salvage their relationship. I would have cut off his balls if he hadn't, but fortunately for everyone involved, that hadn't become necessary.

Now my sweet baby duckling was married and having his baby. And happier than I'd ever seen her.

Which made me happy. Because the only thing I really wanted in this world was for Grace to have everything *she* wanted.

"I think it's just because you're having a Bailey. You know it has to be a stubborn little boy in there. Of course he's kicking you."

She laughed, still rubbing her belly. "I definitely have boy feelings, but who knows. I could be wrong."

They'd decided not to find out if they were having a boy or a girl until the baby was born. It was one of those things that people seemed to put a lot of thought into, and have strong feelings about, which baffled me. Why did it matter whether you found out the sex early or not? It would have been nice for shopping purposes, but it wasn't going to change the outcome. Why make such a big deal out of it?

But I was accustomed to being the odd one with strange ideas about things, so I didn't worry about it. If my boo wanted to wait to find out if Baby B was a boy or a girl, she could wait without any complaint from me. And I'd wring anyone's neck who gave her a hard time about it.

"You got it?" Levi asked in the other room.

"Yeah." Logan's voice was strained, like he was holding something heavy.

Then he grunted.

My hand tightened around the handle of my mug and my inner thighs twitched. The sound of Logan Bailey grunting while he moved furniture was not going to send me into a tailspin of unresolved sexual tension. I was stronger than that. I *refused*.

Gram came back to the kitchen and I used her entrance as an opportunity to shift in my chair, giving my thighs a little squeeze when I recrossed my legs.

She opened the oven, and a fresh wave of yeasty bread smell filled the kitchen. It was her second batch; the first had been sitting on the counter to cool.

Logan grunted again and my stomach turned over. Why did he have to ruin everything? I couldn't even enjoy the scent of Gram's hot-out-of-the-oven bread without him making me sick to my stomach.

Because seriously, why was I suddenly so nauseated? I loved Gram's bread.

My back broke out in a cold sweat. Maybe it was just too hot in here.

"Are you okay?" Grace asked. "You look pale all of a sudden."

I put my tea down and fanned my face. "I think I'm just hot. Maybe from the oven."

"It is warm in here."

Still fanning myself, I nodded.

Gram brought over a plate of thickly sliced bread from the loaf that had been cooling and slid it onto the table.

Grace didn't waste any time. She slathered a layer of butter over the warm surface and took a bite.

"So good," she moaned.

I eyed the bread. My mouth watered, but not in the good way. A hint of bile burned the back of my throat and I had a feeling that if I tried to eat that bread, I wouldn't be able to keep it down.

"Want some?" Grace asked around a mouthful.

"I'll stick with tea for now. I'm not really hungry."

Gram sat next to Grace and moved the bread closer to her—and away from me. Her eyes lifted, meeting mine for a heartbeat. Before I could fathom what her expression meant, she picked up her tea and took a sip. "I hear we're in for a storm."

"Another one?" Grace asked. "I wonder how much more snow we'll get."

Gram lifted her thin shoulders in a shrug and adjusted her grip on her mug. Her hands were wrinkled but looked so soft. "Tough to say. But I think winter's going to give us a tumultuous end. I suspect things will get worse before they get better."

She looked at me again.

Why did she keep doing that?

Maybe she was annoyed that I wasn't eating her bread. Not that Gram seemed like the sort of woman to take that kind of thing personally. I wasn't sure if Gram took anything personally. She was tough as nails, while still being one of the most nurturing people I'd ever met.

I'd lied earlier. Sleeping with Logan wasn't the first thing I'd kept from Grace. I was jealous of her relationship with Gram, and I'd never told her that either.

But honestly, who could blame me for my envy? Gram had those soft brown eyes that made you feel like she understood you on the deepest spiritual level. My grand-mother's gaze had been an icy blue stare of criticism. And don't even get me started on my mom. She'd taken her own mother's talent for judgment and sharpened it to a razor's edge.

Logan grunted again. The sound pulled my thoughts away from my mother—which was a good thing—but I didn't like where they were going. A pulse of heat hit me right between the legs.

"At least I'll have plenty of excuses to wear my new boots." Pointing my toes, I glanced at my feet under the table. I did have a cute new pair of snow boots. Admiring them wasn't nearly enough to get my mind off a grunting Logan Bailey, but I was getting desperate. "Boo, you should let me get you a pair. These have better traction than yours."

Before Grace could reply to my nonsensical suggestion —her boots were fine, and I knew that because I'd bought them for her—Levi and Logan returned to the kitchen.

Levi headed straight for the bread, grabbing a thick slice off the plate. He tore off a piece and shoved it in his mouth, then went for the butter. Logan hesitated next to the counter, eyeing the food like he was hungry too but didn't want to venture too close.

I looked at the table, pretending to ignore both Bailey men.

Why did this feel so tense and awkward? Who cared if I'd slept with Logan once? It was just sex. Drunken sex at that. Was it because we hadn't acknowledged it? Because I didn't know whether he even remembered?

Such an asshole. No one got a piece of this and forgot.

Finally, Logan darted in to grab some bread, but moved away from the table. Grace tried to stifle a laugh. We were so obvious, but at least Grace would only think this was our usual mutual disdain. She had no idea I was sitting there thinking about the fact that I now knew what it felt like to have Logan inside me.

It hadn't been *that* good. I didn't know why I was so out of sorts about it.

Okay, it probably had been that good. Especially since the memory had survived the bottle of bourbon I'd consumed that night.

But it didn't matter. Apparently we'd just keep pretending it hadn't happened and go on with our lives. Easy enough.

The odd roiling in my stomach subsided, so I took a piece of bread and picked at it. I talked to Grace and ignored Logan.

This was fine.

Gram got up and asked Logan and Levi to help her with something upstairs. I let out a breath as they left the kitchen. Pretending not to care was exhausting.

Grace looked at me from across the table. "Are you okay?"

"I'm fine. Why wouldn't I be?"

"I don't know; that's why I'm asking. You seem like something is off."

"I am feeling a little off. I'm probably about to start my period."

She reached over and grabbed my hand. "I know we haven't been spending as much time together as we used to."

I met her eyes. "It's okay. You have a husband and you're growing a tiny person."

"I know, but—"

"Boo, I'm fine." I squeezed her hand. "Pinkie promise."

"Okay. But you'll tell me if you're not?"

"Don't I always? I complain about the slightest discomfort; you know this about me. I'm fine."

"Okay."

I wasn't lying. I was fine. Because I refused to be otherwise.

Logan avoided coming back into the kitchen, although Levi circled back through and fished some cookies out of Gram's cookie jar before they left. Gram came back and Grace and I chatted with her for a while longer. Without the proximity to Logan, the strange tension I'd felt eased. I went back to enjoying tea with two of my favorite people.

We finished up with Gram and helped her tidy the kitchen, then said our goodbyes and left. Grace had picked me up, so she drove me home. I left her with more assurances that I was fine and she hadn't bruised my tender feelings by marrying Asher and getting pregnant.

I went inside, put my things down, and took off my winter coat. It was cold outside, but pleasantly warm in my house.

I loved this house. After I'd bought it, I'd gutted it, remodeling the entire thing from top to bottom. By the standards of my childhood in Southern California, it was modest in size, with only four bedrooms and two and a half baths. But it could have been the size of a shoebox and I would have loved it, even if just for the view of the river. It was spectacular, especially in the winter with all the snow on the ground and icicles dangling from the trees.

It wasn't just this house that I loved. I loved this place. This town. It was small and quirky and they didn't have a decent sushi restaurant. But I loved it here anyway.

I flicked on the gas fireplace and wandered toward the kitchen. I slid onto a stool at the island and poked through the stacks of books I'd been amassing.

One of them had to have an answer. Or something I could use to find an answer.

Grace's concern that I was struggling with the changes in her life, and our friendship, wasn't totally unwarranted. Before Asher had come home, Grace had needed me. She didn't now, not in the same way. Because of all the therapy I'd had, I was self-aware enough to realize I couldn't keep needing her to need me. I couldn't cling to her and insist she enter into a sexless non-lesbian life-partner marriage with me, as much as I'd wanted her to.

Although if she'd been up for it, I would have done it and happily let her have Asher on the side.

Instead, I'd had to let her go—let her spread her wings and fly, like the beautiful tropical bird she was.

The problem was, I didn't have anything in my life to replace her. Not that I wanted a new best friend. But for a while, Grace had been my anchor. Now I was adrift.

Hence the books on my kitchen island.

I picked one up titled *Find Your Passion and Purpose in Ten Easy Steps* and eyed it with skepticism. If there were only ten steps and if they were so easy, why did the guy need to write an entire book about it? Others were about career planning and goal setting and getting your shit together.

One of them had to contain something I could use.

With a sigh, I put the book down. I was the epitome of the spoiled little rich girl. I'd grown up wealthy and inherited enough money that I'd never had a real job. I lived off my inheritance and the money I made as an influencer on social media.

It was stupid, really. I got paid to be pretty. Maybe I could say it had a little bit to do with my photography skills, but that would be a stretch. I wasn't a great photographer; I just knew how to use filters. I knew how to make my social media presence look like everyone's dream of perfection. In that way, I was a skilled liar.

I wanted to be something else. Something real.

But what?

I didn't know. My list of career ideas that I'd discarded for one reason or another kept getting longer. And to be honest, I wasn't sure if it was a career that I was looking for.

I just didn't want to be useless anymore.

3
────

LOGAN

he Rowdy Bear was down near Tilikum College. It wasn't a bad place to get a drink, and it was an even better place to pick up girls. The long wood bar was fronted by stools, and there were plenty of tables and booths with dark red seats.

As usual for a Saturday, it was busy. There were often a lot of college kids, but locals from Tilikum and the surrounding towns hung out here too. The pool tables were all occupied, but there was still some open seating near the bar.

My eyes scanned the crowd as Levi and I walked in, and for a second, I wondered if we were getting too old for this place.

Fuck that. We were twenty-eight. I'd probably have to concede when we turned thirty, but we hadn't crossed that bridge yet. And we didn't look like the oldest guys in here. Not by a long shot.

Levi took off his coat—it was warm in here—and gave the bar a reluctant once over. He looked damn good in his TFD t-shirt and jeans. He'd been working out and had put on some size. I made a mental note to tease him later about using weightlifting as an outlet for his sexual frustration.

Although, as good as he looked tonight, that frustration might soon be a thing of the past. Maybe it was my imagination, but he'd cleaned up. Put in some effort. Maybe my grumpy-ass brother was finally going to let me get him laid.

We already had eyes on us, and we'd barely walked in the door. This was one of the benefits of being a twin. We were handsome as fuck, if I did say so myself, and when we were together, we attracted the right kind of attention.

"I'll get the first round," Levi said.

I elbowed him. "Awesome. Thanks, lambrogini."

He veered toward the bar and I found a table with a good view. I put my coat on the back of the seat and took off my knit hat, then ran my fingers through my hair. I'd probably messed it up more, but girls liked my just-fucked look, so whatever.

A group of girls sat at the table next to me. One of them met my eyes and her lips curled in a smile. I liked where this was going. I was about to smile back—maybe toss a wink her direction—when I realized she was a redhead.

My heart did an uncomfortable thump in my chest and I turned away.

No redheads. Definitely no redheads.

Although that was a stupid thing to get hung up on. Just because *she* was... and we'd... and now I kept dreaming about...

Damn it. Those fucking dreams. They weren't *her*; they were just random sex dreams.

Even if they did feature a woman with red hair.

The solution was simple, and it was the reason I was here. I needed to get laid. Badly.

It had been too fucking long. That was why I kept jizzing

myself in my sleep. The night with Little Orphan Crazy didn't count, and before that, I'd gone... shit, I wasn't even sure how long without any pussy.

Why? Hell, every guy went through a dry spell once in a while. Work had been busy, there'd been shit going on with my family. Plus, I tended to steer clear of local girls. Tilikum was a small town, and there was something about banging a girl you knew you'd run into four or five times a week for the rest of your life that seemed like a bad idea.

Tonight, I didn't care where she was from. I just needed a hot piece of ass.

Who was not a redhead. Another glance at the girl at the table next to me confirmed that. A shudder ran down my spine. No redheads.

Levi came back carrying two shots and had two beers tucked beneath his arm. He set our drinks on the table and sat.

"Thanks, man." I lifted the shot and we clinked glasses.

The whiskey went down easy, burning pleasantly as it slid down my throat.

Except it wasn't just any whiskey. It was bourbon.

She'd tasted like bourbon.

Damn it.

I chased it with a swig of beer to wash away the memory of her tongue in my mouth.

"Did you talk to Evan about Betty yet?" Levi asked.

"Yeah. He's booked for the next month or so, but I'm on his schedule."

"I'm surprised he can get to her that soon. He's been busy as fuck."

Evan *had* been busy as fuck. Ever since he'd restored that 1970 Pontiac GTO and America's Car Museum had bought it for their permanent collection, he'd been in high demand.

"Yeah, well, I'm his favorite brother."

Levi chuckled and took a drink of his beer.

I scanned the bar again, considering my next move. Sitting here wasn't getting us anywhere. The table next to us was a no-go. I didn't like big groups of girls anyway. It was more fun to find a pair of friends, or maybe sisters. We still hadn't fulfilled my dream of hooking up with another set of twins—identical would be fucking awesome—but it wasn't like we ran into hot identical twins who were around our age, single, and looking to hook up all that often. Or ever.

But just because it hadn't happened yet didn't mean it wasn't going to.

A few girls sat at the bar, and one looked particularly fine in her tight jeans. I kept tracking to see who she might be with. A guy in a red flannel sat a few seats down from her. Damn. It was Zachary Haven.

Fucking Havens.

The Rowdy Bear was close enough to campus to be neutral territory, so Baileys and Havens both hung out here. Although we both had a right to be here, I didn't like seeing one of my family's rivals under the same roof as me. The glare that stole over my features was a deeply ingrained response to the generations-long feud.

Our eyes met. His narrowed. So did mine.

I gave him a quick chin tip. I wasn't here looking for trouble. I was here to get laid. And by the look of it, so was he. So I decided not to intrude on a fellow predator's hunting grounds and concede some territory to him.

Zachary returned my nod. He had that side. Levi and I would stay over here.

Levi eyed him for a minute, his hand curling into a fist.

"Just ignore him," I said. "We'll fuck with him another time."

"Yeah," Levi said, although his voice was a low growl.

I'd have to keep an eye on my brother. He didn't usually start shit, but he had a temper.

Two girls at a table nearby caught my eye. They both had a distinct *available* vibe. You could usually tell if a girl had someone fucking her. These two were hot, both showing off their nice tits with low-cut tops.

And neither of them had red hair.

Perfect.

I grabbed my beer and got up. "Come on."

Levi followed my gaze. He hesitated, but before I could ask him what the fuck his problem was—they were hot and this is why we were here—he picked up his beer and stood.

The girls saw us coming and gave each other fake shy smiles. I bet they were the type who said things like *I never do this on the first date* right before blowing you in the back-seat of your car. On the first date.

See? Perfect.

I approached casually, my beer in a loose grip. From the corner of my eye, I watched my brother—tried to gauge which girl he was gravitating toward. Seemed like the one on the left, so I set my sights on the girl on the right.

"Hey." I helped myself to one of the empty chairs without waiting for an invitation. "You two look like you could use some company."

Levi gave me a look. *Did you really just do that?* He was much more of a gentleman than I was—although I wasn't one, so that wasn't hard—and he paused behind the other empty chair.

"Sure," the girl on the right said. "Have a seat. I'm April. This is my friend Mae."

I laughed, and Levi took his seat. "You don't have to give

us fake names, but okay. I'm Logan. This is my brother, Levi."

"No, they're not fake names," Mae said. "Promise. It's why we became friends."

April nodded. "We met freshman year and we've been friends ever since."

"Are you still in school?" Levi asked.

I grinned at my brother. He was actually making conversation? The last couple of times we'd gone out, he'd been about as interesting as a rock. Just sat there glowering at the table, nursing his beer. This was an improvement.

"I graduated already," Mae said. "But April has at least another year, and she's the best roommate ever, so I stayed."

"You think you're the best roommate ever?" I asked, locking my gaze on April. My eyes flicked to her tits and I didn't bother hiding it. "I don't know about that. I might have you beat. I'm a great roommate."

She shifted toward me and I got a whiff of her perfume. It kind of made my eyes feel like they were going to start watering.

Was Levi noticing this?

He didn't seem to be. He and Mae had already broken off into their own conversation. Something about the TFD logo on Levi's shirt.

She touched his chest and I gave him a mental high five. *That's it, buddy. She's putty in your hands.*

"What was that?" I asked April. I'd missed whatever it was she'd just said. "Sorry, I was distracted."

Her eyes flicked to her chest and she gave me a mock scowl. "Logan, were you looking at my boobs?"

I grinned. "Yes." I actually hadn't been, but that was a good excuse. And she did have nice boobs.

Were they as nice as—

I didn't know. I hadn't actually seen Cara's tits.

Fuck, why was I thinking about Cara's tits?

April shifted in her chair, making her body undulate. Which lifted those very nice tits and momentarily distracted me from her perfume.

"You're terrible," she said.

"I really am." I took a sip of my beer. "I'm a total dick. You definitely shouldn't be talking to me."

She leaned closer. "What about your brother? Is he a dick, too?"

I shook my head. "Nope. He's a nice guy."

"Good, because Mae's a nice girl."

"What about you? Are you a nice girl?"

A wicked smile stole across her features and she moved closer again. "Nope." Her full lips popped on the P.

And my dick did... nothing.

I had a girl with nice tits and fuck me eyes giving me every possible signal I wanted to see, and I was as soft as melting ice cream on a hot day.

What. The. Fuck.

I came in my sleep every other night, but I couldn't get it up when I had the real thing in front of me?

Maybe it was the proximity to my brother. I could hear him carrying on a conversation with Mae. That could explain it. That had to be it. Levi was the distraction.

But before I could find an excuse to get April away from her friend, she slid into my lap, draping an arm around my shoulders.

Okay, this should have been good news. April was definitely down to fuck. Why else would she be parking her ass in my lap with her tits in my face?

But damn it, her perfume was terrible. Was it even

perfume? I didn't know what it was, but the scent was making my dick wilt like a dried-up weed.

Levi stood and met my eyes. "We're going to go get another drink."

A flash of panic hit me and I almost blurted out, *Bro, don't leave me alone with her!*

But the last thing I wanted to do was mess with Levi's mojo, especially if he really had a connection with Mae. If I had to take one for the team so Levi could get some ass tonight, I'd do what I had to do.

And why was that such a hardship? I'd literally come here for the express purpose of getting a hot girl to sit in my lap and put her tits in my face—a clear precursor to me fucking the shit out of her later.

"Are you identical?" April asked. Her hand strayed to the back of my neck and she started playing with my hair.

Involuntarily, my back and shoulders tightened. "Yeah."

"Can I tell you a secret?"

Yes, tell me a secret, April. Tell me why my entire body is rebelling at the thought of your mouth around my cock when I should be hard as steel right now.

"Sure."

Her lips brushed my ear and I had to stop myself from flinching away. "I think you're hotter."

I ground my teeth together. Levi and Mae were at the bar. What the hell was I going to do? The more I thought about taking April home with me, the more my muscles clenched and my stomach protested.

My stomach was involved now? What the hell, man?

There was absolutely nothing wrong with her. She was hot. Too much makeup, maybe, but who gave a fuck? And I could tell her to shower first—make it sexy, somehow. That might take care of the way she smelled. Would it be weird if we stopped on the way home and bought some body wash? Got her something better than whatever she was using?

She wiggled in my lap, laughing at her own joke, and I stared at her tits. They really were nice tits. Probably had sweet pink nipples. I rested a hand on her thigh and thought about opening these legs. Sinking my cock deep inside her and—

I recoiled so hard, I dumped her out of my lap and onto the floor.

Somehow, I was standing, although I didn't remember flying out of my seat. But I must have. April looked up at me, rage burning in her heavily made-up eyes.

"What the fuck, asshole?"

"Shit, I'm sorry." I reached for her hand to help her up. "Are you okay?"

She smacked my hand away. "Get off me."

I held up my hands in a gesture of surrender. I didn't want anyone to think I was assaulting her or something. I'd just... freaked out for a second.

"Seriously, April, I'm sorry. I don't know what happened."

"You threw me on the floor, you dick."

Mae was suddenly at her side, crouching to help her up. I stared like an idiot while Mae got April to her feet.

Levi looked alarmed. I gave him a quick shrug—*I don't know what's going on.*

He nodded back and held up a hand—*Stay there.*

"Let's go." April clung to her friend's arm and shot me a nasty glare.

Mae glared at me too, although she looked more confused than angry. She led her friend toward the door.

Levi stepped closer and lowered his voice. "What was that about?"

"I don't know. One minute, she's in my lap and the next, she's on the floor. She just twisted weird and fell, I guess. Maybe she's drunk. I don't know why the fuck that's my fault." I wiped my clammy hands on my jeans. I was babbling, and I needed to shut the hell up. "Let's just get out of here."

"Okay."

We grabbed our coats off the chairs where we'd left them. I hadn't finished my beer, but I didn't care.

"Oh shit, man." I put a hand on Levi's shoulder, feeling like a huge dick. "I just cockblocked the fuck out of you."

"No, you didn't. I was just getting Mae away from the table so you could do your thing with her friend."

"Seriously? You weren't into her at all?"

He shrugged. "Not really. She seemed nice, but it wasn't going anywhere."

"Damn. I still owe you."

"Whatever. Let's just go."

I followed him out into the cold. The temperature had dropped since we'd gone in. It was freezing out here. I zipped up my coat and trudged through the snow to his SUV. Despite what he'd said earlier about driving himself, we'd come together. My truck wasn't running all that well, and it was too icy to trust Betty on the roads after dark.

That made me feel worse about cockblocking him, regardless of what he'd said about not being into Mae. He wasn't always the most fun guy at the party, but he did have my back. Every single time.

I'd make it up to him somehow.

For now, I got in the passenger's side, wondering what the fuck was wrong with me and whether I'd just guaranteed I'd wake up to sticky sheets again tomorrow.

4

LOGAN

$\mathcal{T}$he scent of bacon and toast greeted me as I walked into Bigfoot Diner. Red buffalo check curtains hung in the windows and an assortment of Bigfoot paintings decorated the walls. It was early, especially for a Sunday, but most of the seats were taken. No surprise there. It was the best breakfast place in town.

My shift started in about an hour, but I wanted food first. Good food. And coffee. Tired as I was—I hadn't slept well after last night's bar debacle—I'd probably take my chances with the sludge that passed for coffee at the firehouse later, but I could start the day with something better.

I stopped just inside the door while it closed behind me, cutting off the draft of cold air from outside.

Fuck. It was her.

What the hell was *she* doing here at seven o'clock on a Sunday morning?

Cara sat at a booth next to the window with a plate of half-eaten food across from her, like she'd shoved it away from herself. She had one hand wrapped around a steaming cup of coffee and her eyes were on a book, which struck me as weird. Why, I had no idea. I didn't know what Cara did in her free time, other than drive me crazy. So maybe she read books.

What kind of book was it?

I tamped down the sudden flare of curiosity. Who fucking cared? Hopefully she'd keep her eyes on the page and not notice me coming in. The last thing I needed was a Cara confrontation this early in the morning. I just wanted some fucking bacon.

But apparently my luck was particularly shitty this morning because the only open booth was right next to hers.

A fresh blast of cold air hit me from behind. Someone came in and there I was, standing in the entry like a jackass. The server behind the counter lifted her eyebrows at me in confusion. I ate here all the time; I knew I didn't have to wait to be seated.

I hurried to the open booth. I didn't want the server to say something and make Cara look up from her book. If I were careful, I could slide right into my seat without her—

"Oh perfect," Cara said. "Of course you'd show up here this morning."

Her voice sent a prickle up my spine and my shoulders tightened. I hesitated next to my table. If I took the seat farthest from her, I'd have to face her. But if I had my back to her, there'd be less distance between us.

I decided not facing her was better. There'd be an entire seat and a table between us. It would have to do.

"You're the one crashing my diner," I snapped back as I took my seat.

"Sorry, prince dickhead, but contrary to what you seem to believe, you don't actually own this town."

"I was here first," I grumbled, then wanted to kick myself. That was the best I could do? What was I, ten?

She laughed. "That's all you've got? Here, let me order you some coffee. You're clearly not at your best this morning."

I ground my teeth together. She had no idea how right she was. I'd gone out last night to fix whatever was wrong with me. Instead, I'd only made it worse.

"You're not getting anywhere near my coffee," I said over my shoulder. "I don't know what you'd put in it."

"As if I'd go to that much trouble."

Before I could reply, the server came over with coffee. She took my order—eggs and hash browns with both bacon and sausage—although the longer I talked to Cara, the less appetite I had.

Actually, fuck that, I could always eat.

The server left and Cara didn't say anything. I took a sip of coffee. The hair on the back of my neck stood on end. Maybe putting my back to her hadn't been a good idea. Was she looking at me? Or had she gone back to her book and was ignoring me?

Why did I care what she was doing?

Before I could stop myself, I twisted around. "Why are you here so early?"

She looked up from her book, her eyes blazing. "Why do you care?"

That was an excellent question, but the fact that she'd echoed what I'd just asked myself made me irrationally mad.

"I'm just making fucking conversation, Cara. Sometimes, people do that."

A flash of something—confusion, maybe—crossed her features. "I woke up early and couldn't go back to sleep."

Her honest—and not bitchy—answer deflated some of my anger. But only some. "Then I guess it's just my bad luck that you're here."

She closed her book. "You're looking a little rough. Have you been to bed yet, or did you crawl out of whatever gutter you passed out in and stumble straight here?"

I ran my fingers through my hair. "Whatever. I look great this morning."

"Delusion isn't a good look on you."

No, but you'd look good on me. On my cock, specifically.

Shut up, Logan. Don't say that.

I needed to change the subject. Really, I needed to turn around and stop talking to her, but I couldn't seem to make myself do that.

"What are you reading?"

"Is this you trying to make conversation again?"

I grabbed my coffee and did what was probably the second stupidest thing I'd ever done in my life. I slipped out of my booth and into hers.

What the fuck was I doing?

Playing with fire, that's what.

"Yes, this is me making conversation. What are you reading?"

She had her palm splayed over the cover of the book. Her eyes flicked down, then back to me. But she didn't answer.

"Okay, let me guess." I paused and she raised her eyebrows, like she was ready for me to say something snarky. To be fair, I was. But for some reason, I didn't. "It's one of Skylar's books."

There was a certain satisfaction in seeing her snide expression melt into surprise. It was kind of fun to throw her off by not being a dick for once.

"No, it's not one of Skylar's books."

"That's probably a good thing. Doesn't she write about serial killers and shit? I wouldn't want you getting any ideas."

"She does know at least twenty ways to effectively hide a body."

I shuddered.

Her lips twitched in a smile. "My baby girl is so talented."

Cara's relationships with other women were fucking weird. She talked like she was married to Grace, and Fiona and Skylar were their kids.

Which, okay fine, was kind of cute when I thought about it.

Wait, what the fuck? I took a sip of hot coffee. I did not just think of anything about Cara as cute. She was a viper. A tornado of crazy. There was nothing cute about her.

I put my mug down. "So, not one of Skylar's. What is it?"

With a sigh, she held up the book. It was titled *Find Your Passion and Purpose in Ten Easy Steps*. "Go ahead. Do your worst. I couldn't possibly care less what you think."

"Seems like a thick book for just ten steps, especially if they're easy."

She opened her mouth, like she was about to snap back, then closed it again. "Yeah, I know. That's what I thought, but it's actually pretty good."

Why was Cara reading a book like that? Before I could ask, the server came with my breakfast.

"Would you like this here?" she asked.

Shit. Should I go back to my seat? Or have breakfast with her? This was so weird. I couldn't remember the last time Cara and I had a conversation that wasn't entirely made up of insults. Had we ever?

Actually, we had once, but that was a long-ass time ago.

"Here is fine," Cara said.

I met her eyes and they flashed with heat, like she was daring me to disagree with her and go back to my table. Or maybe she was baiting me, biding her time before picking a fight.

For some reason, I took the bait. I nodded to the server as she placed my food in front of me. "Thanks."

Cara eyed my food with skepticism while I dug in. It was good, although it was mildly uncomfortable to sit there while she watched me eat. She hadn't finished hers. Why was she looking at my plate like that?

I tried to ignore her. She went back to her book but kept flicking glances at my food.

"You want some?" I asked finally.

She scrunched her nose. "No."

"Suit yourself. I wouldn't share my bacon with you anyway."

"The last thing I want is your bacon."

"How about my sausage?" I speared a sausage link with my fork and held it up.

"I don't want your sausage either."

Once when I was a kid, I'd let the flames of our backyard bonfire lick my fingers. I'd known it would hurt and I'd done it anyway. Hadn't been able to resist the temptation of seeing what it would really feel like to touch fire.

I was that kid again now.

I grinned at her. "You sure about that? I seem to recall you liking my sausage."

Her eyes narrowed. "I wouldn't touch your sausage if I was wearing six sets of sterile gloves."

Wait, did she not remember? Or was she fucking with me? We had been pretty drunk.

I leaned forward and lowered my voice. "Come on, you loved my sausage. Your panties are wet right now just thinking about it."

"Shut up, Logan."

Regardless of what it was doing to *her*, thinking about this was making *me* hard. I glanced down at my crotch. *What the fuck, man? Where were you last night when I needed you?*

The fact that Cara was giving me an erection, when tits-in-my-face April hadn't last night, riled me up even more.

"No, I want to hear you say it. I made you come. Admit it."

I shit you not, actual flames lit up her eyeballs. She remembered, all right. She just didn't want to admit I'd done it for her.

"No you didn't. You were so drunk you couldn't even get me undressed."

"I managed. And you came so hard all over me, you could barely move when it was over."

She leaned closer. "You only finished because I have the best pussy you've ever had, and *will ever* have. Unfortunately for you, that was a one-time deal."

"I wouldn't stick my dick in you again if you had the last pussy on earth."

I was lying through my teeth. I wanted to fuck her again. Now. And it pissed me off that I wanted her so badly, I could practically taste her. My cock ached, straining against my pants, and all I could think about was dragging her outside to my car, tossing her in the backseat, and fucking that goddamn smirk off her face.

"Good, because there isn't enough bourbon in the world to get me drunk enough to fuck you again."

"Liar. You're thinking about it right now."

"No, I'm thinking about whether I can make it to the bathroom before I throw up."

"Nice try, Little Mermaid. I see right through you."

"Your brother, though..." She paused, a wicked light in her eyes. "I wouldn't even need to be drunk to fuck Levi."

The heat of lust and anger pulsed through my veins. I practically saw red. "Stay the fuck away from my brother."

"Why?" she asked, batting her eyes in mock innocence. "Are you worried I'll find out he fucks better than you do?"

"No. I'm worried he'll make the same fucking mistake I did."

My stomach dropped. Fuck. I shouldn't have said that.

The hurt in her eyes was like a stab wound to the gut. We said messed-up shit to each other all the time, but that had been a low blow.

Too low.

Damn it.

"Cara—"

She scooped her book off the table and stood, tucking her coat under an arm. Before I could say a word, she swept out of the diner.

I slumped in the booth. That sucked.

What the fuck had I been doing, anyway? Sitting with her, trying to start a conversation. Why? Because we'd fucked once, I suddenly wanted to get to know her? I should have known we couldn't get along for more than a few minutes without going for each other's throats.

I blew out a breath and took out my phone. It was weird that I had her number, considering we never texted each other. But I'd had it for years, under Evil Ariel.

Sorry that I—

Delete.

I didn't mean—

Delete.

That wasn't what it—

Fucking delete.

I tossed my phone on the table. I didn't know what to say to her after that any more than I knew why I cared that she was mad at me. Wasn't *mad at Logan* a state of being for her? She was always mad at me. She hated me, and the feeling was mutual.

But I still felt like shit. So I fired off a quick text before I could overthink it any more than I already had.

Sorry.

5

CARA

*W*eak, Cara. You're weak.

I stomped through the snow to my car, chastising myself for leaving. I should have fired back at him, not walked out in a huff like he'd hurt my feelings. I wasn't some delicate little girl who needed a man's approval to feel worthy. Screw that. What did I care if Logan Bailey thought sleeping with me was a mistake? It *had been* a mistake. What else would either of us call it?

God, he made me so mad.

I hadn't only left because of him. The scent of his breakfast had been messing with my stomach. I'd needed to get out of there and into the fresh air.

Sure, Cara. Keep telling yourself that.

My red Jeep Rubicon was parked up the street from Bigfoot. It was my winter car, something I'd learned my first winter here was a necessity when you lived in the mountains—at least if your rest-of-the-year car was a convertible Mustang. I'd grown up in Southern California and had been woefully unprepared for what it would really be like to live in a completely different climate. But after nearly ten years in this weird town, I had it down. From December through March—sometimes April—I drove my Jeep. When the snow melted, I was back to my Mustang.

Worked out nicely, thank you very much bitches back home who'd told me I wouldn't last six months up here.

My phone buzzed and I glanced at the screen. Oh my god, it was actually him. That was weird; Logan never texted me. I didn't even know why I had his number.

Prince Dickhead: *Sorry.*

I tossed my phone on the passenger seat and kept driving. His short apology took the wind out of my sails and made me feel worse about leaving. He really did think he'd hurt my feelings.

Asshole. I wasn't that precious. It would take a lot more than calling me a mistake to get to me.

I took a corner a little too fast and my tires slipped on the slushy muck that had built up on the edge of the road. I gripped the wheel and steered out of it, but my heart skipped. What was I doing? I was fine. Logan hadn't rattled me so much that I was going to wreck my car on the way home.

The lurch got my stomach acting up again. I took a few deep breaths, trying to calm my racing heart and my churning stomach.

I seriously didn't know what was wrong with me.

By the time I got home a few minutes later, my heart had slowed to a normal rhythm and my stomach was behaving itself—mostly. I hoped it would continue. I didn't want to hurl up the breakfast I'd managed to choke down.

I went inside and tossed my stuff on the kitchen island. My phone buzzed again, but this time it was a call, not a text.

God, Logan, clingy much? I'd answer when I felt like it.

I picked up my phone and my stomach did another somersault. It wasn't Logan. It was my mother.

Buzz.

I stared at the screen, willing my traitorous stomach to behave itself.

Buzz.

Took another deep breath. Did I have time to mix a drink before I answered?

Buzz.

Maybe I'd just call her back.

Buzz.

I groaned, my shoulders slumping. It would be better to just get this over with. Who knew; maybe she wouldn't be calling expressly to deliver a scathing criticism of all my choices while also spilling the latest details of her own spectacular failures at life.

"Hi, Mom."

"There you are. I thought I was getting your voicemail. What took you so long to answer?"

"Nothing. I just got home. What's up?"

"I haven't heard from you in a while. What's wrong?"

I leaned my backside against the edge of a stool. "There's nothing wrong."

"Then why haven't you called?"

"I don't know, Mom. It seems like we just talked the other day."

She huffed. "Cara, you know I had an appointment with Dr. Johnson last week. I would have thought you'd call to ask how I'm doing."

Was Dr. Johnson her plastic surgeon? Her psychiatrist? It was hard to keep track. She had several of each. "How are you doing?"

"Fine, no thanks to that quack I was seeing before. Can

you believe he prescribed the wrong medications twice? I need to write a letter to have his license revoked."

"That's terrible."

"It really is. These doctors take an oath."

"Yes, they do."

"Do you remember Ethel Henderson?"

Her abrupt change of subject didn't faze me. I was used to it. "The woman who lived next door to us my entire life? Yes, Mom, I remember."

"There's no need to get snippy. Her daughter Charity moved back home a few months ago to take care of her. She makes all her appointments, runs her errands, keeps everything on schedule. It's remarkable. She's such a selfless young woman."

This was not the first time my mother had passive-aggressively compared me—unfavorably, of course—to her neighbor's daughter. Charity Henderson was apparently a goddamn saint, who'd given up any hope of having her own life to dote on her aging mother, as if nothing else in the world could possibly be more important.

It was my mother's dream.

And my nightmare.

"How nice for Ethel," I said.

"She's never looked better. I had her over for drinks the other night. She's more than a decade older than me but she looks like she could be my... well, my slightly younger sister. I really think it's how well Charity takes care of her. She never misses her appointments at the medi-spa."

"I'm glad she has someone to take her to her Botox appointments."

"Speaking of, I was looking at your Instagram photos. You should consider a better skin care regimen. It's about time for an eye cream, don't you think? And you're never too young for a little Botox or maybe a chemical peel."

I gritted my teeth. "I'll keep that in mind."

"You should come down here. All the best doctors are in California. I can't imagine you have access to even halfway decent care up there in... wherever you are."

"Tilikum, Mom. The town is called Tilikum."

"Of course it is," she said, her words dripping with distaste, like I'd just suggested she eat rotten meat. "In any case, those bags under your eyes are only going to get worse the longer you leave them."

I resisted the urge to say I'd inherited those bags from her and she made my skin break out every time she called. "I'll work on it."

"See that you do. Your image projects on me too. I have to live with what you put out there in ways my mother never had to deal with when it came to me. Social media is the bane of my existence."

Well, now I knew what I was doing later. Posing for a photo I knew my mother would hate and posting it *everywhere*.

I took a deep breath. My stomach still felt off. Maybe I could change the subject, since she didn't seem to be in any hurry to get off the phone. "We still have snow up here. It's very pretty. I was thinking about taking some photos with the new lens I got. I was watching a tutorial about—"

"God, I hate the cold," she said, cutting me off. Because of course she did. "I don't know how you can stand to live where it snows."

"I don't mind."

"All that freezing air will dry your skin out. I'd shrivel up like a prune if I spent more than a few hours in the snow."

Good thing I'm never inviting you to come up here and visit me, then. "The cold does that."

"Okay, I'll tell you," she said.

I blinked, totally confused. Was that another subject change? That had been abrupt, even for her. "I'm sorry, did I miss part of our conversation?" *Or are you on pills again?*

Great, it was probably pills again. How many times was I going to have to pay for that outrageously expensive spa that masqueraded as rehab?

"I've been trying to hold back, but it's too exciting. And it's why I want you to take better care with your image."

"Mom, what are you talking about?"

"I spoke with Barry Stein last week."

"The producer? Why?"

She took a deep breath. "He wants you to come read for him."

Oh god. Not this again. "Mom, we've had this conversation at least eight hundred times. I'm not reading for anyone. I'm not going to any auditions. I'm not interested."

"Don't be ridiculous. Of course you'll read for him. He's one of the biggest producers in Hollywood."

"I know who he is."

"I'll set something up for—"

"Mom," I said, not willing to sit through the next ten minutes of her trying to bully me into flying to L.A. to meet with a lecherous movie producer who'd probably want me to audition by sucking his dick. "No. I'm not an actress. That's not what I do."

"Cara, you've made this nearly impossible, what with your insistence on living in that godforsaken town in the middle of nowhere."

"It's only impossible from your perspective because you don't listen to me when I tell you I don't want to be an actress. I've been telling you for years, so I don't understand why you never hear me."

She burst into tears.

Fuck me running.

"Mom," I said in the most soothing tone I could manage. "Mom, stop crying."

More sobbing.

My raw stomach protested and now I had a piercing headache. I pinched the bridge of my nose and held the phone away from my ear to lessen the impact of her hysterics. At this point, I had two choices. Hang up on her, in which case the next phone call would be ten million times worse. Or wait for her to stop crying and figure out how to give her something she wanted without agreeing to anything I wasn't willing to do. Like going to an audition.

This one might require a trip to L.A., though. Damn it.

I wandered over to the couch and flopped down letting my arm rest on one of my throw pillows. And waited while she cried.

Toddlers everywhere should take notes on how to throw a tantrum from Layla Goulding.

Finally, her sobbing eased, turning into hiccups and sniffles.

"Mom?"

"What?"

I took another deep breath. "Listen, I don't want to upset you—"

"We need this, Cara."

"No we don't. Maybe you think you need this, but *we* do not."

"Yes, we do." Her voice went shaky again. "This could be your chance, and you don't understand what it could mean financially."

Financially?

Oh no.

That's what this was really about. She needed money. Again.

"How much, Mom?"

"How much would the role pay? I don't know for sure, but if it led to—"

"No. How much do you need?"

She went quiet and for a second, I wondered if she'd hung up on me.

"Honey, I..."

"It's okay, Mom," I said, once again adopting the soothing tone of a mother talking to a young child. "You can tell me."

"It isn't my fault. You realize it's not my fault."

"I know it isn't."

She paused again. I leaned my head back against the couch cushion and waited for her to come clean. What was it this time? A six-figure plastic surgery bill? Another bad real estate investment? Had she gilded her entire house in solid gold? Nothing would surprise me at this point.

"I owe some money."

"Okay."

"There are always so many events that I have to attend and obviously I can't wear the same outfits or jewelry that I've worn before. What would people think? And I couldn't pass up that Mediterranean cruise. How would it have looked if I were the only one of my friends who didn't go? And the kitchen needed all that work. I can't live in a house with travertine tile. It's so ten years ago."

I sighed. I'd known about the cruise but she hadn't told me she'd remodeled her kitchen yet again. That meant she'd probably replaced all the furniture in her house to make sure everything matched. Plus who knew how many other trips and purchases she wasn't telling me about. She spent like a millionaire, even though she was broke.

"How much?"

Silence from her once again. That meant it was bad.

There had been a time, not too many years ago, when I'd had what I called *fuck you money*. I did whatever I wanted with it without thinking twice and knew I didn't run too much risk of running out. I didn't spend like my mother did, so chartering a flight when I had to see her in L.A. or treating Grace to luxury spa weekend getaways hardly put a dent in my bank account. My college education had, as had buying and remodeling this house. But for a rich girl, I lived simply. I liked to spoil other people, but there weren't very many people in the world I actually liked, so that didn't cost too much. And I didn't spend a lot of money on myself, so it should have lasted.

But now, I no longer had fuck you money. It wasn't like I was about to be destitute, but over the past seven or eight years, I'd bailed out my mom so many times, it showed.

She always claimed she'd find a way to pay me back. I knew she never would.

And I also knew I couldn't say no. Because the reason I'd once had fuck you money riddled me with guilt.

My grandparents had been Hollywood royalty—my grandmother one of the most famous and sought-after actresses of her day, my grandfather the biggest producer/director of his time. And when they'd died, instead of leaving their estate to their only daughter, they'd left it to me.

My mother had never forgiven me for that.

So now, whenever she had money problems, I fixed them.

"How much, Mom?" I asked again, my voice just above a whisper.

"Several hundred... thousand."

"What does several mean?"

"Nine."

Letting out a breath, I closed my eyes. I didn't ask how she could possibly have gotten herself almost a million dollars in debt. I didn't want to know. Because it didn't matter. I was going to pay it.

"Okay, Mom. I'll take care of it. Just send me the details."

I didn't wait for her reply. If I did, she'd just leave more scars than she already had. Because she wouldn't say thank you. She wouldn't tell me she was grateful, or I was a wonderful daughter for always taking care of her. She wouldn't tell me she loved me. She'd probably just change the subject back to the bags under my eyes and how my social media presence was ruining her life.

So I hung up on her.

Deep breaths, Cara. Deep breaths.

For some reason, I swiped back to Logan's text. *Sorry.* It was so weird, but seeing that little word, knowing he'd typed it, made me feel better. Because okay, maybe he had hurt my feelings a tiny bit. And seeing this little apology, sent almost immediately after I'd walked out of the diner, eased the hurt.

A lot.

Suddenly, my stomach lurched and bile rose in the back of my throat.

Oh no.

I was going to—

I ran, sprinting for the closest bathroom with my hand clamped over my mouth. I made it in time, but only just.

There went my breakfast. God, throwing up was the worst.

Was I sick? I cleaned up and pressed the back of my hand to my forehead, then my neck. I didn't feel hot. And now that I'd emptied my stomach, I felt better.

The same thing had happened this morning, which was the real reason I'd been at Bigfoot Diner so early. I'd woken up to a roiling stomach, then rushed to the bathroom and puked. I hadn't been able to go back to sleep, so I'd decided to try diner food, as if my raw stomach had been the product of a hangover.

Although I hadn't had a drop of alcohol since Skylar's book launch party.

When I'd gotten so drunk, I'd—

Oh my god.

Oh.

My.

God.

What day was it?

I rushed to the living room to grab my phone and swiped to the calendar. When had I last? And what day was it now? And when had Logan and I...?

Bile rose in my throat again, but it wasn't because my stomach was queasy. It was because I'd just realized something.

Logan and I hadn't used a condom. And my period was late.

6

<hr>

CARA

*T*apping my foot, I waited while Grace's phone rang. And rang. And rang. I was about to hang up —I didn't trust myself to leave a coherent message right now —when she answered.

"Hey, sorry. My phone was in the other room."

"Are you busy?"

"We were just setting up—it doesn't matter. What's wrong?"

"I'd apologize for interrupting whatever you were doing, but I don't have it in me to be sorry right now. Can you come over? Like, right this minute?"

"Honey, what's the matter?"

"I don't know. No, I do know but I need to talk to you in person."

"I'm putting my shoes on. Do you need me to stay on the phone until I get there?"

"No, that's okay."

"Are you sure?"

"I'm sure. But maybe Asher should drive you. The roads—"

Her laugh cut me off. "The roads are clear. But—" She stopped talking just as abruptly as I had. I could hear Asher's voice in the background. "Okay, so apparently you and Asher are on the same team today. He's driving me. We're leaving right now."

"Tell him I love him."

"Cara loves you."

Asher grumbled something.

"We're on our way."

"Thank you," I whispered. My voice seemed to have gone out.

I ended the call and was about to set my phone on the kitchen counter when my thumb swiped—completely of its own accord—back to Logan's text.

Sorry.

Logan. Thinking his name made my heart beat too fast. This couldn't be happening.

I was always careful. Always. I'd never let a guy put his dick in me without a condom before. Ever. Not even when I was young and stupid and making bad decisions left and right. Drunk, stoned, sober, it didn't matter. I never took that chance.

God, why had I let that stupid doctor take out my IUD? Other than the obvious, which were the horrible side effects. I should have gone back on the goddamn pill. Why hadn't I gone back on the pill?

The fact that I hadn't been sleeping with anyone in... well, way too long... had something to do with that. I hadn't needed it. And despite my reputation—I knew what people said about me because I said it about myself—I wasn't nearly as promiscuous as people thought.

I was too picky to be as slutty as I appeared.

Kind of slutty. But not that slutty.

My feet ate up the hardwoods between the kitchen and the big windows showcasing the view of the river. I hadn't even realized I was pacing until I'd done several laps. My feet were heavy. Why were they so heavy?

Right, I was still wearing my winter boots.

Calm down, Cara. You're stronger than this.

I was stronger than this. A late period shouldn't have been enough to make me lose my mind. I hadn't been regular since getting the IUD out. This was very likely a false alarm.

That thought calmed me down. I was just riled up from talking to my mom, so everything seemed like an emergency. She always did that to me.

I took off my boots and put them away. Then went to the kitchen to make myself a mimosa.

Except if I was pregnant, I shouldn't be drinking.

But I wasn't. There was no way.

I stood in front of the open refrigerator, holding a bottle of champagne, until I heard Grace come in.

"Cara?" she called, hurrying into the kitchen.

I put the champagne away and shut the door.

When I turned around, the sight of the concern on my best friend's face just about broke me. Tears sprang to my eyes, and I was not a crier. I'd only cried in front of another person a handful of times, and two of those had been at weddings—Grace's and Fiona's—which didn't count because those had been happy tears.

"What happened?" She rushed to me, gathering me in her arms. "What's wrong? Is it your mom?"

I let her hold me. Closed my eyes and took a few slow breaths. "She did call, but that's not what's wrong."

She pulled back and took my hands. "Come on."

I felt oddly dazed as she led me to the couch. I was

almost light-headed. At least my stomach was behaving—
for now. She took off her coat and we sat.

"Talk to me."

I glanced toward the front of the house. "Is Asher here?"

"He dropped me off."

I nodded. Good. I didn't want an audience for this. Especially a Bailey brother audience. "My mom called, but it was
just the usual from her. She thinks I need an eye cream. Or
Botox. I don't know."

"Is that what has you so upset?" Grace sounded
confused.

I shook my head. Why was this so hard? I could tell
Grace. I could tell her anything. "I haven't been feeling
well."

She pressed the back of her hand to my forehead. God,
she was going to be such a good mom. "You don't feel fever-
ish. Do you have a cold?"

"No." I lifted my eyes to meet hers. "But I threw up twice
this morning."

"You didn't eat at Lucky's, did you? A whole bunch of
people got food poisoning there last week."

"No, I hate that restaurant. But you know, the more I
think about it, the more certain I am this is nothing. You're
probably right: I ate something that disagreed with me. It's
not a big deal. And the period thing is just because I got my
IUD taken out and my periods aren't regular yet."

Grace went very still. "What period thing?"

I shrugged, as if I could cast off the dread that had
settled in my stomach with a flick of my shoulders. "It's
nothing. I'm late. But I doubt I'm actually late. Like I said, I
haven't been regular."

"Cara, are you telling me your period is late and you
threw up this morning?"

"Twice, but who's counting?"

Her eyes filled with tears and her lower lip trembled. "Oh, Cara."

"What?" I grabbed her hands in alarm. "Why are you about to cry?"

"I didn't even know you were dating someone. I've been neglecting you so much, I had no idea." She swiped beneath her eyes. "Sorry, this isn't about me. I swear, this baby makes me so emotional. It's like a roller coaster. But I am sorry I didn't know you were dating someone. Wait, are you dating someone?"

"No."

"Okay, so one night stand?"

I nodded once.

"And now you're late?"

Another nod.

"And you threw up." That last one wasn't a question. "So you think you're—"

"Don't say it." I put my fingers over her lips. "Please don't say it out loud. If you say it, then I'll have to say it, and then it's going to seem real."

"I think we need to say it."

"Do we have to?"

She gave me a sympathetic smile and nodded.

I slumped into the couch. "I might be pregnant."

The word hung in the air like a spritz of cheap perfume.

"Here's what we're going to do." Grace was using her no-nonsense, we-can-fix-anything tone, which was precisely what I needed right then. "We're going to find out one way or the other. Like you said, maybe you're just irregular, not actually late. But we need to know; otherwise all we're going to do is sit here obsessing over your symptoms. Do you want me to text my doctor? She'll come in on a Sunday for something like this."

"No, no doctors. Not yet. Then there will be a record of it. Can't I just take a home pregnancy test? Do you have any left?"

She glanced away. "No, I sort of took them all."

"I thought you had extras."

"I did. I kept taking them because I was afraid the first positive was a fluke."

"You're the cutest thing in the entire world." I sat up and took a deep breath. I was tougher than this. I'd be fine. "Okay, I need to take a test. We'll run to the Quick Stop."

"Are you okay to drive?"

"I might be pregnant, boo; I haven't been drinking. Okay, so I had the champagne out and ready to pour a mimosa when you got here, but I thought better of it."

She laughed. "I don't think you've been drinking. I mean are you too upset to drive?"

I stood and smoothed down my shirt. "I'm not upset. Whatever is going on with my body, I'm sure I can handle it."

She stood, eyeing me with skepticism. "Okay."

We bundled up against the cold, then went into the garage to my Jeep. I was absolutely not too upset to drive.

Maybe I should have replied to Logan, though. Because if we were—

Stop. I was going to take a home pregnancy test, get a negative, and spend the rest of the day drinking gin and tonics. Or maybe vodka sodas. Just not bourbon. I couldn't even think of bourbon without remembering—

Nothing. Logan did not have that kind of power over me. I'd drink an entire bottle of bourbon and not think of him once.

My stomach protested, as if the mere thought of alcohol bothered it.

Seriously?

Maybe it was thinking about Logan that was so nauseating. That had to be it.

I got Grace talking about the nursery they were decorating on the way to the Quick Stop. They'd been setting up the crib when I called. Which was perhaps not the best topic to distract me from my current predicament, but it sure made her happy. Since they didn't know if Baby B was a boy or girl, they were sticking with gender neutral decor to start. Then they could add things that fit the baby's personality once he or she was here.

Did babies have personalities?

That might have been a weird question, but I honestly didn't know. I'd never been around a baby before. I'd never even held a baby before.

Oh god. This was bad. This was so, so bad.

Panic started to rise again. I gripped the steering wheel and turned into the Quick Stop parking lot, the tires crunching in the icy slush.

Deep breath. Stay calm. This is fine.

Grace reached over and gave my hand an encouraging squeeze. I turned off the engine and we climbed out.

The Quick Stop had unpleasant fluorescent lighting, and the same soft rock playlist they'd used for as long as I'd lived here pumped from the speakers. Two steps into the store, I wished we'd driven to another town. I knew everyone in here.

Lacey Hanson stood with her little girl in front of a nail polish display, pointing out various shades of pink. I'd probably see Lacey tomorrow night at Stitch and Bitch. Doris Tilburn turned over a box of hair dye, like she was contemplating what it would do to her hair. I went into her bakery once every week or so.

In the snack aisle, Gerald McMillan stood rubbing his thick beard, as if it would help him decide on a package of cookies. Olive Hembree was at the checkout counter. Sandy Chen was cashiering. Kaitlyn Peterson perused the makeup aisle.

How did I know so many people? I didn't even like people.

But the worst was the sight of Mason Flynn in line behind Olive, waiting to pay for a tube of toothpaste and some deodorant.

Mason was TFD.

He worked with Logan.

"We need to go." I grabbed Grace's arm and tried to twirl us around.

"Calm down." Her voice was soothing and she tugged on my arm, leading me deeper into the store. "It's going to be fine."

"There are a lot of people in here."

"So?"

"You remember where we live, right? If I'm seen buying... what we're here to buy, everyone in town will know by dinner."

"We'll just say it's for me."

I stopped. "You're visibly pregnant. No one's going to believe you need to take a pregnancy test."

"Then we'll buy a bunch of other stuff and no one will notice that one little thing."

"Good plan. In fact, we should buy as many embarrassing products as we can find. If we're both holding tampons, yeast infection creams, douches, and adult diapers, even the biggest gossipy bitches will avert their eyes."

She laughed, but I was not kidding.

Plus, grabbing more items would ensure Mason was long gone before we got in line to pay. The last thing I needed was someone at the fire station mentioning that Cara Goulding was in line behind him at the drug store to buy a pregnancy test.

So we walked up and down the aisles, grabbing every personal product we saw. Condoms—and the irony wasn't lost on me. Lube. Stool softener. Adult diapers. A wart removal kit. Tampons. Extra-large super-absorbent maxi-pads—with wings. Yeast infection cream. UTI test strips. And a bottle of anti-diarrhea medicine.

Grace grabbed the one thing we actually needed and kept it tucked beneath a package of hemorrhoid wipes.

By the time we got to the front, Mason was gone and there was no one in line. My heart only beat a little bit too fast and my fingers only tingled with a hint of adrenaline.

This was fine.

Grace chatted with Sandy while she rang up our purchases. My back tightened when she got to the box of home pregnancy test. But she didn't even look. Just swiped it over the scanner and dropped it into a bag.

I let out a breath and stuck my credit card in the machine so Grace wouldn't try to pay.

The total reminded me that I probably needed to stop wasting money.

Tomorrow. I'd stop wasting money tomorrow. This was an emergency.

"Thanks, Sandy," Grace said. "I'll see you later."

I grabbed most of the bags and Grace picked up the last one. I didn't know which contained the box of doom. Not that it mattered. But something told me the sharp corner of a box hitting me in the thigh as we walked was the box containing a trio of pregnancy tests, mocking me.

After stuffing everything in the backseat, we got in and drove to my house. We went inside and dumped everything on the kitchen island.

I picked up a douche and rolled my eyes. "Do women still buy these? I thought everyone knew they were bad for your vag."

Grace shrugged and picked up the box of home pregnancy tests. "Are you ready for this?"

"Clearly not because I'm trying to start a conversation about douching."

"Cara."

"You know what we should do? Bake cookies. I bet I can do it on my own now."

She shoved the box at me. "Go. Get it over with."

"Okay, okay, I'm going. But get out the gin because I'm going to need a drink after this."

The Bombay Sapphire was already on the counter. She smiled, her hand on the bottle.

"God, I love you," I said. "There are limes in the fridge, but I can slice if you don't want to."

"Go." She pointed in the direction of the bathroom. "Or no drinky."

"I can't believe you're holding my liquor hostage. Fine, I'll take a stupid test. But we both know I'm a drama queen and completely overreacting." I clutched the box to my chest, willing that to be true. "I probably started my period in the drug store and just haven't felt it yet."

"Go."

My heart thumped uncomfortably hard as I walked to

the bathroom. I kept my back straight, shoulders back. No hurry. I was fine. I wasn't panicking. I was tougher than that.

The instructions were simple enough, so I followed them and waited. Ninety-nine-point-nine percent accuracy seemed reliable. In three little minutes, all this would be a thing of the past. A story Grace and I would laugh about later.

Remember that time I thought I was pregnant? Oh my god, that was so funny. We bought all that stuff so no one would see the pregnancy tests, and after all that, of course it was negative.

Maybe I'd even tell her who the father would have been.

After three minutes, I took a deep breath and picked up the test. And almost threw up right then and there. A single word, clear as day, declared the truth. And with that one word, my entire life changed.

Positive.

7

LOGAN

I pulled my phone out of my pocket and glanced at the screen. Again. She hadn't replied, and I didn't know why the fuck I kept checking. I was acting like an idiot.

Work had been eerily quiet today. We'd responded to a call downtown first thing this morning—some out-of-towner had backed their car into Lola, the pinup statue in front of Bruce Haven's Dame and Dapper Barber Shop. No injuries, so we'd left one of Sheriff Jack Cordero's deputies to handle it.

Since then, nothing.

I could have really used a distraction. Checking gear, washing the engine, and losing at poker to Jacob and Eric over lunch hadn't done much to help. I was still thinking about what I'd said to Cara at breakfast and the way she'd walked out.

And how she hadn't acknowledged my apology.

Why did I give a shit? I'd been asking myself the same question over and over since this morning. Why did it matter if I'd hurt Cara's feelings? Did she even *have* feelings?

In all the years we'd known each other, I'd never obsessed over her like this. We saw each other, we said shitty stuff, and we left. End of story. I didn't think about her afterward, or send apology texts, or agonize over why she hadn't replied yet.

So why was I doing it now? Had one drunken fuck messed me up that much?

Apparently, it had.

Tones rang out. Time to move. Fucking finally. Not that I wanted something bad to be happening to anyone. But I needed to do something other than brood over whether a girl I hated was still mad at me.

I went to gear up, listening as dispatch relayed the information. Residential address, potential structure fire. Call came through a security company. They were attempting to contact the resident, but no response so far.

That wasn't good.

I climbed in the engine with the rest of the crew, including Levi, and we headed out.

"Standby for cross streets," dispatch said through the radio.

When dispatch came back on, giving us the cross streets, my back stiffened. We were heading toward Cara's house.

She had a monitored alarm system. If the company hadn't been able to reach her, that meant a fire alarm was going off in her house and she wasn't responding.

Fuck.

Levi met my eyes. He was thinking the same thing I was.

Okay, so not exactly the same thing. He was probably thinking that Grace would kill us if we let anything happen to her bestie.

I was too consumed with a sharp rush of adrenaline to

think much of anything, other than we needed to fucking get there. Now.

A few minutes later, we pulled down Cara's long driveway. No cars outside. If she was home, hers might be in the garage. I jumped out and did a visual sweep. No smoke or other sign of fire.

"It's probably a false alarm," Levi said, smacking me on the back.

Jacob and Christian went around the side of the house to check the back, leaving me and Levi to try to make contact with Cara.

Levi knocked on the front door.

"Hold on!" Cara's muffled voice came from inside. It didn't sound like she was in distress. I breathed out a sigh of relief.

The door opened, revealing an unusually disheveled Cara. Her red hair was in a ponytail, but wispy strands had come loose around her face. She had something all over her shirt—probably food, but it was hard to tell.

She was hot when she was messy.

Damn it, no she wasn't.

That was a lie. She really was.

Her eyes flicked between the two of us. In our turnouts, we were probably harder to tell apart at first glance.

"What are you two doing here?" she asked. "And why are you dressed like that?"

"We got a call that your fire alarm activated," Levi said. "Your security company was trying to contact you but didn't get a response."

"Are you serious?" She patted her back pockets. "I can't remember where I left my phone."

A whiff of smoke reached my nose and I whipped my

face around to look at my brother. He gave me a quick nod. He smelled it too.

"Is something burning in there?" I asked.

She looked at me again, but only for a second. Why did it seem like she didn't want to meet my eyes? "Everything is fine. I mean, yes, something was burning, but I put it out."

"Put it out?" I asked. "Cara, what the fuck is—"

Levi stopped me with a hand on my shoulder. "Can we come in and take a look? Just to make sure."

For a second, I thought she might argue. But with a resigned breath, she stepped aside to let us in.

It was cold inside, which was odd because Cara's cheeks were flushed, like she was hot. Windows were open—probably to let out the smoke. I could smell it, but now that I got a better whiff, it didn't have the acrid scent of a structure fire. It just smelled like something had burned in the oven.

And judging by the state of her kitchen, that's exactly what had happened.

A heap of burned... something... filled the sink, along with a blackened cookie sheet. The counters were littered with mixing bowls, dirty utensils, and spilled ingredients. A dusting of white made me wonder if she'd put out a fire with an extinguisher, but on second glance, it was just flour.

"I was baking," she said, her voice strangely high-pitched. "The fire alarm in here is so sensitive. It's stupid. I was in the bathroom and the alarm went off, so I came out and opened the windows. I didn't think the security company would call 911. I just wanted cookies."

I listened to her ramble with growing confusion. She looked like she was about to burst into tears.

"Sorry you guys came all the way out here for nothing. I'd offer you a cookie, but they look like lumps of coal, so I'm sure they taste terrible. Plus, I had to run water on them, so now they're soggy lumps of coal."

Wait, what the fuck? Now she was crying.

"Hey." I had the strangest urge to wrap her in my arms and hold her. "It's not a big deal. We're just glad you aren't hurt."

She sniffed and swiped beneath her eyes but seemed to pull herself together. "I'm fine. I burned my wrist a little, but—"

In an instant, I was in front of her, gently grasping her hand. I turned her arm over to inspect her wrist.

"It's fine."

"Let me look."

She had a small burn on the inside corner of her wrist. She'd probably gone for the baking sheet and touched her skin to the hot metal. It would have only taken a second.

"Did you run this under cold water?"

"Of course I did. I know how to handle a burn."

I held her hand, palm up, and swiped my thumb across the inside of her wrist, taking care to avoid touching the burn. "It doesn't look bad. No blistering, but it might leave a scar."

"It wouldn't be the first."

I met her eyes. They shone with unshed tears. I could see her fighting to keep herself together, but I had no idea why she was so upset. So she'd ruined some cookies and gotten a quarter inch burn on her wrist. Why was that such a—

She yanked her hand out of my grasp. "Can you go now, or is there a fine for false alarms?"

Something was wrong with her. I didn't know how I knew, but I did. I could feel it with every fiber of my being.

And I wanted to fix it.

"No one's going to fine you," Levi said.

"Be careful with the oven," I said. "Most residential fires start in the kitchen."

Anger flashed across her face, like she wanted to argue with me. But I wasn't trying to chastise her. I just didn't want her to get hurt—or burn her fucking house down—because she left some goddamn cookies in the oven too long.

But the flare in her eyes passed and she didn't snap at me. "I'd say I know what I'm doing, but clearly I have issues. I blame Gavin. He taught me to bake."

I laughed. "Well there's your problem, gingersnap. Everybody knows not to listen to Gav."

The corners of her mouth lifted in the hint of a smile. Kind of made me feel awesome. Her smile was pretty when it wasn't laced with evil.

Jacob and Christian knocked on the open front door and came in.

"Everything looks good outside," Christian said. His eyes flicked to the mess in the sink. "Kitchen fire?"

"Just a little mishap with some cookies," I said. "It's Gavin's fault."

His eyebrows knitted together, but he didn't ask what the fuck I was talking about. "If we're all clear, we should head back."

Levi met my eyes and I tipped my chin toward Cara. *I'll wrap up.*

He lifted his eyebrows. *Are you sure?*

I nodded. *I've got this.*

The three of them left while I hesitated near the kitchen. Cara wrung her hands together, like she was nervous about something. I didn't understand what was going on with her. I'd never seen her act like this. Well, once, but that had been a long time ago, and I'd always assumed it was a fluke.

Something pulled me to her, like an unseen force drawing us together. I knew I should get out of there before we started fighting again. Because we always started fighting when we were in the same room.

But I didn't like the way she kept looking away. The way her eyes still glistened, like she might cry. I wanted to gently kiss her wrist where she'd burned herself. And maybe run out to the bakery to get her some cookies if it would cheer her up.

"Are you sure you're okay?" I asked finally.

Her spine snapped straight and that momentary hint of vulnerability was gone from her face. "Yeah. Fine. I guess I'll just go to the store if I need carbs."

"All right." I searched for something else to say, or maybe I was looking for an excuse to stay a little longer. But I didn't come up with anything. "I'll get out of your way then."

She didn't say a word as I turned and walked to her still-open front door. I needed to go. The guys were waiting for me.

I stepped outside and glanced back, reaching for the handle so I could shut the door.

She stood with the light from the big windows behind her illuminating her silhouette. But she didn't say anything.

I shut her front door and walked out to the engine. Climbed on board.

This had been a weird fucking day.

We got back to the station and put away our gear, making sure everything was ready for the next call. I checked my phone and felt a tug on my chest. I tapped the screen to read her message.

Evil Ariel: *It's okay. And I wouldn't really fuck Levi.*

A big-ass smile stole over my face. I didn't know why I cared so damn much, but it felt like the weight that had been sitting on my chest since breakfast had finally lifted.

We were good.

8

CARA

*F*or the first time in the history of my attendance at Stitch and Bitch, I wasn't drinking.

I'd brought my usual pitcher of Long Island iced tea. I'd even poured one for myself. Grace had raised her eyebrows at me, and I'd just shrugged. It wasn't like I was going to drink it. But if I hadn't brought booze, and didn't pour a drink for myself, the ladies would notice. And they might ask questions.

Questions I didn't want to answer right now.

I'd have to answer them eventually. I'd thrown up three times this morning. It was like my body had decided I needed a daily reminder of the predicament I was in. But I needed a little time to process.

The fire alarm debacle yesterday had made that incredibly clear.

I stirred the drink I wasn't sipping. After confessing to Grace that the test was positive, she'd stayed for a while. But I hadn't freaked out. I'd been oddly calm. Eventually I'd convinced her I was okay to be alone and she could go back to decorating Baby B's nursery. I was fine.

All those acting classes my mother had forced me to take as a child had apparently left their mark. I hadn't been fine.

But Grace had her own life, and I wasn't about to go dominating it with my drama.

So naturally, I'd almost burned my house down trying to bake cookies.

I'd been in the bathroom puking again when the alarm had gone off. Smoke had been pouring out of the oven. Once I'd taken my sad attempt at cookies out of the oven and dumped them in the sink—the flames hadn't been that bad—I'd opened all the windows to get the smoke out. Then stood beneath the first-floor smoke alarm waving a pillow under it, trying to push the smoke away so it would stop blaring.

Just when I'd thought everything was under control, the TFD had showed up at my door.

Not just the TFD. Logan Bailey.

Seeing him on my doorstep dressed in all his gear—and no, being a firefighter did not make him hot—had almost made me crumple to the floor. I'd wanted to run at him and land in his arms. Beg him to make me feel better. To give me another fucking orgasm because god, my body could not decide whether it wanted to be sick or horny.

The entire thing had been a mess, from the moment I'd opened the door to the moment he'd left. I'd cried in front of him. *Cried.*

It felt like I was losing control. I needed to get my shit together.

I was doing a decent job of it today. I hadn't burned anything, yelled at anyone, cried, or called Grace in a panic.

What I had done was take the rest of the pregnancy tests that had come in the box, just in case. Suddenly I realized why my boo had gone through so many.

All positive, by the way. No ambiguity there.

I'd hoped coming to Stitch and Bitch—technically it was called Stitch and Sip, but I liked my name better—would help. And maybe it had. Sitting here listening to the ladies gossip had been better than staying home by myself, peeing on more pregnancy tests.

In fact, Violet and Tillie arguing over the relative merits of shortening, lard, and butter for pie crusts was actually an interesting conversation to listen in on.

Then Gram shut them down when she said, "I use butter."

Gram was the reigning pie queen of Tilikum. No one questioned her methods.

Thinking of pie made my stomach start to act up again. Although thinking about food in general had been doing that to me today.

Eventually, the drinks had been sipped and conversations died down. One by one, the Stitch and Bitch ladies packed up their yarn in their sweet little tote bags and left.

I was about to do the same—although I hadn't bothered to take anything out of my tote tonight, which wasn't unusual for me—when Grace gave me a sharp look. She wanted to talk without an audience.

Grace pretended to take her time gathering her things while everyone else left. I took my drink to the bathroom, and with my lower lip protruding in a pout, dumped it down the sink. I could have really used that drink.

When I came out, she pointed to one of the armchairs. I put the empty glass on the table and sat.

"I haven't heard from you all day," she said. "Are you okay?"

I gave my hair a flippant toss over my shoulder. "I'm fine. Why wouldn't I be?"

"Cara. I heard the guys had to come out to your house because you burned a batch of cookies."

"Does nothing stay quiet in this town?"

"You know it doesn't."

I blew out a breath. "It wasn't a big deal. I set off the alarm and the security company couldn't reach me because I was busy puking. Again. I thought that was a morning thing, by the way."

"I've read it can happen anytime."

"But you don't throw up multiple times a day?"

"I haven't thrown up at all. I've actually felt great the whole time." She winced. "Sorry."

"If you were anyone else, I'd hate you for that. But because you're you, I'm glad your baby is being nice to you." And I meant it. Grace had been through enough. She deserved an easy pregnancy.

"I know you have so much to think about right now, and I don't want to put pressure on you. But if you need to talk, you know I'm here."

I reached over and squeezed her hand. "I know you are. You always are. You're my person."

"Do you think... do you think you'll keep it?"

I pressed my lips together. I already knew the answer. I'd known it since yesterday, which was surprising. I wouldn't have thought it would be such an easy decision, but strangely, it was.

"Yes."

She nodded slowly. "So this is happening. We're doing this. Okay, for starters, you need to take prenatal vitamins."

We're doing this. God, I loved her so much. "Vitamins. Got it."

"And you'll want to see a doctor to confirm everything and get on the schedule for regular prenatal visits."

I blew out a breath. Shit was getting real.

"I'm sorry. I don't want to overwhelm you."

"No, you're not. But maybe let's stop before we get to cribs and diapers and all that stuff. I'm not ready for that yet."

"I'm still in shock about this. I can't imagine how you must feel."

"Honestly? I don't know how I feel. I have these moments when I think oh god, this is really happening. That's usually followed by vomiting. But then sometimes I think okay, maybe I can do this?"

"You can definitely do this."

"I'm glad one of us has faith in me."

Glancing down at her lap, she picked at a little piece of yarn.

"Go ahead," I said.

"What?"

"You can ask. It's fine."

"Why do you think I want to ask you something?"

"Because I know you're wondering when I'm going to tell you. And I would have asked you already if the tables were turned." I swallowed, because truthfully, I was dreading this moment, when I'd have to answer her unspoken question. *Who's the father?*

But she was going to find out eventually.

"I'm sorry I even have to ask, but—"

"Don't be. How would you know? It was a one night stand I didn't tell you about."

"So..." She raised her eyebrows.

"It's Logan's."

A mix of surprise and confusion passed across her features. Then she laughed. "Come on, Cara. Seriously. Who is it?"

"I'm being completely serious."

"If you don't want to tell me, it's fine."

"No, I'm telling you it's Logan. We were both drunk at Skylar's book launch party and wound up banging in the guest room upstairs."

The look of disbelief on her face almost made me laugh. "Logan? As in Bailey?"

I brushed a strand of hair away from my face. "Yes, Logan Bailey."

"But you hate him."

My throat clenched tight and for a second, I couldn't respond. Now was not the time to unpack any feelings I had for Logan Bailey, good or bad. "Yeah, well, apparently drunk me didn't hate his dick."

She stared at me open-mouthed for a long moment. "I'm sorry. I didn't think I could be more surprised than I was yesterday when you said the test was positive."

"You and me both. But here we are."

"Have you told him yet?"

I glanced away. "No."

"But you're going to, right? Soon?"

"Yes, I know I need to tell him." I rolled my eyes, like I was terribly put out. "He's not going to be happy about it, but I'll tell him."

"You never know. He might surprise you."

I gave her an incredulous look. "Grace, he hates me. He's not going to be happy to find out I'm having his baby."

"I don't think he hates you nearly as much as you think he does."

I thought about his text. *Sorry.* He'd never apologized to me before. "A girl can hope. This kid is already doomed with me for a mother."

"No, he or she is not," she said, her voice emphatic.

"You're an amazing person with a huge heart and you're going to love this baby so much."

Tears sprang to my eyes and I glanced away again. "Will you stop? I'm very unstable emotionally right now. More than usual, which is really saying something."

"It's rough, isn't it?"

I sniffed hard. "I don't know how you deal with this every day. It's like PMS on steroids."

"I'd say it gets better, but I think mostly you just get used to it." She paused for a moment. "You know what this means, right?"

"I'm going to get stretch marks and I should start saving now for the tremendous amount of therapy this kid is going to need with me as a mother?"

"No." Her smile lit up her whole face. "Our babies are cousins."

I stared at her, dumbfounded. Because in all the thinking I'd done since yesterday—pondering everything from whether or not I could actually do this to how Logan and I could possibly make any of it work—that little fact had not occurred to me.

So, naturally, instead of hugging my best friend—because not only were we pregnant at the same time, our babies were related—I burst into tears.

Grace wedged herself, belly and all, into the armchair with me. And she held me while I cried.

And cried.

And cried.

Because I really didn't know if I was cut out for this.

9

LOGAN

*J*t was the weirdest thing. I had a text from Cara.

I'd been staring at it off and on for the last few minutes. Princess Squeaker purred in a contented nap on the couch next to me and noise I was choosing to ignore came from Gavin's bedroom. Skylar was here, so I didn't want to know. I'd been about to turn on the TV to drown it out, but my phone had buzzed.

Evil Ariel: *Can you come over?*

What was that about? Cara had asked me to come over literally never. When she threw parties or had people over, it was always someone else who told me about it—one of my brothers, usually. *Hey man, we're all going to Cara's for a thing tonight. You coming?* I usually went just because they were, even though being at her house made me want to drink until it was time to go. Which is exactly what I'd done the last time I'd been there. And wound up drunk-fucking her upstairs.

At least, I think it had been upstairs. That part was still fuzzy.

But she wasn't having people over—not that I knew of, anyway. And if it was just one of her parties, she wouldn't have phrased it like that.

And it was eleven o'clock in the morning.

Was this a booty call?

Seemed like kind of a delayed response. We'd fucked like three weeks ago. If she'd wanted more, wouldn't she have asked for it sooner?

Then again, this was Cara we were talking about. She was probably that stubborn.

The question was, if this was a booty call, did I want to answer?

My dick had a very strong opinion about that. I adjusted my pants. *Stand down, big guy. I can't trust you with anything.*

And if it wasn't a booty call, what did she want?

There was only one way to find out, and it wasn't by sitting on my couch, staring at my phone like a pussy.

Me: *Sure. Be there in a few.*

I was wearing a plaid flannel over an old Tilikum College t-shirt and a pair of workout shorts. It was cold as shit outside, but whatever. My legs didn't usually get cold. So I put on a coat, tugged on a pair of boots, and left.

The gray sky threatened snow, so as much as it pained me to leave her at home, I didn't take Betty. I hopped in my pickup—it was kind of a piece of shit, but it had four-wheel drive and I could take it anywhere. As long as it would start. Today it did, first try even, so I headed out.

My route took me past the outskirts of downtown and for a second, I thought about swinging through Angel Cakes Bakery to get her some cookies. She'd wanted cookies the other day. Maybe she still did.

But she also might think I was being an ass and making fun of her for burning the ones she'd tried to bake.

That actually made it more tempting to stop. Fuck with her by handing her some cookies? That would be hilarious.

But weirdly, I didn't want to fuck with her. So I didn't stop.

I pulled up to her house and felt a strange twinge of nervousness. Things had been different between us lately. I didn't particularly want to admit that, but it was true. And as I walked to her door, a sense of foreboding stole through me. The wind rustled in the trees and a crow cawed somewhere behind me.

That was weird.

I was probably overreacting and all she wanted was a booty call.

With a deep breath, I raked my fingers through my hair and knocked.

Cara opened the door, dressed in a slouchy red sweater and distressed jeans. Her hair was down and this time, she didn't have splotches of cookie dough on her clothes.

A few weeks ago, I would have hardly noticed what she was wearing. Except, fine, I would have noted how good her ass looked in her jeans, because damn, that ass. I also wouldn't have noticed the circles beneath her eyes or the paleness of her cheeks.

I wasn't sure why I noticed now—why sleeping with her once suddenly meant I worried about why she looked so tired—but I did.

"Hey." I probably looked skeptical, like I assumed she'd lured me here to prank me.

"Come in." She turned and walked away, clearly assuming I'd follow her.

I went inside and shut the door.

A fire flickered in her gas fireplace and candles burned on the mantle. She had more candles sitting on the kitchen island. Their scent filled the air, something soft and floral. It was nice.

Was this ambiance?

Looked like she wanted a romantic booty call. I could work with that.

She stood with her back to me, looking out one of the big windows. I wanted to sidle up behind her and slip my hands around her waist. Bury my face in all that red hair while I felt her up from behind.

Did she want me to? Was I supposed to get this started?

Because this *was* a booty call, right? I was wracking my brain here and I couldn't think of any other reason she would have asked me to come over. And the fire was on, and those candles...

I decided to start by taking my coat off. One less layer of clothing. I put it on a stool next to the kitchen island, then toed off my boots. I had my flannel halfway off when she turned around.

"What are you doing?"

"Taking stuff off."

"Why?"

"Because you've got the fire going, so it's warm in here. And I assume you want my clothes off eventually."

Her eyebrows drew together. "Why do you assume I want you to take your clothes off?"

"If you want me to keep them on, I can do that too."

"What?"

"I'm just saying, I'm flexible. We can do this however you want."

"What are you—oh my god." She pressed her palm over her eyes. The girl fucking facepalmed. "You think I asked you to come over so we could have sex?"

"What am I supposed to think? Why else would you ask me to come over?"

"Not for that. That's not happening again."

I had to work pretty hard to keep the sudden flare of disappointment off my face. Not happening, as in never? "Then what are all the candles for?"

"Nothing. They smell good."

My brow furrowed. "Okay. So what the hell am I doing here?"

She didn't answer immediately. Her mouth opened and closed, like she was struggling to get out whatever it was she wanted to say.

"It's a simple question, Cara. What the fuck am I—"

"I'm pregnant."

I stared at her, unblinking. Waiting for my brain to catch up. Because she couldn't have just said what I thought she'd just said. There was no way I'd heard that word come out of Cara's mouth.

Pregnant?

Under normal circumstances, I would have had at least five wisecracks on the tip of my tongue. I could make a joke about anything. Lighten the mood, ease the tension, get people laughing. I was awesome at that.

But I had nothing. She'd shocked me into silence.

"You're..." I blew out a breath. "Did you just say *pregnant?*"

Her face was full of vulnerability as she nodded. In that moment, I knew what I said next mattered more than anything I'd ever said in my entire life.

Which is why I did not launch into a joke about how hard it was going to be to figure out who the father was.

I knew. She knew.

It was me.

"It's mine."

Something happened when I said those words. I didn't just speak them. I felt them. Something inside me shifted to this new reality. I was having a baby with Cara Goulding.

My baby.

Her back straightened and she lifted her chin. "Don't start with me about proving it. If you want a DNA test, that's fine, but I'm telling you it's yours. I haven't been with anyone else in fucking forever."

"I'm not questioning you."

"Good, because it's physically impossible that anyone but you is the father."

"I get that. I believe you."

"And don't ask me why I wasn't on birth control. Since when is it the woman's responsibility? You went in bareback and now we both have to deal with the consequences."

She'd really put a lot of thought into all the ways I might argue with her. All the ways she thought I'd try to get out of this.

But I wasn't going to try to get out of anything.

Cara seemed to glow with an unnatural light—a warmth emanating from deep inside her. With that one phrase—*I'm pregnant*—my perception of her had completely changed. She'd gone from the woman I loved to hate to the most important person on the planet. She hadn't changed. She was still crazy as shit. But who she was to me had been forever altered.

"It's my baby. I'll deal with the consequences."

She crossed her arms. "Why are you being like this?"

"Like what?"

"So agreeable. I just told you I'm knocked up and it's your fault."

"It is my fault."

"Why aren't you arguing with me?" The pitch of her voice rose with every word.

"Because there's nothing to argue about. We got drunk and had sex without a condom and now you're pregnant. What am I supposed to argue?"

"I don't know."

"Did you expect me to say it didn't happen? We both know it did. That you're not pregnant? You're crazy, but I don't think you're fake-a-pregnancy crazy. That it's not mine?" I stepped closer. "I know we've never gotten along, but I don't think you'd lie to me about this."

"I'm an awful person, but I'm not that awful."

"That's what I'm saying."

Her chin tilted up again. "And I'm keeping it. I'm going to have the baby."

Relieved to hear her say that, I exhaled. "Good."

"Good? You think this is good? This isn't *good*, Logan. This is a giant fucking mess. How are we supposed to have a baby together? All we do is fight. If it's a girl, you're probably going to try to name her after your favorite stripper, and my kid is not going to be named Destiny."

"Okay, first of all, my favorite stripper is Cherry, but you're crazy if you think my daughter is going to have a name that dooms her to the pole."

"Why are you so sure it's a daughter? It might be a boy, and oh god, it would be a *Bailey* boy. He's going to come out wearing boxing gloves and already know ten dick jokes by the time he can speak."

I grinned. "That's my boy."

"Will you stop? This is serious. You got me pregnant."

I took a slow breath and lowered my voice. She was bordering on unhinged. I could see the crazy light in her eyes. Cara was about to lose it and one of us needed to stay calm. "Yes, I know, and I'm being serious. I got you pregnant and we have a lot of shit to figure out."

"So that's it?"

"Yeah. I know you think I'm an asshole, but you could have a tiny shred of faith that I'm man enough to do what's right. I won't walk out on you."

The fire in her eyes cooled and some of the tension in her body seemed to melt. She'd been ready for a fight—probably psyching herself up to hate me more than she already did. I didn't like that she'd assumed the worst about me, but it wasn't like I was the guy she would have chosen to get her pregnant. She didn't want to be having a baby with me any more than I wanted to be having a baby with her.

Although was it really that bad? Maybe our kid would be a redhead like her.

"You're just acting very calm," she said, her voice returning to normal. "I thought you'd freak out."

"I'm freaking out a little bit on the inside." I raked my hand through my hair. "But this is happening, so I guess we just figure out how to make it work."

"Like, together?"

I nodded. "Yeah. Together."

"So... no stripper names?"

"No stripper names." I held up my hand, palm out. "On my honor."

"And no names of exes or previous sexual partners."

"You're very concerned about names."

She stepped closer and smacked my arm. "Just agree."

"Okay, okay. I agree if you do."

"Yes, I agree. And I better not find out this kid has a half-sibling who's practically the same age."

"Wait, what?" I asked. "How would this kid have a half-sibling? I don't have any other kids."

There was that defiant chin lift again. "So there's no chance? Not even with Skylar's friend?"

"Ginny? No. I hung out with her a few times, but we never slept together. Actually, I haven't been with anyone other than you in... quite a while."

"Oh. Well, that's good to know."

Without thinking, I brushed her hair back from her face. "Anything else?"

"Not right now, but I'm sure I'll think of something."

"Fair enough. Are you feeling okay? Do you need anything? I don't know how any of this works."

For a second, I thought she might step into me and rest her head on my chest. I was ready to wrap my arms around her—taking care to avoid her claws—but she broke eye contact and walked toward the kitchen. "I've lost count of the number of times I've thrown up and everything smells terrible. I thought I wanted toast this morning, but I couldn't choke it down, and then all I could smell was the toast I couldn't eat."

"Is that why you're burning thirty scented candles?"

"Yeah. It seems to help. But other than morning sickness that's really all-day sickness, I'm okay. I have the right vitamins and a doctor's appointment, thanks to Grace. Other than that, I don't think there's much to do right now."

"Grace knows?"

She crossed her arms. Man, she was quick to put up her defenses. "Of course she knows. She's my best friend and she's also pregnant, so naturally I confided in her immediately."

I put my hands up. "I'm not complaining that you told

her. I'm just wondering who else knows about this so I can be prepared."

"Oh." She dropped her arms to her sides. "No one else. I did buy a pregnancy test at the Quick Stop, but I don't think anyone noticed."

"Do you want me to keep it quiet for now? I don't mean I'm going to spread it around town, but can I tell my family?"

"Yeah, it's fine. Besides, everyone will find out sooner or later. It's going to be hard to hide once I start turning into a whale."

An image of a very pregnant Cara flashed through my mind. I didn't know why that was so appealing, but apparently my dick liked the idea.

Seriously, stay out of it. You're the one that got us into this mess.

"You're not going to be a whale. You're going to look cute with a baby belly."

Her eyes filled with tears. She clapped a hand over her mouth and turned away.

"Cara, I'm sorry. I just meant—"

"It's fine." Her voice shook and she held up a finger, like she needed a minute.

Fuck this. I walked into the kitchen and scooped her up, one arm supporting her back, the other beneath the crook of her legs.

"What the fuck are you doing?" she asked through her tears.

I didn't reply. Just took her to the couch, sat down with her in my lap, and wrapped my arms around her. Tight.

She wiggled.

I didn't move.

"Logan, what the hell?"

She tried to thrash.

I held on.

"What. Are. You. Doing?" she asked, gritting out each word in between attempts to break out of my arms.

"Holding you until you relax."

She struggled again. "Why?"

"Because you need a fucking hug and I'm going to give it to you as soon as you stop thrashing around like a feral cat."

"I don't need a hug."

"Yes you do."

"Not from you."

"Well, there's no one else here, so that's what you're getting," I said, my voice strained as I tried to keep her from wiggling out of my lap.

Finally, she stopped moving. With a shaky breath, she sagged against me. I pressed her head into the space where my neck meets my shoulder and held her close. I didn't know what it was, but she smelled amazing.

Fear tried to settle into my gut. To be fair, I had a damn good reason to be afraid. An unplanned pregnancy would scare anyone—even Gavin, and nothing scared him. And an unplanned pregnancy with crazy Cara? That was some terrifying shit.

But I pushed the fear aside. I was a Bailey. We never backed down from a challenge, even when the going got tough. Especially when the going got tough. And we didn't bitch out on our responsibilities. My dad hadn't. And my grandad had taught me better than that. I had to be a man.

A father.

Okay, there was the fear again.

I cradled Cara in my arms, knowing this was a rare moment of peace between us. She was right: We did fight all the time. I wasn't sure how we were going to make this work.

But one thing was certain: I wanted this baby. I wanted to be a part of his or her life. From this moment on, that would be my focus. I didn't know why the switch inside me had flipped so easily, but it had. I was going to do whatever it took to take care of Cara and our baby. I had to.

Because this baby was *mine*.

10

LOGAN

*I*t was weird to sit at Gram's dinner table with my family and nothing seemed different—no different than last week, at least. Obviously a lot had changed in the past couple of years. Asher was home. The women were starting to balance out the men, what with Grace, Fiona, and Skylar joining our family. But everyone sat around the table, enjoying the meal, talking about the usual stuff—the latest prank on the Havens, who was going to put a beard on Lola, whether the squirrels were planning an uprising.

My life, on the other hand, had been turned upside down.

I assumed Asher knew. Cara had told Grace, so Asher had probably known before I did. And it was a safe bet that Gram already knew—or at least suspected. She wasn't giving me any knowing looks, but I'd bet good money that it wasn't going to surprise her. She had intuition that bordered on creepy.

"Has anyone heard if they've found out anything more about the Haven House?" Fiona asked.

Her question caught my attention. The Haven House, an old home turned local history museum, had burned down late last fall. Gavin had been on the call—we'd almost lost him that day. The fire had been ruled an arson, but so far, they hadn't figured out who had done it. Or why.

It couldn't have been a feud thing. None of us would ever go that far. And despite the name Haven House, it had been built by Ernest Montgomery, one of Tilikum's founders. It didn't have anything to do with the Havens, and even if it had, no Bailey would have burned it down.

A Tilikum Historical Society volunteer had been inside, but there was no reason to suspect anyone had targeted Sally Oliver. She was just a sweet older lady who loved local history.

Why anyone would burn down a historic building was beyond me. But the evidence for arson had been clear.

"Not as far as I know," Levi said. "I think the sheriff's office is still investigating."

The whole thing pissed me off. My brother had almost died in that goddamn fire. So had several other TFD guys. As firefighters, we knew the risks, and we took them. Accidents, natural disasters, forest fires, those were one thing. But arson in my town? That was not okay.

"I still think someone wanted to get rid of something that was in the basement," Skylar said.

After the fire, Gavin and Skylar had admitted they'd snooped around the Haven House about a week earlier. They'd found a storage room in the basement and discovered a trunk full of artifacts, including a diary written by Sarah Montgomery that mentioned Eliza Bailey—the mysterious owner of the antique mirror Grace had found hidden beneath the floorboards of her house.

There was a legit mystery going on here. Who was Eliza

Bailey, and what had happened to her? Did her disappearance have anything to do with John Haven, a guy they'd found mentioned in connection with her disappearance? A Bailey and a Haven had both gone missing. Was that how the feud had started? And what did Sarah Montgomery, and her family's fortune, have to do with it?

Truthfully, I was a lot less interested in all that—even if the answers explained the origins of the Bailey-Haven feud —and a lot more interested in who the fuck had almost killed my brother by setting that building on fire.

"You might be right, but whatever was down there is gone," Levi said.

"Yeah, I saw the floor collapse," Gavin said. "There's no way anything survived."

"I still don't understand why they'd burn down a building," Grace said. "If they knew something was in there, why not just take it and hide it somewhere else?"

"If something gets stolen, it can be tracked and found again," Asher said.

"True."

The conversation quieted. We'd talked about this before, multiple times. None of us had any more answers than we did when it had happened.

The lull made my heart beat harder. Should I tell them? Cara was okay with it, and I didn't want them to hear it from someone else. But how did a guy tell his family that he'd knocked up his mortal enemy?

This was going to be awkward.

"So, I have some news," I said, breaking the short silence.

Grace's eyebrows lifted. So did Asher's. Gram's expression didn't change, and everyone else just looked at me like they expected me to say something normal, like I'd seen Bigfoot again.

I took a deep breath. "Cara's pregnant. And the baby's mine."

Fiona gasped, then clapped both hands over her mouth. Gavin and Skylar both stared at me, their eyes wide. Evan's brow furrowed, like he was confused, or maybe waiting for the punch line. Levi gave me a similar look. Grace and Asher didn't react, but of course, this wasn't news to them.

And Gram? Her eyebrows lifted, but her expression remained serene, like it was nothing to be alarmed about.

"Before you guys say anything, I know how huge this is. Obviously it wasn't planned, but she's going to have the baby and I'll be involved every step of the way. I'm not sure how that's going to work, exactly, but she and I will figure it out. And try not to kill each other in the process."

Grace's eyes filled with tears. "I knew she could count on you."

"Thanks, Grace. That's more than I can say for her, but whatever. She knows where I stand now."

"Hold on," Levi said. "You're not kidding? A baby? With *Cara*?"

I tapped my finger on the table a few times. "Yeah. With Cara."

"I knew it." Gavin pointed at me. "I knew you secretly liked her and that's why you guys fight so much."

"Shut up. I didn't secretly like her, we just..." I stopped, my eyes flicking to Gram. "Things just happened."

"When?" Gavin asked.

"Too personal, broatmeal." I shook my head. I was not about to get into detail in front of Gram.

"You seem really calm about this," Levi said, still giving me the side eye. "Are you okay?"

"Why does everyone expect me to freak out?"

"To be fair, I think most people would freak out," Gavin said.

"You'd freak out if I got pregnant?" Skylar asked.

"No, not now." He twisted in his chair to face her. "Why? Are you pregnant?"

She laughed. "No. I just mean theoretically."

"I'm not going to freak out," I said. "It happened and now I have to figure out what comes next. Like I said, I don't know how this is all going to work, but as soon as she told me, I felt... I don't know. It's a baby. There are a lot of things that could happen to a guy that are worse than having a baby, even with Cara."

Gram's expression softened into a smile. "That, right there, is the truth. Having a baby, even one that wasn't planned, is far from the worst thing that can happen to a man. In fact, it just might turn out to be the best thing."

I sat up straighter and leaned forward. "Right, that's what I was thinking. So you don't think it's weird that I'm okay with this? Because, Gram, let's be real, this is complicated. You know Cara."

"I do. And I know you, Raven. A trickster you might be, but you'll fly to the ends of the earth to take care of those you love."

Damn. That had to be the nicest thing anyone had ever said to me. And coming from Gram, it meant more than I knew how to say. "Wow. Thanks, Gram."

"You're in for a wild ride," she said, a knowing smile playing on her lips.

I blew out a long breath. "No kidding. I don't know anything about babies. Although, to be honest, I'm more worried about the baby's mom than anything else. I can learn to change a diaper. I'm not sure if I can learn to handle the princess of fire without getting burned."

"She's not that bad," Grace said.

I raised my eyebrows with skepticism.

"She's not. She's just... misunderstood."

Asher put an arm around his wife and squeezed her.

"Well, I'm getting a crash course in understanding Cara. Hopefully I come out alive."

"You're both going to do just fine," Gram said.

Her calm assurance helped. "Thanks, Gram."

Actually, everyone at the table helped, whether they realized it or not. We didn't always get along, and my brothers and I had spent a fair bit of our lives beating the crap out of each other. But this was my family, and I knew they had my back. If and when shit got hard, they'd be there to help me through it.

And right now, that meant everything to me.

11

CARA

I pried my eyes open, momentarily disoriented. Where was I? Lifting my head, I glanced around. I was on my couch and daylight streamed in through the windows. A book I'd been reading lay face down on the floor. Apparently I'd fallen asleep and dropped it.

My cheek felt wet. Lovely. I'd drooled on myself.

Still feeling out of it, I pushed myself up to a sitting position. I couldn't seem to stay awake lately. How nice to add mind-numbing exhaustion to the all-day sickness this baby had given me. At least I hadn't fallen asleep in the bathroom again. I'd done that twice in the last week.

This was so Logan's kid.

My stomach growled, but not with nausea for once. Was I actually hungry? Seemed that way. I checked the time on my phone—I had a doctor's appointment later this afternoon—and got up.

Finding food that wouldn't make me sick was getting harder. What worked for me one day smelled like garbage the next. I couldn't even look at some foods without feeling nauseated.

I poked around in the fridge, grabbing things and sniffing them. Last night's leftover taco meat—which had tasted fine yesterday—now made my stomach turn over. Nope. Vanilla yogurt was also a no. So was cottage cheese. Finally, I settled on a slice of cheddar and an apple. Not exactly an Instagram-worthy charcuterie board, but if I could keep it down, I'd call that a win.

I checked my messages while I nibbled on my snack. I had an email from one of my mom's creditors, but fortunately it was just to verify that payment had been received. I didn't know what I was going to do if she asked me to bail her out again. I was sure she had no idea how much money I'd already given her. She had a conveniently selective memory. The last time I'd talked to her, I'd made it clear I couldn't afford to help her again. She'd assured me she wouldn't need it.

I knew that was bullshit.

Thinking about my mother reminded me that I had yet to tell her I was pregnant. It was still early. No one could blame me for waiting. But regardless of when it happened, I was not looking forward to that conversation.

And then there was my father.

He hadn't been in my life when I was growing up, but I'd been in contact with him as an adult. He lived in eastern Washington—odd how we'd both ended up in the same state—but I'd never met him in person.

Ever since finding out I was pregnant, I'd had the strangest urge to call him.

I didn't know why. I barely knew the guy.

But maybe he'd want to know he was going to be a grandpa.

I finished the rest of my snack, happy that it wasn't causing another stomach upheaval. There was nothing like crappy pregnancy symptoms to foster gratitude in the smallest of things, like finding something I could eat that wouldn't make me vomit.

Grace would have pointed that out, so it made me happy that I'd thought of it myself. Maybe my boo's goodness had rubbed off on me a little bit.

My appointment was soon, so I left to pick up Grace. She'd offered to come with me and hinted that I could ask Logan to be there, too. I'd considered telling him. In fact, I'd started texting him several times, asking if he'd come with me. But for some reason, I'd deleted the text each time.

Maybe I wasn't giving him enough credit. But I was afraid of how I'd feel if he said he couldn't go. Would it be a couldn't, or a wouldn't?

I was way too emotional from all these hormones. It was better if I just went with Grace. She was a sure thing.

She came out of her house wearing a coat that clearly wouldn't zip over her belly and the cutest maternity shirt that said *Baby* in glittery letters. We drove to the clinic and went inside.

I checked in at the front desk and they told me a nurse would be out shortly to bring me back. Grace and I chose a pair of chairs in front of a coffee table littered with magazines and sat. Plants that were obviously fake—Fiona would be horrified—stood in the corners, and an aquarium bubbled pleasantly.

Grace handed me a trashy magazine. I thumbed through the pages. Lots of juicy celebrity gossip. I paused on the *who wore it better* page. I had that same dress.

How long would it fit me? Would I ever be able to wear it again?

I took a slow breath. It was just a dress.

"Are you okay?" Grace asked.

I tossed the magazine on the coffee table. "Yeah, fine. Being here is making me nervous."

She reached over and clasped my hand. "You're going to be fine."

I squeezed back. "Thank you for coming."

"Of course."

A nurse in blue scrubs came out with a clipboard. "Cara Goulding?"

My heart lurched and my stomach turned over.

Calm down, Cara. How bad could this be? You already know you're pregnant.

Grace and I stood and followed the nurse.

She made small talk while she made me step on a scale, then sent me off to the bathroom to pee in a cup. I came out and she led us to an exam room.

On the outside, I was cool as a cucumber. Calm and collected, like I wasn't facing an unexpected pregnancy. I answered her questions and even made a joke about cutting down to one bottle of wine per week since finding out I was pregnant. She'd looked alarmed until Grace had assured her I was kidding.

"The doctor will need you to undress from the waist down." The nurse handed me a paper sheet. "You can drape this over your lap. And your friend is welcome to stay if you'd like. That's completely up to you."

"Yes, she's definitely staying."

"Great. Doctor Murthy will be in shortly."

The nurse left and the door clicked shut behind her.

I slid off the exam table and unfastened my jeans. "Is it weird that my pants are already tight?"

"Not really. I didn't start showing for a while, but I was bloated at first."

"If you didn't start showing right away, that probably

means I'll be borrowing your maternity clothes next week. I seem to be having the opposite of a Grace Bailey pregnancy."

"Just invest in some yoga pants. You'll be fine."

I stepped out of my heels, took off my jeans, and folded them. I set them on the chair next to Grace, then took off my panties and folded those. I tucked my panties in my jeans so they wouldn't be sitting out.

"You do that too?" Grace asked.

"Yes, although I have no idea why. Your lady doctor is well acquainted with the inside of your vagina. Why worry about them seeing your panties?"

She laughed. "I know, but I do the same thing."

I got back on the exam table and laid the crinkly blue paper over my lap. "At least it's not just me."

There was a soft knock on the door. "Are you ready for me?"

"Come on in."

Dr. Murthy had straight black hair, deep brown eyes, and dark skin. She wore a cream-colored blouse and gray slacks and had a stethoscope draped around her neck.

She introduced herself and said hello to Grace. Her calm and friendly demeanor put me at ease. She had the air of a person who knew exactly what they were doing.

"Well, we did a pregnancy test just to be sure, and it was positive," Dr. Murthy said. "According to the first day of your last period, you should be about six weeks along. That puts your due date around October fourth."

My heart was beating too fast, but Grace gave me a reassuring smile.

Dr. Murthy spent some time examining me and asking questions. She was sympathetic to my all-day sickness and gave me a few ideas of things that could help. The way things had gone so far, I was going to be buying crystallized ginger in bulk.

"Let's take a look and see how things are progressing," Dr. Murthy said. "Go ahead and lie back."

She stood in front of what I presumed was an ultrasound machine. But the wand she picked up didn't look right. It was long with a large handle and a round bulb on the end.

Why was it so long?

"I'm going to have you put your feet in the stirrups," Dr. Murthy said. "And then just relax."

"Wait, why am I opening my legs?" I asked.

"I need to do a transvaginal ultrasound. That way I can take accurate measurements and make sure the baby's growth is progressing properly."

I glanced at Grace, my eyebrows drawing together. "Did she stick one of those up your vag?"

"Yeah, it's not bad."

I eyed the wand with skepticism.

"It looks worse than it is," Dr. Murthy said. "I don't have to use the entire length. And I'll be gentle, especially if you're experiencing any sensitivity."

"My lady garden's no stranger to medical grade plastic. I just wasn't expecting..." I gestured to the wand. "All that."

She just gave me that calm smile.

I leaned my head back on the pillow and opened my legs. Dr. Murthy inserted the wand, and it wasn't exactly a night with Mr. Bigshot, but it didn't hurt. I had no idea what we were seeing on the screen. Shapeless blobs and wavy lines. Certainly nothing that resembled a baby. Then again, it must still be so tiny. Maybe we wouldn't be able to see anything recognizable yet.

It made me wonder what the heck she was doing.

And then I saw it.

She held the wand still and clicked her mouse. But that wasn't what had my attention. I couldn't tear my eyes away from a tiny little flutter in the center. It was moving. Was that the—

"So Cara, if you look right here, you can see the baby's heart beating."

She kept talking. Something about the measurements tracking with being six weeks into the pregnancy and confirming the due date. But I barely heard her. All that existed was that little blip, blip, blip on the screen.

There really was a baby in there.

My baby.

Our baby.

And I could see the heartbeat.

My eyes flew to Grace. Without me having to say a word, she took out her phone. She knew exactly what I was thinking.

Logan needed to see this. He should be here.

"Dr. Murthy, as much as I'd rather not have an ultrasound wand up my coochie for any longer than necessary, would it be possible to—"

"He's on his way," Grace said.

"Wow, that was fast."

Dr. Murthy smiled. "The father?"

"Yeah."

"Of course." She slid the wand out. "I can come back and give you another peek when he gets here."

"Thanks."

"No problem. Just let the nurse know when you're ready."

After cleaning the ultrasound wand, she gave us both another smile and left.

I blew out a breath. "Is he really coming that fast?"

"It's possible Asher told him you had an appointment and he's been sitting in his truck waiting to see if you'll call him."

"Seriously?"

"Yes, seriously. He's a good man. Obnoxious sometimes, but good."

"I guess if someone had to knock me up, it could have been worse."

Wait, had I really said that? Worse than Logan Bailey?

Yeah, I'd said it. And meant it.

I had no idea what was happening to me.

12

LOGAN

*S*he wasn't going to call.

I was sitting in my truck, waiting like a dumb-ass. Cara had a doctor's appointment. I wanted to go with her, but she hadn't asked me to. There was a line between being involved and intruding on her privacy, and I wasn't quite sure where it was. Because I wanted to drive my ass down to the clinic and go to that appointment with her whether she wanted me to or not. But that was probably over the line.

Asher had said it was over the line, and his wife was pregnant, so he'd know.

Damn it.

I wished she would have at least asked. She probably figured I'd blow her off. I had a long way to go to prove to her that I was in this for the long haul, no matter what.

But I couldn't shake the feeling that she might call. And if she did, I wanted to be ready.

Which was why I was sitting in my truck.

I picked up one of the pregnancy books I'd ordered. When I'd searched on Amazon, I'd come up with thousands of titles. Talk about overwhelming. Grace had given me some suggestions, so I'd bought those, plus half a dozen others, just in case. I hadn't been kidding when I'd told Cara I didn't know how any of this worked. I had no clue what I was doing, and even though she was doing all the work at this point, I wanted to know what was going on.

My phone buzzed with a text and I almost dropped it between the seats. Damn it. I fished it out, but it wasn't Cara.

Grace: *Can you come?*

Me: *On my way.*

Finally. I tossed my phone on the passenger seat, started up my truck, and drove to Tilikum Family Medicine.

One of the benefits of living in a small town: Everything was close. I was at the clinic and rushing inside in no time. Grace was in the waiting room.

"Is she still here?" I asked. "Is everything okay?"

"She's fine," Grace said. "I'll show you back."

I followed her through a door, past the nurse's stations, to an exam room. A wave of nervousness washed over me. I didn't know what I was so worried about. But this felt like a big deal.

She paused in front of the closed door and met my eyes.

"Are you going to let me go in?"

"Yes."

She didn't move.

"What?"

"Be nice to her. Don't pick a fight with her today and don't take the bait if she tries to pick a fight with you. This is a lot, and she's more fragile than she seems."

"Okay, I'll be nice."

"I'm serious, Logan." Her blue eyes went icy. "If I find out you were mean to her, I'll cut your balls off, dip them in wax, and turn them into a candle."

I flinched backward. I'd never seen Grace look so fierce. "Okay, I get it. I'll be nice to her."

She pointed toward her eyes with two fingers, then swung her hand around to point at mine. "Watch yourself, Bailey."

"Can I go in now?"

Her eyes narrowed but she finally moved out of the way. "I'll tell the nurse you're here."

No wonder Gram called her Mama Bear.

I went in and found Cara on an exam table. The back was angled so she was partially sitting up and she had a piece of blue paper covering her lap.

My mouth hooked in a grin. "Are you naked under there?"

"Shut up, Logan."

I put my hands up. "I'm just asking. How is everything? Are you okay? Is the baby okay?"

She smoothed out the paper, making it crinkle. "Yes, fine. The doctor took measurements or whatever it is she does. The baby looks... well, there's not a lot to see, but apparently that's normal."

"So you're all right? Everything is fine?"

"If by fine, you mean unexpectedly pregnant with your baby but otherwise healthy, then yes."

"Good." I put up my hands again. "I know, I know. You're pregnant, so this isn't *good*. I'm just trying to make the best of the situation."

She glanced up—not quite an eye roll, but close. "Well, maybe it's not all bad. But listen, the doctor is going to come back and to do the ultrasound. She has to—"

A knock on the door interrupted whatever she was about to say.

The doctor came in, a woman with straight black hair

and dark skin. "Hi, I'm Dr. Murthy. You must be the baby's father?"

I puffed out my chest. Hell yes, I was the baby's father. "Logan Bailey."

"Nice to meet you. Okay, Cara, are you ready to take another look?"

"Let's ride the dildo-cam," she said.

Wait, what? What was a dildo-cam?

Dr. Murthy moved in front of the ultrasound machine and picked up a long... thing. It had a large handle with a stick that ended in a round bulb. It was reminiscent of a sex toy, although skinnier than I would have thought.

And longer. A lot longer.

"Is that going in your—"

"Yes," Cara hissed. "Just stay up here by my head."

I wanted to make a joke about having seen the good stuff before, but Grace's crazy-eyed threat made me bite it back.

"Now Cara, just relax," Dr. Murthy said.

Cara bent her knees and tipped her legs open and of course I didn't try to sneak a peek beneath the paper covering.

Yeah, I totally did. But I couldn't see anything.

Dr. Murthy moved the paper a bit and, I assumed, stuck the dildo-cam into Cara's vagina. I kept my eyes on the screen and tried not to think about what the doctor was doing to her. It was slightly weird to be standing next to her while a doctor shoved a wand up her vag.

"There we go," Dr. Murthy said. With her other hand, she pointed to a round shape on the screen. "That's the baby's head. And here you can see the outline of the body. And this little flicker right here is the baby's heart beating."

All the air left my lungs and I stared at the screen in awe. Holy shit. It really was a baby. I could see it.

"Whoa," I breathed.

"Is it weird that I could just sit here and stare at it?" Cara asked.

I wasn't sure if she was asking me or her doctor, but I knew exactly what she meant. Without quite meaning to, I grabbed Cara's hand, twining our fingers together. Maybe it was because she was mesmerized by our baby's heart beating, but she let me.

"Not at all," Dr. Murthy said. "I'll record it for you and have a link for you to download the video in your online chart. I can send you home with some pictures as well."

"Thank you," Cara said.

I gazed at the screen—at the little flicker of movement. It was so tiny.

"Can you tell if it's a boy or a girl yet?" I asked.

"Not yet. We can usually tell by ultrasound around eighteen to twenty weeks. Cara's pregnancy is measuring six weeks right now."

I nodded, still not taking my eyes off the screen.

Cara turned to look at me and suddenly I didn't know what was hitting me harder, the sight of my baby's heart beating or the look in her eyes. For once in our very tumultuous relationship, we were on exactly the same page.

Scared, but also a little bit excited.

"Me too, Tiger," I said softly.

She squeezed my hand. I squeezed hers back.

Maybe we really could do this.

13

CARA

*L*ogan held the clinic door for me and we stepped out into the cold. I hadn't been prepared for that appointment. I'd thought it would be simple— they'd give me another pregnancy test, then hand me some pamphlets or something. But seeing the baby on the ultra- sound had been intense.

And seeing Logan see the baby on the ultrasound had been even more so.

I was glad he'd come. It was his baby, too, and he really did seem to want to be involved. But his response to the news of our unexpected pregnancy was starting to whittle away at my firmly held antagonism. When he'd held my hand, it had felt like we'd had a moment.

I wasn't prepared to be having *moments* with Logan Bailey.

He stopped in the slushy parking lot and turned to face me. "Do you want to get some food?"

Yes. No. I was hungry, but I didn't know what I'd be able to eat. And after that brief hand-holding incident in the exam room, I wasn't sure if I should spend any more time with Logan today.

But my stomach did feel more hungry than nauseated, and we did have a lot to talk about.

"Yes, but I have to warn you that the baby has very strong opinions about food smells."

"Okay. How about we park downtown and give some restaurants the sniff test. When you smell one you and the baby like, we'll go in."

"That's actually a really good idea."

He grinned. "I'd take credit, but I read it in a book."

"What book?"

"One of the pregnancy books I bought."

"You bought pregnancy books?"

He shrugged. "Yeah. I know the pregnancy is mostly your thing, but I figured I should read up."

Goddammit, why was he being so sweet? It was driving me nuts. "Father of the year already. I'll drive myself so I don't have to come back for my car."

A flicker of disappointment passed across his face, but I ignored it. It didn't make sense to drive together. My house was in the opposite direction. Why circle back to get my car?

"I'll meet you at Bigfoot Diner," he said. "It's not open this late, but there should be parking. We can start our search there."

"Okay."

I walked to my Jeep and got in. My hands trembled as I put in the key. Why was I so jittery?

Maybe I was just hungry.

Logan followed behind me as I drove the short distance to Tilikum's little downtown. There was indeed parking outside Bigfoot Diner. I was mildly disappointed they weren't open this late in the day. Waffles sounded good.

I parked and got out. Another diner, The Copper Kettle, was right across the street. Thanks to the weirdest aspect of Tilikum life—the Bailey-Haven feud—I'd never been inside. The Havens went there, which meant people on the Bailey side didn't.

And right then, a Haven walked out.

It was Josiah Haven, looking like a burly bearded mountain man in flannel. I'd never cared about the feud—not for my own sake, at least. I was loyal to the Bailey side because Grace was so fiercely attached to them. If anything, I'd always been slightly disappointed that the feud put all those hot Haven men in the do not touch zone.

But seeing the narrow-eyed glare that Josiah Haven gave Logan made my hackles rise.

Go ahead, asshole. Say something. I'll claw your eyeballs out.

"Whoa, Cara bear." Logan gently grabbed my elbow and steered me back to the sidewalk. "You can put the claws away."

"What's his problem?"

"I'm a Bailey. He's a Haven. That's always the problem."

"Dick," I muttered.

Logan chuckled softly and kept his light grip on my arm. "Let's just find a restaurant that smells good."

The first one we tried immediately made me gag. The second seemed okay on the first inhale, but my stomach protested on the second. We walked a little farther and tried another. I recoiled away, shuddering at how bad it smelled.

Logan didn't seem annoyed that I was taking picky to a level that was extreme even for me. He just moved on, walking with me to the next place.

Although this town was small, and we were running out of restaurants.

"I think the baby wants onion rings," he said, gesturing across the street to the Caboose.

I crinkled my nose. "I guess we could give it a try."

We walked to the Caboose and as soon as he opened the door, I knew this was it. I inhaled deeply, taking in the strangely appetizing scent of greasy comfort food.

"I don't want to admit that you're right, but this place smells good."

He held the door and gestured for me to go in. "Baby Mama."

I smacked him as I walked by. "Don't call me that."

He just laughed.

Asshole.

The Caboose was decorated with an assortment of railroad décor, including old signs and model trains. We picked a booth on the restaurant side. There were plenty of open tables, and I didn't want to sit in the bar if I couldn't drink. And that little flicker on the screen had certainly confirmed what I'd already known. There was definitely a baby in there.

A Bailey baby.

How the hell was this my life?

A server walked by with something that smelled like what I needed to eat. I twisted around, trying to see what it was. He put two plates down in front of a couple at a table on the other side of the restaurant, then went back to the kitchen.

"You okay?" Logan asked.

"What was that? Whatever it was, that's what I want."

I was about to get up and go ask the lady what she was eating, but Logan was already standing. He walked across the restaurant to their table and spoke to them for a moment. He came back and slid into his seat.

"Meatloaf with mashed potatoes," he said.

"No, what the woman is eating, not the guy."

He glanced at the other table again. "That is what she's eating. They both ordered the same thing."

"Meatloaf? I don't even like meatloaf. It looks like a bunch of ground beef mixed with mystery ingredients designed to use up the stuff that no one wants."

"I guess the baby wants meatloaf." He shrugged. "By the way, is there anything you don't want me to order? I read that some women don't even like the sight of some foods, especially if they're having a lot of morning sickness. You know what, never mind, I'll just order what you're having so we don't have to worry about it."

I stared at him. He really needed to stop being so nice to me.

"What?" he asked.

"Nothing."

"I'm just trying to make sure you don't puke all over the table."

I rolled my eyes. "I won't."

"Good, because that's a first date deal breaker for me. Girl vomits up her meal, I'm out."

"Whether I puke or not, this isn't a date. Besides, if I puke, it's your fault."

"It's kind of my fault, but I feel like you should take fifty percent of the blame."

Before I could fire back—although he wasn't wrong— the server came to take our orders. He confirmed that the meal that had smelled so tantalizing was indeed meatloaf, so despite my usual disdain for bread-shaped meat, I ordered it. So did Logan.

"Anything to drink?" the server asked.

"Just ice water for me," I said. "But only half the ice, and a slice of lemon on the rim."

"No problem. What about you?" he asked Logan.

"I'll take a Hein—" He stopped mid-sentence. "Never mind. Just water for me."

"Would you also like lemon?"

"Sure, why not."

The server left with our orders and I eyed Logan for a moment.

"What?" he asked.

"Why didn't you order a beer?"

"You can't drink, so I figure I can live without it."

"You don't have to do that."

The corner of his mouth lifted. "I know."

A chaotic mix of emotions swirled inside me. Maybe I should have gone home. I was having a hard time holding myself together, and the last thing I needed to do was lose it in front of Logan. Again. But my feelings were all over the place. I wasn't sure if I wanted to go sit on his side of the booth so I could curl up next to him or bite his head off.

This was all very confusing.

"What do you think of the name Brolin?" he asked.

"Brolin? For a baby? No."

"Just like that and it's off the table?"

"Yes, just like that."

He scowled, but this was good. For some reason, thinking about names wasn't too overwhelming. And if I suggested names Logan would object to...

"I was thinking something more like Bear."

"Bear?" His brow furrowed. "First, no. Second, bears are Asher's thing."

I tapped my lips. "What about Cooper?"

"Cooper?" he asked, and the irritated skepticism in his voice was music to my ears. "Like Grace's brother, Cooper?"

"Exactly. He'd make a great namesake. Smart, hard-working, funny, plus he's hot as hell."

Logan crossed his arms. "No. I veto Cooper."

"Why?"

"Because we're not naming our kid after a man you think is hot."

"He's married; what are you worried about?"

"Doesn't matter. No."

"Fine. What about Roland?"

He rolled his eyes. "Let me guess. Because he's Grace's other brother, and he's also hot."

"It's not my fault her brothers are all gorgeous hunks of man candy. And I heard Roland has a piercing."

"You want to name our baby after a guy because you think he's hot and he has a piercing?"

It was hard to keep a straight face. "No, I just like the name."

"God, I hate you sometimes," he growled.

"I'm glad something hasn't changed."

His expression shifted into a smug grin. "If it's a girl, I say we name her Ginny."

I ground my teeth together, anger flashing hot. "Absolutely not."

"Why? It's a cute name."

It was all I could do to stay on my side of the booth. I wanted to throttle him. "We already agreed no names of exes or previous sexual partners."

"Ginny is neither of those."

"You dated her."

"I didn't *date* her. I took her out a few times and, I'll remind you, did not sleep with her. That doesn't count."

"Still no."

By the way he kept trying to hide his smile, I knew he was fucking with me. And of course I was fucking with him by suggesting Cooper and Roland.

But still. I was the pregnant one. He shouldn't fuck with me.

"We should really consider the baby's full name," I said. "Whatever we choose has to go with Goulding."

"Hold up there, gingersnap. You mean Bailey."

"Why should the baby's last name be Bailey? We're not married."

"Because it's *my* baby."

Something about the way he said that, in that growly voice with so much emphasis on *my*, made me clench my thighs. A flush hit my cheeks and I almost told him he was skipping the meatloaf and having me for dinner.

Now.

The server came with our meals and set them in front of us. As soon as the scent of that meatloaf hit my nose, my body's intense need for sex was suddenly replaced by an intense need to shove every bite of this food in my mouth as quickly as possible. I didn't wait for the server to ask if we needed anything else before grabbing my fork and attacking my dinner.

Four or five—or maybe ten—bites later, I paused. "Oh my god, this is the best thing I've ever eaten. And I once had a plate of thousand-dollar sushi that made me want to weep."

Logan laughed. "That good, huh?"

"I don't even like meatloaf and this is so good I could die."

I felt no shame at the speed with which I inhaled my

meal. It tasted like heaven and it felt so good to eat without causing waves of nausea.

In fact, by the time I finished the last of the mashed potatoes, my brain buzzed with contentment. I glanced up at Logan—he seemed to be enjoying his meal, too—and a strange sense of euphoria washed over me.

But it wasn't because I liked Logan. After struggling to keep anything down for the last few weeks, I was just happy to be able to eat. I was high on meatloaf endorphins.

I had no illusions about him. Yes, I could admit he was going to be a good father to this baby. Fine. But that was all. We'd make things work because we had to.

I wasn't going to set myself up for disappointment by imagining anything more.

14

LOGAN

*B*etty's engine rumbled as I pulled to a stop in front of Evan's shop. A pang of sadness hit me. I'd imagined this day for a long time—driving Betty out here to leave her in my brother's capable hands. Only in my dreams, I'd be getting her back, fully restored.

That wasn't why I was here.

"I'm sorry, baby." I caressed the steering wheel. "I wanted to keep you forever, but things change."

And in my life, *things* hadn't just changed. Everything had.

I pulled out my phone and swiped to the video Cara had sent me. It was only about thirty seconds long, but I'd probably watched it a thousand times since her appointment a few weeks ago. My baby's heartbeat on the ultrasound.

With a deep breath, I got out and shut the door.

Evan's dog, a huge German shepherd named Sasquatch, stood guard in the open garage bay door. I stopped in my tracks and eyed him. Sasquatch was the scariest fucking dog. He always looked at me like the only reason he wasn't ripping my throat out was because his human had told him not to—but he could, and if Evan ever gave him the go-ahead, he damn well would.

I shuddered.

My brother came out dressed in a long-sleeve shirt and jeans, holding a cup of coffee. He was the tallest of the five of us, with broad shoulders and a perpetual scowl. Although since Fiona—especially since *marrying* Fiona—he'd been in a much better mood.

With a quiet command, he sent Sasquatch into the shop.

"Why does your dog hate me?"

Instead of arguing that his dog did not in fact hate me, he just shrugged. "What's up?"

"I need to talk to you about Betty." I placed a gentle hand on her hood.

"I'm only a couple of weeks from having a spot in the shop for her."

"Yeah, I know, but that's not why—"

The office door burst open and Fiona danced her way out, singing at the top of her lungs. She had a wrench in her hand and used it like a microphone. After pausing to spin on one of her tiptoes, she stopped, her wrench-microphone still in front of her open mouth.

Evan smiled at her. I still wasn't used to seeing that expression on his face.

"Sorry," Fiona said, lowering her hand. "I didn't know anyone else was here. Morning, Logan."

"Morning, Fiona."

She looked past me and her eyes lit up. "Is it time? Do we get Betty? I'm so excited to get to work on her. She's going to be such a hot car when we're done."

I put my hand on my chest. Ouch. She would have been a hot car—my hot car. But I had bigger things to worry about.

"Yeah, I know you guys would make her look amazing." I took a deep breath. "But I'm not going to have her restored. I was hoping you could help me find a buyer."

Evan's brow furrowed. "If it's the money, you know I'm going to give you a big discount. We can work it out."

"I know, and I appreciate it. But I need something reliable that I can drive year-round. Something that will fit a car seat."

"Aw." Fiona clutched her hands to her chest. "You're going to sell Betty to get a family car? That's so romantic."

Evan's brow furrowed. "Romantic?"

"He's giving up his dream car to be a responsible daddy," she said. "That's extremely romantic."

"It's *not* about romance," I said. "Cara and I are not... No, this isn't about her. I'm going to have a kid, and I have a busted-ass pickup and a muscle car that needs a shit ton of work. Neither of those are practical."

Evan rubbed his jaw. "Yeah, it makes sense. Are you sure, though? I could hold onto her for you."

"I thought about that, but who knows when I'll have the money to put into her. I'm going to use up what I have buying a daddy wagon."

"What are you thinking about getting?" Fiona asked. "Amy at Stitch and Sip loves her minivan—"

"Whoa," I said, holding up a hand. "No minivans."

"I know they're not cool, but have you seen the automatic doors on those things?" she asked. "They're pretty slick."

Evan met my eyes and gave me a subtle head shake.

"No. No minivans. I've been looking at Explorers."

"So you're sure?" Evan asked, gesturing to Betty. "You want us to find a buyer?"

I caressed her hood again. "Yeah. I could use the money.

And like I said, if I keep her, she'll just go back to sitting in my garage. It's not fair to her. She needs to live her best life."

Fiona came at me with open arms and wrapped me in a sisterly hug. "You're such a good guy. I know how hard this is."

I hugged her back. "Thanks."

"Do you want to leave her here?" Evan asked. "I can run you back to town."

"Yeah, that's probably for the best. Thanks, brotastic."

He patted my shoulder.

After leaving Betty behind, I felt a sense of peace. I was going to miss her, but I also knew without a doubt that this was the right call. And that afternoon when I took my pickup down to a dealership in Wenatchee to trade it in for a Ford Explorer, it actually felt pretty great. Maybe it wasn't the muscle car I'd been dreaming about since I was a kid, but it wasn't a bad ride. And my baby's car seat would fit comfortably in the back.

That mattered a lot more.

I PULLED INTO MY DRIVEWAY, parking next to Levi's blue Explorer—glad I'd chosen a dark red. It hadn't occurred to me that I was buying the same car as my twin, but he had the same model, just a few years older. Figured. We did shit like that all the time.

Gavin stood in the front window, holding a bowl and shoveling food into his mouth. Levi appeared next to him. Nosy assholes.

I opened the front door and they both looked at me, then out the window.

"Holy shit, you really did get a new car," Gavin said

around a bite of cereal. Sometimes it was hard to reconcile the fact that my younger brother—who still sometimes ate cereal with marshmallows for dinner—was getting married.

"How did you know I bought a new car? I just left the dealership."

"Skylar heard something at the coffee shop. She called me to see if I knew."

I didn't know why I was surprised. As soon as I'd rolled into town, tongues must have started wagging. A guy with a new SUV was apparently an interesting piece of news around here.

"Whatever. Yes, I bought a new car."

"Nice choice," Levi said.

"Thanks, bro diddly. Figured I needed a daddy wagon, so I might as well get it over with. I traded in my truck, and Evan's going to help me find a buyer for Betty." I took off my coat and tossed it on the back of the couch.

"A buyer?" Levi asked as I headed for the kitchen. "You're selling Betty?"

"Yep." I went to the fridge and rooted around. It was surprisingly well-stocked, considering the three of us lived here. I grabbed a beer and when I turned around, he was staring at me. "What?"

"I just can't believe you're selling your car. You love that car. Like, more than is healthy."

I grabbed a bottle opener and popped off the top, my back clenching with a spike of annoyance. "So?"

"I'm just surprised, that's all."

"You're surprised I'd make a mature decision? Why does everyone assume I'm a total fuckup? My baby mama thinks I'm going to flake out on her. You assholes assume I'd rather keep my car than have a safe ride for my baby. Seriously, what the fuck?"

Still holding his bowl and spoon, Gavin held up his hands. "I didn't say anything."

I gestured at him with my bottle. "You were thinking it."

"That isn't what I meant," Levi said. "I know you're not a fuckup. I'd trust you with my life. In fact, I do all the time."

Okay, so that was true. You had to trust the guys on your crew. Sometimes your life literally depended on it.

I nodded to Levi in acknowledgment.

"This calls for a celebration." Gavin added his bowl and spoon to the pile of dirty dishes in the sink and got two more beers out of the fridge. He cracked them open and handed one to Levi. "To Logan's new daddy wagon."

I lifted my bottle and took in a mouthful, then almost choked on it. I ran to the sink and spit it out.

"Dude, what's wrong?" Gavin asked.

I set the beer down and wiped my mouth with the back of my hand. "I said I wouldn't drink because Cara can't. I grabbed the stupid beer without thinking."

The front door opened and Asher walked in. "Hey. So you really did buy a new car?"

"Is that why you came over?" I asked.

"I saw it in the driveway."

I rolled my eyes, but I couldn't even be mad. The nosiness in this town was baked into all of us. "Yes, it's mine."

Gavin took the beer and handed it to Asher. "We're celebrating Logan's new daddy wagon."

"Nice." He took a drink. "Congrats, man."

"Thanks."

Asher helped himself to a seat in one of our armchairs. The rest of us followed and sat around the coffee table. I was only slightly envious of their beers.

"Did you guys talk to Gram today?" Asher asked.

"No, I actually haven't talked to her in a few days," I said. "Is she okay?"

"I think so. She asked me if I knew of any good accountants."

"I thought she had an accountant," Levi said.

"She did," Asher said. "I guess she went to her yearly tax appointment and the guy was a no-show."

"No shit?"

"Yeah. She said no one was at his office. She went home and left him a message, but if he doesn't call her back tomorrow, she's going to find someone else. You know how she is when it comes to manners."

I did know. Gram was the only reason the five of us hadn't gone feral after our parents died. Even when we were beating the shit out of each other, we were still polite about it.

"Do you know anyone?" Levi asked.

"Grace might, but she's not home yet," he said.

"Isn't Darcy Klein an accountant?" I asked.

Levi glanced at me and raised his eyebrows. *Didn't you date her?*

I scowled at him. *Yes, shut up about it.*

"Yeah, I think she is," Levi said.

Luckily for him, he left the rest out. For some reason, it was grating on me to be reminded of an ex.

Also, note to self, don't suggest Darcy as a baby name.

"Thanks," Asher said. "I'll look her up."

My phone rang, the screen lighting up with *Baby Mama*. I'd changed it from Evil Ariel after the ultrasound.

"Hey, baby mama, what's—"

"Are you at work?" she asked, cutting me off.

The urgency in her voice made my back stiffen and I sat up. "No. What's wrong?"

"It's probably nothing, but I'm bleeding a little and my doctor told me to come in."

"Stay where you are. I'll come get you."

"You don't have to—"

"Cara," I snapped. "Are you at home?"

"Yes."

I was already stepping into a pair of shoes. I had no idea who they belonged to, but I didn't give a shit. "I'm on my way."

"What's going on?" Levi asked.

"I have to take Cara to the doctor," I said, then flew out the door.

15

LOGAN

*I*t was March, but still cold as shit in the mountains. Light snow fell and the sky looked gray and heavy, like it was about to dump a lot more. I hadn't grabbed my coat, but I didn't give a fuck. All I could think about as I drove toward her house was Cara and the baby.

Bleeding a little. What the fuck did that mean? My heart hammered in my chest and a sick knot of fear sat heavy in my gut. I'd read enough about pregnancy to know bleeding could be nothing serious—or it could be worst-case scenario bad. What had she meant by *a little*? Was she doing that thing she did where she tried to act like nothing was wrong? Or was it actually a small amount and this trip to the doctor was just a precaution?

She'd sounded scared.

In the back of my mind, I wondered if she'd called me first, or if she'd tried to call Grace and hadn't gotten through.

I pulled up outside her house and dashed to her front door, leaving the SUV running. Her door was locked, so I banged on it a few times. "Cara?"

When she answered, she had her fake-ass *everything is fine* face on. I used to think that was just her—that she didn't give a shit about much of anything, which was why she walked around looking like the world bored her. But now that I'd seen behind her mask a few times, I was starting to recognize her bullshit.

"You didn't have to come get me. It's not like I can't drive." She shouldered her purse and came out, shutting the door behind her.

I bit back a sharp reply. "Let's just go."

She took a few steps toward the driveway but paused. "Whose car is that?"

"It's mine. I picked it up today." I went around to the passenger side and opened the door for her.

She climbed in without any snarky remarks about my choice of color or complaining that I didn't need to open doors for her.

That seemed like a bad sign.

I got in and backed out of her driveway. "So what's going on? You're bleeding?"

"A little. Not like a period, but enough that I noticed." Her voice was casual—almost flippant—but I didn't miss the way she twisted her purse strap in her hands.

I glanced at the clock. It was after seven. "Are we going to the clinic or the ER?"

"Clinic. Urgent care is still open and my doctor is meeting me—" She paused for half a second. "Meeting us there."

"Are you experiencing any cramping?"

"Well, Dr. Bailey, I'm bloated and I noticed my labia are a bit swollen. But no cramping."

I shot her a glare. "I just want to know if you're feeling okay."

She let out a breath. "I feel fine. No pain or cramping."

"Good." I hesitated for a moment. "Are you really swollen down there?"

"Shut up, Logan."

"I'm just asking."

"The state of my labia is none of your business."

"Okay, okay." I hung a right at the bank. My heart still beat too hard, but I didn't want to stress her out, so I stopped myself from asking more questions.

Finally, we pulled into the almost-empty parking lot outside the clinic.

She didn't wait for me to come around and open her door. The urge to grab her hand while we walked inside was strong, but I had a feeling she'd just smack me if I tried.

But goddamn, I wanted to hold onto her.

She checked in at the front desk. Most of the seats in the waiting area were empty, but a woman with a toddler in her lap sat near an aquarium. I hung back, cataloging all the reasons for bleeding in early pregnancy that I'd read about. She was a little over nine weeks, still in the first trimester. Still at a time when, statistically speaking, a lot of things could go wrong.

"Dr. Murthy is already here," the woman at the front desk said, getting up from her chair. "I'll take you back."

I hesitated behind her, not sure if I should follow. Every cell in my body screamed at me to go with her—to make her let me if she tried to refuse.

But the desire for her to want me to be there was just as strong.

Come on, Cara. Turn around and snap at me to hurry up or something.

My feet felt glued to the floor as she started toward the door that led to the exam rooms. Her back was straight, nothing in her posture to suggest she was concerned. No sign that she might be scared for our baby.

I knew it was an act. She was scared. And it pissed me off that she was trying so fucking hard to hide it.

The front desk lady opened the door and Cara finally looked back at me over her shoulder.

"You can come with me. Or stay here if you want."

Her voice betrayed nothing—she sounded like she really didn't care either way. But I saw the truth in her eyes. They pleaded with me. I caught a glimpse of the real her—the Cara she kept hidden away deep inside. That woman was afraid, begging me to blow past her defenses and help her through this.

So I checked my irritation and followed her back.

A nurse met us at the exam room, followed closely by Dr. Murthy. I took a seat in the corner, trying to stay out of the way.

Dr. Murthy asked a series of questions while the nurse checked her vitals. Her answers didn't give me anything I didn't already know and even Dr. Murthy's calm voice didn't do shit to slow my heart rate.

What if we lost the baby?

That question had been hovering in the back of my mind since Cara had called. Now I finally allowed myself to actually think it.

There was no doubt everything would have been easier if this hadn't happened—if I hadn't gotten her pregnant in the first place. This was complicated as hell.

But fuck, I didn't want to lose our baby.

The doctor continued to examine Cara and the nurse took some blood. Cara cast quick glances at me, never quite holding my gaze. I shook my leg, the only outlet I had for all the adrenaline coursing through my veins.

Finally, Dr. Murthy and the nurse both left with instructions for Cara to get undressed from the waist down.

"I won't watch," I said. "Or I can step out if you want."

"No, don't go." She finally seemed to allow a little of her fear to show.

I waited, eyes on the floor, while she undressed and climbed back on the exam table with the blue paper across her lap.

"Who knew I'd be looking forward to the dildo-cam again."

I stood and risked the tiger's claws. Slipped her hand in mine and squeezed. And I didn't make a joke about how the ultrasound wand couldn't be a big deal to a woman who must have an extensive collection of dildos at home.

But I did chuckle.

"You were going to say I must have bigger dildos at home so what's the big deal, weren't you?"

"No."

"Liar."

"I was actually thinking about the quantity of dildos you own, not the size. But size is funny too."

The corners of her mouth lifted.

"Besides, you've had me inside you. The dildo-cam is nothing compared to that."

That made her laugh. Sure, she was laughing at me—at my dick, no less—but it was worth it.

Dr. Murthy knocked and came back in.

"We'll have the results of your blood work soon. We're looking to see if your hCG level has risen to where we'd expect. In the meantime, let's take a look."

I waited with my eyes glued to the screen while Dr. Murthy performed the ultrasound, desperate to see that little blip. Cara's grip on my hand tightened.

Finally, we saw it. That tiny little flutter—although it looked a bit less tiny this time. Cara squeezed my hand again. I leaned over and kissed her temple.

Thank fuck.

"Everything looks great, Cara," Dr. Murthy said. "Baby is measuring right on time at just over nine weeks. Heartbeat is strong. Your placenta is low, which is probably why you started spotting. That might happen on and off for a little while. If it gets worse or you experience any cramping, let us know right away. Otherwise, just take it easy and it should resolve itself. The baby looks great."

I felt her body shudder as she took a shaky breath. "Thank you."

"We'll call you with the results of your blood work, but I don't expect we'll find anything out of the ordinary." She paused and met my eyes, then Cara's. "You're doing a great job."

I kissed Cara's temple again. "Yeah, you are."

The fact that it took her about ten seconds to elbow me away felt like progress. Toward what, I wasn't sure. Obviously I wanted us to figure out a way to co-parent this kid without killing each other. Beyond that, her not hating my guts would be nice.

Except... did I actually want more than that? Would not hating me be enough? Maybe I wanted her to actually *like* me.

Dr. Murthy left and I waited with my eyes on the floor while she got dressed. Didn't even peek once. I was too busy contemplating the impossible.

Could Cara Goulding ever like me?

Did I want her to?

Did I like her?

I could still make a list of a thousand ways she pissed me

off. But every glimpse I got of the real Cara—every moment of honesty, however brief—was a crack in my resolve to hate her. Truthfully, I hadn't hated her since I'd found out she was having my baby. I could even admit that sometimes I kind of liked her.

I grabbed her coat and helped her slip it on.

"Thanks." She pulled her hair out from the collar.

"Of course. I'm glad you called."

I waited for her to tell me she'd called Grace first. Hell, that she'd called Fiona and Skylar, too, and I'd been a last resort.

But she didn't. She just smiled. An honest, no bullshit smile. "Me too."

Fuck, she was beautiful when she did that.

We left the clinic, and my head was full of too many thoughts to sort out. Mostly I was just glad the baby, and Cara, were okay.

But a sense of discontent still thrummed through me. I knew why—knew exactly what was bothering me. But I wasn't sure what I was going to do about it.

16

CARA

I had no idea how to deal with the level of relief I felt.

Because, let's be honest, wouldn't it have been easier if I'd lost the baby?

I was a horrible person for thinking such a thing, but I had thought it. And who could blame me? It was a completely unplanned pregnancy with a man I could barely stand. It was practically a worst-case scenario. I wouldn't have been human if I hadn't asked myself that question.

And me as a mother? I still hadn't figured out how the hell that was going to work.

But as soon as I'd seen that first smear of blood, I'd been consumed with fear. Because I did not, in fact, want to lose the baby.

It was a sobering realization, one I was still trying very hard to keep locked inside me while Logan drove us through the dark streets of Tilikum.

"What do you need?" he asked, glancing at me. "Meat-loaf again?"

My first instinct was to roll my eyes and say something shitty. *I don't need anything from you, Logan. Just take me home.*

But I didn't. Because I did want meatloaf.

More than that, I didn't want to chase him off.

"Actually, yes."

"You got it, Tiger."

I watched the lights glint off the snow as we drove to the Caboose. My hand kept straying to my stomach. There was no baby belly yet—no outward sign that I was carrying a tiny flicker of life inside me. But I knew it was there, and not just because I'd seen the heartbeat for the second time.

Because I loved the little intruder.

So much.

It was terrifying. How could I love this baby so much it hurt already?

But I did. It was inescapable. It was possible that I loved this baby as much—or maybe even more—than I loved Grace, something I'd thought was impossible.

I decided to wait in the car while Logan went in to get our food to go. I fiddled with the half-empty water bottle in the cupholder and took a deep breath, enjoying the new car smell. My stomach was telling me meatloaf was going to be just as inexplicably good this time as it had been a few weeks ago when we'd eaten here together. But I also knew my sensitive nose could find fault with anything. After the day I'd had, I didn't want to risk puking in public.

While I waited, I pulled out my phone to call Grace.

"Hey, sweetie," she said. "How are you feeling?"

"Before I tell you what happened, I'm okay and the baby is fine."

"Oh my god, what happened?"

I gave her the full story and somehow managed to keep my voice calm the entire time.

"That must have been so scary," she said. "I'm so glad everything is okay."

"Me too. I won't lie: I had a moment when I saw the heartbeat again."

"I bet you did. Do you need me to come over?"

"That's okay, boo. Logan's grabbing dinner at the Caboose. Hopefully the baby still likes meatloaf."

"All right. Let me know if you change your mind."

"Thanks. I'll be fine."

We chatted for a few more minutes while I waited for Logan to come back. He came out of the restaurant and I let her go with promises to talk to her the next day.

Logan opened the door and held up the to-go bag. "Smell okay?"

The fact that he waited for me to smell the food before bringing it all the way into the car almost made me burst into tears. I bit the inside of my lip to keep from losing it and nodded.

"Yeah, fine," I managed to say.

"Awesome."

He put the food in the backseat, then got in. It didn't just smell fine. It smelled incredible.

It figured that Logan's kid would make me crave food I normally hated.

But food wasn't the only thing I was craving. And it wasn't the only thing in this car that smelled amazing.

So did Logan.

There had to be a scientific explanation for that—a biological reason a woman would be physically attracted to the man who'd gotten her pregnant. It was probably some evolutionary holdover from a time when a pregnant woman would have needed to stay close to her caveman for protection from wild animals or other cavemen.

It was not because I liked him.

Although if any man was going to get me pregnant, I could have done a lot worse than Logan Bailey.

Not that I was going to do anything about the frustrating pressure between my legs. I'd just been to the doctor for spotting; I wasn't about to risk having sex.

And I wasn't having sex with Logan again anyway.

No.

Definitely not.

Not an option.

Although...

No.

The meatloaf was going to have to do it for me tonight. That and a quick DIY session if my swollen lady parts didn't calm the fuck down.

I was seriously considering an ice pack. That's how bad it was getting.

Logan took me home and we unpacked our dinner on the kitchen island. I dove in and it was basically the best meal I'd ever eaten in my life. Again.

Pregnancy was so weird.

Logan was oddly quiet while we ate. I caught him casting glances at me, like maybe there was something he wanted to say. Whatever it was, he didn't say it.

It took me until I'd inhaled almost every bit of my dinner before I realized how big of a jerk I was being.

This had scared him, too. And I hadn't acknowledged that.

I stared at my almost-empty plate. No matter how hard I tried to be different, I was still my mother's daughter. Spoiled and self-absorbed. Regardless of how I felt about Logan under normal circumstances, he cared about this baby. And he seemed to care about me, even if just by default.

With a deep breath, I put my fork down and turned on my stool to face him. "Thank you."

He paused midchew, his eyebrows lifting. "No problem."

"I don't just mean dinner. I mean thank you for coming to get me and for being with me at that appointment." I paused. Maybe I'd stop there. I was terrible at the kind of raw honesty that was trying to come out of me. But I kept talking, my voice starting to break. "I was so scared there was something wrong and I'm glad I didn't have to be there by myself."

He held my gaze and his dark brown eyes were deep pools of feeling. "Me too. I was really scared."

"I want to have this baby," I said, barely above a whisper.

"Yeah." He nodded slowly, staring at me with a hint of confusion on his face, like he wasn't sure who I was. "I do too."

"It's weird, right? I can't feel anything. All I have are food aversions, cravings, and nausea." I left out the persistent horniness. "But I love this little thing already."

"I know what you mean." His mouth hooked in a grin. "I do too."

My throat tightened and I felt like I was about to burst into tears. These pregnancy mood swings were a killer.

Logan shifted and started to reach toward me. I knew if I let him, he'd wrap his arms around me again. Maybe even carry me to the couch and hold me in his lap until I stopped struggling.

And I wanted him to. God, I really did.

But if I gave in to that urge, I'd wind up with my head on his chest. With those annoyingly muscular arms holding me, his infuriatingly delicious scent surrounding me. And

I'd probably lose all semblance of control and do something monumentally stupid. Like beg him to make me come.

Goddamn, I bet he could do it fast.

I shot off my stool and grabbed my plate, turning away before he could touch me. This was already complicated enough. I didn't need to make it worse in a moment of weakness.

I was stronger than that.

Keeping my back to him, I put my plate in the sink next to the mug I'd used earlier for my ginger tea. The tension between us was thick. I could feel his eyes on me. I wasn't trying to be a jerk. I'd thanked him. I just knew my mood was liable to flip as easily as a light switch and suddenly I'd be biting his head off.

Or fucking his brains out, but there were several reasons that couldn't happen.

For a second, I fantasized that he ignored my attempt to keep distance between us. That he sidled up behind me and slid his arms around me. Kissed my temple again and murmured that I was doing a good job.

A tear slid down my cheek and I swiped it away, hoping he wouldn't notice.

"Are you going to be okay tonight?" He was still on the other side of the island.

Because of course he was. If I'd wanted comfort from him, I could have taken it. I hadn't.

And it was better that way.

"Yeah." Another tear broke free as I turned around. I didn't bother hiding that one. Just wiped it with my fingers. "I'm just not used to being so emotional all the time."

"Grace said she was too. Especially at first."

"Hopefully I'll start feeling like myself again soon. I'm in love with meatloaf and everything makes me cry. It's ridiculous."

"You are kind of freaking me out. We made it through an entire meal without fighting."

I rolled my eyes. "I don't even know who I am anymore."

The corner of his mouth lifted. "That makes two of us, Tiger."

Thankfully, the surge of emotion passed and I didn't burst into tears.

Logan got up and brought his plate to the sink. "We should probably quit while we're ahead."

I came so close to blurting out, *please don't leave me alone tonight*, but somehow managed to keep control of myself. "Good plan."

A flicker of something I couldn't quite read passed across his features. Then he opened his arms. "I think we should hug it out."

"Hug it out?"

"Yeah. Today was rough. We had a scare—you more than me, although it freaked me out too. So I think we should hug."

I hesitated.

"For fuck's sake, Cara. It's a hug. It won't hurt you."

Oh, but it could. He had no idea.

I rolled my eyes like he was being dumb. "Fine."

He wrapped me in a tight hug and all that firmly held resolve started to melt. He was warm and safe and he smelled so good, I wanted to roll around in his clothes and get that scent all over me. I wanted to break into his house and steal his pillow and only give it back when the scent wore off, just so I could steal it again after he'd slept on it for a while.

His hands caressed my back and he kissed the top of my

head the way he'd kissed my temple in the exam room. "See? That wasn't so terrible."

He stepped away and I instantly missed him.

I had officially gone insane.

The pregnancy books were missing something very important. Why did none of them warn you about the hormone-induced insanity? Because that had to be what was wrong with me.

"I go on duty tomorrow at eight, but I'll text you before I go in. Just reply when you get up and let me know how you're doing, okay?"

I nodded. I was about to crumble again, and I didn't want to do it in front of him.

He didn't say anything else. Just nodded back and said a quiet goodbye. Then he turned and left.

As soon as the front door closed behind him, I fell apart.

17

CARA

*T*he weight of the day—of my fear and all these stupid crazy feelings—finally crushed me. My knees shook and my vision blurred.

Great, I was crying again.

Not just crying. Sobbing.

I almost called Grace. But it was getting late and she was probably tired. If I called, she'd come over, and as much as I wanted an impromptu slumber party with my bestie, I didn't want to pull her away from her life like that. She wanted to spend the night wrapped in her husband's big, tattooed arms, not listening to my pathetic sobs.

Plus, I was gasping for breath. If I called her now, she wouldn't be able to understand a word I said.

Without bothering to lock up, I went up to my bedroom. Fell on the bed and curled into the fetal position. And cried.

And cried.

And cried some more.

"I fucking knew it."

Logan's voice jolted me out of my sob fest. "What the hell are you doing here?"

He shook his head while he toed off his shoes. "You're impossible, you know that? Fucking impossible."

I hiccupped. Oh my god, I'd cried so hard, I'd given myself the hiccups.

Why was I so weak? I was stronger than this.

"No, I'm not."

"You really are. Move over."

"Why? No."

He sighed. "Can we just skip the part where you physically resist me? I'd like to avoid getting kicked in the nuts."

I watched him approach the bed, probably with a look of abject horror on my face. But I wasn't horrified. I was confused.

The only light in my admittedly large bedroom came from the bathroom. He took off his jacket and tossed it on one of the armchairs by the big window.

What was he doing?

He climbed on the bed, shoving several throw pillows out of his way, and rolled me onto my other side. Manhandling me like I was a bendable doll, he moved me into the position he wanted, then tucked himself behind me. Suddenly I was the little spoon to his big spoon—my back to his front, my legs slightly bent with his following the same curve. His hand slid around my waist and he grunted as he shifted.

Oh god, Logan, don't grunt while you're touching me. Especially when we're on a bed.

But then the weirdest thing happened.

I relaxed.

His steady breathing was more powerful than any pill I'd ever taken. My heart rate slowed and the tension in my body melted away. I didn't even want to cry anymore, nor did I feel shame for having done so. I just felt calm. Secure.

Safe.

Too exhausted to keep fighting his effect on me—or what it meant—I went to sleep.

I WOKE to the sound of my shower. I was nestled in my bed, still dressed in the clothes I'd worn yesterday. And my back was cold.

Had I slept in Logan's arms all night?

I couldn't decide if I hoped I had, or hoped I hadn't.

It was early—a little after seven—and I rolled over carefully. If I moved too fast in the morning, it tended to trigger my stomach. Of course, I usually threw up in the morning no matter what I did.

It was so Logan's baby. Totally had it in for me.

The shower turned off. I sat up and a wave of nausea poured over me. Sweat broke out on my forehead. I closed my eyes, taking slow breaths, hoping it would pass this time. If it didn't, Logan was going to have to deal with it. He was in the closest bathroom.

By some miracle, the nausea's grip on me eased. I knew it would be back, but at least I might not have to puke in front of him.

"You okay?"

I opened my eyes at Logan's gentle voice. He stood in the bathroom doorway, a towel wrapped around his waist. His dark hair was wet, and moisture beaded on his broad chest and across his defined abs. A droplet of water trailed down his tattooed arm, following the lines of the red and orange flames.

I could not escape the simple reality that Logan Bailey was hot.

So hot.

I'd always thought so, although I'd never admitted it.

Get it together, Cara. It's bad enough that you lost your mind last night.

"Yeah, I think so," I said finally. "It comes and goes. I'll probably puke soon."

He winced. "That sucks. I hope it goes away."

"Me too."

"Sorry if I woke you. I need to run home before I go on duty, but figured I'd grab a shower first."

"It's fine."

He adjusted the towel, hitching it up a little higher on his waist. "Okay, so I'm going to move in."

I blinked. Had he just said *move in*? Did he mean with me? "What did you say? Because it sounded like you just said you're going to move in, but I have no idea what you're talking about."

"You heard me right. I don't mean move into your bedroom. Unless you want me to." He winked, goddamn him. "But I think I should move in."

"Why the hell would you do that?"

"So I can be here if anything happens or you need help. Plus, when the baby's born, it'll be easier if we're both here. How else are we going to manage a newborn? Neither of us know what the fuck we're doing; it's going to take both of us. And if I move in now, we have time to get used to being around each other before the baby comes."

There was a strange and surprising logic to his argument. But I couldn't let Logan Bailey move in with me. That was crazy. We couldn't stand each other. This would never work.

Except... I didn't actually hate him.

And we were having a baby together.

And he was right: It would be easier to take care of the baby if we lived in the same house.

Was I about to agree with him? Crazy. Pregnancy had made me crazy.

"Plus, maybe it would be better if you weren't alone right now," he said.

His stupid, sweet, gentle voice almost broke me again. But I was not going to have another meltdown.

"I thought Gavin was supposed to be the brother without fear," I said. "You really want to move in with me?"

He shrugged. "I'm on duty for twenty-four, sometimes forty-eight hours at a time. I'd only be here in between. Plus, this house is big. There's plenty of space."

"Fine." I threw the covers the rest of the way off and got up before I could come to my senses and refuse. "But I need the bathroom now, so get your stuff."

"You got it, baby mama." He ducked into the bathroom and grabbed his clothes off the floor.

"Don't call me that." I swept past him into the steamy bathroom, my stomach starting to churn. "Bye, Logan."

"Bye, roomie," he called as I closed the door. "See you tomorrow."

I closed my eyes. God, he was infuriating.

Sexy, charming, and utterly infuriating.

And on that thought, I puked.

MY BOOTS CRUNCHED in the ice-crusted snow as I made my way down the slope toward the river. Chunks of ice clung to the banks, but the naked tree branches had signs of new life. Little green buds glistened with cold moisture.

It really was beautiful here.

I snapped a photo—a close-up of a tiny droplet of water hanging off a leaf. My new lens was amazing, and I felt like I was finally getting the hang of using it. A great photographer I was not, but there was something satisfying about taking photos of the world around me. Of capturing a bit of the beauty I saw in this weird little town.

It was better than more filtered selfies and photos staged to look like someone followed me around, documenting my life with a camera while I suggested products my followers might enjoy.

My life was so dumb.

The temperature had started to drop as afternoon waned and the sun dipped closer to the mountain peaks. My fingerless gloves were no longer enough to keep my hands warm, so I decided it was time to go inside.

After the turmoil of the previous day, today had been blessedly quiet. I'd slept better than I had in weeks—which I was sure had nothing to do with Logan—I'd stopped spotting, and I'd only thrown up once. I'd even managed to eat an entire meal that wasn't meatloaf, and kept it all down.

The fact that I'd agreed to Logan moving in with me was the only hitch in an otherwise nice day. But he wouldn't be back until tomorrow.

It wouldn't be so bad, right? Logan and I could exist under the same roof for...

How long?

Until the baby was sleeping all night? Until he or she could walk? Until when?

I didn't know how this was going to work. And maybe we'd just cross that bridge when we got to it.

But what if Logan started dating someone?

My hands tightened around my camera. I got to my back door and stomped my boots—just to get the snow off, not because I was suddenly furious at the thought of Logan with another woman.

But seriously, was my kid going to have a stepmom someday?

That almost made me cry again.

Almost.

I sucked it all in, sniffing back the tears, and forced myself to calm the fuck down. I was being ridiculous.

Inside was warm and after stripping off the layers of winter clothing, I made myself a cup of ginger tea. My phone rang, Grace's name lighting up the screen.

"Hey, boo."

"Is Logan moving in with you?" she asked.

"How do you know that? Never mind; don't answer that. This is Tilikum. Yeah, I guess he's moving in."

"You guess?"

"I don't know. He caught me when I was vulnerable. I'd just woken up."

"Wait. Why were you with him when you'd just woken up?"

I slid onto one of the stools. "I'm not hiding anything from you, sweet sunflower. After the spotting incident, he stayed at my house last night."

"I'm sorry, honey. I'm not trying to accuse you of anything. It's just... I didn't know you'd been with him in the first place and now..."

"Now you're wondering if I'm banging my baby daddy behind your back."

"You can, obviously—as long as the doctor says it's okay after the spotting, I mean. And in a way, you might as well. He already got you pregnant, so it would be kind of like a freebie."

I made a gagging sound. "Stop. I've only puked once

today. I'd like to keep it that way."

"I'm just saying."

"I know, and please tell me I won't spend the rest of my pregnancy a giant raging hormone masquerading as a woman. Because my fucking word, Grace, I've never been so horny in my life."

"No, that just gets worse."

I almost dropped the phone. "Shut up."

"I'm serious. I'm starting to worry about Asher. I think I'm wearing him out and we have eight more weeks until the baby's due."

"I'm going to die. This is why pregnancy used to kill so many women. There must have been quack doctors telling them not to have sex and they died of it."

She laughed. "I know, right? Is taking care of it yourself not helping?"

"No. No, it's really not."

"Well, there's always—"

"Don't say Logan."

She didn't reply.

I decided to change the subject. Just thinking about sex was making me ache. "You know, you have seemed remarkably sane throughout your pregnancy. Have you been hiding the crazy from me? Is Asher taking the brunt of it?"

"What do you mean?"

"I've lost my mind. That's the only explanation. I agreed to let Logan Bailey move in with me. He calls me crazy all the time, but I'm starting to think he's right."

She laughed again. "You're not crazy. It makes sense for him to move in with you for a while. It'll make taking care of the baby a lot easier."

"That's what he said. And he said he should do it now so

we can get used to being around each other before the baby is born."

"Also a good point. It'll be good for you."

Good for me? It was going to be torture. And not because we'd fight. We would, but I could deal with that. It was going to be torture to be this horny and have not just a man, but the man I was drawn to as wildly as the Caboose's meatloaf, living under the same roof.

I wasn't sure if I could take it.

"I guess what doesn't kill you makes you stronger," I said.

"There's a lot of truth to that."

Grace and I chatted for a few more minutes, then said goodbye. A few seconds later, I got a text.

Prince dickhead: *Just checking in. Feeling okay?*

No, I'm desperate for an orgasm and suddenly I'd kill for a cold slice of watermelon.

Watermelon? Where had that come from?

Me: *Yep. Feeling fine. No more spotting.*

Prince dickhead: *Good. I have my phone on me, so let me know if you need anything.*

Me: *Okay, thanks.*

There he went again, being annoyingly sweet. Maybe I needed to put his actual name in my phone.

I let out a long breath. The truth was, I was glad he wanted to move in. The prospect of bringing home a newborn and being expected to keep it alive was slightly less daunting knowing I wouldn't be doing it alone. And I could admit he wasn't terrible to snuggle with.

And if that snuggling led to—

No. Not that. Too complicated.

But who knew, maybe we had a shot at making this work. I just had to learn to live with Logan Bailey.

18

LOGAN

I dug through the stuff I'd brought over to Cara's and threw on some clean clothes—an old TFD t-shirt, a pair of gym shorts, and socks. The only time I paid attention to what I wore was when I had to work. On my own time, I couldn't have cared less what my clothes looked like. I just grabbed whatever was clean.

I ran the towel over my damp hair one last time, then hung it up in the bathroom. I was not the tidiest guy, but Gram had drilled certain things into us. Hanging up towels was one of them.

It had been a little over a week since I'd moved in with Cara—into one of her guest rooms, specifically. So far, we'd managed to keep from killing each other. Actually, we hadn't seen each other very much. For someone without a regular job, Cara kept herself busy. She carried a camera around a lot, but I hadn't asked why. We crossed paths occasionally and once or twice I'd wondered if she was avoiding me on purpose.

It was hard to tell.

After my shift had ended this morning, I'd stopped by

my house to get some more of my stuff. I'd tried to convince Gav to let me bring Princess Squeaker with me—she liked me best, even if he wouldn't admit it—but he'd shot me down. Maybe I'd have to get my own cat. Although with a baby on the way, a pet probably wasn't a good idea.

It was weird to have moved out of the Bailey bachelor pad, even temporarily. I'd never not lived with Levi. When we'd moved out of Gram's house, we'd gone together. We hadn't even discussed it, really. It had been a foregone conclusion that we'd be roommates. Then Gavin had started crashing on our couch and never left.

We'd had a good run, the three of us. But things were changing. Gav was getting married, and he and Skylar were going to move into Jack and Naomi's house, next door to Gram. Assuming I could survive living with Cara, I'd be here for the foreseeable future. The baby was due in October, and who knew how long it would make sense for us to live together. Not forever, obviously. But maybe as long as a year or two.

I was worried about Levi. Not that he couldn't handle living alone. And we worked the same shifts a lot, so we'd still see each other. But there was something wrong with my brother, and I didn't know what it was. Whenever I tried to dig into it with him, he deflected my questions like a goddamn ninja.

Was he going to lapse into being a broody recluse without me around to force him to have fun? I didn't know.

I threw a flannel on over my t-shirt and went downstairs. Before I'd reached the bottom, I heard Cara's voice. She was talking to someone on the phone.

And she sounded exhausted.

I crept closer, walking softly across the hardwood floor, and peeked around the corner. She stood in the kitchen, one hand holding her phone to her ear, the other on the counter, like she needed support to hold herself up. Her head drooped and she took a deep breath.

"Yes, I know that."

I waited, wondering if I should go back upstairs until she was done.

"Mom, this doesn't have anything to do with you. I don't —" She stopped talking. I couldn't hear the other side of the conversation, but her mom had obviously interrupted her.

Her body language screamed at me. She looked hurt. Defeated. This was worse than finding her sobbing on her bed. That night, I'd known she was upset and was trying to hide it from me. I'd barged back into the house, fully aware of what I'd find. Prepared to make her feel better—to force her to *let me* make her feel better.

Those tears had been an expected and understandable reaction to the events of the day. She'd been afraid we were going to lose our baby. But this was different. She was talking to her mom and it was clearly fucking her up. The wrongness of that ate at me.

"No, that's not going to happen," she said with little more heat to her voice. "It was never going to happen and you need to let it go. This is... Okay. You know what? I'm done. I have to go."

She ended the call and I would have bet all the money in the world that she wanted to throw her phone across the room. But she didn't. Just set it down, held onto the counter, and let her head drop.

"Hey." I approached carefully, like I would if she were a wounded animal.

As soon as I spoke, her spine snapped straight. Her shoulders lifted with a deep intake of breath and she swiped the few tears she'd let fall. When she turned around, whatever had bothered her about that phone call was buried behind her *I don't give a fuck* mask.

"If you need the kitchen, it's fine," she said. "I'm not doing anything in here."

Well, at least she hadn't led with something shitty. "I was going to make some breakfast. Are you hungry?"

Her hand strayed to her stomach. It made me want to step in close and put mine over hers. But I didn't want to risk her claws. I knew she had them sharp and ready.

"I think I am hungry."

"Any food I should avoid?" I asked, heading for the fridge.

"No, there's nothing left in there that will make me vomit on sight. I think I've figured out my triggers."

I opened the fridge and perused the contents. "Good to know. And hey, I haven't had a chance yet, but I'll get some more groceries and stuff. I'm not here to freeload."

"I'm not worried about that."

I glanced over my shoulder. "Can I be blunt about something?"

"Since when do you ask first before being blunt?"

"I'm just trying to have some manners."

She leaned her hip against the counter. "Okay."

"I know you're loaded, but you're my baby mama, not a sugar mama. You don't need to worry about me trying to get in on whatever you've got going in your bank account."

She gazed at me, her expression bewildered. "I didn't think you would."

"Good." I went back to the fridge and took out some eggs and cheese. "Scrambled eggs?"

"That sounds good, actually. You know how to cook?"

"Gram raised me. Of course I know how to cook."

She went around to the other side of the island and sat on a stool. "I should have known."

"She always said we weren't leaving her house until we knew how to take care of ourselves." I rooted around until I found a glass bowl. Her kitchen was fully stocked, like a gourmet chef lived here. Copper pots and pans gleamed from hooks above the island, and half the stuff in the cupboards looked like it had never been used.

"Gram has to be the wisest woman alive."

I grinned as I started cracking eggs into the bowl. "No doubt. And one of the toughest. She managed to get all five of us to adulthood. That was no easy feat."

"She's a saint."

"Can't argue with you there."

I kept working—mixed the eggs and got them in a pan to cook. A low hum of tension hung in the air, but so far, Cara and I weren't fighting. This was good. Progress.

When the eggs were almost done, I sprinkled a bit of cheese across the top and gave it a minute to melt. Cara got up and grabbed plates. Maybe it was stupid to get excited about the two of us cooperating to put breakfast on the table, but with our track record, this was a big deal.

I slid our plates across the island. "Look at us, acting all civilized."

"Who would have thought?"

We sat down next to each other and started eating. I made a mental note that feeding Cara something she liked was a good way to keep her tiger claws retracted. Maybe I'd go get her meatloaf from the Caboose tonight. See if I could keep this getting along streak going.

But I also wanted to know what was up with her mom. I wasn't a total idiot. I knew I had to tread carefully. She hadn't meant for me to hear that conversation, but something about it had upset her. Had she told her mom about the baby? Was her mother mad? Judgmental? Excited for her and ready to move up here to help her out?

I knew next to nothing about Cara's family. But now that we were having a baby together, I needed to be at least somewhat in the loop.

"Was that your mom on the phone earlier?" I asked, and I didn't miss the way my question made her stiffen.

"Yeah, she called."

I decided I needed to just come out and ask. "Does she know about the baby?"

"She does now."

Irritation poked at me. *Come on, Cara. Why is getting anything out of you like pulling fucking teeth?* "How does she feel about it?"

She paused, poking at the remnants of her eggs with her fork. "It's hard to say. At first, she said she saw this coming ten years ago and wondered how I made it to twenty-eight without getting knocked up. She didn't like being reminded that I'm twenty-nine."

"Jesus."

"And then she proceeded to lecture me on all the ways I've ruined my life and how she hopes I don't expect her to swoop in and take care of the baby for me. That she had to do it on her own, so I can too."

Anger simmered hot in my gut. What the fuck was wrong with that woman? "Seriously?"

"As if I'd let her anywhere near this kid."

No wonder she'd looked so exhausted. Her mom sounded like a piece of work.

And Cara was starting to make a little more sense.

"What about your dad?" I asked. "Was he not around?"

"No." She got up and took her plate to the sink.

"Do you talk to him now?"

"Sometimes."

"Does he know about the baby?"

She whirled around, her eyes full of fire. "No, he does not know about the baby. But I'm sure that conversation will be about as much fun as the one I just had with my mother, so thank you for bringing it up."

I held my hands up. "Sorry. I was just wondering."

"It's none of your business."

"Actually, it is my business. Your parents are my kid's grandparents, so if there's shit going on between you and them, it might help if you'd at least clue me in."

"My mom's crazy and I barely speak to my dad. There. You're caught up."

"I'm sorry this is hard for you, but—"

"This isn't hard for me. It's just life. I have a shitty family. A lot of people do. We can't all be raised by a saint like Gram. It is what it is, and I'll deal with it like I always do."

Grinding my teeth together, I stood. "But you don't have to deal with it alone."

She crossed her arms. "I don't need your help, so stop trying to be some kind of knight in shining armor."

"Yeah, that's me, riding up on my white horse. Except your crazy ass would have the dragon trapped in the tower instead of the other way around. And I'd fucking turn around and go back to my own damn kingdom."

"Good. At least you're smart enough to figure that out." She turned, whipping her hair, and stomped out.

I gripped the back of the stool, growling with frustration. Fuck, that woman was infuriating.

I was just trying to—

And she kept—

Fuck.

I didn't know why I thought we had a chance at living together peacefully. Maybe this whole thing was a big-ass mistake. I should move back home and we'd figure out how to co-parent like divorced couples did. I didn't like that idea, but if this was how she was going to be, I didn't know if I wanted to deal with her crazy.

19

CARA

*T*rying to find places to hide from myself was an exercise in futility, but one I actively engaged in all day. I felt like shit. I didn't want it to be my fault. But I knew it was.

The hum of the TV through my closed office door told me Logan was still home. When I'd walked out on him this morning, I'd thought he might leave, at least for a while. But he hadn't, and his presence in the house had been a constant reminder that the feeling in my stomach wasn't morning sickness.

I felt guilty for being a jerk to Logan.

It was easy to fall back on blaming my mom. I was always on edge after talking to her, and this conversation had been particularly awful. I hadn't expected her to be thrilled to find out she was going to be a grandma, but I also hadn't counted on her rant about all the ways this baby was going to ruin my life.

She'd know. I'd ruined hers.

So when Logan had poked at that sore spot, I'd lashed out.

The problem was, he was right. He did deserve to know what he was dealing with when it came to my family.

I hated it when he was right.

But because I was a stubborn bitch, instead of owning up to it and apologizing, I'd avoided him and hoped he'd go away.

He hadn't, the jerk.

I was pretty sure he'd stayed home all day to piss me off.

It had worked.

Anger was a great way to smother guilt, and I was well-practiced at being angry at Logan Bailey.

It wasn't helping that as I started to feel better—I hadn't thrown up once today, nor had I fallen asleep anywhere awkward—the other effect of pregnancy kept getting stronger.

My hormones were on fire. I wanted sex. Badly.

Mr. Bigshot had no chance of satisfying this raging need. None. There was only one thing that would.

Dick.

I needed the real thing.

And I didn't just want any dick. I wanted Logan's.

I'd thought about it all day. Gone through a mental list of the men I could call to satisfy my desperate need to be fucked. There were a few who fit the bill, assuming they were still single—which they probably were. Men I'd been with before, who'd be happy for another shot at me.

And I didn't want any of them.

Not only did I not want them, the thought of sleeping with any of them made my nausea come back with a vengeance.

Was this a pregnancy thing? Was it normal to be completely repulsed by the thought of a dick that didn't belong to the father of my baby?

Because I was violently repulsed.

But Logan? I could easily imagine fucking Logan Bailey. It pissed me off.

And why was the TV so damn loud?

I shot a glare at the door, as if I could make Logan feel the heat of my ire from here. Anger felt good. It felt normal. I was used to being mad at Logan—fuming at him for being so fucking irritating.

And now here he was, in my house, watching my TV so loud I couldn't hear myself think.

Yep, that was what I needed. All those other inconvenient emotions burned away to ash as I started losing my grip on my temper.

I got up and marched down the stairs, feeling stronger than I had all day. Logan lounged on the couch, dressed like a sloppy teenager in a flannel, t-shirt, and shorts. He had one sock pulled up to his shin, the other bunching toward his ankle.

God, I hated his stupid tube socks with their stupid white cotton and stupid red stripes.

But I still wanted him to fuck me senseless.

"Do you have to have that so fucking loud?" I snapped.

His gaze swung to me and the flash of anger in his eyes riled me up even more. It made the heat between my legs flare.

"You could just ask me to turn it down."

I nudged an unlit scented candle aside, grabbed the remote from the coffee table, and shut it off.

"What the fuck is your problem?" he asked.

"You're my problem."

He swung his legs onto the floor and stood. "Awesome. The mood swing queen strikes again. Glad to see you're still crazy."

"If I'm crazy, it's your fault."

"How the fuck is it my fault? Don't blame the pregnancy. You were nuts before I knocked you up."

He was absolutely right. In fact, he had no idea how crazy I really was. Because what kind of woman got off on starting a pointless fight with a man she wanted to sleep with? Me. I did. Every word out of his mouth was like a stroke across my sex-starved clit. Maybe I'd get him to keep yelling at me, then let Mr. Bigshot bring it home.

No. I wanted the D. But I didn't want him gentle. I wanted him angry.

"Maybe I was, but you like my crazy. You want it, but you're too afraid to admit it."

He hesitated, lust flashing in his eyes. I was right. He did like my crazy. He craved it like I was craving him.

"I fucked you because I was drunk," he said, but there was no resolve in his words. He didn't mean them.

"No you didn't." I stepped closer. "You fucked me because you wanted to, and the whiskey made you brave enough to do it."

He moved toward me. "You're a pain in the ass."

"You're obnoxious."

"You're a spoiled brat."

I got right in his face. "Then spank me."

With a deep growl, he manhandled me onto the couch —knees on the cushion, hands braced against the back. Before I could take another breath, he yanked down my lounge pants, leaving me in nothing but a thong, my ass in the air.

Then he smacked it.

Hard.

The sting was exquisite. I could hear his ragged breaths as he skimmed his palm over my ass. But he didn't strike again. Because he was an asshole who loved to torture me, he took his time, methodically wrapping my hair around his hand.

He held my hair in a tight grip. "What do you want, Cara?"

"Spank me. And make it hurt."

Smack!

I sucked in a breath through clenched teeth, the sting everything I needed. He smacked me again, right in the same spot, leaving my skin hot.

He yanked on my hair. "You like that?"

"Yes," I breathed.

Smack!

I cried out, arching my back hard. Instead of winding up to spank me again, he slid his fingers beneath the thin scrap of my thong and traced them along my slit.

His voice was a low growl. "This is what you really need, isn't it?"

"Yes." I sounded desperate and needy. And I did not care.

I was desperate and needy. There was no point in hiding that now.

Bracing himself with a knee on the couch, he leaned closer. "You need to get fucked, don't you?"

"Yes."

"Ask me nicely."

My temper flared hot. "Fuck you, Logan."

"No, sweetheart." His voice was smooth and controlled, but I could hear the undercurrent of lust. He wanted this as much as I did. "That's not how you ask nicely."

"Fuck me. Right now."

"Nicely," he crooned.

Oh my god, I was going to kill him.

"Logan if you don't fuck me—"

He yanked on my hair. "Ask. Nicely."

I smiled, reveling in the tug on my scalp. In the way he wasn't going to take a single bit of my shit. If he didn't make me work for it, I wouldn't want it so bad.

But I was still going to fight him.

"Fuck me now," I said in a syrupy sweet voice, "or get the hell off me."

Without warning, he smacked my ass again, so hard I yelped.

"Please," I cried out. "Please fuck me."

He smacked me again. "What was that, sweetheart?"

"Please," I begged, so giddy I almost laughed. "Oh my god, please fuck me."

"Good girl."

His hand released my hair, leaving it to fall around my shoulders and face. He caressed the spot where he'd spanked me, leaning down to pepper soft kisses over the stinging skin. Then he slipped my thong down, tugging it and my pants the rest of the way off.

I looked back at him over my shoulder, watching while he pulled his shorts down. His thick erection jutted out, swollen and veiny.

He still wore those stupid socks.

I didn't care.

He took himself in his hand and rubbed the tip along my wet slit. Up and down, slicking himself. Torturing me.

"Logan, please."

"I know, baby," he said, his voice growly and low. "I'll give you what you need."

When his dick was good and wet, he lined himself up with my opening, grabbed my hips, and rammed himself in.

My arms went stiff against the back of the couch and I

threw my head back, moaning in ecstasy. His violent thrust and impressive girth stretched me open, skirting the line between pain and pleasure.

He slid out and slammed into me again, grunting hard. I'd been aching for this. Dying for it. And now that he was giving it to me, it was better than I'd hoped.

It was everything.

He pounded me hard and deep, showing not the slightest hint of mercy. His fingers dug into my hips, jerking me backward with each thrust. His thickness filled me like nothing ever had. The pressure and friction had me spiraling, my body racing toward climax within minutes.

"Don't stop," I said. "Don't fucking stop."

"I knew you loved my cock," he said, then slammed it in again. "Say it."

He wasn't wrong, but the urge to argue was too strong. "No I don't."

Smack!

He spanked my ass cheek again and I cried out.

"I can't stand it," I said, my voice on the edge of hysteria. "And I can't stand you."

Smack!

"I hate you for feeling so fucking good."

Smack!

"I know you do, baby," he growled. "I hate you too."

Raw pleasure consumed me. I was dizzy with it. High on the heat and pressure of Logan's thick cock plunging in and out of me.

And he was relentless.

I gasped, struggling to hold onto the back of the couch, but he refused to give an inch. He pounded me from behind, his primal grunts feeding my lust. I tightened around him, the pulses of my impending orgasm rippling like a warning.

He could feel it. I knew he could. His hands tightened and his movements grew frenzied.

We were losing our minds.

"Give it to me, Cara," he growled. "Give me what I want."

Yes, Logan. I'll give you anything you want if you keep doing this. "No. Not yet."

"Let go," he said through clenched teeth. "Come on my cock, baby. Do it now."

I moaned, trying to hold myself back. To show him he couldn't tell me what to do.

But god, I wanted him to keep telling me what to do.

Fight with me, Logan. Make me do it.

"You can't make me come," I said, almost laughing at the lie. I really was crazy.

He growled again, still thrusting hard, and the sound almost made me lose my mind. "No?"

I couldn't even answer. My body teetered on the edge, the pleasure so intense, it hurt. Why was I torturing myself? If I just did what he said and—

His hand slid around the front of my thigh and on his next thrust, he pinched my clit between his fingers.

I burst into a million pieces, the explosion so intense, I couldn't breathe. I felt his cock pulse inside me, thickening against my spasming walls. Oh god, he was coming too. He grunted and thrust while I came, shock waves rippling through me.

We slowed to a stop, and like the aftermath of a thunderclap, the resulting silence seemed to echo through the room. All I could hear was our breathing. He stepped back, letting his cock slide out of me. I blinked, trying to get my bearings, and climbed off the couch, still facing away from him.

Was I trembling? God, what was wrong with me?

I turned and met his eyes. They were glassy and a sheen of sweat covered his forehead.

"Feel better?" he asked.

I brushed a strand of hair off my face. "Yes."

His gaze flicked up and down. Then he grabbed his shorts and tugged them on. "Good."

Without another word, he left, his footsteps fading upstairs. A few seconds later, his bedroom door shut.

I let out a long breath, then went to the bathroom to clean up.

20

CARA

*P*hysically, I felt better than I had in weeks. My body was sated, the persistent ache between my legs finally soothed. My ass hurt where Logan had spanked me—he'd really gone all out. But I loved it. It was satisfying to feel the rawness he'd left.

Emotionally, however, I'd been better.

Without the flames of anger singeing me, I was back to feeling shitty. Guilty for being a bitch to Logan, although letting him come in me like that had to count for something. Worried about whether my mother was right and this baby was going to ruin my life.

More than that, I worried I wasn't cut out to be a mom at all. And this poor kid was going to pay the price.

Kind of like I had.

Lying on my bed, I texted Grace to see if she could talk. She called me right back.

"Hey, honey," she said, her voice cheerful. "How are you feeling today?"

"I picked a fight with Logan on purpose so he'd have angry sex with me."

"Did it work?"

I shifted one of my pillows. "Yes. Surprisingly well."

"So... do you feel better?"

"Yes and no. I won't lie; he's so good at it. Don't tell him I said that. But now that I'm calm, I can think. And I don't want to think."

"What are you thinking about?"

"All the reasons I'm going to be an awful mother."

"Cara, stop. You're not going to be an awful mother."

Usually, I would have answered that with something flippant. But this time I didn't. "I don't know what I'm doing, Grace. At least you had a good example. Your mom is great. I'm flying blind."

"You don't need to know what you're doing. You just need to love your child and be willing to learn."

My hand slid over my stomach. "I'll be eleven weeks tomorrow. That means I have less than thirty to figure this out. I don't know if that's enough time."

"Just keep taking things one day at a time. You'll be ready. And remember, you're not alone."

I smiled, but the little tug on my chest wasn't for the love I had for my best friend. It was for the man in the room down the hall.

He'd told me the same thing. I didn't have to do this alone.

"Thanks, boo. I feel better. Love you."

"Love you, too."

I ended the call.

And found myself at a crossroads.

I could keep ignoring Logan. Pretend I didn't care. Or I could stop being such a psycho and go talk to him.

Maybe even accept his help.

Because if we were going to make this work, I needed to give a little.

I'd spoken to my mom, but I still needed to call my father. And Logan had said I didn't need to do this alone. Maybe I needed to take him up on that.

With my phone still clutched in my hand, I got up and went to Logan's room. His door was shut, so I knocked.

"Yeah?"

I opened it and peered inside. "Can I come in?"

He lay on the bed with one hand behind his head, eyeing me like he didn't trust me. Not that I blamed him. "Do you need something?"

"Maybe." I stepped inside.

His eyebrows lifted.

I took a deep breath. "I hope that was as good for you as it was for me. Because it was really good for me."

The corner of his mouth lifted. "Yeah, it was fucking amazing."

I smiled. "Good. But that's not why I came in here."

"What's up? You want meatloaf again?"

"No, I'm not hungry for once. Actually, I need to call my father."

He didn't look confused or ask what that had to do with him. He sat up and motioned for me to come sit on the bed. "Do you want to call him now?"

It was exactly what I wanted from him—exactly what I needed—and the power of that little question almost unraveled me.

"Yes." I lowered myself onto the bed next to him. "He wasn't a part of my life when I was a kid, but we've been in contact since I was eighteen or so. My mom hates him, although honestly, that doesn't mean much to me. My mom's crazier than I am."

"Damn."

I laughed softly. "I know, right? I don't know him very well, but I talk to him once in a while. And he inexplicably sends me birthday cards. He has since I was nineteen. Anyway, I don't really care what he thinks about all this, but I figure he should know."

"Okay." He tucked my hair behind my ear. "Go for it. I'll be right here."

"All this buildup, and I'll probably get his voicemail." I brought up his number and hit send.

My father answered on the second ring. "Hi, Cara."

Anxiety flashed through me. I met Logan's eyes. He reached over and squeezed my leg.

"Hi, Dad. I know this is out of the blue. Are you busy?"

"No." Something clanked in the background. "Not at all. It's good to hear from you."

"You say that now. You don't know why I'm calling."

"Is everything okay?" he asked, alarm in his voice.

"Yes, I'm fine. Except for the fact that I'm pregnant."

"Oh," he said, and I could tell he didn't know what to make of that bit of news. "Well, congratulations."

I stared at Logan. Congratulations? "I know I'm not a teenager or anything, but this wasn't planned."

"Oh," he said again. "Then what do you need? Are you still in Tilikum?"

"Yes, but—"

"I can be there this evening."

"No, Dad, that's not why I called. I don't need anything."

"Are you sure? Is the father around?"

Logan hadn't lifted his hand from my leg. He squeezed.

"Yes, the father is involved. We're not together, but we're making it work. He's..." I trailed off, my eyes straying to Logan's again. "He's a good man."

"Good. I'm glad to hear that." He paused, like he was trying to figure out what to say. "Do you know when the baby's due?"

"The beginning of October."

"Okay. So you've got some time. Does your um... does your mother know?"

I sighed. "Yes. She's less than thrilled that I'm ruining her life yet again."

He made a low noise in his throat. "That's... I'm sorry, Cara."

"It's all right." My voice was casual, like it didn't matter in the least. Maybe if I could convince him of that, I'd convince myself. "I'm fine where I am. The father is doing everything he can, and I have good friends here. I just wanted you to know."

"Thank you for calling. I'm glad you're all right."

"You're welcome." I needed to be finished with this call. His non-judgmental reaction was stoking my emotions. It felt like my mood was on the verge of flipping, and I didn't want to go crazy Cara on Logan again. "Anyway, I have to go."

"Okay. Bye, Cara."

"Bye, Dad." I ended the call.

"That wasn't so bad," Logan said.

I let out a breath. "If it weren't for the fact that he blew off my entire childhood, I'd say he's not a bad guy."

Logan's eyes flicked up and down. "You need to spoon again."

It wasn't a question. It was almost a command, and of course my first urge was to argue.

But he was right.

I nodded.

He grinned and my tummy did a little flutter. "Come here, Tiger."

I didn't resist when he hooked his arm around my waist and dragged me next to him. I nestled back against him and took a deep breath. He was warm and strong, his presence calming. How was it that he could rile me up so much but still make me feel so relaxed?

He took a slow, deep breath, his chest expanding against me. A surge of pressure bloomed between my legs. Before I could stop myself, I arched my back, pressing my ass into his groin.

With a grunt, he pushed his hardening erection against me. But there was no urgency to it. "Already?"

Part of me was tempted—my hormones were seriously out of control—but mostly I just wanted him to hold me.

Which also had to be due to my out-of-control hormones.

"No, this is good," I said.

"Wow, did that hurt?"

"What?"

"Admitting that you like cuddling with me."

Before I could roll away, his arm tightened, locking me in place.

"What makes you think I like cuddling with you? Maybe you're just a warm body."

He chuckled.

"We do need to discuss something, though."

"What's that?" he asked, his voice starting to sound sleepy.

"I'm going to need your dick again."

Another chuckle. "Two compliments from you in one day? I should go buy a lottery ticket."

"It's not a compliment. It's just reality. Pregnancy is

turning me into a monster and if I don't get regular dick, I'm going to be impossible to live with."

"More than usual? That's terrifying."

I elbowed him. "And since it's your kid inside me, I can't have someone else's dick."

He made a growly noise in his throat.

I tried to ignore the way that possessive sound sent a jolt of electricity through me. "That leaves me with one option. Yours."

He was quiet for a moment. He wasn't actually going to turn me down, was he? Would he say no to regular sex just to be stubborn?

"I guess this is my fault," he said, his voice casual. "The least I can do is help keep you comfortable."

"But no sleeping in my room. I like the bed to myself."

"Whatever you say, ruby red. You're doing all the hard work."

A wave of sleepiness swept over me. I *was* doing all the hard work; making a human was exhausting. My eyes closed and I let myself relax into his warmth.

His hand splayed over my belly. If I hadn't been so tired, I might have gotten up. Because despite how good this felt, that little gesture reminded me of the simple truth I couldn't ignore.

I didn't deserve Logan Bailey.

21

LOGAN

*T*he scents of coffee and popcorn—both burnt—lingered in the air in the firehouse kitchen. I sat at a round table nursing a cup of coffee, eyeing a few questionable-looking pastries on a paper plate. A row of clean mugs sat in the dish dryer and there was a red stain above the stove from a pasta sauce incident involving Gavin last year.

I was looking forward to getting off my shift. Two calls in the middle of the night had meant I'd barely gotten any sleep. I needed to head home and take a nap.

Of course, if Cara were home, she'd probably want a piece of me before I could rest.

Pregnancy had made her insatiable. I'd probably had more sex in the last month than in the previous year. Not that I was complaining. Sober me liked fucking Cara even more than drunk me had. She was a wildcat, and I had the scratches and bruises to prove it.

They were worth it.

I did wonder how long this was going to last. She was

about fifteen weeks into her pregnancy, which meant we still had more than halfway to go.

I swiped my phone screen to a photo I'd taken of her a few weeks ago. She'd decided the baby had needed waffles, so I'd taken her to Bigfoot Diner. What my baby wanted, my baby got. I'd caught her looking out the window, her expression unusually serene. A rare glimpse of the Cara on the inside—the one she almost never let anyone see.

She was beautiful.

"Hey," Levi said, lowering himself into a chair.

I clicked away from the photo before he could see it. "Hey, bro mein. How's life at home without me? You're bored off your ass; you can admit it."

"It's all right. I do miss kicking your ass at video games."

"Dude, you only kicked my ass maybe fifty percent of the time. Fifty-five, if I'm being generous."

"Unlike grappling, where I kick your ass all the time."

"Bro." I crossed my arms.

He shrugged. "You haven't been to the gym in a while. That's okay. You're going to be a dad; you can get soft. Embrace the dad bod."

"I do not have a dad bod." I stood and yanked my shirt up. "See?"

From across the room, Mason whistled. "Nice abs, buddy."

I scowled at him and tucked my shirt back in.

"Not yet," Levi said.

I dropped back in my seat, thinking about all the shit I'd been eating lately. I probably did need to get to the gym more often. And maybe stop eating like I was the one who was pregnant.

Was I getting soft?

"Fine. Are you going to the gym later?" I asked.

"Yeah. I'll text you."

Gavin swept into the kitchen—he was about to go on duty—and set a container on the counter. "I made cookies with Sky yesterday. I'd grab some before the rest of the guys realize they're here."

My eyes lit up. Cookies did sound good. But I caught Levi's smug-ass expression and all I could think were the words *dad bod*.

Crossing my arms again, I slumped in my chair. "I'm good."

"How's Cara?" Gavin asked, leaning against the counter while he shoved a bite of cookie in his mouth.

"She's fine, I guess. I still can't keep up with what she will or won't eat, since it seems to change on a daily basis. But at least she's not puking all the time anymore."

"That's good."

"How's Princess Squeaker? She doesn't miss me too much, does she?"

"I doubt she even remembers you, dude."

"Fuck off. Of course she does."

Gavin took a bite of his cookie. "I'm her cat mom. You were just a guy who fed her sometimes."

"Whatever. I'm going to go visit her after this."

"Cool. She'll be happy to see you," Gavin said.

I got up, and Levi followed. "You just said she doesn't remember me."

"Since when do you take anything I say seriously?" Gavin asked. He grabbed the container of cookies and held it up. "Sure you don't want one? Breakfast of champions."

"No, I'm good. I need to avoid getting a dad bod."

Gavin laughed, then poked my stomach. "Yeah, good call."

I was about to tackle him, but Levi put a hand on my shoulder. "Save it for the gym."

Gavin's shit-eating grin made me want to take him down. But Levi was right.

He and I left Gavin with his cookies and ran through our last gear check before handing everything off to the incoming crew. I went out to my SUV and decided I was going to visit Princess Squeaker. And maybe take a nap while I was at it.

Spring had swept over Tilikum, the warmer days melting the snow. White still topped the mountain peaks surrounding the town, but at our elevation, everything was turning green.

The change in weather seemed to have coincided with a change in Cara's pregnancy. She still had issues with food, but she seemed to be feeling a lot better in the last couple of weeks. At least I didn't hear her puking in the morning anymore. That was an improvement.

I felt bad that this had been so hard on her. She tried to hide it from me, but I knew she felt like shit a lot. And no matter how many pregnancy books I read, or late-night food cravings I helped her indulge, there was only so much I could do for her.

All the orgasms had to help, though.

I followed Levi home and pulled into the driveway behind him. We went inside and Princess Squeaker came out to greet us.

She purred as I scooped her up. "See? I knew you didn't forget me."

I took her to the couch and tossed my phone on the coffee table. Like usual, it was cluttered—littered with video game controllers, a few gum wrappers, and a scattering of loose change. The cat tree Levi had built stood in front of the window, but a few strokes down Princess Squeaker's back and I knew even her favorite perch couldn't tempt her away from the warmth of sleeping on my chest.

Levi went back to his bedroom and a few minutes later, I heard the shower turn on. My eyes were already heavy. I wanted to take a nap, but a nagging voice in the back of my head kept bothering me.

Should I text Cara and let her know I wasn't coming home right away?

Would she give a shit?

We generally told each other what we were up to. She knew my work schedule and I knew when she had stuff going on. So why did this seem like an important decision all of a sudden?

I didn't know what we were to each other. We weren't dating. But we were definitely fucking. And we were living together. But not sharing a bedroom.

And then there was the whole having a baby thing.

It was just... weird. And I was starting to feel oddly unsettled about it.

I shifted the cat so I could reach my phone and send her a text.

Me: *I'm off work but I stopped at my place. I'll be back later.*

Baby Mama: *Okay. I might be in town running errands.*

Me: *Do you need me to stop anywhere on my way back? Save you a trip?*

Baby Mama: *That's okay. I'd like to get out of the house.*

Me: *Sounds good. See you later today then.*

Baby Mama: *Have a nice nap.*

Me: *How did you know I was going to take a nap?*

Baby Mama: *Lucky guess.*

With a grin, I put my phone back on the coffee table.

Look at us, texting like normal people who knew how to get along.

Actually, we'd been getting along more often than not. We still had our moments, and Cara's mood could flip like a light switch. But for the most part, we'd been coexisting peacefully. When she did pick a fight with me, it was usually more playful than angry—because she wanted sex. And she liked it rough.

Goddamn, so did I.

Thinking about sex—about yanking her hair, pinning her to the bed, smacking that ass—made a nap seem a lot less enticing. Maybe I would just go home. Catch Cara before she left to run her errands.

Someone knocked on the front door. Asher poked his head in.

"Good, I'm glad you're here." He came in and shut the door behind him. "Where's Gav and Levi?"

"Levi's probably getting dressed. Gavin's on duty."

There was a flash of something in Asher's eyes. Disappointment, maybe. He should have been a firefighter, too. His felony conviction hadn't just robbed him of seven years of his life, it had taken his career goals with it. He was doing fine, working as an MMA coach. And he was great at it. But I knew a part of him was still pissed he had to give up his dream.

It pissed me off, too. Life wasn't fucking fair.

Levi came out, dressed in gym clothes. "Hey, Ash. What's up?"

"We have a problem." Asher sat in one of the armchairs. "I was going to text everyone, but it's complicated. You know how Gram was looking for a new accountant because hers missed an appointment?"

"Yeah."

"The guy missed the appointment because he skipped town. He took off and no one knows where he is."

"What?" I felt a sinking feeling in my gut. "Why?"

"Did that make her late on her taxes or something?" Levi asked.

"It's a lot worse than that," Asher said. "I just got off the phone with Darcy Klein. Gram hired her to take over and she started digging into Gram's finances. Something went seriously wrong."

Despite Princess Squeaker's protests, I sat up, a sense of alarm surging through me. "No shit?"

"Darcy's still working on sorting everything out, but Gram's taxes haven't been paid in years. Not her property taxes or her personal taxes. And it doesn't make sense, because Grandad set up a trust to take care of all of that. She just had to approve the payments. There was plenty of money and all the paperwork her accountant was showing her looked legit."

"So who dropped the ball?" I asked. "Her old accountant?"

Asher took a deep breath. "We don't know for sure, but it looks like he might have done more than drop the ball. We think he cleaned out her trust account. In fact, Darcy thinks he might have been stealing from her for years."

Fiery anger tore through me. "Who the fuck is this guy?"

"Mike Phillips. Grandad originally hired someone else, but when that guy retired, Mike Phillips took over most of his clients."

"So he fucking disappears and now her money is gone?" I asked. "What the fuck?"

"How much does she need?" Levi asked.

"Darcy's working on that, too. But it's going to be a lot. We're talking back taxes, penalties, and interest." He paused and my stomach dropped. "She might lose the land, her house, everything."

"What can we do?" I asked. "Should we call Jack?"

"Gram already did. He's looking into it."

"Is Gram okay?" Levi asked.

"She's pissed," Asher said. "I was just there and she was banging things around in the kitchen."

"Mad is good." I felt a hint of relief. "If she wasn't mad, I'd be worried about her."

"That's what I was thinking," Asher said.

I met Levi's eyes, then Asher's. "We'll figure this out. There's no way she's losing her house. Over my dead fucking body."

Levi nodded back, undisguised anger all over his face. He and I were on the same page. We'd gut that fucker if we had to. And we weren't going to let anything happen to Gram.

I didn't know what we were going to do about it, exactly. But there had to be something.

Cara sprang to mind, and I was pissed at myself for even thinking it. I had no idea what kind of money she had, and I hadn't been bullshitting when I'd told her I didn't want any of it. Granted, asking her to help Gram wasn't the same as treating her like a sugar mama. But still. This was our problem. We'd figure it out.

"I need to get back to Grace," Asher said. "I'll call Evan and fill him in if you guys want to talk to Gav."

"Sure, I'll tell him," Levi said.

"Is Grace okay?" I asked. If Cara hadn't been pregnant, I probably wouldn't have even remembered when Grace's baby was due. But I was keenly aware that Grace's pregnancy was rapidly approaching the finish line. She only had a few weeks left.

"Yeah, she's doing great," Asher said, his face lighting up. "She doesn't want to rub it in because she knows Cara's had a hard time, but she's loved being pregnant. I think she's going to miss it."

"I don't think Cara loves anything about being pregnant," I said. "Although, I swear, her boobs are insane. Did Grace's boobs get next level awesome?"

Asher glared at me—a very clear message not to talk about his wife's boobs. But then he nodded. "Yeah, they're amazing."

"See, it's a thing," I said to no one in particular. "Are her nipples really sensitive, too, because—"

"We're done here." Asher stood.

Levi shook his head at me. "Too far, man."

"I was just asking."

"I'll keep you guys posted about Gram," Asher said as he headed for the door.

"Thanks, brofessor."

Asher left, and Levi and I looked at each other.

"This could be bad," Levi said.

"Well it's not like she's going to be on the street," I said. "We'll all take care of her."

"Yeah, but that's not enough. That house is her whole world. She's not Gav; she can't just crash on someone's couch. And Grandad—" He stopped, glancing away.

"It's like Grandad is still there," I finished for him. I stood and put my hand on his shoulder. "We're not letting her lose the house. Between the five of us, we'll figure something out. There has to be a way."

He nodded. "Yeah. There will be."

There had to be. We couldn't let this happen to Gram.

22

CARA

I glared at my phone, as if it could be held responsible for my sudden bad mood. Not that a reason existed—not a reason that made any sense, at least. So what if Logan wasn't coming home right away? Why did I care? It wasn't like I'd spent the morning lost in daydreams where he burst in and ravaged me as soon as he got off his shift.

Fine, yes I had.

This was what I'd been reduced to. Fantasizing about Logan Bailey.

Although to his credit, he lived up to every one of my fantasies.

I could have just been up front and told him to get his ass home so he could give me the D. But I refused to allow myself to be ruled by the ebb and flow of my surging hormones. I was stronger than that.

So I finished getting ready for the day. Blow-dried my hair and put on a little makeup. Choosing clothes was becoming trickier, but I found a cute tunic and leggings, and paired it with knee-high boots. Flats, though. Heels were no longer my friend.

And boots hid the fact that I was starting to get cankles.

I paused in front of Logan's half open door on my way downstairs. He'd left the bed unmade and a few of those damn tube socks were strewn around the floor. I wanted to be irritated at the mess, but mostly I just wanted to go in there and sniff his sheets.

But I didn't. Not this time.

I got halfway down the stairs before I turned around, marched into his room, picked up his pillow, and smashed it against my face so I could smell it. The deep inhale flooded me with endorphins and I let his pillow drop to the bed, feeling a little drunk.

And I resolved, not for the first time, to never, ever tell anyone that I did that.

Food was getting easier to deal with, although I still couldn't look at—let alone smell—anything with chicken. Especially raw chicken. I had to avoid the meat section at the grocery store or I risked purging my stomach contents. But I'd been dealing with this long enough, I didn't have anything questionable in my kitchen.

I grabbed a quick breakfast and thumbed through a pregnancy book while I waited to make sure my stomach would accept the food. I'd abandoned most of my self-help and career planning books in favor of a growing stack on pregnancy and parenting. It was a lot of information, so I was taking things one chapter at a time.

When I was sure my breakfast would stay put, I headed into town. I parked in front of Nature's Basket Grocery and got out, taking a deep breath of the fresh spring air. Although I'd lived in Tilikum for nearly ten years, after growing up in L.A., the clean mountain air was still a luxury. It was like I could smell that it was spring.

I grabbed a small cart on the way inside and pushed it while I perused the produce section. The little store made up for its size with cuteness and selection. Who knew a small-town grocery store would carry kumquats and star-fruit alongside the thirty different types of apples? And their gourmet chocolate selection was the best I'd seen anywhere.

But I wasn't in the mood for fancy produce or organic dark chocolate sweetened with monk fruit and stevia. Oranges were my current favorite food. I'd been eating five or six a day, which meant I ran out quickly. I put two large bags of them in my cart and was contemplating adding another—although there was the risk that I'd flip and hate oranges tomorrow—when I noticed Lorraine Montgomery standing by a mountain of apples, eyeing me.

Lorraine was the town librarian, and not the sweet kind who lived to share her love of books with her community. She was the glare and shush you type who loved to collect library fines. She'd once shushed me in a parking lot.

Of course, Lorraine Montgomery was not my biggest fan.

Her eyes swept over the swell of my stomach. By now, everyone in town knew I was pregnant. I'd gone past I-can't-button-my-jeans and was firmly in leggings-and-loose-shirts territory, with a baby belly that visibly protruded. I hadn't surrendered to actual maternity clothes yet, but I had a feeling I'd be in them sooner than Grace had.

Of course, Grace's body had lovingly complied with the demands of pregnancy. Mine was in a constant state of revolt. So it didn't surprise me that less than halfway through this ordeal, I'd already grown out of my normal clothes.

I could feel the judgment in Lorraine's gaze. Her high and mighty attitude wasn't helped by the fact that her husband Harold was Tilikum's mayor. She clung to every shred of small-town authority and status she could grab.

And for some reason, she hated me.

Actually, I knew why she hated me. It had started when I'd posed for a figure drawing session in a community art class at Tilikum College.

Yes, I'd posed naked while students drew me. And why not? I looked great naked. Or I had before I'd been possessed by Logan Bailey's spawn.

Harold and Lorraine had taken that class, and apparently Lorraine had been unhappy with how much her husband had enjoyed my modeling session. She'd been glaring at me ever since.

Meeting her eyes, I gave her a fake smile and put a hand on my belly. If she wanted to judge me for being pregnant, she was welcome to. I wasn't ashamed, so she could fuck right off.

I finished my shopping and took my groceries out to my car. On a whim, I took my camera out of my handbag and took a few photos of the sky. It was pale blue with fluffy white clouds. I walked up the street, toward Lumberjack Park, to get a different angle.

"There's not much time," a gravelly voice muttered behind me. "Not much time at all."

I turned to find Harvey Johnston, Tilikum's resident oddball, poking at the air with a finger. He wore a faded gray flannel shirt with a leather vest over it. The knees of his jeans were dirty, like he'd been kneeling on the ground. Gardening, maybe. Or digging for the treasure he was convinced he'd find.

I loved Harvey. He was one of my favorite people in this

town. Always had been. He was weird as hell, but he took care of himself just fine. I'd been to his house—a cabin on the outskirts of town—many times to make sure he had everything he needed. He always did. I had no idea how he paid his bills, but he had running water, electricity, and a kitchen full of food and supplies. For a guy who wandered around talking to himself, he did okay. And the fact that he did wander around talking to himself was why I loved him so much. This guy did not give a fuck, and I adored that about him.

"Not much time for what, Harvey?" I asked.

He turned to me, his eyes lighting up with surprise, as if he'd just realized there were other people in the world. "Hi, Miss Cara. Time to find it."

"Find what?"

"His treasure," he said with a decisive nod. "Time is running out and then it will be too late."

I just smiled. Harvey was always talking about finding the so-called Montgomery treasure. Town lore claimed one of the town's founders had left treasure in the mountains for someone to find—and more than a hundred years later, no one had.

Town lore also claimed Bigfoot lived just north of Tilikum, so there was that.

"Have you found any clues yet?" I asked. "Anything new to report?"

He shook his head. "Nothing new. Someone will. Soon, I think. I'm not crazy. It's there."

"If it is, I sure hope you're the one to find it."

He met my gaze and the lines around his eyes crinkled. I lifted my camera and took a photo, right as he gave me a gap-toothed smile.

"Did you take my picture, Miss Cara?"

"I did. Is that okay?"

He shrugged. "Sure. Don't know why you'd want to, though."

I took another photo. His face was so interesting. "You have a nice face."

His face lit up with another smile. "Do I?"

"Yeah, you really do. I wouldn't lie about that."

"Well, thank you. You and that baby have a nice day."

"Thanks, Harvey. Be careful out there."

"Always am." He glared at a squirrel that darted by and started grumbling about thieves as he walked away.

I wandered over to a bench and took a seat. A squirrel stopped in front of me, nibbling on a dog treat. He must have stolen it from the dish outside Happy Paws. I lifted my camera and took a few pictures. I'd have to send these to Fiona. Unlike most people, who thought they were a ruthless gang of thieves, Fiona loved Tilikum's squirrels.

My phone rang. I pulled it out of my purse and my smile faded. So much for my good mood. It was my mother.

"Hi, Mom."

"I've been thinking about your pregnancy."

"Oh?" I braced myself for whatever she was about to say. It was unlikely to be good.

"You're on your own and you're so far away from home. I'd come there, but we both know that's not practical."

My stomach went queasy at the thought of my mother deciding she needed to move to Tilikum to be closer to me. "No, it's not practical. You need to stay in L.A."

"Of course I do. My whole life is here."

"I agree. Your doctors and your therapists and all your friends. I'm sure you don't want to leave all that behind."

"I wouldn't dream of it."

Thank God.

"Which is why you need to move home," she said, her tone decisive.

And there it was.

"I don't think that's such a good idea," I said.

"Why not? You don't have any family there."

"No, but I have friends. And the baby's father is here."

She huffed. "What does that have to do with anything?"

"It's his kid."

"Men don't care about that sort of thing. If he was planning to marry you, there might be a chance he'd stick around. Is he?"

"What, planning to marry me? No, but that's not—"

"See? He already has one foot out the door."

"He isn't Dad."

"No, but I can tell you what's going to happen. As soon as he gets a taste of how much responsibility this is, he'll be on his way."

"He's not like that."

"Don't be naïve."

"I'm not being naïve. You're jumping to conclusions about a man you've never met. Logan isn't going to bail on me."

She let out a heavy sigh. "I don't understand why you always insist on learning things the hard way."

I bit back a scathing comment about how I didn't need advice from a woman whose own life was a smoldering dumpster fire. "You have the wrong idea about Logan."

"Who?"

"Logan Bailey. The father of my baby."

"No one's saying he can't come visit once in a while."

"Mom, I grew up without a father. Why would I intentionally make it harder for my kid's dad to be a part of his or her life?"

"I'm just trying to protect you," she said, and I could hear the hysteria in her voice starting to rise. "I know what it's like to be a single mother. I raised you all on my own, even though it cost me everything. I did what I had to do."

"Yes, I know."

"You have no idea what you've done to your life. I only want to help."

"Thank you, I guess, but I don't need to move to L.A. for this to be okay. Logan and I are making it work. We're figuring out how to parent together."

"That's not the point."

"Then what is the point?" I asked, ready to smash my phone on the pavement.

"You can't raise my grandchild in some backwoods town."

"It's actually a very nice town."

She huffed again.

"It really is. Besides, it's where I live, and it's where Logan and his family live. I'm not leaving."

"I should have known he'd get in the way."

"Get in the way of what? He's going to be a dad to his kid. Why are you acting like that's a bad thing?"

"Like I said, I'm just trying to protect you. But if you don't want my help—" She hung up.

I dropped my phone back in my purse and took a long, deep breath. The fresh mountain air helped a little. I shouldn't have been surprised that my mother wanted me to move home. I'd chosen Tilikum largely because it was the sort of place she'd hate—and therefore would never come visit.

But if I didn't live in L.A., she didn't have control. And that was the real reason she wanted me to move back.

It was never going to happen.

I probably needed to call my therapist to set up a session. It had been a while, and the challenge of maintaining a somewhat peaceful relationship with my volatile mother was getting harder.

But today, I could let it go. The sun was shining, the air was fresh, and when Logan did get home, he and his glorious dick were going to make me feel so much better.

FOR A WOMAN with serious smell issues, the Knotty Knitter was one of my favorite places. It smelled great. No threat of food scents that would send my stomach into a frenzy. Just the calming aroma of paper and yarn with a hint of tea in the air.

Stitch and Bitch was quiet tonight—just me, Grace, Skylar, and Fiona, plus Amy Garrett, Tillie Bailey-Linfield, and Marlene Haven. We all sat on the well-worn couch and armchairs that had been set up in a circle in the back of the store.

I was so used to seeing Marlene here, I rarely thought about the fact that she was a Haven, and therefore supposed to be the enemy. But it wasn't like that at Stitch and Bitch. Leave it to the women of Tilikum to go around the feud while the men were still coming up with an endless stream of juvenile pranks, all for reasons no one could remember.

I'd stopped bringing Long Island iced teas to our weekly gathering, but the others had picked up the slack. Tonight there was an open bottle of wine and a steaming pot of tea.

Fiona occupied one of the armchairs. Her hair was back to dark brown, after a short stint as a blond, and she wore it up in a cute messy bun. She had a smudge of what was probably grease on her cheek. Skylar sat next to her. She was the prettiest little thing with straight dark hair and dark brown eyes. But that sweet face hid a wicked, and sometimes morbid, imagination.

I'd thought my adoption of those two would be as close as I'd ever come to motherhood. Joke was on me, apparently.

The conversation had been breezing by me. I was focused on the hat I was attempting to crochet. At least, it was supposed to be a hat. It wasn't turning out quite the way I'd planned.

I'd never been any good at this.

But I was determined to not suck at everything anymore. I was tired of being the eccentric rich girl who rolled into the small-town knitting group with nothing to contribute but alcohol and sass. I was going to be a mother, for fuck's sake. I needed to learn to do something other than mix cocktails.

I held up the hat, trying to figure out why it was so crooked.

"You okay, honey?" Grace asked.

"I just don't know what I'm doing wrong."

"You're doing fine," Tillie said. She was probably in her sixties and wore wire-rimmed glasses and bright pink lipstick. "It just takes practice."

"Don't worry; you're not alone." Skylar held up a blue and gray... something. I didn't know what she was trying to make. "I can't get this right either."

At least I wasn't the only one. But Skylar was a successful novelist. Whether or not she figured out how to crochet, she had plenty of talent.

Wincing, Grace placed a hand on her belly. Even sitting, Grace looked huge. To be honest, looking at her made me twitchy. She was only a few weeks from her due date, and a vivid reminder that not only was I going to be just as enormous, I was going to have to get this kid out of me somehow.

I was already dreading that part.

"Are you okay, boo?" I asked. Freaked out or not, my concern for her overrode everything else.

"Yeah, I'm okay."

"Are you having contractions?" Marlene asked.

"Just Braxton-Hicks," Grace said. "Not the real thing yet, but I sure feel them."

Marlene clicked her tongue. "I had those for weeks with Annika. They can get uncomfortable."

Grace shifted in her seat. "I had an appointment this morning and it doesn't look like I'm ready to go into labor yet. But things are definitely changing."

"I'm so excited to meet my first niece or nephew," Fiona said.

"When are you going to join the fun?" I asked, winking at Fiona. "Apparently getting knocked up by a Bailey is all the rage."

Fiona laughed. "I don't know. We've talked about it, but I'm not sure if we're ready."

"Gavin brought it up the other day," Skylar said. "We're not even married yet, but he says we should consider it because he doesn't want his brothers to show him up. I told him having babies shouldn't be a competition and he looked at me like I was crazy."

I laughed. "Sounds like Gavin."

"Sounds like all the Baileys," Fiona said.

I dropped my crochet hook and my sad excuse for a hat in my lap. "I'm done for tonight. If I'm going to keep failing at making this into something that's roughly hat-like, I at least need alcohol."

Stitch and Bitch had been winding down anyway. The

other ladies put away their projects and we cleaned up the drinks. Despite the fact that my project was on the wrong side of awful, I felt a little glimmer of pride. It needed work, but it was better than anything else I'd attempted to crochet.

I gathered up my things and followed Grace out to her car. She put her tote in the passenger side, then stepped in and gave me a big hug.

"What was that for, boo?"

"For being my best friend. And because I had a feeling you needed it."

"You know me so well."

"How's everything at home?" she asked.

"Surprisingly okay. Living with Logan isn't the worst thing ever."

She gave me a knowing smile. "Not the worst, huh? I'm guessing it's a lot better than that."

I rolled my eyes. "Fine. The regular orgasms are a plus."

"I knew things were going to work out between you."

"Don't get the wrong idea. Sleeping with Logan is simply fulfilling a physical need. We're not together."

She raised her eyebrows, clearly skeptical. "You say that now, but first comes sex, then comes baby, then comes more sex, and the next thing you know, you're in love."

"Hardly. The only people I'll ever love are you and this kid." I brushed my hair back from my face. "I think Logan and I will be able to navigate this co-parenting thing, but that's all. Besides, I already know we won't end up together."

"Why do you say that?" Grace asked.

"Because I'm not his fated mate."

Her brow furrowed. "What does that even mean?"

"You know, in some books the couple is fated to be together and once they find each other, they instinctively know. Although in this case, it's Gram that knows." I could tell she still wasn't following my logic. "Take you, for example. Gram knew you'd end up with Asher. I'm convinced she knows who all her grandsons will be with."

"How could she possibly know that?"

"I don't know *how*, I just know that she does."

"So what makes you think she hasn't always known that you and Logan will end up together?"

My throat felt tight and I had to swallow before I could keep going. "She's never given me a nickname."

"What?"

"You're Gracie Bear, or Mama Bear. She likes you so much, she gave you two. She calls Fiona Cricket, and Skylar is Sparrow. She's never called me anything but Cara."

"That doesn't mean things won't work out with Logan."

"No, it does. Has she ever given someone other than her grandsons or their fated mates a nickname?"

"Fated mates," she said with a laugh. "Okay, no, I don't think she has. She doesn't give nicknames to just anyone."

"And is she ever wrong about anything?"

Grace opened her mouth to answer but closed it again. "I'm sure she is, but I just can't think of a specific example right now."

"She's never given me a nickname, so I know I'm not meant to be with Logan."

"Maybe she did and she just hasn't told you yet."

I arched an eyebrow. "I doubt it. And it's okay. It's not like I'm in love with Logan and pouting because I know he's never going to marry me. At best, we'll be friends who can make parenting decisions without fighting first. That's all I'm hoping for."

It was all I could hope for.

I felt the telltale signs of my mood changing. I'd joked about how moody I was before, but old me had nothing on pregnant me. Tension knotted my back and a smoldering heat flared to life inside me. I reached out and grabbed it. Mad was better than sad. I wasn't going to let myself be sad over this.

I almost felt sorry for Logan. He was going to have to deal with my moody ass when I went home.

Grace narrowed her eyes. I could tell she wanted to argue with me, but she knew I was right.

And it was fine. My baby would be a Bailey, but I'd always be an outsider.

23

LOGAN

*B*y the amount of cabinet slamming I could hear from the kitchen, Cara was in a mood. Why was anyone's guess. Had I left a mess downstairs and she was annoyed with me? Maybe she was annoyed with me for no reason. That was another solid possibility. Or had something happened while she was at Stitch and Bitch that had pissed her off?

Then again, maybe she was just hungry. Or horny.

A smarter man would stay in his room. Wait it out until it was safe to emerge.

But I liked playing with fire.

I crept down and hesitated at the bottom of the stairs. Light flickered from the gas fireplace in the living room. Cara moved around the kitchen, opening cabinet doors and slamming them shut. Her white shirt and leggings showed the swell of her pregnant belly and it was weird how much I liked it. The way her body was changing was sexy in ways I never would have predicted.

A deep, primal urge stole over me. I'd felt protective of her since the moment she'd told me she was pregnant. But it was morphing into something else. Every time I looked at her, one word came to mind.

Mine.

Did every guy feel this way about the mother of his child? And would I still feel like this after our baby was born?

Was it really just the baby?

Of course it was. I couldn't get wrapped up in possessive feelings for Cara.

But I could fuck the fight out of her. That was definitely what she needed right now.

She opened the fridge, looked inside for about two seconds, then slammed it closed again.

"What are you so pissed about?" I asked, sauntering into the kitchen.

Her green eyes flashed. "Not now, prince dickhead."

I casually leaned my hip against the counter. "I'm just asking. You're the one down here banging shit around for no reason."

"It's my kitchen. If I want to bang shit around, I will."

"Okay, crazy."

"Why are you so annoying?" She took a step forward and her eyes flicked up and down. "Look at you. You can barely even get yourself dressed."

I glanced down at myself. I was wearing a t-shirt and gym shorts. "What's wrong with my clothes?"

"Your stupid socks don't even match."

"They don't?" I stuck one foot out, then the other. One sock had a red stripe, the other blue. "Huh. I guess they don't."

She gritted her teeth. "I hate those socks."

"No you don't."

"Yes, I really do."

I moved closer. "You love my socks because you love the way I annoy you."

"Shut up, Logan."

"Is that all you've got? Shut up? Come on, princess, you can do better than that."

"I hate you."

I took another step, getting right in front of her. She had to lift her chin to look up at me. "No you don't."

"Yes I do."

"You don't hate me." I ran my fingers through her hair and grabbed a handful in my fist. My gaze locked on her mouth and it occurred to me that she almost never let me kiss her. Whenever I tried, she found ways to avoid it. "You like me and it pisses you off that you do."

She rolled her eyes but didn't try to back away. Not that she could with the grip I had on her hair.

"You wish."

I leaned my face closer, sliding my nose along hers. She stiffened, but I didn't give an inch. "You like the way I fuck you."

Her only answer was a soft whimper in her throat.

"You do, don't you?" I let my lips brush against hers as I spoke. "Say it. Tell me you like the way I fuck you."

"No."

I smiled. I knew she'd say no. I wanted her to. My body was on fire for her already, my dick hard as steel. There was nothing hotter than fighting as foreplay. I fucking loved it.

"Don't lie to me, sweetheart." My tongue flicked out and touched her lips. "You love getting fucked."

"No I don't. You don't do it for me at all."

"No? That's too bad." With one hand still in her hair, I cupped one of her tits and squeezed. It was a low blow. I knew how sensitive they were.

A moan escaped her lips.

"That's what you need, isn't it?" I rubbed my thumb across her nipple. "You need me to make you come. Tell me."

"I hate that you do this to me," she whispered.

"I know." I brushed my lips against hers again, not quite kissing her, and bent one knee to push my thigh between her legs. Like the horny monkey she was, she straddled my thigh and rubbed herself against me.

I had her right where I wanted her. So I slanted my lips over hers and kissed her.

She planted her hands on my chest, like she was about to push me away. But I invaded her mouth with my tongue, kissing her deeply.

And she melted.

A shudder ran through her body and she wound her arms around my neck. I let go of her hair, instead maintaining a gentle hold on the back of her head, my fingertips massaging her scalp.

Something was happening. The lightning strikes of anger that usually jolted between us became soft ripples of pleasure. No fingernails, no fists pulling hair. She even stopped dry humping my leg, although I kept steady pressure with my thigh.

Her full lips were warm and pliant against mine and our tongues tangled in a slow dance. I slid my other hand around to cup her ass, pressing her tighter against me.

The kiss went on longer than I thought she'd allow, but eventually, she put her hands back on my chest and pushed.

I broke the kiss and let her go.

"You shouldn't kiss me like that," she said, her voice breathy.

"Why not?"

"You just shouldn't."

Maybe she was right. Without the spark of anger lighting a fire between us, what was left suddenly felt real and raw. I still wanted to fuck her brains out. My dick ached to be inside her. But my chest felt full and an emotion I didn't want to acknowledge tried to claw its way to the surface.

We needed to go back to being mad. This was too fucking much.

I shrugged, like that kiss hadn't just wrecked me. "I guess you don't want an orgasm, then."

Anger once again made her green eyes shine. "You're going to give me one."

"I don't know, sweetheart. I don't think you want it."

"Now it's two."

Oh yeah. I liked where this was going. Tension crackled in the air between us. "Try three. But I'm going to make you beg."

"I won't beg you for anything."

"Yes, you will." My voice was a low growl. I crowded her against the counter, caging her with my arms. "I'm going to make you lose your fucking mind until you beg me to stop. Until you're so desperate to come, you can't stand it."

She put her hands on my chest and curled her fingers so her nails bit through my shirt. "You aren't that good."

"Wanna bet?" I deftly slid my hand under the waistband of her leggings. "This greedy pussy will come for me right here."

My fingers slid between her legs and she hissed in a breath. Her panties were soaked.

"See?" I growled, letting my fingers glide along her wet slit. "You want me."

"I don't want *you*. I just want an orgasm."

I grinned, pushing two fingers inside her while she dug her nails into my shoulders. "No one could fuck you like I do."

She moaned as my fingers slid deeper. "I've had so much better."

"Dirty little liar," I growled in her ear. "Tell me you love this."

"No."

I grinned again as she rocked her hips, grinding against my hand. "Tell me you don't want me to stop."

Another moan, and her eyelids fluttered. "You can stop. I don't care."

Her inner muscles tightened. I fingered her faster, pressing against her clit with the heel of my hand, driving her to a frenzy. Her breath came fast and she rolled her hips, riding my hand.

And then I stopped.

Her eyes went wide and she gasped as I pulled my hand out of her pants.

"What the fuck?"

"You don't need me. I'm not that good anyway."

"Logan."

I slid my fingers in my mouth and sucked off her taste. Fuck, that was good. "Too bad. You taste fucking amazing."

Taking ragged breaths, she gripped the counter. "Logan. You better…"

"What?" I asked, struggling to sound nonchalant. Because despite this game I was playing, I was ready to turn her around, rip off her pants, and slam my dick inside her. It was all I could do to hold back. "What do you need?"

"You know what I need."

"Then ask nicely." I traced a line from her neck to one of

her tits. Moved my finger in a lazy circle around her nipple. Even through her clothes, my touch made her gasp.

She grabbed my erection and squeezed. Hard. "Give me a fucking orgasm."

Despite myself, I grunted, my hips jerking. "All you have to say is please."

Her hand tightened. I gritted my teeth. She basically had me by the balls, but I didn't give in.

Instead, I kissed her again.

That really pissed her off.

But she did kiss me back.

She threw her arms around me and dug her nails into my back. I grunted at the sharp pinch and delved my tongue into her mouth while I fumbled to get my hand back in her pants. She bit my lip, refusing to let go until my fingers plunged inside her.

"Please," she said between messy, teeth-clashing kisses. "Please, Logan. Please."

I pumped my fingers into her while I kissed her hard, giving in. Giving her what she needed. Her pussy tightened, spasming around my fingers with quick pulses.

One orgasm down. And I was just getting started.

I pulled my hand out of her pants and she sagged against me for a few seconds, catching her breath.

She straightened and brushed her hair out of her face. "That was barely adequate."

"I guess I better try again." I grabbed her chin so she couldn't turn away and kissed her again. This one was soft— almost tender. A strange contrast to the urgency thrumming through my body and the hardness of my voice. "Get your ass to my room and take your clothes off."

She hesitated, her eyes locked with mine, and I wondered if she was going to keep arguing.

"Now," I said.

She loved it when I told her what to do. Her lips twitched in a smile. She planted her hands on my chest and shoved me away—she had to find some way to fight me on everything—but with a toss of her hair over her shoulder, she started up the stairs.

I followed her up, my hands all over her hips and ass. As soon as we got to my room, she did what I said—peeled off her clothes and let them drop to the floor. She turned and looked at me while I undressed, heat and defiance burning in her eyes.

Fuck, she was beautiful.

I backed her up toward my bed and she climbed on. As much as I wanted to be inside her, I wasn't letting her leave until she'd come for me at least two more times.

Plus I really loved eating her pussy. This was a total win-win.

She lay with her head on my pillow. I settled on the bed and pushed her legs open. Tasted her with a few long drags of my tongue.

So fucking good.

With my hands on her thighs, I went to work, licking and sucking while she gasped and moaned. She could insult me all she wanted—claim I didn't give her the best orgasms of her life. Her body told the truth. Here, she couldn't hide from me. I knew what I did to her, and we both fucking loved it.

Moaning, she slid her fingers through my hair. I flicked her clit in a steady rhythm while she rolled her hips against me. I loved getting her to this point—where she was enjoying herself enough to relax. No longer desperately chasing an orgasm, or hurling insults at me, she was lost in the feel of my tongue between her legs.

Her breath came in quick gasps as I licked and sucked, driving her crazy. I knew exactly what she liked and I used that knowledge mercilessly. She writhed against the sheets, clutching my hair, and let her legs fall open wider.

I sucked on her clit, making her cry out, then slid two fingers inside her. She was almost there. I could feel the heat, the tight pulses as the tension in her body rose to a breaking point.

"Don't stop," she pleaded. "Please don't stop."

I could have. Sometimes I did, just to make her beg for more. But this time, I kept licking her, driving her relentlessly toward another orgasm.

Her walls pulsed and her taste flooded my mouth. Lust blazed through me, making my erection ache and almost involuntarily, I rubbed myself against the sheets. I was going to fuck the shit out of her. She'd be lucky if she could move when I was done.

"Oh my god," she said breathlessly, her body going limp. She draped an arm over her forehead. "That was... Oh my god. I don't know if I can take any more."

I sat up on my knees and wiped my mouth with the back of my hand. "I'm not done with you yet."

Her eyes flicked to my swollen cock, then back to my face. "I have to admit, you're very generous."

Pushing her legs open, I moved closer. "Consider me your orgasm dealer. Like drugs, only better for you."

"So much better."

"Do you still need to get fucked after all that?" I grabbed my cock and started to stroke.

Licking her lips, she watched my hand move up and down my hard length. "I really do. But I like watching you do that."

"Yeah?" I stroked faster. "You like to watch, you filthy little girl."

"That's so hot."

Groaning, I tightened my grip, still stroking fast. Her taste lingered in my mouth, and the sight of her beautiful body spread out before me only made this better.

But I needed to be inside her like I needed air.

Still on my knees, I grabbed her ankles to hold her legs up and thrust inside her. I groaned as I sank into her wet heat. Fuck, she felt good. So hot and tight around my swollen cock.

I drove my hips, pounding into her, banging the headboard against the wall. She braced herself with her arms over her head and her tits bounced.

Damn those tits. They were insane.

Her body was amazing. It had changed, giving her curves where she hadn't had them before. And I loved it.

I fucked her hard, growling like an animal. My abs flexed and my chest glistened with a sheen of sweat. Pressure built in my groin as I thrust in and out, the hot pressure almost unbearable.

Her eyes rolled back as her slick walls clenched around me and she murmured a stream of barely coherent yeses as she started to come again.

That was three. Time to let loose.

A few more hard thrusts and I was done for. I came unglued, grunting with each pulse as I unleashed inside her. Waves of pleasure burst through me as I came, the intensity overwhelming.

Holy shit.

I pulled out and set Cara's legs back on the bed. Her eyes were closed and she draped an arm over her forehead while she caught her breath. I crumpled onto the bed next to her, my heart still racing, my entire body saturated with endorphins.

We lay there for a minute, just breathing. Then she pushed herself up, moved to the edge of the bed, and stood.

"Goodnight," she said as she swiped her clothes off the floor.

"Night."

I watched her finish gathering her clothes and I almost said it. Almost told her—no, asked her—to stay.

Because she never did. We had sex. She left. Even when it was in her room.

And once again, I asked myself why I cared. We both knew what this was. We were just making the best of the situation. We weren't a couple.

She brushed her hair back over her shoulder and for a second, I thought she might look back. And if she had, maybe I would have said it.

Stay.

But she didn't.

So I didn't.

She left my room with her clothes hanging off her arm, and this weird hole in my chest got a little bigger.

24

LOGAN

For the first time ever, I'd brought a girl to Tuesday night dinner at Gram's.

Granted, it was Cara, so maybe that didn't count. It wasn't like she was my girlfriend, which was why I hadn't brought her before. But a few days earlier, Gram had asked if she was coming. That was her way of saying, *You better invite her.*

It was never a good idea to cross Gram. Plus, I liked the idea of bringing Cara to dinner. It seemed fitting. Maybe we weren't a couple, but we were having a kid together, so she was stuck with us now. It made sense to integrate her into the family.

Fortunately for both of us, I'd always been the lone Cara-hater among the Baileys. Evan and Levi seemed to more or less ignore her, but they didn't dislike her. She got along fine with Gavin, although most people did, and she and Asher seemed to have accepted each other. And Gram liked her, so she certainly wasn't walking into hostile territory.

But I'd sensed her anxiety as soon as we'd left to come

over. And even though she'd probably been to Gram's hundreds of times with Grace over the years, I could still feel her anxiety as we sat at the big farmhouse table with the rest of the family, picking at the remnants of our dinners.

I'd been living with Cara for almost two months and in that short time, I'd figured out a lot about her. I knew that food or sex could cure even her worst bad moods. Bonus points if I gave her both. I knew she spent long afternoons editing photographs she'd taken—and they were gorgeous. I knew her mother was ten times crazier than she was, and that I still had a lot of questions about her dad. I knew she was picky about almost everything, from food to the way her clothes fit, and she had weird taste in music. She watched a lot of YouTube videos, trying to learn how to do things, and cooking was not her best skill.

I'd also figured out that her cool nonchalance was a façade and she hated feeling vulnerable.

Maybe that was why she'd chosen a seat next to Grace instead of me. She didn't want to lean on me for anything, even though she needed it.

God, she drove me crazy sometimes.

Grace leaned back in her chair and rested a hand on her belly. She had less than a week until her due date, but despite how big she was, she always looked content and comfortable. Unlike Cara, who kept shifting in her chair. Her hips had started aching, especially after she'd been sitting for a while. The books said it was her joints loosening in preparation for giving birth. She said her body hated being pregnant and was finding new ways to make its dissatisfaction known.

I'd have to give her a back rub after we got home.

I glanced at Gram. There wasn't even a hint of stress in

her expression. No one had brought up the subject of her finances, although I knew we were all thinking about it. But she'd probably say it wasn't dinner table conversation. I'd have to ask Asher about it later.

"So, the Bailey flag is still up," Gavin said with a grin. "Whoever put it up there did a good job."

I straightened in my chair. "What Bailey flag?"

Levi's brow furrowed. "The giant blue flag that says Bailey on it that's been flying over city hall for the last two days. You didn't see it?"

"No." That was weird. How had I missed that? "Why didn't you guys let me know? I could have helped."

"We didn't do it," Gavin said casually.

Gram snorted.

"What?" Gavin asked while Skylar snickered behind her hand.

"How have the Havens not taken it down?" Fiona asked. "It's massive. They must hate it."

"I suppose it's possible whoever put it up, and I have no idea who that was, might have booby trapped it," Gavin said. "That's just what I heard."

I caught Levi trying to hide a grin. He'd been in on it, too.

Damn. I didn't know how to feel about the fact that I'd completely missed this. Not only had I not been in on the prank, I hadn't even noticed the flag. But I had been preoccupied lately.

My life was changing. And it wasn't a bad thing, necessarily. Just different.

"Well, nice job to *whoever* did it," I said, making air quotes. "Booby traps were a nice touch."

"Thanks," Gavin said with a smile. "I mean, yeah, I agree."

"It would be funny if someone reloaded the traps," Levi said. "Again."

Gram got up and took her plate to the sink. "My peckers sure do lay a lot of eggs. More than I can give away sometimes. Not sure if you boys have a use for them, but you're welcome to some if you do."

Gavin and Levi shared a quick grin. I stared at Gram. Had she just offered to help prank the Havens? She never did that. My eyes flicked to Cara and she gave me a quick wink. I could have sworn I understood what she was saying —*Gram is a badass*—just like I always had with Levi.

That was weird. I'd always figured that was a twin thing. Did I have it with Cara too?

Before I could keep pondering any potential nonverbal communication ability I had with her, everyone started getting up and taking their dishes to the sink. I followed suit, then elbowed Gavin out of the way so I could help clean up.

Evan and I did the dishes while Gram chatted with the girls at the table. When we finished, I grabbed a chocolate chip cookie out of the cookie jar and went out to the back porch.

The evening air was still warm. Asher stood looking out over the backyard with his forearms resting on the porch railing. Gram's chickens had all settled into their coop and the only sound was the rustle of the wind in the trees and some frogs croaking down by the creek.

"Hey, brotee." I leaned against the railing and took a bite of my cookie. "Any news on the money situation? Gram hasn't said a word to me about it."

"Darcy's still working on it. Unfortunately, the IRS doesn't particularly care why Gram owes back taxes."

"That's such bullshit."

"I know. But we'll figure something out."

I nodded, hoping he was right. This place wasn't just a house on a bunch of land. It was acres and acres of history. It was Gram's world.

"So you're in full-on baby watch," I said. "Any day now, huh?"

"Every time she moves, my adrenaline shoots through the roof because I think it's time."

"Are you ready?"

He hesitated, like he needed to think about it. "As ready as I can be, I guess. We have everything we need and we took the baby classes. But how ready can you be?"

"Good point. I won't lie: Seeing Grace freaks me out. I keep thinking about how that's going to be Cara in a few months. And before I know it, a doctor is going to hand us a tiny human and expect us to keep it alive."

He laughed. "Exactly. It's some heavy shit. I'm excited, though. At first, I wanted Grace to get pregnant because I knew she wanted a baby. It was about her, you know? But now I can't wait to meet my son or daughter. For a while, I didn't think I was going to get this chance, so starting a family with her feels like the final step in getting my life back."

I slapped him on the shoulder. "You deserve it, man. You're going to be a great father."

"Thanks." He met my eyes. "So are you."

Hearing that from him meant a lot. I kind of wanted to make a joke, or tell him to shut up, just to deflect all the emotion hanging between us.

But I didn't. Instead, I owned it.

"Thanks, Ash." I held out my arms and gave him a back-slapping hug. "That means a lot."

We stepped apart and Asher cleared his throat.

"Want one?" I asked, holding up the last of my cookie.

"Sure. Thanks."

I went back inside, casting a quick glance at the table. Cara sat with Gram and the girls. Someone had made tea and there was a plate of cookies in the center. I grabbed one, then went for the fridge to see what else she had to drink.

"Fortunately, I'm not completely dense," Cara said, her voice nonchalant. Which meant she was hiding how she really felt about whatever they were talking about. "I'll figure it out."

"Don't worry, Tiger," Gram said. "It will be fine."

I froze in front of the open fridge. Had Gram just called Cara *Tiger*?

I called Cara Tiger all the time. She was a wildcat with red hair. It fit. But I called her lots of things. Nicknames rolled off my tongue, kind of like my brocabulary.

But had Gram just given Cara an animal name? It wasn't native, and all our animals had their origins here, in the Pacific Northwest.

Tigers were foreign. Exotic.

Kind of like Cara. She was as foreign to our weird little town as a tiger would be in the Cascades.

But hell yes she was a tiger. She was fierce, protective, and territorial. Wild and impossible to tame. And as I stood there, reeling in shock, I realized something.

I liked her. A lot. In fact, I had a crush on her crazy ass. And I had no idea what I was going to do about it.

25

CARA

"Don't worry, Tiger. It will be fine."

Wait, what?

Had Gram just...

I could feel Grace looking at me, but I avoided her eyes. Because I knew exactly what she was thinking. Fated mates. Gram knew.

She always knew.

No, that couldn't be what had just happened. I'd known Gram for years, and she'd always called me Cara. She was just referring to my red hair. Or it was because of the baby. That made sense. She'd finally resigned herself to the reality that she was stuck with me since I was going to be the mother of one of her great-grandchildren. So she'd relented and made up an animal name for me. Maybe she'd even heard Logan call me Tiger and decided to just borrow his nickname for me.

It couldn't be because...

Logan was in the room. I could feel his presence behind me. He was looking for something in the fridge, so had he heard her? What was he doing over there? Probably contemplating whether he could sneak a beer, even though he'd promised to give up alcohol with me while I was pregnant.

He probably hadn't heard.

Why was I freaking out about this?

Fiona was saying something, but I'd lost track of the conversation. My eyes were glued to the table, my usual cool aloofness on the verge of crumbling.

And something happened inside me.

In my belly, to be precise. Until this moment, I'd felt like I was harboring a slowly expanding balloon, not a baby with arms and legs who could move, kick, or poke me.

I laid my hand just below my belly button. There it was again. It felt like bubbles swirling around and popping inside me. Was that the baby? It had to be.

Not quite sure what I was going to say, I looked up and opened my mouth. But before I could get a word out, Grace's eyes went wide. Gasping, she put her hand on her belly.

"Oh wow," Grace said on an exhale. "I'm having a really big contraction."

A powerful mix of excitement and concern poured through me. Oh my god, was it time? I grabbed her hand. "Is it still going?"

She nodded and I waited while the seconds ticked by. Her forehead tightened and she started to breathe harder. After what felt like an eternity, but had probably been about a minute, she took a slower breath and her grip on my hand relaxed.

"It stopped. But that was so much stronger than they've been."

"Than they've been when? Today? How long have you been having contractions?" I asked.

"Since about noon."

My eyes widened. "Grace, that's almost seven hours. Have they been regular? How far apart?"

"Pretty regular," she said. "And getting stronger. The last few were about six minutes apart."

"You've been sitting here in labor and you didn't say anything?" I gaped at her in disbelief.

"I've been having little ones for the last couple of weeks. I didn't want to get everyone excited over—oh." She hissed in another breath. "Yep. There's another one."

"Looks like baby bear is coming sooner rather than later," Gram said, her voice pure serenity.

"Hey, Ash," Logan called. "You might want to get in here."

The back door flew open and Asher rushed in. "Is it time?"

Grace held up a hand while she breathed through her contraction. "That was a big one. What did they say in the baby class about when we should go to the hospital?"

"Five minutes apart, lasting for a minute, for an hour," Asher rattled off like he'd memorized it.

He probably had.

"Well, they've been about six minutes apart, and now—" She stopped again, obviously in pain.

I held my breath while she squeezed my hand.

"They're coming right on top of each other," she said when it was over.

"You need to go," I said.

Asher was already there to help her up out of her chair. "Let's go, Mama Bear."

I got up, grabbed her purse, and followed them out to their car. The night air had a bite to it and stars twinkled across the clear sky. They had their hospital bag with them, just in case. Because of course they did. They were ready.

The bubbly feeling in my belly reminded me how *not* ready I was.

Asher helped her into the passenger side, then closed the door. I handed him her purse. A part of me wanted to tell him to keep her safe. To make sure she made it through this.

But I didn't need to. He had this. He had her.

I loved him for it.

He met my eyes. "Thank you."

I knew he didn't just mean thank you for the purse. There was almost a decade of thank yous in that one little phrase.

"I'll be there if she needs me," I said.

"I know."

We looked at each other for another second, then he stepped forward and wrapped me in a tight hug. I hugged him back, tears stinging my eyes.

I stepped back. "Go, before she ruins your interior by having a baby in the car."

The corner of his mouth hooked in a small smile. Then he ran around to the driver's side.

I watched him back up and a few seconds later, their car disappeared down the private drive, heading toward town.

"She'll be fine," Logan said behind me.

He rubbed a few circles across my back while I stood motionless.

It felt good.

Really good.

And for once in my very rocky relationship with Logan Bailey, I didn't make a sharp comment or pull away. I accepted his gesture of comfort without fighting him first.

"So, to the hospital?" he asked, dropping his hand.

I turned to face him. "Yes. And I'm camping out in that

waiting room until she has her baby and they let me see her. I don't care what they say about visiting hours."

His mouth twitched in a subtle smile. "Yeah, I know."

His eyes held mine, and for a second, I thought he might kiss me.

But he didn't move.

Obviously I didn't want him to. Things were complicated enough. Letting him kiss me while we had sex was one thing. But kissing in front of Gram's house was something else entirely.

Tiger. Why had Gram called me Tiger?

As if to make sure I left her house as confused as humanly possible, Gram caught my eye. She stood on the porch, a knowing smile on her face.

She was just smiling because her first great-grandchild was about to be born. That had to be it.

"Gram, are you driving yourself over, or do you want a ride?" Logan asked.

"I'll take my car and meet you there," she said.

Everyone else filed out of the house and climbed into cars to head to the hospital. Apparently this entire branch of the Bailey clan was going to hang out in the waiting room while Grace gave birth.

Of course they were. They were that type of family.

Logan dropped me off at the hospital, saying he'd be right back. I didn't know what he was up to, but I wasn't particularly worried about it. I just wanted to be as close to Grace as possible.

It wasn't that I thought Asher would come running out to the waiting room looking for me, insisting I come back to labor and delivery to be with Grace while she had the baby. As close as we were—closer than sisters—I'd known she wanted it to be just her and Asher in the delivery room. I didn't begrudge them that in the least. It was their baby. And it was time for Asher to shine.

But I'd be in that room as soon as they'd let me.

I went in the main entrance and followed the signs to the childbirth wing. It was upstairs, on the fourth floor. The waiting room was empty, although that was about to change. Gavin, Skylar, and Levi came in right after me, followed closely by Gram. Evan and Fiona were behind her. A few minutes later, Naomi and Jack, Grace's mom and stepdad, joined the group.

So many people here who loved my boo. It warmed my cold heart.

A slight antiseptic smell hung in the air, and the jungle print on the furniture made no sense. Gram got comfortable in a chair with a pile of knitting in her lap. I gazed at her from across the waiting room, wondering if she was okay. I got the sense that something was wrong but she was working hard to keep it from showing.

I'd know. I was an expert at that.

Logan's brothers congregated in a knot of chairs. They all had their phones out—probably watching random YouTube videos. Once in a while, one of them would angle his phone so the others could see. They'd all chuckle and nod, then go back to their own screens.

Skylar and Fiona shared a small couch, so I scooted a chair closer.

"I'm so excited, I could pee my pants," Fiona said.

Skylar fiddled with her hands in her lap. "I hope Grace is okay."

I hoped so too, but I didn't want to let Skylar go down one of her morbid tangents. "Grace is a warrior. Plus, she's had such an easy pregnancy, the kid will probably walk out on his or her own."

Fiona laughed. "What do you guys think? Boy or girl?"

"Boy," Gavin said from across the room.

"I wasn't asking you, Gav," Fiona said.

Gram looked up from her knitting. "Boy."

"Well, that kind of settles it, doesn't it?" Skylar said.

"I think she's right," I said. "I'll be shocked if it's not a boy."

"What about your baby?" Fiona asked. "Do you have any feelings one way or another?"

"I have no idea," I said as casually as I could manage. I didn't want to have a preference—that seemed unfair to the child, somehow. So I had yet to admit it out loud, but I hoped it was a boy.

Which probably meant I'd have a girl.

Fiona tilted her head. "Can I ask you a personal question?"

"Of course, pretty starfish."

"Did you want to have kids? I mean, at some point? Don't get me wrong; I'm not saying you don't want this baby or you won't love it like crazy. But did you think you'd have kids someday?"

I looked down at my hands because that wasn't a simple question. "Honestly? I didn't think I would, but not because I didn't want to. I didn't think I should."

"Why?"

It was all I could do to maintain my give-no-fucks façade, but I managed a shrug. "My childhood was a shit show. I figured I didn't have any business being a parent. But here we are."

"You don't give yourself enough credit," Skylar said, her voice soft. "You're going to do fine."

"I agree." Fiona gave me a bright smile. "And you've already had a little bit of practice with us."

"This is why I adopted you. You're so adorable."

Skylar's eyes moved to something behind me. I glanced over my shoulder to find Logan standing with a big throw blanket from my couch and a pair of slippers dangling from his hand.

"I thought you might want to get comfortable in case it's a long wait," he said.

I gaped at him. Why was he always so goddamn nice to me?

In some ways, life had been easier when we'd hated each other. At least I hadn't been flooded with a constant stream of confusing emotions.

Then again, maybe that was just hormones.

He gestured to an open couch. I got up and followed him over, then took off my shoes and put on my slippers. He sat next to me and draped the blanket over our laps.

"Thanks." I drew the blanket up higher. "This is nice."

"No problem," he said. "Can I ask you a question?"

"Sure."

"Why was your childhood a shit show?"

I opened my mouth to answer, but I wasn't sure what to say. "That's a random thing to ask."

"I heard you talking to Fiona and Skylar. And I've heard you say it before, but I don't know why it was bad."

"It's a long story."

"I've got time."

I glanced away. I didn't particularly want to dig into this, but he probably deserved to know. "To understand my childhood, you have to understand my mother and her parents. My grandparents were basically Hollywood royalty. Grandpa got his start as an actor but made his fortune as a producer. My grandmother was the star. So when my mother came along, she grew up in the business and everyone assumed she'd be a star too. Including her. Maybe especially her."

"Let me guess. It didn't work out that way."

I shook my head. "As a child actress, she got small parts. It was probably steady work, but she wasn't getting the recognition or fame my grandparents expected of her. Then, when she was eighteen, she landed her first lead role. It was a big budget film with one of the major studios. And then she found out she was pregnant."

"Oh, shit."

"The studio wasn't willing to work around her pregnancy. She wasn't a big name; to them, she was replaceable. So they replaced her." I shrugged. "After that, her career never went anywhere. She kept auditioning until I was in my teens, and she got some bit parts. Eventually she was offered a recurring spot on a soap opera, but when she realized it was as the mother of one of the main characters, she quit for good."

"Damn."

"I'd have more sympathy for her if she hadn't made my life miserable. As soon as I was old enough, she started sending me to auditions. Apparently if she couldn't live her dream, I was going to. So I spent most of my childhood being carted around like a show pony. She tried to get me into modeling, commercials, TV shows, anything she could find."

"Did you want to act?"

"Never. I hated it."

"But she made you do it anyway," he said.

"She didn't give me a choice. And maybe I could have gotten through all that more or less unscathed, but she was my biggest critic. She'd sit in on auditions when they'd let her, and if they wouldn't, she'd drill me about them afterward. When I got a role, she'd ride my ass about it until the job was over. Nothing was ever good enough for her. By the time I was thirteen, she was already talking about fixing my nose and getting me a boob job."

"What the fuck?"

"Layla Goulding is a serious piece of work. To be fair, it's not entirely her fault. In a lot of ways, her mother was worse. She was so disappointed in her daughter, she changed their will to leave her money to me instead."

"No shit?"

"And my mother has never forgiven me for it." I paused and glanced around. I didn't want anyone else to hear me, so I lowered my voice. "The truth is, she treated me like an accessory. Only, she wanted a designer purse and she got stuck with a cheap knockoff."

"You're not a cheap knockoff." He took my hand and traced his thumb along the back of it. "And you're not her."

"I know."

"Do you, though? You act like nothing can hurt you, but I know you're scared."

I didn't answer. He was right. But I hated feeling so vulnerable.

"You're going to be a good mother, Cara." His gentle tone warmed me from the inside. "You're not the terrible person you claim to be. You're crazy, but you're good. You have such a big heart and I know you're going to be a great mom."

"Shut the fuck up," I whispered. "If you make me cry right now, I'm going to punch you in the balls."

"There's my girl," he said.

We spent the next couple of hours waiting for news. Gram knitted. Skylar and Fiona talked quietly. The guys chuckled at more YouTube videos. Logan rubbed my feet until I started to get sleepy.

Finally, the door opened and Asher stepped into the waiting room. By the look on his face, I knew. Their baby had been born.

A hush settled over the room, as if we all held our breaths.

"It's a boy," he said.

Cheers erupted around me and everyone surged forward to hug and congratulate Asher. I hung back while his brothers wrapped him in bear hugs, while he kissed a teary-eyed Gram and embraced his in-laws.

He met my eyes. This Asher was almost unrecognizable from the man I'd met just over two years ago. That man had been broken. Grace's love had put him together again. Now he looked like the happiest man who'd ever lived.

Would Logan look like that when our baby was born?

"She wants to see you," he said, then turned to the rest of his family. "Thanks for being here. You guys can come back a few at a time to meet him."

After a few more hugs, Asher gestured for me to follow him to the room.

My heart beat hard and the bubbles in my belly were back. "So she's fine? Everything went well?"

"She's great." He had so much pride in his voice. "She's tired, obviously, but everything went perfectly. She was amazing."

I shuffled into the room, still in my slippers, and Asher squirted hand sanitizer into my palm. I rubbed it in, gazing at my Grace. She sat up in the hospital bed with a bundle in her arms. Her cheeks were a healthy shade of pink, and although I could see the exhaustion in her eyes, she looked so happy, it made me want to cry.

Stupid pregnancy hormones.

Her smile lit up her whole face. "Hey. Do you want to meet him?"

I went to stand by the bed and looked down at the baby in her arms. He was wrapped in a white blanket and wore a little blue hat. His eyes were closed, his tiny lips pursed.

He was perfect.

I brushed a tendril of hair back from her face. "He's beautiful, boo. You did so good."

"She was incredible," Asher said.

She pulled back the hat, revealing a tuft of dark brown hair. "Look at all this hair."

"God, he really is cute, isn't he?"

"Did you expect him to be ugly?"

"No, of course not." I gazed at him, fascinated by his tiny features. "Did you name him yet?"

"We decided on Charles after Asher's father. We'll call him Charlie."

"I love that."

"Do you want to hold him?"

My heart jumped. Oh my god. I'd never held a baby in my life. What if I held him wrong? What if I dropped him? The baby classes we'd started hadn't done shit to prepare me for the reality of holding a tiny human in my arms.

"Here," Grace said, lifting the bundle. "Take him."

Without giving me a chance to protest, she deposited her newborn baby in my arms.

He was so light. So small. I adjusted him so his head was supported—I'd read that in the baby books—and gazed at him. Holding him felt good in a way I couldn't explain.

"Grace, he's perfect."

"I love him so much, I don't even know what to do with myself."

Asher stood on the other side of the bed and lovingly

stroked his wife's hair. I was surprised he wasn't right next to me, ready to step in and grab little Charlie if I did something wrong.

It was oddly touching that he trusted me to hold his baby.

The bubbles in my belly continued as I held Charlie, and I couldn't help but imagine the moment when my own baby was born.

And for the first time since I found out I was pregnant, that thought didn't completely terrify me.

26

CARA

*a*fter the night at the hospital, I was exhausted. I didn't know whether it was being up half the night, all the emotions involved, or a combination of the two, but I basically slept for the next three days. I'd get up to eat, tell myself I was going to do something other than snack and nap, and eventually go back to bed.

Apparently I'd needed it because I woke up Friday morning feeling more like myself than I had in months.

I was eighteen weeks pregnant, definitely showing, and feeling more and more movement. And somehow, holding baby Charlie hadn't terrified me. It had certainly made this whole pregnancy thing feel more real than ever. But holding him had felt good—more natural than I would have thought.

Maybe I did have a maternal instinct or two.

I hadn't seen Logan much over the last few days. He'd come home this morning after a forty-eight-hour shift and gone straight to bed. Sometimes when he got off duty, he seemed energized and ready to go. Other times, he went to bed and would get up a few hours later to eat half the food we had in the kitchen in one sitting. I had a feeling today was going to be one of the latter.

I took my tea into my office and sat down at my desk. It was white with matching built-in bookshelves on either side. I scooted my fuzzy peach ottoman closer so I could prop up my feet. I'd been editing some photos I'd taken in downtown Tilikum. Not that I had any idea what I was going to do with them. Tilikum had an art walk every fall, but that seemed like a leap. From Instagram girl to art show exhibitor? Even a small-town art walk seemed like a stretch, like I'd be outed as a big fake in front of everyone I knew.

But I was proud of how they'd turned out, especially the ones I'd taken of Harvey Johnston. He had so much personality. The creases in his skin told a story, and there was a light in his eyes. Granted, I'd enhanced the lighting so it looked like he had an actual twinkle. But the spark was his. It was real. I'd just gotten lucky enough to capture it.

There was a soft knock at my door, so I swiveled my chair around.

"Hey," Logan said. His hair was disheveled and he wore a dark blue t-shirt and a pair of what looked like lime green swim trunks. As usual, he wore those dumb tube socks, and only one was pulled up to his shin.

But there was something about his sleepy eyes and his lopsided smile.

"Have a good nap?" I asked.

"Yeah. How have you been?"

"Better than usual, actually."

The other corner of his mouth lifted, making his smile less lopsided but no less cute. "Good. That's awesome to hear. Still feeling the baby kick?"

I placed my hand on my belly. "Only from the inside, but yeah."

"I can't wait until I can feel it too."

"Me too."

"So, I was thinking..." He trailed off and ran a hand through his hair, messing it up more. "We should go out."

"Go out? Where?"

"No, I mean go out. On a date."

I stared at him, my mouth slightly open. "You want to... date me?"

There was that lopsided smile again, and no, it was not the sexiest grin ever.

That was a lie. It was.

"Yeah, I do. Can't I take my baby mama out on a date?"

I didn't want to smile at his use of the term *baby mama*— I was supposed to hate that—but damn him, he was so cute when he said it. "Fine. We can go out on a date. I guess."

"You guess? Wow, so much enthusiasm. Don't get too excited."

I rolled my eyes. "What are we doing on our date?"

"What does the baby want to eat today?"

Okay, he was really getting to me with the sweetness. He was always so concerned about what I could or couldn't eat. And he never complained about my ridiculous level of pickiness.

"I think the baby wants meatloaf. I've been trying to deny it for the last couple of days because seriously? Bread-shaped meat again? But it's the only thing that sounds good."

"Done. And I figure we can go do something fun afterward."

I glanced away, as if I needed to think about it. A strange, eager giddiness tried to bubble its way up, like I was a virginal schoolgirl and Logan was the boy I'd been crushing on from afar.

What was wrong with me?

"Okay," I said, trying to keep my voice level. "I'll go out with you."

"And it's a date," he said. "A real date."

"Yes, I get it. You said date."

"I'm just making sure we're clear. This isn't just to appease your meatloaf fetish."

I grabbed a pen off my desk and tossed it at him. "It's not a fetish; it's a craving."

"Oh, that's right. You have a Logan fetish."

"Shut up."

He grinned. "I need to run into town, but I'll be back to pick you up."

"Just tell me one thing."

"Sure, what?"

"What are you going to wear? Not that, right?" I gestured up and down with my finger.

He looked down at himself. "What's wrong with this?"

"Are those swim trunks?"

"I don't know. Maybe."

"You don't even know if they're swim trunks? Do they have a mesh liner in them?"

He pulled open the waistband. "Huh. Yeah, they do. I guess they are swim trunks."

I rolled my eyes. "You're ridiculous."

"Yeah, but you love it."

"No swim trunks on our date."

"Fine. Oh, hey, I was thinking, what about the name Brody if it's a boy?"

I wrinkled my nose. "Not a fan."

"Seriously?"

"No. How about Leo?"

He scowled. "No more hot brothers of your best friend."

I raised my eyebrows innocently. "Oh, does Grace have a brother named Leo? I'd totally forgotten. Wait, I have it."

"You do?" He looked skeptical.

"Chase."

"No."

I tried not to smile. "Have we considered Miles, though?"

He opened his mouth, like he was going to say no, but paused. "Okay, Miles is actually a kick-ass name. But I still think you're trying to name our kid after a guy you think is hot. Or in this case, multiple guys you think are hot. So, no."

"Fine." I stuck my lower lip out in a pout.

"Tell you what. I'll make it up to you with meatloaf and the best date you've ever had in your life."

"Wow. Are you sure you're up for that?"

"You bet I am, Tiger," he said with a wink.

"We'll see," I said, casually tossing my hair. But I had a sudden case of butterflies, and it wasn't the bubbly feeling of the baby moving.

Was I really this excited to go on a date with Logan Bailey?

Apparently I was.

I HAD no idea what to wear. I stood in my closet surrounded by a pile of discarded clothes. And yes, my closet was probably the size of a small bedroom, but I needed the space for all my heels. That I could no longer wear because pregnancy had robbed me of my balance.

And my ankles.

None of my regular date attire fit. But I didn't want to wear my usual tunic and leggings. I wanted something that made me feel a little more like the old Cara. Or at least made me feel cute, not like I'd given up on fashion in favor of stretchy fabrics and slip-on flats.

Finally, I settled on a wrap dress that had enough room to accommodate my baby belly. It did make the hem ride higher than normal, but I had great legs, so why not? And it made my boobs look fabulous, so I couldn't argue with that.

If I got to keep any part of my pregnant body, I hoped it was my boobs. They'd never looked this good.

When I was satisfied with my outfit, I went downstairs. Logan waited for me in the kitchen, seated on one of the stools at the island.

He looked up from his phone and his eyes widened. "Holy shit."

"It's the best I could do. Nothing fits."

"Fuck, Cara. You look amazing."

The awe in his voice made me feel fidgety. "Thank you."

His eyes swept up and down, taking me in. I had to admit I liked the way he looked at me, and that my changing body didn't bother him.

Granted, any guy would appreciate the way my boobs looked in this dress.

Finally, he stopped staring at me and we left. I'd been right about the meatloaf. It was definitely what the baby wanted tonight. It tasted just as good as it had the first time. Would I ever enjoy anything as much as my pregnant self enjoyed meatloaf?

After dinner, we left the Caboose and drove across town. Logan parked in front of Crazy Shotz Mini Golf. I eyed the sign with skepticism. One of the letters was broken and another was hanging off the sign.

"What's wrong?" Logan asked. "Don't like mini golf?"

"I can't think of the last time I played, but that's not the issue. Are you sure this place is still open?"

"Yeah, there's someone in the booth."

That was true. There was a wooden shack with a price list tacked above the window. A bored-looking teenager sat inside, looking at his phone.

We got out and despite my love of high heels, I was glad I'd opted for flats. Although the sun had gone down, the spring air was warm and the mini golf course was well-lit by string lights. Logan bought our tickets and the kid handed us putters, two balls, a score card, and a small pencil.

"I'll go first," I said when we got to the first hole. The obstacle looked like it had once been a fairy tale cottage, but the colors were faded and there was a crack in the roof. I put my ball down, set up my shot, and hit. The ball rolled in a wider arc than I'd intended and stopped several feet from the hole.

"Nice shot," Logan said.

"Let's see you do better."

"Oh, I will. That's a given."

I rolled my eyes.

He took his turn, sending his ball rolling past the cottage. It stopped at least a foot closer to the hole.

"Damn it," I said.

"Your turn, Tiger."

I managed to keep from overshooting the hole, but I didn't sink the ball. "I blame the belly. It's making me off balance."

"Okay, sure."

I smacked his arm as he walked by to take his turn. He just laughed. And sank his ball in the hole.

"And Bailey takes the lead."

Fortunately, I got the ball in the hole on my next turn, so I wasn't too far behind.

We tied the next two holes, and then I caught up by

winning the fourth. We got to the fifth hole and paused in front of what looked like a large rabbit holding its chest.

"Is it just me?" Logan asked.

"No, it looks like a bunny holding its boobs."

"That's... creepy."

"This entire place is creepy."

He looked around. "Okay, fine, I'll give you that. I haven't been here in a while and I didn't remember it being this dilapidated."

"It looks like something out of a horror movie."

"I'll have to tell Gav. I bet Skylar would love it."

I smiled, feeling a new appreciation for the creepy mini golf course. "Aw, she would, wouldn't she? My morbid little ray of sunshine."

"So what do you think of Bronwyn for a girl?" he asked.

"Is that a serious suggestion? Because it's pretty."

"Yes, it's a serious suggestion."

"I don't know if it feels like the one, but I like it."

"Goes well with Bailey." He winked.

That gave me an idea. "How about we make this more interesting?"

"Winner gets oral?"

"No. If you win, the baby's last name is Bailey. If I win, the baby takes my last name."

He narrowed his eyes. "You're on."

He pulled ahead by two and on the next hole, I closed the distance by one. The rest of the course was just as weird as the beginning. Faded forest animals in awkward poses. Ramshackle windmills and castles.

But despite the course's need for renovation, we were having a lot of fun. I couldn't remember the last time I'd laughed this much—especially sober.

We got to the final hole and the score was tied. I took my shot, sending the ball rolling through a tunnel and down to the green. It stopped about six inches from the hole. Logan went and his ball rolled toward the hole. It looked like he'd get a hole in one, but it circled around the rim and didn't go in.

"Damn it," he said.

If I put the ball in the hole on this turn and he made his next shot, we'd tie. And if he missed, I'd win.

He stood off to the side and crossed his arms, glaring at his ball like it had betrayed him.

I lined up my shot, my eyes moving from the ball to my target. I cast a quick glance at Logan, then hit the ball too hard.

On purpose.

Oh my god, I'd just thrown the game so Logan could win.

"Ooh, so close," he said. "You realize what this means?"

"You haven't won yet."

He tapped his ball in without even looking. "Brodacious Bailey."

"We are not naming our kid Brodacious."

"But it'll be a Bailey."

I rolled my eyes, trying to hide my smile. "Fine. The baby's last name can be Bailey."

"Thanks, Tiger." He tapped my ball in for me, then plucked them both out of the hole. "So be honest. This is the best first date you've ever had."

It actually *was* the best first date I'd ever had. But I wasn't letting him off that easily. "It was probably in my top five."

He flashed me a grin. "Bullshit."

"Fine, top three. It was an impressive effort, especially

considering you only asked me out because you're stuck with me."

He gazed at me for a long moment, his expression unreadable. "That's not why I asked you out."

A wave of emotion washed over me. Because I was afraid I was right, and I didn't want to be. "It's not?"

"No." He put the balls down and leaned his putter against a bench, then stepped close enough to touch me. "We both know we don't have to be together as a couple to make this work. A lot of people co-parent for one reason or another. And I didn't go into this thinking we'd have a shot at anything more than coexisting without killing each other. So I didn't ask you out because I feel like I'm stuck with you. We are stuck with each other, but not like that. We could both go on to date other people, get married if we want, whatever."

The idea of either of us dating someone else sent a surprising jolt of anger through me. Like hell he was going to date someone. And as for me, ew. The thought of another man touching me was still remarkably revolting.

"I wouldn't want you to settle for me just because I knocked you up," he continued, tucking a piece of hair behind my ear. "And I don't want you to think I'm settling for you, because I'm not."

"Then why did you ask me out? This isn't because of Gram, is it?"

His brow furrowed. "What about Gram?"

"You know, what she said the other day." I had a sudden flare of doubt. Maybe when she'd called me Tiger, it hadn't been special. God, I was such an idiot. It probably hadn't even been a real nickname.

"Do you mean when she called you Tiger?"

I shrugged, trying to maintain my nonchalance. "Yes, but that didn't necessarily mean anything."

"No, it did."

"Really?"

"Oh yeah."

"So what does it mean? Now you can ask me out on a date because Gram gave her blessing in the form of an animal nickname?"

"You think I asked you out because Gram gave me permission?"

"I don't know. I don't know what any of this means, or if it means anything. I didn't grow up with a wise grandmother."

"This isn't about Gram. I've never waited for her permission to ask someone out before, and I'm certainly not going to start now." He placed his hand on the side of my face. "I wanted to take you out on a date because I have a crush on your crazy ass and I thought fuck it, why not date her?"

"So you're telling me you like me enough to date me, even if I wasn't currently harboring your offspring?"

"That's exactly what I'm telling you."

"God, when did that happen?"

He grinned again and my insides turned to mush. "I don't know. But it did. You hooked me good, Tiger."

Maybe I was crazy, because I liked him too.

A lot.

He leaned down and pressed his lips to mine. I let it happen. No resistance. No fighting. Just our mouths tangling, his hands sliding into my hair.

I was kissing Logan Bailey on our first real date. And I had to admit, for the first time in a while, I was actually happy.

27

LOGAN

The world had officially gone crazy. I was dating Cara Goulding.

Actually, dating my baby mama was great. She was the first woman I'd ever dated that I wanted to keep dating. Since that night at mini golf four months ago, we'd morphed into a real couple—not just two people having a baby who lived together like roommates and fucked when she was horny.

I'd abandoned the guest room and moved into Cara's bedroom. In fact, I'd cleared the rest of my stuff out of the Bailey bachelor pad months ago. All that was left over there was my old bedroom furniture. Gavin joked that I was never coming back, and although Cara and I hadn't exactly discussed the long-term future, I was pretty sure he was right.

Cara and I had started off hating each other, but it was amazing what a drunken fuck and an accidental pregnancy could do to bring two people together.

It wasn't just the baby that was mine. Cara was too.

Convincing her of that was another issue. Sometimes

she still acted like she only tolerated me because I had good dick game.

But I understood her. That cool, casual thing she did was just her way of protecting herself. It was going to take some time to show her she could trust me, not just to be a good daddy to our kid, but to be a good man to her.

I was willing to wait. She'd come around.

Cara came downstairs with freshly dried hair, wearing a long shirt and leggings. Her baby belly was something else. She had about seven weeks to go, give or take, before her due date, but she was huge. Not that I would have said so out loud.

Besides, she was still hot as fuck. The belly made sex tricky, but it was just a good excuse to get creative.

And we were great at getting creative.

I looked up from my spot at the kitchen island and smiled. "Morning, birthday girl."

She smiled back. Not a smirk, or her *I give no fucks* lip curl. A real smile.

I didn't think I'd ever get tired of being the guy who got to make her do that. Pleasing her sexually had been great, but damn that smile looked good on her.

I got up and gave her a kiss. I liked being the guy who got to do that, too.

She kissed me back and ran her hands up my chest. "I don't know how I feel about this birthday."

"Why? Because you're turning thirty and that basically makes you a cougar since I'm still in my twenties?"

"Ass." She shoved me away. "You're not that much younger than me."

That was true. Levi and I would be twenty-nine soon, and that year between us didn't seem the least bit significant.

But it was still fun to tease her.

"You know, they say women hit their sexual peak later than men do. So you're smart to be with a younger guy. I have plenty of stamina."

She just rolled her eyes and went to the fridge.

I followed her just to grab her ass. Because damn, that ass. "Don't worry. Even though you're getting up there, I'm still incredibly attracted to you."

She glanced over her shoulder. "Of course you are. Who wouldn't be?"

"Exactly." I squeezed her ass again and leaned close so my lips brushed her ear. "But this is mine."

Her back arched slightly and she purred like the wildcat she was. I gave her ear a quick nibble, then smacked her ass. I thought about hauling her upstairs, but I had a lot to do today. I needed to swing by Gram's, then come back here and finish getting ready for Cara's birthday party tonight.

We'd fought for a week over whether to have this party before she'd finally given in. She'd insisted it wasn't necessary. I'd insisted that was bullshit and I was throwing her a goddamn birthday party. She threw parties for other people all the time; she could damn well let her boyfriend throw one on her thirtieth.

Of course, I had no clue what I was doing. Bailey parties were usually of the casual, everyone brings something variety. Bonfires, drinks, tons of food. Cara parties had themed decor and fancy catering. Hopefully I could pull this off and make it something she'd like.

"I have to run out for a little while, but I'll be back this afternoon."

She closed the fridge and turned toward me, so I crouched down to kiss her belly.

"Bye, baby Bailey. Be good to Mommy today."

"Baby kicked right here." She took my hand and placed it to the right of where I'd kissed her.

I held my breath. A second later, I felt it. A distinct nudge against my palm.

"There you are, little one," I murmured and kissed her belly again. "Daddy loves you."

We still didn't know whether we were having a boy or a girl. At our last ultrasound, baby Bailey had kept his or her legs crossed. We probably wouldn't find out until the big day.

Cara ran her fingers through my hair. "You really need to stop being so cute."

Glancing up, I met her eyes. "Makes it hard to hate me, doesn't it?"

"I guess I can admit you have other good qualities besides your dick and generosity with orgasms."

I stood and kissed her lips. "I knew you'd come around."

"Don't get too full of yourself. I still hate your socks."

"What socks?"

"They don't match. And why do you always have only one pulled up?"

"Do I?" I looked down at my feet. Sure enough, one of them was pulled up to my shin while the other was bunched around my ankle.

"Yes. Are you really unaware of that? It's like your thing."

"I don't know. I have more important things to worry about than my socks. Making you the happiest birthday girl ever, for example." I kissed her nose. "I'll see you later."

She said goodbye and I left her to decide what the baby wanted for breakfast. Probably a chocolate protein smoothie with peanut butter, pineapple, and half a banana. It sounded gross as shit to me, but she swore it was delicious.

Her pregnancy food preferences were weird, though. I was used to it.

I headed out and drove over to Gram's house. She had some extra folding chairs I wanted to borrow for tonight. My Explorer bumped along the private drive to her house, kicking up dust behind me. I pulled up in front of her big front porch and parked next to a pickup truck. Who was here? Because the truck looked like Josiah Haven's, but it couldn't be. He'd have no reason to be here.

But just as I turned off the engine, Josiah fucking Haven walked out Gram's front door.

He was a big guy with thick arms and a beard. His red flannel shirt had the sleeves rolled up and he wore jeans and brown work boots.

What the hell was he doing here?

I got out and shut the door, keeping my eyes on him. He glanced at me but didn't stop or say a word. Just got in his truck, turned it on, and left.

That was fucking weird.

I went inside and shut the door behind me. "Gram? Are you okay?"

"In the kitchen," she called.

I hurried down the hall, past the wall of family pictures, and found her standing at the counter stirring batter in a bowl as if nothing was wrong. But I could tell as soon as I saw her face that something wasn't right.

"What was he doing here?" I asked.

She didn't answer right away. Just kept stirring. There was a stoop to her shoulders and a tiredness in the way she moved the wooden spoon through the batter.

"He wants me to sell," she said finally.

"Sell your house?"

She nodded slowly. "My house, my land. All of it. Word

is getting around that I can't afford to keep it and the vultures are circling."

"I thought Darcy was helping you get things sorted out."

"She's doing her best, but the numbers are what they are."

I stared at her. "It's that bad?"

"It's that bad." She moved the spoon in a few more circles. "Never thought I'd see the day, but sometimes life takes unexpected turns."

"Gram, you can't sell. Especially not to them."

"I'm not in a position to be choosy about the buyer, Raven."

"There has to be a way. You haven't committed to anything, have you?"

"No. Sometimes I'm too stubborn for my own good. Josiah wasn't exactly happy with me when he left just now."

Despite the seriousness of the situation, that made me smile. "Good. Screw that guy."

The corner of her mouth lifted.

I gently took the spoon out of her hand and set it in the bowl. "We're not going to let this happen. This land is yours and no one is going to take advantage of you like this."

"It's a lot of money, Raven."

"Yeah, well, we'll figure it out. Just don't agree to anything, especially if it's coming from Josiah."

"I've spent a lot of time looking for a solution. We might have to accept that there isn't one. Not one that we like, at least."

"No." I shook my head. "I refuse to accept that. There's a way out of this that doesn't involve losing your home."

She raised her eyebrows.

"I'm serious. You've been looking for a solution, but you

haven't unleashed your cubs. We're going to make this right."

She patted my cheek, but I could tell she didn't think we could fix this. But she was wrong. We'd find a way. All five of us had inherited our dad's stubbornness. He'd inherited it from Grandad. It was basically a Bailey tradition.

I fired off a text to my brothers, telling them we needed to get together ASAP. While I waited for them to reply, I loaded the folding chairs into the back of my SUV. By the time I finished, we'd agreed to meet at Asher and Grace's place.

Levi and Gavin were already there when I arrived, sitting on the couch in the living room in front of a wall of family photos. It was hard to believe their house was the same dilapidated heap Grace had bought when Asher had still been in prison. They'd worked their asses off to restore it and had turned it into a great little home.

There was baby stuff everywhere. A swing in the corner, car seat near the door, a diaper bag hanging from a hook alongside their coats. It even smelled like baby, but in a good way. Like that baby shampoo that was supposed to be gentle on their skin.

Asher sat in an armchair, holding a sleeping Charlie against his shoulder. Grace wasn't home, but Asher had been a hands-on dad since day one. He looked like a natural with a baby on his chest, even with his big, tatted-up arms.

Evan came in a few minutes behind me. Once we were all there and seated, I jumped right into it.

"We need to talk about Gram. Did you guys know she thinks she needs to sell her house?"

"Since when?" Asher asked.

"Ash, I thought you were in the loop on this," Levi said.

"So did I," he said. "Last I heard, they were crunching the numbers to figure out a payment plan."

"She probably kept you out of it so you wouldn't worry," Evan said. "With the baby and everything."

"Apparently she hasn't been keeping any of us in the loop and it's worse than we thought," I said. "Josiah Haven was there today, trying to convince her to sell. To them."

"What the fuck?" Levi muttered.

"She's not considering it, is she?" Gavin asked.

"She told me she's been trying to figure out a solution, but she hasn't found one. So yeah, I think she's considering it."

"No," Gavin said, his voice firm.

"Do you have the money to bail her out, Gav?" Evan asked.

"No, but there has to be a way to help her that doesn't involve losing her home. Especially to those fuckers."

"Maybe they think they're helping," Levi said.

My brow furrowed. "Helping? How the fuck is trying to convince an old lady to sell the home she's had for decades helping?"

"I'm just saying we don't know what they're offering. If it's fair market value—"

"Shut the fuck up right there, bromeo. Are you defending the Havens now? Is that what's happening here?"

"I'm just trying to be rational. This doesn't have anything to do with the goddamn feud."

"Of course it does. Everything has to do with the feud when it comes to that fucking family."

"Logan, think about it. This isn't a prank."

"No, it's worse. They're coming at Gram when she's vulnerable."

"It is a shitty thing to do," Asher said. "Although Gram isn't some senile old lady. She can hold her own."

"I know she can, but those assholes shouldn't swoop in and try to take her land when she's in trouble. That's bullshit. Can you imagine if the tables were turned? They'd be all over us."

Gavin clenched his fists. "We should go down to the Timberbeast right now and fuck shit up."

"No, we shouldn't," Evan said, and the weight of his deep voice kept me from piling on with Gavin. "Like Levi said, this isn't a prank. We can't unleash a bunch of squirrels on them to make this go away."

"Then what the hell do we do?" Gavin asked.

"We find a way to pay her debt," he said.

"And how the fuck do we do that?" I asked.

No one answered. Because none of us knew.

A minute ticked by. Yeah, I was thinking about Cara and her big bank account. I didn't want to admit I was thinking about it, but I was. Did she have the funds to help? Maybe a loan and we could pay her back? Was there any way to bring this up without it being totally shitty?

"There was gold in the basement of the Haven House," Gavin said, breaking the silence.

"What?" I asked.

"When Skylar and I were down there snooping around, we found gold coins."

"We know, but what's your point? Even if we could get them, they aren't ours. And we can't get them. They're buried under what's left of the burned-out building. And it was only a few anyway, right?"

"Yeah, but what if there's more somewhere? What if that was just a clue?"

Asher adjusted Charlie, switching him to his other

shoulder. "Are you seriously suggesting what I think you are?"

"Hear me out," Gavin said. "I know Sky has an active imagination, but the stuff we found down there was real, and someone set that fire right after we were there. I'm telling you, somebody's hiding something. What if it's money? What if it's—"

"The Montgomery treasure," I said, slowly nodding.

"Guys, there's no Montgomery treasure," Asher said.

"The coins had an M on them," Gavin said.

"A handful of coins doesn't mean there's actually a treasure," Asher said. "Even if they had an M."

"What if it does?" I asked.

"If there was a treasure, someone would have found it by now," Evan said.

"Not necessarily," I said. "No one's found Bigfoot yet and people have been looking for decades."

Levi rolled his eyes. "Dude, not this again. Bigfoot doesn't exist."

I pointed at him. "You were there. You saw it."

"I didn't see shit."

"Liar." I'd swear to the day I died that I'd seen Bigfoot when we were ten. Levi had been with me, but now he denied there had been anything out there. "But think about it. Stories like the Montgomery treasure usually start with a grain of truth, right? So maybe it turned into a Tilikum tall tale over the years, but what if there was something that started it in the first place?"

"You aren't actually suggesting that we start looking for buried treasure so Gram doesn't lose her house," Asher said.

"I'm not suggesting that's *all* we do," I said. "I'm not an idiot. But I think Gav is right. There's something going on and if we can get to the bottom of it, maybe we'll be the ones to finally find Montgomery's missing fortune."

"You're nuts," Evan said.

"Big problems call for big solutions," I said.

Levi met my eyes and raised his eyebrows. *Maybe?*

I tipped my chin. I knew he'd have my back, even if he still denied seeing Bigfoot.

"So this is our plan?" Asher asked. "Try to find a treasure that may or may not exist?"

"No, this is just our hail Mary," I said. "We keep doing things the right way with accountants and lawyers and all that. And if they can fix it, great. But if not, we have to do whatever it takes to save her land."

Asher absently rubbed Charlie's back. The kid was out cold. It was pretty cute, actually, seeing my brother holding his little four-month-old baby.

"Okay, I'm with you on the *do whatever it takes* thing," he said.

"Me too," Levi said. "The treasure idea sounds nuts, but if there's a chance, we should take it."

"I think you're all crazy for thinking it's crazy," Gavin said. "It's a fucking brilliant idea."

"Agreed, brotastic."

Maybe it wasn't the best plan, but at least it was something. We couldn't just sit around while the Havens swooped in and bought Gram's land out from under her. I still didn't know what the fuck Josiah was thinking. This wasn't a prank, even a big one. This was so much worse. This was personal.

But I wasn't going to let it happen.

28

CARA

*E*xhaling slowly, I put my phone down on my desk. My mother had called, and one would have thought it would have been to wish me happy birthday. But really, she'd wanted to badmouth Logan and hound me about moving to L.A. again. I'd deflected her attempts to talk me into it without making her cry or hang up on me, which was probably the best I could have hoped for. I decided to call that a win.

I heard the front door open and shut, then Logan came into my office. I couldn't seem to help the smile that stole over my face. It was so silly. We lived together, so I saw him all the time. I didn't know why I got so giddy after even brief absences.

That feeling triggered my instinct to pull away. To slam a metaphorical door in his face and keep him out.

Not for the first time, I fought against the messed-up urge to sabotage our relationship.

He came in and flopped down on the couch, rehoming a few of my throw pillows onto the floor in the process.

"Are you okay?" I asked.

He took a deep breath. "I'm just stressed. We've got some family stuff going on."

"Really? What's wrong?"

"Gram's having financial issues. We're working on it, but it's worse than we thought."

That sounded uncomfortably familiar. But Gram was nothing like my mom. "What kind of financial issues?"

"Her accountant was embezzling money from her— money that was supposed to go toward paying her taxes. She's in over her head and no one seems to give a shit that she's the victim. She owes a lot and now she's talking about selling her property. As if that wasn't bad enough, the goddamn Havens are sniffing around, trying to get her when she's vulnerable."

I sat up straighter, my protective streak flaring to life. "Get her? How?"

"Josiah Haven was over there earlier, trying to talk her into selling to them."

"Are you kidding? Why would he do that?"

"Because he's a fucking shark and he smelled blood in the water, I guess. This is low, even for them."

I opened my mouth to say I'd pay it. Whatever she owed, I'd pay it all.

But I stopped.

Because I didn't know if I could.

Heat rushed to my cheeks and my stomach dropped. I'd bailed out my mom too many times. I didn't have fuck you money anymore. I couldn't throw it around like it was nothing.

I couldn't fix this.

"I can help, but I don't know how much," I said. "My mom keeps running up debt and I keep paying it and—"

"Don't." His voice was firm but gentle. "I'm not asking you for money."

"I know you're not. But if I can help make a dent in her debt, I will."

He held my eyes for a moment. "You're so good. You know that, right?"

I sniffed away the tears threatening to gather in the corners of my eyes. "I'll talk to Gram about what I can do. I don't know if it will be enough, but I'll do what I can."

There was pain in his eyes but I didn't know how to fix that either. The baby chose that moment to kick me in the ribs.

Thanks, kid.

I rubbed my belly absently. "Who was embezzling money?"

"A guy named Mike Phillips. He took over for her old accountant."

I narrowed my eyes and heat smoldered inside me. "Where is he now?"

"Easy, Tiger."

"If you don't tell me, I'll find out on my own."

"We don't know where he is. He skipped town a few months ago."

I crossed my arms as icy cold anger flowed through my veins. This guy was ruining Gram's life. I was going to ruin his. "I'll find him."

"Should I be concerned?"

"No."

He looked skeptical. "Anyway, I do have an idea about how to help her. It's a long shot, but Levi doesn't think it's crazy, so that's something."

"Are you saying Levi is the sensible one?"

"Usually, yeah."

"So what's your idea?"

He tapped his thigh a few times. "I know what this is going to sound like, so don't roll your eyes too hard. I wouldn't want you to get dizzy and fall over."

"Oh my god, just tell me."

"I kind of think the Montgomery treasure could be real. And maybe we could find it."

"You think one of the oldest stories in a town that can spin a tall tale out of anything might be the solution to Gram's financial crisis?"

"Well, not when you say it like that."

"How else am I supposed to say it?"

"We're already doing all the stuff you're supposed to do. Gram has a new accountant working on that side of things, we'll get her a lawyer, and Jack and the sheriff's department are looking for Mike Phillips. But what if none of that is enough? What if she's still stuck with all this debt and can't afford to keep her house and her land? If there's even the tiniest possibility we could avoid that, it's worth trying."

I paused, letting that sink in. On the surface, looking for treasure as a solution to Gram's problem did seem ridiculous. But if there was even the smallest chance of finding it, maybe it was worth doing.

Or maybe I'd lived in Tilikum too long.

Still. I'd do anything to help Gram. And I really was going to find that asshole accountant and burn down his life.

"Here's the thing," I said. "I still have some money after my last Layla bailout. I'm going to make Gram let me help her. But if that's not enough, you might have a point about looking into the Montgomery thing. And I'd kind of like to know if it's real anyway."

"See? Something weird is going on in this town.

Whoever set the Haven House fire had to be trying to hide something. There's no way it's a coincidence."

I leaned back in my chair. "Skylar said they found a few gold coins and a journal written by Sarah Montgomery. Do you know who she was?"

"No."

"But it sounded like she was friends with Eliza Bailey. And we know Eliza disappeared."

"Maybe because of a Haven."

"Or with a Haven."

"Ginny was looking into this when she was in town," he said and my back stiffened at the mention of Skylar's friend. "I think she found an engagement announcement for Sarah Montgomery and John Haven. And they were supposed to inherit the Montgomery fortune."

I pushed aside the rush of jealousy at his mention of Ginny. "So Sarah was supposed to marry John, but he disappeared and so did her friend Eliza."

"And we don't know who inherited the Montgomery money after all that."

"Hence the hidden treasure story," I said.

"Meanwhile, something sparks a feud between the Bailey and Haven families. Could be related."

"It's not impossible. And I've always been convinced Harvey Johnston isn't as crazy as he seems. Maybe he's right about there being a treasure."

Logan grinned. "You know, if we actually find something, we'll have to give him a cut. Just for keeping the story alive."

"Absolutely." I tucked my hair behind my ear. "I'll talk to Libby again. She was helping me do some research when Grace was trying to find out about Eliza and her mirror. I'll see what I can find out."

"Thanks, Tiger. But I don't want you to worry about this for the rest of the day. All you need to do is show up to your party and look beautiful. You've already got the second one covered, so just be there."

"I look like a whale."

"You don't look like a whale. You look like the crazy hot redhead I knocked up."

I had to admit, the way Logan still enjoyed my body eased my self-consciousness about how much it had changed. I was huge, but somehow he still thought I was sexy.

He got up and came over to kiss my forehead. "I have work to do. Go up to your room. As of right now, you're banned from being downstairs until it's party time."

"What if I get hungry?"

"Text me."

"What if I get horny?"

He gave me his best lopsided grin and a little spark of heat burst between my legs. "Just shout. I'm never too busy to give you a much-needed orgasm."

"That's very generous of you."

"It is your birthday."

"How about now?"

His grin widened as he reached out to help me to my feet. "Anything you want, Tiger."

I took his hand and let him lead me to the bedroom, and I couldn't help but think this was going to be the best part of my birthday.

I CROSSED my arms and looked out my bedroom window. The river meandered by, slow and lazy this time of year.

Daylight faded as the sun dipped toward the mountain peaks surrounding Tilikum. I checked the time again. Logan was taking forever. I wished he'd let me come downstairs already.

For the first time since I was little, someone else was throwing me a birthday party.

When I was a child, my grandmother had hosted lavish parties with lengthy guest lists and elaborate decorations. Ostensibly they were for me, but that was mostly for show. My birthdays were a way for her and my mother to network and show off. I was just another accessory.

After I moved to Tilikum, I started throwing parties— but rarely for myself. I threw Grace a birthday party every year, and I hosted cocktail and dinner parties all the time. Or I had before all my pregnancy-induced food issues popped up. It was fun to treat people to a delicious meal and too much alcohol. But I usually let my own birthdays pass with just champagne and cake with Grace.

This year, Logan had insisted on throwing me a party.

So there I was, sequestered in my bedroom, dressed in a black maternity dress Grace had helped me pick out for the occasion. My hair was down, and whether it was my hormones or all the vitamins, it was thicker than ever. Big boobs and lustrous hair were admittedly nice perks. They almost made up for the fact that, despite what Logan said, I looked like a whale.

Almost.

I'd made some calls this afternoon to get the ball rolling on finding the piece of shit who'd stolen from Gram. I knew a private investigator who was perfect for this kind of job. It didn't matter where Mike Phillips had gone. He wouldn't stay hidden for long.

Then I'd burn down his life.

Logan opened the door and I did a double take. Not only did his clothes match, he wore a button-down shirt with the sleeves cuffed, and a pair of dark slacks.

"Hey, birthday girl. You look beautiful."

"Thanks. You don't look bad yourself. Who knew you cleaned up so well?"

He glanced down at his clothes. "I do make this look good, don't I?"

"It's better than the tube socks."

He grinned. "Ready?"

I took the hand he offered, and he led me downstairs.

The main floor of my house looked like a party store had exploded. Multicolored balloons littered the floor and a bright red *Happy Birthday* sign hung on the wall. He'd draped streamers around the furniture and covered the dining table with a paper tablecloth and shiny confetti.

It was a mess. And completely adorable.

He rubbed the back of his neck. "It didn't exactly turn out like I pictured. Decorating for a party is harder than I thought."

I gazed at the mess of decorations. "I love it."

"You don't have to lie to me. I know it looks like shit."

I stepped off the bottom stair and nudged a bright pink balloon out of the way. "I'm not lying. I really love it."

"The good news is I ordered food and the cake, so I know those will be good."

"It's perfect."

He slipped his hand around to the small of my back and pulled me close. His lips brushed mine. "Happy birthday, Tiger."

"Thank you."

As if on cue, the doorbell rang.

"Party time," he said. "I'll get it."

Grace and Asher were the first to arrive, along with baby Charlie. In his four months of life, he'd gone from a tiny newborn to a round little chunk with chubby cheeks, dark hair, and eyes that seemed to be turning brown like his dad's. I'd never been much of a baby person, but even I couldn't deny how cute he was. And happy, too. He smiled at everyone.

Watching Grace navigate new motherhood had made me start to look forward to meeting this kid of mine. Although knowing my luck, I'd have the baby who never slept, and instead of bouncing around town with my adorable mini-me, I was going to be a zombie for the next few years.

Evan and Fiona came a few minutes later, followed by Levi. Logan had been bugging him about bringing a date, but he showed up alone. Skylar and Gavin were a few minutes behind, and then Gram arrived with two pies. The scent of peaches and cherries filled the air and thankfully they smelled good. You never knew with me. Food smells could still unexpectedly send my stomach into a fit of protest.

Logan had invited the Stitch and Bitch ladies, too, although Marlene Haven was an unsurprising no-show. Apparently the Knotty Knitter truce didn't extend to birthday parties, especially when the tension between the two families was at an all-time high.

Hank from the Caboose arrived with the food and Logan was so getting lucky again later. He'd ordered mini meat-loaves, mashed potatoes in little cups, and the Caboose's signature gravy for dipping. There was other food too, but I ignored it in favor of that stupid, magical meatloaf our kid seemed to love so much.

I wandered around, chatting with people, letting my

girls feel the baby kick, and eating too much. We had cake and Logan insisted on lighting candles and making everyone sing happy birthday. It felt sort of silly, but I made a wish before I blew out the candles.

It was a stupid wish, but I did it anyway.

Everyone agreed the cake was delicious—Angel Cakes Bakery was the best—and I didn't even miss my usual party cocktails. Music played in the background and Levi and Gavin started a game of poker at the table while Gram and the Stitch and Bitch ladies sat in the living room and gossiped.

I put my cake plate down. Logan sidled up next to me and rubbed slow circles across my back. I gazed at the party in progress. At the silly decorations, the pregnancy craving-inspired food. At the house full of guests. He'd done all this for me. Not to show off or to appear important. Not to get in my pants or to lord it over me later, expecting favors in return. He'd done it simply to make me happy.

A sliver of fear poked at me, like a rock in an otherwise comfortable shoe. How long was this really going to last?

How long until he realized I wasn't worth the trouble?

I knew I wasn't easy to love. I was temperamental and difficult even when I wasn't pregnant. Grace was the only person who'd managed it, and she was basically a saint.

But maybe Logan...

I gazed at him. Was it possible? Did he actually—

My thoughts were interrupted by the doorbell. That was odd. Who else had Logan invited? Wasn't everyone I liked already here?

"I'll get it," I said.

Logan followed me as I walked over to answer the door. A tall man with auburn hair and a beard stood holding a gift bag. It took me a second before I realized who I was looking at.

My father.

We stared at each other like a couple of deer caught in the glare of oncoming headlights. Logan put a steadying hand on my lower back.

"I'm sorry," he said. "I probably should have called first."

"What are you doing here?"

"It's your birthday and I thought..." He trailed off.

Conflict raged through me. As a little girl, this had often been the wish I'd whispered to myself just before blowing out birthday candles. For my dad to appear.

But the first time he decided to show up was when I turned thirty? Twenty-nine previous birthdays, no dad. Why the fuck was he here now?

I was caught between snapping at him so he'd leave and inviting him in so he wouldn't. So I decided to be honest. "I don't know what to think about this right now."

"That's fair," he said. "Maybe I shouldn't have surprised you like this."

Logan squeezed me against him, then held out a hand toward my father. "I'm Logan Bailey."

They shook hands. "Nate Broderick. Are you the uh..."

"Yeah. I'm Cara's boyfriend."

He held Logan's eyes for a moment, then gave a short nod.

Cara's boyfriend.

Not *Cara's baby daddy* or *the guy who knocked up your daughter*. Her boyfriend.

For some reason, that calmed me. I wasn't ready to do this with my dad—not with a party Logan had worked so hard on in full swing. But my father was here and I could give him a little bit of credit for that. At least enough to hear what he had to say.

"Are you staying in town?" I asked.

"Yeah. I got a place. I could meet you tomorrow somewhere."

"How about coffee?"

"That sounds great."

"There's a place downtown called the Steaming Mug. I can meet you there around ten."

He smiled. "I'll be there. Thanks, Cara. Happy birthday."

"Thank you."

He nodded to Logan again, then turned and left. He hadn't given me the gift bag, but I wasn't worried about that. I still didn't know what to think about the fact that he was here, in Tilikum.

Why? Why now?

Logan didn't give me a chance to pretend to blow this off. He shut the door, then gathered me in his arms and held me firmly against him.

I gratefully accepted his comfort, remembering when he'd told me I didn't have to do this alone.

And I was so thankful for that.

29

LOGAN

*C*ara sat on the couch with her feet propped up on the coffee table. The light was dim and she'd lit one of her scented candles. It smelled nice. It kind of reminded me of her.

The party had wound down and the last guest had gone home. And it wasn't even eleven. I was a little tired, but completely sober—unlike the last time I'd been at a party in this house.

Funny how things had changed.

I plopped down on the couch next to her, dislodging one of her eighteen million throw pillows. I grabbed another one and tossed it on the floor to get it out of my way.

"Thank you," she said.

"For what?"

"The party. It was fun."

"Yeah? You had a good time?"

She smiled and goddamn, it looked good on her. "I had the best time."

I'd been worried her dad showing up would ruin her evening. But we'd come a long way. She'd actually let me hold her without arguing or trying to thrash her way out of my arms. Afterward, she'd seemed to enjoy the rest of the party. And not with her fake-ass *everything is okay* face on. It had been genuine.

She reached for one of my feet and pulled it into her lap. I groaned as she dug her thumbs into the ball of my foot.

"Damn, that's good." I leaned my head back against the couch cushion. "I didn't even realize my feet were so tired."

"You did a lot of work today."

"It was worth it."

She kept rubbing. "You know what I'm thinking about?"

"What?"

"Having cake for breakfast."

I cracked a grin. "It was good, wasn't it?"

"It was delicious. So were the mini meatloaves."

"I thought you'd like those."

"I loved everything. It was the best birthday party I've ever had."

I turned to glance at her. "You mean that literally, don't you?"

"Absolutely."

I puffed up a little at that. "Thanks, Tiger."

She pushed my foot out of her lap and shifted closer. Her hand skimmed up my thigh. "No. Thank *you*."

A whiff of her scent and her hand on my leg were enough to get me instantly hard. How did she do this to me? I grunted as she grabbed me through my shorts and squeezed.

"Happy to see me?" she cooed in my ear, then planted a soft kiss on my neck.

"Always. In case you hadn't noticed, he really likes you."

She kissed my neck again. "That works out well. I like him, too."

Even through my shorts, her hand around my cock felt great. She squeezed while her tongue darted out to lick my neck. I was about to haul her into my lap so I could at the very least start dry humping her, but she slid off the couch and got on her knees in front of me.

Oh, fuck yes.

She nibbled her bottom lip and looked up at me with a wicked gleam in her eyes as she helped pull my shorts down. My heavy erection jutted out, thick and swollen.

"He's so pretty." She traced her finger around the tip.

"Pretty?"

"I mean that as a compliment." She leaned closer and pressed a kiss on the shaft. "A pretty dick is a very good thing."

Her tongue slid lazily along the ridge around the tip and fuck it, she could call it anything she wanted as long as she kept doing that.

"You're always so good to me." She kissed the tip again. "Let me be good to you tonight."

She slid my cock past her lips without giving me the chance to reply. Not that I was going to argue. Her mouth was warm and wet. Fuck, that felt good.

I groaned as she played with me, alternating between long, slow licks and sucks on the tip. She grabbed the base and squeezed while she lavished wet kisses along the shaft.

"So good to me," she murmured, giving me a good, long stroke.

Leaning my head back, I grunted. "Fuck."

She took me in her mouth again, deeper this time. I ran my hands through her hair, holding it gently while she plunged up and down. The sight of my thick cock sliding between her lips was fucking amazing.

Her eyes lifted to meet mine, but she didn't stop. My hips

jerked with her rhythm, the pressure in my groin building fast. She kept going, her mouth relentless.

This woman was pure magic.

I growled as she moved faster. The tip of my cock slid along the roof of her mouth and just when I thought she couldn't possibly take me any deeper, she did.

"That's it, baby. I love watching you suck my cock."

She plunged down again. I was about to lose my mind. Her mouth was slick and hot and her fingers dug into my thighs. I held her hair and rolled my hips, feeling my balls draw up tight.

I was right on the brink, ready to unload down her throat. Her wet mouth worked me faster, her head bobbing in my lap. Fuck, this was hot.

"Fuck, Cara. I'm gonna come." My voice was strained.

I held back in case she didn't want it in her mouth. But she moaned, plunging down harder.

And I came fucking undone.

The pressure exploded and my cock throbbed between her lips. I grunted with each pulse, my hips jerking. The white-hot intensity almost knocked me out cold. I'd never felt anything like it.

When I finished, she let my cock slide out of her mouth and swiped her hand across her lips.

She was such a badass.

"That was..." I let my head drop back against the cushion. "I don't even know."

"I'm glad you enjoyed it."

She climbed back on the couch and I hauled her against me, tucking her under my arm. My eyes were heavy and I felt like I was floating.

"Just give me a minute. That was... fuck."

Her arm slid around my waist and she rested her head on my chest. "Don't worry about me. That was just for you."

"Are you sure?"

She laughed softly. "Logan, you gave me two orgasms earlier today. Besides, I wanted to do that for you. I want you to know how much I appreciate you."

Damn. Hearing that felt good. "Thanks, Tiger."

"You're welcome."

My shorts were still off, but it didn't really matter. I was happy and sated, and not just because of the fantastic blow job. I'd wanted to throw Cara a great party and I'd done it. She'd had fun. We'd had fun together. The rest was just a bonus.

I tightened my arm around her, squeezing her against me. She let out a contented sigh. And man, all I could think about was how fucking happy she made me.

30

CARA

*D*espite my father's surprise appearance, last night had been the best birthday party I'd ever had. I'd thanked Logan profusely after the guests had left—with his dick in my mouth, to be precise. And unlike parties of the past, we'd been in bed just after eleven.

That was pregnancy for you.

Of course, there was something to be said for not being hungover the next day.

Logan had gone on duty this morning, but before he'd left, he'd tried to talk me into postponing coffee with my dad so he could be there. I was so grateful to him, but I needed to do this alone.

I had a little time before I was supposed to be at the Steaming Mug, so I decided to drop into Happy Paws to see if Libby Stewart was there. When she wasn't working at the local pet store, she was a part-time library volunteer, and she'd helped me do some research when Grace had found Eliza Bailey's mirror and those love letters. Libby had found a newspaper clipping about Eliza's disappearance and it had mentioned John Haven. Fiona had later discovered that

John had also gone missing after winning prize money in a race.

I wasn't quite sure what to think about Logan's idea to find the Montgomery treasure, but I was curious enough about the whole story to dig deeper. Grace had once told me I was like a cat—usually disinterested, but if you dangled a string in front of me, I just might follow it.

This was my string.

For all I knew, the treasure story was just another Tilikum tall tale. This town loved their stories like other places loved sports teams. Gossip was the town pastime and stories from the past were a particular favorite. I figured that was why no one knew how the feud had really started. People had made up so many versions over the years, no one knew which story was real anymore.

But, like the cat I was, I wanted to follow the string to see where it led. And I had a feeling whatever had happened to Eliza and John was related to both the Montgomery family fortune and the origins of the Bailey-Haven feud. I knew firsthand how easily money could become a wedge between people. My relationship with my mother had always been rocky, but it had gotten a million times worse after I'd inherited my grandparents' estate.

The door to Happy Paws jingled when I walked in. I didn't see the owner, Missy Lovejoy, or Libby, so I wandered up an aisle filled with cat toys. Maybe I'd buy one for Gavin's cat, Princess Squeaker.

"Sorry about that," Libby said from behind a box she was carrying. She set it on the front counter. "What can I do for—"

She stopped abruptly and her customer service smile melted. Apparently she wasn't happy to see me. I wasn't too surprised. I'd tried to pay her to do more research for me but she'd stopped, telling Grace there wasn't anything left to find. That had always struck me as odd. There was always something else to find. People hid their skeletons in closets, basements, attics, and crawl spaces. They buried them deep, but they were still there if you dug far enough.

Until now, I hadn't cared enough to find out why she'd claimed she couldn't keep helping me, despite the money I was paying her.

Now I wanted to know.

"Hi, Libby," I said, keeping my voice friendly.

She hesitated behind the counter, her blond hair in a ponytail. She was around my age, give or take, and wore a pink Happy Paws t-shirt and jeans.

"Hi, Cara. Can I help you?"

"Possibly. Do you remember a while back when you did some research for me? Town history stuff."

"Um..." She glanced down, like she was trying to recall. "I think so?"

I'd never been one to beat around the bush. I approached the counter. "Sure, you do. Eliza Bailey, John Haven, love letters, a disappearance."

"Right, that. I already found everything."

I took my wallet out of my purse and set a twenty on the counter. In the past it would have been a hundred but I was trying to be more careful with my money. Hopefully this would be sufficiently motivating.

"Are you trying to bribe me or something?" she asked. "I already told Grace—"

"I know. And no, I'm not trying to bribe you. I want to pay you for another piece of information."

Her eyes lingered on the bill. "What information?"

"Why did you really stop researching?"

"I found everything I could. There aren't a lot of records from back then. I didn't want to waste your money."

I almost believed her. She was right: There weren't a lot of records left. Half the town had burned down in a fire. But she'd shaken her head slightly while she spoke—as if she didn't believe her own words—and there was a slight tremor to her voice.

Keeping one finger on the bill, I slid it back toward me. "I'll pay you for the truth, not the story you told Grace."

She hesitated, which meant I was right. There was another reason. In the back of my mind, I wondered if she knew anything about the Haven House fire. That seemed like a stretch, but—

"It's because of Lorraine," she said, lowering her voice. "She told me not to."

"Lorraine Montgomery?" I asked. "Why does she care?"

"I don't know. She didn't tell me. She just told me to stop helping you and Grace."

"Why did you listen to her? She's not even your boss. You're a volunteer."

Her shoulders lifted in a weak shrug. "She scares me."

I raised my eyebrows. Lorraine Montgomery wasn't exactly pleasant, but scary? Although I got the impression that Libby was easily intimidated.

"Do you have any idea why Lorraine would care whether Grace looks into the history of someone in the Bailey family?"

"I don't know."

I lifted my finger off the bill. Libby was a sweet little mouse and she'd told me what I wanted to know. Not that it was going to help. I had a feeling I knew exactly why Lorraine Montgomery had told her not to help Grace. Because she hated me.

"Thanks, Libby."

"I can't keep that. There was hardly anything I could tell you."

"It's a start," I said cheerfully. "Take it. And don't worry. I won't say a word to Lorraine."

She nodded and took the bill. "Thanks."

"My pleasure. Have a lovely day." I turned and swept out of the store.

As much as I wanted to keep playing ginger Nancy Drew, I needed to head to the coffee shop. I'd pushed aside my anxiety over seeing my father, but as I walked to the Steaming Mug, it came back with a vengeance. The baby moved, almost like he or she was reacting to my increased heart rate.

"Sorry kid," I muttered, resting a hand on my belly. "You're being born into a fucked-up family."

But I was going to protect my baby from the worst of that, no matter what I had to do. This kid wasn't going to grow up like I did.

With a deep breath, I went inside.

The Steaming Mug was the cutest coffee shop in the history of ever, and not just because Grace used to run it before she had Charlie. It was objectively adorable, with a mint green counter, soft lighting, and big chalkboard menu against an exposed brick wall.

My dad was already here, waiting at a table. He'd aged well, with hair that was the same rich auburn as mine and lines around his eyes that made him look distinguished rather than old.

I had no memories of seeing him in person, although I knew he'd seen me when I was very young. He'd reached out to me after I'd turned eighteen and I'd eventually agreed to give him my address. Hence, the birthday card he sent me every year. But mostly he'd been a mystery. The man who'd gotten my mother pregnant, then disappeared from our lives.

But I also knew my mother. I only had one very biased side of the story, which was why I was willing to see him at all.

He stood when I walked in, giving me a hesitant smile. I went to his table and we both sat down.

"I'm sorry about last night," he said. "It seemed like a good idea when I left home, but I misjudged it."

"It's okay. You didn't know I'd have a house full of people."

"Did you have a nice party?"

I hesitated before answering. "Yes, but I'm averse to small talk. I'd rather get things out in the open."

He nodded once. "That's fair. In that case, I showed up yesterday without calling first because I was afraid you'd tell me not to come."

"And it would be harder to refuse to see you if you were already here."

"Something like that."

"Why are you here?"

"I should have done this a long time ago, but the times I reached out to you before, you didn't exactly seem receptive. Not that I blame you for that."

That was true. A memory of an eighteen-year-old me yelling and hanging up the phone came to mind. "I suppose I wasn't. But let's be honest: You're not exactly in the running for Father of the Year."

He glanced down. "No, I'm not. I don't suppose it helps to know I have a lot of regrets."

"That's better than a callous disregard for the child you fathered."

He met my eyes. His were green, just like mine. "I've thought about you every day since I found out you existed."

"That's sweet, I guess, but if you thought about me so much, why stay away?"

"It was never my choice."

"So it was my mother's fault? Is that your excuse?"

"It's a reason, not an excuse."

I crossed my arms. I was all too familiar with my mom's brand of crazy. It was easy to imagine her making things difficult for my father. She'd never had anything good to say about him, which had always made me wonder why she'd been with him in the first place.

Getting knocked up by Logan Bailey had made me slightly more sympathetic to my mother's own unexpected pregnancy. Maybe they'd been like me and Logan, only they'd never figured out how to get along. Not even for my sake.

Which brought me to the crux of my problem with my father. If he'd given a shit, why hadn't he fought harder to see me?

"Look, I don't know what brought on this sudden desire to mend family ties. Maybe it's the baby or you realized your daughter is thirty and you barely know her. Or maybe you're dying and you're looking for forgiveness, I don't know."

"I'm not dying."

"That's good. But you can't just waltz into my life and expect to suddenly be my dad."

"No, I know that. That's not why I'm here."

"Then why are you here?"

He picked up the gift bag he'd brought last night and set it on the table. "Because I have to start somewhere. When you were little, I didn't have a choice. And when you got older, I thought I'd let you take the lead. If you wanted to see me, you'd reach out and let me know. But now I realize that I need to do what I can to make this right. It took thirty years to get to this point, and if it takes another thirty for you to feel like I'm your father, then I'll just have to wait and hope I live that long." He pushed the bag toward me. "In the meantime, I'd like to come back and get together again."

I left the bag where it sat. The little girl who still lived inside me perked up. He wanted to see me again?

"Well, if you come back to Tilikum, we won't be able to avoid each other."

He gave me a warm smile. "I'll take that as a yes, then. I won't take up any more of your time right now. But I'll see you again soon. Happy birthday, Cara."

"Thank you."

He stood and went to the counter to drop a few dollars into the tip jar, then glanced back at me. There was sadness in his eyes, but no malice. No deceit.

I fought down a surge of emotion as he left, but I refused to turn into a weepy mess again. Especially in public. I was stronger than that.

Curiosity as to what was in the bag got the better of me. I set the pink tissue paper aside and pulled out a stack of envelopes. They were varying sizes—cards, not letters—and they were all sealed. Each one was addressed to me, at my mother's address. The return addresses varied, but all had my dad's name.

The first one had once been pink, but now it was faded and pale. The postmark was twenty-nine years ago, but it had been marked *return to sender*. I popped it open, the brittle glue snapping easily, and took out a card.

A birthday card for a one-year-old child.

It felt as if my heart was lodged in my throat as I opened the next one. A second birthday card. Then a third. The next one didn't have a year on the front, but it said *happy fourth birthday* inside.

All were signed *Love, Dad.*

Eventually, the envelopes no longer had stamps. The early cards had all been returned, so he'd given up mailing them. But he'd kept buying me birthday cards, year after year.

The last one was when I turned eighteen. After that, we'd been in contact by phone a couple of times and he'd had my address. He'd started mailing them to me.

Had he kept them all these years, thinking he'd one day have the chance to finally give them to me?

I wasn't sure what he hoped to accomplish with these. It wasn't like a yearly birthday card made up for everything. How much effort did buying a card really take? A trip to a drug store, then a quick stop at a post office?

But it did mean he'd been thinking about me. I didn't know why he hadn't tried harder, or whether there was enough to build any sort of relationship now—if I even wanted one. I didn't know what to think and I kind of wished I'd postponed so Logan could have been here.

I touched the stack of cards, still fighting the lump in my throat, wishing I was tough enough not to care.

31

LOGAN

The August heat beat down on me as I sprayed off the engine. I'd gone on duty at eight and although there hadn't been any calls yet, there was never a shortage of things to do. But all I could think about was Cara.

She was probably with her dad right now. I'd tried to talk her into rescheduling so I could go with her, but she'd insisted she'd be fine. It was typical Cara—always attempting to be cool and untouchable. Her dad showing up out of nowhere had rattled her, but she hadn't wanted to talk about it, even after the party guests had gone home. Plus, I was on a forty-eight hour shift, so it would be a couple of days before I had time.

I just hoped he wasn't an asshole.

On the one hand, it seemed like he'd have to be. Cara clearly had some daddy issues, and this guy was the reason. Or part of the reason, at least. Based on what I knew about her mother, she wasn't exactly a ray of sunshine. Cara's past was complicated, and I had a feeling there was more to her dad's story.

But if he was a dick to her, my brothers and I were going to demolish him.

My crew and I finished our cleaning detail just as a call came in. It wasn't an emergency, but there was suspected gang activity out at the Timberbeast Tavern.

Squirrel gang, to be exact.

That was the thing about being a small-town fire department. We got all kinds of calls.

I wasn't exactly looking forward to this one as we drove out there. The squirrels in Tilikum weren't normal. There was a lot of wildlife out here, but I was with Harvey Johnston on this one. The squirrels were fucking scary and no one was going to convince me otherwise.

We stopped out in front of the Timberbeast. It was the Havens' hangout, but there was an unspoken rule about the feud. It never interfered with safety. So when I was in uniform, the feud didn't exist.

But the squirrels did. I hopped off the engine and picked up a foot so a squirrel could run by.

"What the hell?" I asked as another one darted past.

Mason shot me a surprised glance. "You're really scared of them, aren't you?"

"Fuck yeah, I'm scared of them. They're evil."

"He had a bad experience when we were kids," Levi said.

"It was more than a bad experience," I said. "They tried to maul me."

"You were the one who sat in the tree with a container of Gram's cookies. What did you think would happen?"

"They knocked me out of the tree. I could have broken a leg."

Levi shot me a skeptical glance. "They didn't knock you out of the tree. You freaked out and fell."

"Same thing," I grumbled. "Let's just figure out what's going on and why they called us instead of animal control."

"You know animal control doesn't do squirrel calls," Levi said.

"Because they know the squirrels are evil."

Levi patted me on the back and leaned closer, lowering his voice. "You realize this is probably our fault, right?"

That had occurred to me. It had been a while since our squirrel-pocalypse prank on the Timberbeast, and they'd had an ongoing problem with squirrels trying to get in ever since. Not that we were going to admit to knowing anything about it. Prank denial was part of the deal on both sides.

By the way Rocco, the Timberbeast owner, glared at me and Levi, he was well aware of the reason for his squirrel problem.

He stood outside the open front door, hairy arms crossed over his barrel chest. He was a burly guy with a thick, dark beard and an intimidating scowl. If he hadn't been on the Haven side, I probably would have liked him. Seemed like a decent guy.

"Squirrel problem, Rocco?" Mason asked.

"You could say that. I thought they'd given up, but they found a new way in this morning and now I can't get them out."

Levi glanced at me. "Maybe we should call Fiona."

"Good idea, broffeur."

I pulled out my phone and brought up Fiona's number.

"Hey, Logan. What's up?"

"We're out here at the Timberbeast, and for some reason, I have no idea why, it looks like squirrels found their way inside. I don't know how they would have learned to do that. But you're the Disney princess around here. Do you have any advice as to how to get them out?"

"They're still breaking into the Timberbeast? That worked better than we thought."

"Nope, no idea why they keep going in."

"Oh, right, the owner is probably standing there."

"Yep."

"Got it. Sorry. Well, they're smarter than most people give them credit for, but they also have pretty basic instincts. You just need to lure them away with something better than what they're finding in the tavern."

"Any suggestions?"

"Peek and Boo have a thing for those cookies with peanut butter that you can get at Nature's Basket. Crumble those up and mix in some nuts and it's squirrel crack."

"Got it. Thanks, Fiona."

"No problem. And be careful. Don't hurt any of them."

"I know. We won't."

"Promise?"

"Yes, I promise." I ended the call and stuck my phone back in my pocket. "As long as they don't climb on me."

"Did she have a suggestion?" Levi asked.

"Peanut butter cookies. We'll lure them away and hopefully they find something else to do once they've decimated their squirrel crack."

Rocco grunted, like he wasn't convinced.

It didn't take long to run to the grocery store and grab a few bags of cookies, along with some nuts. We brought them back to the Timberbeast and Rocco helped us make a trail of squirrel crack out the back and into the woods. We spread out the goods so the squirrels would have to work for it and hopefully keep them out of the tavern for a little while.

By the time we finished up, we were hungry, so we headed over to the Caboose for lunch.

Gavin's truck was in the parking lot and Levi and I spotted him as soon as we walked in. He was just about to sit down at a table with Skylar and Skylar's friend, Ginny.

I'd gone out with Ginny a couple of times when she'd been in town last year, but nothing had ever come of it. She was pretty, and at the time I'd been somewhat attracted to her. But there hadn't exactly been any heat, and I think both of us had known it.

So it didn't feel awkward to smile and give her a friendly wave. And she didn't seem surprised to see me.

Levi nudged me with his elbow and raised his eyebrows. *Is this cool?*

I furrowed my brow. *Why wouldn't it be?*

He shrugged and I followed him over to Gavin's table.

"You guys want to join us?" Gavin asked.

"Yeah, why not?" I said. "Hey, Skylar. Hi, Ginny."

Ginny smiled. "Hey. It's good to see you again."

"You too."

There was a larger table nearby, so we all took a seat. Said our hellos, placed our orders, and told them about the squirrel issue over at the Timberbeast. Skylar hadn't heard the story about the squirrel-pocalypse prank, so Gavin filled her in.

Although ever since we found out the Havens were sniffing around Gram's land, trying to get her to sell, even just talking about our usual pranks didn't feel the same. The tone of the feud had changed. None of us had been planning to put a beard on Lola or flamingo all the Haven brothers' yards, and we were overdue. But until we figured out this mess with Gram's land, and made sure the Havens stayed out of it, pranking them again seemed wrong.

Our food came out and it was delicious. Cara's meatloaf

craving had rubbed off on me. I ordered it every time I was here.

"So, I heard you're having a baby," Ginny said. "That's big news."

"Yeah. A lot has changed since you were here last."

"No kidding. Congratulations."

I smiled. "Thanks."

"How's Cara?"

"She's hanging in there. It hasn't been the easiest pregnancy, but she's tough. She's handling it."

"Poor thing."

"So how about you? Are you in town for long?"

"No, just a few days. I'm in between projects and Skylar invited me to come visit. Although honestly, any excuse. I love this town."

"Yeah, it's not a bad place to be."

"Great place to raise a family," she said.

I smiled at her use of the word *family*. I kind of liked hearing it. "It sure is."

We finished up lunch, then Levi and I met the rest of our crew to head back to the firehouse. Our route took us past the Timberbeast. Things looked quiet—from the outside, at least. Hopefully Rocco could keep the squirrels out.

Pesky little suckers.

By the time we got back, I had a text from Cara. She said her meeting with her dad had gone okay and she'd tell me about it later. That was a good sign. She was willing to talk to me about it instead of blowing it off like it hadn't meant anything.

Progress.

My phone rang and I didn't recognize the number. That was weird. I stepped out a side door to take the call.

"Hello?"

There was a woman's voice on the other end. "Is this Logan Bailey?"

"Yes, it is."

"Logan, so nice to finally meet you," she said, her tone syrupy sweet. "I'm Layla Goulding, Cara's mother."

Alarm bells went off in my head. Why was Cara's mother calling me?

"Nice to meet you, too," I said carefully.

"I understand you're the father of Cara's baby?"

That was an odd way to word it. "We're having a baby together, yeah."

"And what are your plans regarding my daughter?"

I hesitated. "Are you asking if I'm going to marry her?"

"Oh my god, no. At least, I hope not."

"Excuse me?"

"Cara's not the marrying type. No, I'm wondering what kind of expectations you have about your role in this child's life."

"My role? I'm the baby's father. That's pretty self-explanatory."

"One would think, but that's not how the real world works, now is it?"

My brow furrowed. "I'm not sure what you're getting at."

"I want what's best for my daughter and her child. I can't give her that if she's living there, and I'm not interested in my grandchild growing up in some backwoods town. I can't fathom why she insists on staying there, other than to irritate me. But you also seem to be part of the problem."

"Wow. I'm not sure what to say to that."

"Let's be open with each other, shall we Logan?"

"Isn't that what you're doing already?"

"You might think you have good intentions, but I know

how difficult Cara can be. Do you really think you're equipped to handle her for the next eighteen years?"

"That's a spectacularly crappy thing to say about your daughter."

"It's just the truth. Cara has plenty of good qualities but she's adept at accentuating her flaws."

"I'm not sure what you're hoping to accomplish, other than pissing me off, but you don't need to worry about my intentions. Not that it's any of your business anyway."

"Of course it's my business. This is my grandchild. I'm already getting too many awkward questions about the baby and its upbringing."

What the fuck was she talking about? "Look, Cara and I are the baby's parents, so his or her upbringing is our responsibility. You don't need to worry about it."

"Obviously I'm not making myself clear."

"Apparently not."

"You seem to have some quaint notion that you'll do the right thing, so to speak. But I know what's really going to happen. In a few months, maybe a little more, you're going to realize what you got yourself into. You're going to discover that the sleepless nights and constant crying are just the beginning. And you're going to regret your attempt at chivalry and wish you could be free."

"You have got to be kidding me."

"Perhaps I sound callous, but I'm simply being realistic. You're with my daughter now because of the circumstances, but doing the right thing is about to get considerably more difficult. Which is why I'm calling. To offer you a way out."

"I don't need a way out."

"Logan," she said, and the contempt in her voice crawled up my spine. "I know what happened and it's nothing to be ashamed of. You had a fling with my daughter and the unexpected occurred. I applaud your attempt to be involved, I really do. But in the long run, wouldn't you rather have your life back?"

"No. Cara and the baby are my life now. Seriously, lady, you're barking up the wrong tree if you think you can chase me off. And don't insult me by trying to bribe me, either, in case that's where you're going with this nonsense. You might be my girlfriend's mother, but I'll hang up on your ass and block your number."

She took a slow breath, and if she were anything like Cara, I could imagine the fury burning in her eyes. "You're making a mistake."

"No, letting Cara go would be a mistake. Not being a father to *my* child would be a mistake," I said. "And letting this conversation continue would also be a mistake, so on that note—"

I ended the call.

32

CARA

I wasn't in a good head space, and I didn't like it.

Ever since my father had showed up in town, I'd been off. It was like the first trimester all over again. I bounced around between wanting to cry, eat, possibly puke, and curl up in bed. I wouldn't have said no to an orgasm, either, but Logan was still on duty.

I'd thought my hormone-induced mood swings were over, but apparently they'd just been dormant for a while.

I sat curled up in the corner of Grace's couch with a soft knit blanket covering my lap. Or what was left of my lap. It was mostly baby now. And I still had more than six weeks left. How big was I going to get?

I didn't want to think about that. I was fragile enough without worrying about stretch marks.

"Did you get stretch marks?" I asked, apparently unable to control myself.

Grace sat on the other side of the couch with the blanket covering her no-longer-pregnant lap. Baby Charlie napped in the other room. "Oh yeah. Lots of them. But they're already fading."

"I guess you are a normal human, then. I was beginning to wonder."

She laughed. "I'm sorry this has been so hard on you."

"Don't be. It's nothing I can't handle."

"Are you going to tell me what's wrong yet, or are we going to keep pretending?"

"Pretending what?"

"That you're not about to cry."

"I'm not about to cry."

She raised her eyebrows. "Liar."

"I'm really not. I was about five minutes ago, but I think the urge passed."

"Is it about your dad?"

I took a deep breath and fiddled with the blanket. "Probably."

"I know a bunch of old birthday cards don't excuse his absence. But it's okay if it makes you feel a little better to know he bought them."

"He tried to send them at first. Some of them were post-marked, but my mother returned them. Which makes me wonder how much of his absence was his fault versus hers."

"Do you think she kept him away from you?"

"I'm starting to think so. I know she wouldn't have made it easy on him. That's just how she is. But she wouldn't even let him send a birthday card?"

"That's pretty harsh."

"I guess it's possible she was trying to protect me. If those cards were his only attempt to be in my life, then maybe it's understandable. But I also know my mother, and if she'd decided to cut my dad out, she would have done so. Mercilessly. I'm convinced the only reason she still talks to me is because I keep giving her money."

"Oh, honey." She grabbed my foot and squeezed. "I'm sorry, but your mom doesn't deserve you."

"Whether she does or not, I'm the daughter she's stuck with."

"It's the other way around. She's the mother you're stuck with, and it wouldn't be wrong to set tougher boundaries with her."

"So my therapists have told me."

"They're right. Her happiness isn't your responsibility."

"Ouch." I put a hand on my chest. "That's a truth that hurts."

"I just hate the way she treats you."

"I'm not exactly Layla's biggest fan, either. But it's complicated."

She squeezed my foot again. "I know. Do you want to talk about something else?"

"Yes, please."

"Okay. Have you settled on any names?"

"Not really. I'm pretty sure we'll still be arguing about it in the delivery room."

A knock on the door interrupted whatever Grace was about to say. Gavin walked in without waiting for an answer.

"Ladies," he said, flashing us a wide smile.

Grace held a finger to her lips. "Careful. Charlie's asleep."

"Sorry," he whispered. "Do you have any eggs?"

"I think so. Why?"

"I'm proving to Ginny that I know how to bake."

My fists tightened around the blanket. I didn't want to react to her name, but apparently my hormones had other ideas.

"What?" Grace asked.

"Ginny is in town for a few days visiting Skylar, and

since I'm off, they're hanging out at my place. I don't know how the subject came up, but Ginny doesn't believe that I know how to bake. Actually, I think she's messing with me just to see if she can get me to make a batch of cookies because I know she's had my cookies before. But cookies sound good anyway, so why not? Only, we're out of eggs."

Grace blinked at him a few times. "Okay, then. Help yourself."

"Awesome." He disappeared into the kitchen. "Hey Cara, do you know if they got the squirrel situation taken care of?"

"What squirrel situation?" Grace asked.

"Squirrels were getting into the Timberbeast Tavern again." He came out with a carton of eggs. "The girls and I had lunch with Logan yesterday and he'd just been over there, trying to lure them out."

I tried to keep my face neutral. He *and the girls* had lunch with Logan?

That meant Logan had lunch with Ginny yesterday. I'd talked to him since. He'd told me about the squirrels at the Timberbeast, but he'd neglected to mention having lunch with Ginny.

"I think the peanut butter cookie trick worked," I said, keeping my voice even.

"Cool." He held up the eggs. "Thanks for these. I'll bring some cookies over when I'm done."

"Thanks, Gav," Grace said.

He left and I forced myself to open my fists and let go of the blanket.

Logically, I knew there was probably nothing to worry about. He hadn't said Logan had lunch with Ginny by himself. There had obviously been a small group. Although if it had been Gavin, Skylar, Ginny, and Logan, that was an awful lot like two couples having lunch.

I needed to stop it. My hormone-soaked imagination was getting out of control.

But what if I wasn't being paranoid?

Ginny was in town. A woman who Logan had liked. A woman who was not currently the size of a beached whale, with cankles and stretch marks and wicked mood swings and enough baggage to fill a Greyhound bus with all her issues.

Somehow, I kept my expression from betraying the storm that raged inside me. Grace didn't ask what was wrong. Or maybe she was just used to me looking like I was on the verge of an emotional breakdown and assumed it was the pregnancy hormones again. And maybe it was.

Or maybe I was setting myself up to get hurt and it was only a matter of time before the other shoe dropped.

Because for me, it always did.

LOGAN CAME HOME the next morning while I was eating breakfast. He looked happy to see me. And the way he brushed my hair back from my face and kissed me felt wonderful. It felt real.

But he didn't mention Ginny.

What if I was kidding myself and we were just playing house?

He poured a bowl of cereal and milk and started eating. I picked at my food, my appetite suddenly nowhere to be found.

"So, I kind of need to talk to you about something," he said.

I swallowed hard. That phrase was rarely followed by something good. "Sure. What's up?"

"Your mom called me the other day."

Great. Another thing to add to the already chaotic tumble of emotions inside me. "What did she want?"

"I think she was trying to get rid of me."

"What do you mean?"

"She didn't quite bribe me to break up with you, but I'm pretty sure that's what she was getting at. She asked some questions about my intentions with you and said she wanted to offer me a way out."

I gaped at him, my mouth hanging open. "She what?"

"Yeah, that was my reaction. Has she been trying to get you to move back to L.A.?"

"She has, actually."

"I think that was her angle. She wants to get rid of me so you'll move home and bring the baby. She doesn't like the idea of her grandchild growing up in... what did she call it? A backwoods town? Something like that."

"If she offered you money, I'll lose my mind. She doesn't have any money."

"She didn't specifically mention money, but it sounded like she was working up to that. I hung up on her before she got that far."

He'd hung up on my mother? That was kind of amazing. "Wow."

"Sorry if I made things worse by pissing her off. But I wasn't going to take that shit from her."

"It's okay."

At least he hadn't taken her offer.

But god, I came with a lot of baggage. How long was he going to want to deal with shit like this?

Maybe it wouldn't be Ginny, but some girl was going to come along who wasn't a total pain in his ass with a family that was worse.

A familiar smoldering heat rose up from deep inside me. I didn't know if I was just moody again or if I had any right to be mad. I was too emotional to care whether I was about to turn into a jealous psycho, and I felt my temper snap.

"So how's Ginny?"

His eyes darted from side to side, like he wasn't sure what the fuck I was talking about. "Fine, I guess? I don't know. Why?"

"Were you at some point planning to mention that you had lunch with her?"

"Lunch with her?" he asked, as if he had no idea what I was talking about. "Oh, that. I didn't have lunch with just her. I was with Levi and she was with Gav and Skylar. We all had lunch together."

"Where?"

"The Caboose..."

My eyes widened. "Our restaurant? Did you have meatloaf?"

"Yeah, but—"

"Oh my god." I tried to fly out of my seat, but it was awkward with this belly. "You had lunch at the Caboose with Ginny and you ordered meatloaf?"

He stared at me like he had no idea why I was mad.

Which was probably fair. I was losing it over something stupid. But I couldn't seem to stop, which only made it worse. Because every irrational word I spewed at him confirmed what I already knew.

He wasn't going to want to stick around. Not with me.

"Maybe my mom was right and you do need a way out."

"Slow down, Tiger. Where did that come from?"

"I'm sitting here at home getting fat because you knocked me up and you go out to eat with your ex? You even had meatloaf. No wonder you didn't tell me about it."

"She's hardly my ex. And are you more mad that Ginny was at lunch or that I ordered meatloaf? Because I can go to the Caboose right now and get you the fucking meatloaf if it'll calm your ass down."

"It's morning."

"I'll call Hank."

"I don't want meatloaf."

"Then what the fuck do you want?"

I didn't know. Reassurance? A hug? For him to just leave me already so I could get it over with?

Fighting with Logan was easy. It was familiar. I wasn't vulnerable when we were fighting. I was tough.

On the outside, at least. Inside was another story.

"I don't want anything," I snapped and stomped out of the kitchen and up the stairs.

33

CARA

I slammed my bedroom door. What was I doing? Why was I picking a fight with Logan over something so stupid? He hadn't done anything wrong. I did wish he would have told me about seeing Ginny, but it wasn't that big of a deal.

The problem was, I wasn't really mad about Ginny. I was annoyed, but that was shallow—and covering something a lot deeper.

Logan burst through my bedroom door. "I know what you're doing."

"What are you talking about?"

He crossed the distance between us, leaving me no choice but to meet his eyes. "You're upset about something else. What is it?"

How could I possibly explain? I hated feeling so afraid. I was tougher than that.

He ran his fingers through my hair. His touch tender, but his eyes blazed with frustration. "I didn't tell you I had lunch with Ginny because I forgot I'd seen her. I'm sorry it hurt your feelings and I'm sorry I ate meatloaf without you."

I hesitated for a moment, teetering between being sane and accepting his apology, and being crazy Cara and making this worse.

In the end, his touch calmed me. "I know the Caboose isn't really *our* restaurant."

"That's a start," he said, his expression softening. "Did your dad do something? Because if he did, I'll fucking break him."

"No. Just the birthday cards I already told you about."

"Then what's wrong?" He massaged his fingers into my scalp.

I wanted to melt into him. To trust him with the weight of all my stupid issues.

"I'm too much," I said, my voice barely a whisper. My eyes closed. I didn't want to see him agree with me.

"You're fucking infuriating. But you're not too much."

"Logan—"

"Shut the fuck up, Cara."

Before I could snap back at him, he silenced me with his lips on mine. I threw my arms around his neck as he delved his tongue into my mouth. This was what I needed. Logan taking control, fucking all these raging emotions out of me.

We made quick work of our clothes, tearing them off in a frenzy. My belly pressed awkwardly between us, but we were well-practiced at working around it. He cupped my breast, sliding his thumb over my sensitive nipple, and I gasped into his mouth.

His hands roved over me, every touch sending bursts of sensation through my body. I was needy and raw, but he handled me like an expert. He knew where to caress and linger. Where to pinch and tug.

God, he was good at this.

We climbed onto the bed and he rolled to his back, guiding me on top of him. I straddled his hips and sank onto his erection. My eyes fluttered at the feel of him stretching me open, filling me.

I rolled my hips, dragging my clit against him. He held my thighs and thrust up into me, matching my rhythm. His muscles flexed and his brow furrowed. He was sexy and real and mine.

For now, at least.

Bracing my hands on his broad chest, I dug my fingernails into his skin. Although my body had changed, his was still a glorious specimen of firefighter hotness. His hard planes of muscle tightened and contracted, his abs rippling. He was gorgeous.

I squeezed my thighs to slide up his hard length and dropped down again. Up, then down, reveling in his low growls as I rode his cock. His thickness was intoxicating, the pressure of him inside me intense. He grunted, thrusting harder. Deeper. Giving me everything I needed.

"Touch your tits," he commanded. "Grab them and squeeze."

I wasn't going to argue, but before I obeyed, I clenched my thighs and dug my fingernails into his chest, leaving red marks. His eyes burned with the heat of lust and he smacked my ass.

"Be a good girl, Cara."

I slid my hands up my body and palmed both tits. As soon as my hands brushed my nipples, I hissed in a breath. I was so sensitive.

"That's it, baby. Squeeze those tits."

I did what I was told, caressing myself while I rolled my

hips. Logan watched, holding my thighs and driving his cock inside me.

My inner walls tightened and heat pooled in my core as I spiraled toward my climax. I chased it, riding him hard. I was desperate to come—to relieve this aching pressure.

A few more thrusts and he had me. I braced myself against his chest and threw my head back as the intense pleasure washed over me in waves. He grunted, still driving into me, as if he were enjoying my orgasm as much as I was.

I slowed down and he didn't push for more, although he hadn't come yet. He waited, caressing my thighs while I caught my breath.

"Better?" he asked.

I brushed my hair back from my face. "Yeah."

"Good."

I climbed off him, but instead of manhandling me onto my knees so he could pound me from behind, he guided me so I was lying on my side. He stayed behind me, caressing my back, and leaned in to pepper kisses up my spine.

"You're so fucking sexy," he said between kisses. "I can't get enough of you."

He took his time, kissing and touching me until I was drunk on him. Relaxed and warm, my body both primed and sated. I purred like a cat, arching my back while he rubbed his cock against me.

"Don't you want to fuck me?" I asked.

His teeth grazed my shoulder. "I want to devour you."

He lifted my thigh and slid his cock inside me. This angle was intense in an entirely different way. I moaned as he bit down harder, the pinch of pain mixing with the pleasure of his thickness once again filling me.

I loved the way this felt. The heat of his skin on mine.

The drag of his cock as he thrust in and out. The sound of his rough grunts in my ear.

I didn't want this to end.

"Don't stop," I whispered.

Was that too much to wish for?

Emotion flooded through me, making tears spring to my eyes. I squeezed them shut, trying to focus on the feel of Logan fucking me.

Don't stop. Please don't ever stop.

He drove into me, hard and rough, making the headboard bang against the wall and my body jerk with the force of his thrusts. I braced myself against the bed, clutching the sheets. I was helpless, totally in his power.

I'd never wanted to be owned by anyone. To be at their mercy.

To be so vulnerable.

But I was. Logan owned me. And I loved it.

He growled in my ear and the pressure of his cock sent sparks of pleasure racing through me. I let go, crying out, surrendering to the power of his body joined with mine.

"Fuck, you feel so good," he said, his breath hot on my neck. His fingers dug into my thigh. "I'm going to come so hard."

I moaned. "Yes. Come inside me."

He grunted again, driving in deep. A second orgasm rolled through me and I clenched tight around him.

I loved the way he lost control, pounding into me as he found his release. He held me in a strong grip as his hips jerked and his cock pulsed inside me.

So good.

We gradually slowed and he slid out, but he didn't let me go. He kissed my shoulder, his mouth making a warm trail on my skin.

"Better?" he asked again.

I nodded. "Yes."

"Good."

I nestled against him and he wound his arm around me, holding me close.

"I'm sorry," I said.

"It's okay. You're hot when you're jealous."

I shot him a look over my shoulder. "Is that why you didn't tell me? You wanted to make me jealous?"

"No. Just an unexpected benefit."

"I hate you sometimes."

He kissed my neck. "I know."

I paused for a moment, basking in the warmth and security of his arms. "I'm sorry about my mom. I'll call her and tell her to leave you alone."

"You don't have to apologize for her."

"Still. And I'm not moving back to L.A." I wasn't sure why I said that, but as soon as the words left my mouth, I was glad. I wanted him to know. "I don't want you to worry that I'm going to take off with the baby or something. I wouldn't do that."

His grip around me tightened and he kissed my shoulder again. "I know you wouldn't."

"And I'm sorry I'm so crazy."

"Tiger, I wouldn't have you any other way."

Hearing that settled my raw nerves even more than the two orgasms.

I knew I was hard to love, but if anyone had a shot at it, it just might be Logan Bailey.

Was that too much to wish for?

Maybe.

But as I lay in his arms, I wished for it anyway.

34

LOGAN

*T*he door to the bedroom down the hall from ours stood half-open. A sliver of light peeked into the hallway, catching my attention.

The baby's room.

I paused in the doorway and glanced inside. Over the last few months, we'd been gathering the stuff we were going to need after the baby was born, and the girls had thrown Cara a baby shower. For a while, most of it had sat in there, untouched. Still in boxes. But the other day, Cara had gotten a bug up her ass about setting up the nursery.

So I'd put the furniture together and placed it where she wanted it. She'd put sheets on the crib and started filling drawers with baby clothes.

This was starting to feel awfully real.

I wandered into the room and ran my hand along the edge of the crib. The sight of all the baby stuff made my chest ache, the old scar of my parents' death throbbing. I missed my mom and dad. And my grandad. At least one of them should have been here to help me figure this out. To teach me how to be a father.

I hoped I was up for it.

Until recently, I hadn't worried a lot about whether or not I could handle being a father. I was too focused on the here and now—helping Cara through her pregnancy and figuring out how to navigate my often rocky relationship with her.

But it wasn't going to be long before we moved into the next phase. She was going to have the baby, and then it was on. Time to show up, step up, and be a dad.

"It's weird, isn't it?" Cara asked behind me.

"Do you think we'll be ready?"

"Probably not."

I loved her blunt honesty. "Nope, probably not."

"Although I don't think we'll be completely terrible parents. Between the two of us, we must have enough redeeming qualities to equal at least one good one."

"That's probably fair." I stepped closer and brushed her hair back from her face. "Then it's a good thing we have each other."

Her mouth lifted in a slight smile. "You're okay, I guess."

"Yeah, I don't totally hate you."

"You're lucky I keep you around." She poked my chest but kept her other hand behind her back.

"I know I am."

She smiled again and light danced in her green eyes. "I made you something."

"It's not muffins again, is it?" Her attempts at baking were very hit or miss.

"You said you liked my muffins."

"I was probably lying to keep you from stabbing me."

She rolled her eyes. "I wouldn't stab you."

I raised my eyebrows. "I don't know. You can go from sweet to psycho in two seconds flat. You were probably holding a butter knife and I didn't want to take any chances."

"Fine, I take it back. I didn't make this for you." She took a step backward.

"Oh, come on. I'm teasing. What did you make me?"

A flicker of vulnerability passed across her features. She drew her hand from behind her back and handed me something made of blue yarn.

For a second, I almost panicked. What was it? By the hopeful look on her face, I was supposed to know. I turned it over, like I was admiring it. The stitches were loose in some places, tight in others, making for an odd pattern of holes. But it had a basic shape that almost looked like—

"It's a hat," I said, relieved it hadn't taken me too long to figure it out.

She beamed at me. "I thought blue would look good on you. I know it's not perfect, but it's the first crochet project I've ever finished."

I held it up to decide which side would work best as the front. It was roughly beanie shaped, so I settled on a direction and put it on. "What do you think?"

She reached up and tucked a piece of my hair underneath. "It looks great."

"I'm going to go look."

I took her hand, leading her to the bathroom with me, and stood in front of the mirror. The hat was crooked and the sizes of the little holes didn't match. But I didn't care. She'd made it for me, so I fucking loved it.

Her hopeful gaze faltered. "It's a little messy, but—"

"Don't care." I adjusted it, although that didn't help much. "I love it."

"Really?"

"Absolutely." I leaned over and kissed her. "Thank you."

That brightened her up. "You're welcome. Gram says I just need practice and I'll get better."

"She'd know. So are we ready to go?"

"Yeah, but you don't have to wear it today if you don't want to. It's hot out."

"Of course I'm going to wear it. It feels well-ventilated." I gave it one last adjustment in the mirror. "Let's go."

My quest to find the Montgomery treasure was probably pointless. I knew that. But at least it gave me something I could do. And because Cara was awesome, she'd come up with a brilliant idea.

Talk to Harvey Johnston.

He wasn't exactly playing with a full deck, but he'd been searching for the Montgomery treasure for years. Maybe he was just a crazy old mountain man and he wouldn't be able to tell us anything. But who knew; Harvey might be able to give us a clue. It was worth a shot.

We drove through town but didn't see him anywhere. He might have been out in the hills, wandering around, but we decided to check his house.

He lived in an old but tidy log cabin at the end of a long dirt road. My brothers and I came out here once in a while to check up on him—make sure he had supplies and firewood.

The cabin sat in the center of a clearing. A few tools had been left strewn around and the wood pile near the door was well-stocked. He had bunches of tin cans hanging from tree branches all around the clearing. He claimed they helped keep the squirrels away.

The front door was wide open, which could have meant he was here. Or it could have meant he'd wandered off and forgotten to close it.

Hard to tell with him.

I parked in front of the cabin and Cara and I got out. It sounded like he was home. Someone inside the cabin was whistling.

"Do you know how long he's lived here?" Cara asked.

I shrugged. "As long as I can remember. I'm pretty sure he was born in Tilikum."

The whistling grew louder and Harvey poked his head out the door. He was dressed in an old t-shirt with a brown leather vest and dusty jeans. It looked like someone had given him a new hat—tan with a wide brim.

His face broke out in a gap-toothed smile. "Hi there, Miss Cara. Logan."

"Hi, Harvey," Cara said. "Mind if we come in?"

He patted his vest pockets, like he was looking for something. "Sure. Come in, come in."

Cara and I followed him inside. The interior was clean, if a little bare. He had a small kitchen, a wooden table and two chairs that he'd probably made himself, and a twin-sized bed. A door led to a small bathroom and he had a faded rug on the floor.

"We were hoping we could pick your brain a little," I said. "About the treasure."

His eyes lit up, which didn't surprise me. The Montgomery treasure was one of his favorite topics. The evils of the Tilikum squirrel population was probably a close second. "What do you want to know?"

"What makes you think it's real?"

"It is real."

Cara and I glanced at each other.

"A lot of people in town say it's just a story," Cara said. "So how do you know it's really out there?"

"No one asks." He gave her a wide grin. "No one ever asks. If they asked, I'd tell. I don't need to keep secrets."

He kept muttering to himself about no one asking and keeping secrets while he went to a wooden chest and started rooting around.

"We're not trying to take it from you," I said. "If it's real and we actually found it, we'd make sure you got in on it."

He twisted around. "I don't want to keep it."

"You don't?"

"No, no." He straightened with an armful of stuff and brought it to the table. "Don't want to keep it. Don't need it. Just want to find it."

"Why?" Cara asked.

His blue eyes were unusually clear and he smiled at her again. "The finding is the point. The solving. But there's not much time."

He unceremoniously dumped everything on the table and spread it out. He had old maps, photocopied newspaper clippings, a brown leather pouch, and a battered spiral notebook.

Cara and I glanced at each other again. She shrugged. Best to just let him do his thing and see what he had to say.

He opened a folder and took out a photocopy of a newspaper clipping. It was an old article about treasure hunters descending on Tilikum, searching for the Montgomery treasure. There was a big group photo outside city hall.

Harvey pointed to a face on the end. "My granddaddy."

"May I?" Cara asked.

He handed her the paper and she held it carefully. "That's amazing. Did he come here just to find the treasure?"

"Yep. He looked with the rest of them. Didn't find it. Found a wife instead."

"That's not a bad trade," I said. "So this is how your family came to Tilikum? Treasure hunting?"

Harvey nodded. "My granddaddy always said it was out there."

"What about your parents?" Cara asked. "Did they look, too?"

His expression darkened. "No. They didn't believe him."

"So you want to prove your granddaddy right," Cara said.

"Yes, ma'am."

He dug through the mess and pulled out another piece of paper. It was an old photocopy of an even older picture showing three men in suits.

"Did you make these copies?" Cara asked.

"At the library, long time ago. So the originals wouldn't get ruined." He pointed to the man on the left. "That's Ernest Montgomery. He left the treasure."

"Who are the other two?" I asked.

"Frederick Bailey and Arthur Haven. The three of them founded Tilikum."

"A Bailey and a Haven," Cara said. "They don't look like they're feuding. This must have been before it started."

"They worked together. No feud then," Harvey said and it didn't escape my notice that he seemed more coherent the longer we talked. "Arthur Haven started the timber company and the Baileys built the railroad. Ernest Montgomery was in banking and he owned a lot of the land 'round here."

"Did your grandaddy ever talk about the feud?" Cara asked. "Had it started by the time he came here?"

"Oh yeah. It was worse back then. No pranks. Lot of fights."

"So this Ernest Montgomery guy," I said. "He made a bunch of money and helped found a town. But where does the treasure story come from? Why wouldn't he just leave his money to his kids or grandkids or something?"

"He left it to his granddaughter, but she died before he did," Harvey said.

"Was his granddaughter Sarah Montgomery?" Cara asked.

"Yeah, Sarah." Harvey sorted through his pile again and retrieved another photocopy, this one of an old newspaper obituary. "Sarah Montgomery. Died of the flu. But I did find something."

He rustled through the pile and pulled out the leather pouch. He loosened the opening and motioned for Cara to hold out her hands, then dumped a tarnished silver pendant into her open palm.

She pinched the chain between her fingers and held it up. The pendant was roughly the size of a quarter. There was something engraved on both sides, but it was hard to make out. She caught it with her other hand and peered at it.

"There are initials on one side. SJM." She turned it over. "But I'm not sure what this is. A squirrel?"

"A clue," Harvey said, his voice triumphant. He dug through his pile again, this time producing what looked like a charcoal rubbing.

I eyed it with skepticism. Harvey might have gone off the rails with this one. "Is that a squirrel too?"

"Yes, yes." He took the pendant from Cara and held it next to the rubbing. "See? The same."

He was right, the squirrel-shaped design on the rubbing was the same as the engraving on the pendant.

"This was Sarah's," Harvey said, gesturing to the pendant with a finger.

"Did you make this rubbing?" I asked. "Where'd you find it?"

"I did, I did. I saw it. Found it. Same as the necklace."

"Where did you find it?"

"Haven House," he said. "On a wooden chest. Couldn't pick it up. Too heavy. So I made this." He pointed to the rubbing.

Harvey seemed convinced this was significant, but it seemed like a longshot to me. Although maybe I'd seen the squirrel design before, I just couldn't think of where. "How do you know the necklace belonged to Sarah? The initials match, but it could have been someone else's."

He glanced away and rubbed the back of his neck. "Oh, it's hers. I took it out of the Haven House. Meant to put it back. Didn't mean to keep it."

"Too late for that now," Cara said.

He shuffled through his pile again. "After Sarah died, there was a big to-do over Ernest's money. Man wasn't even dead yet and people were fighting over it."

"That's awful," Cara said.

"Ernest died later, but then there was the big fire," he continued. "Half the town burned down. Lots of stuff was lost."

"Do you know if Ernest himself said that he was leaving a treasure somewhere?" I wanted to know if this was just another Tilikum tall tale. Maybe wishful thinking from a town that had just been devastated by fire.

Harvey's face scrunched up, making the wrinkles around his eyes deepen. "My granddaddy said Montgomery did it to teach people a lesson."

I glanced at Cara. "Maybe because people were fighting over his money before he was even gone. Or maybe it had

something to do with the feud. The Baileys and Havens
could have been fighting over his money."

"But if it was Montgomery money, why doesn't the feud
include them?" she asked. "Wouldn't they have been mad at
both sides if they were after Ernest's inheritance?"

"It doesn't all add up."

"Montgomerys don't want it found," Harvey said, a
sudden urgency in his tone. "No they don't."

"Why not?"

He shook his head vehemently. "No. Don't trust 'em.
Don't do it."

"Do you know why?" Cara asked gently.

"It's almost too late." He was muttering again. "Too late
and it's gone. Not much time. Need to find it first. They don't
want it found."

"Harvey, do the Montgomerys know where the treasure
is?" Cara asked. "Are they hiding it?"

Intensity blazed in his eyes as he met her gaze. "Don't
know. But you be careful, Miss Cara. Don't trust them. Don't
trust anyone. Greed makes people bad. It's why I don't want
it. Just want to find it. Prove he was right."

"Greed does awful things to people," Cara said. "Don't
worry; we'll be careful."

Another part of Harvey's mutterings had caught my
attention. "Why is time running out? What happens if no
one finds it?"

He shook his head. "No. Need to find it. Not much time."

Cara and I glanced at each other again while Harvey
continued muttering. His moment of clarity seemed to be
passing.

"Thank you for sharing this with us," Cara said.

"Yeah, thanks, man."

Harvey looked up. "No one asks. But we need to find it."

"Okay," she said. "We'll do our best."

He took the pendant and gently put it back in the leather pouch, then held it out to Cara. "You take this. Might help."

"Thank you, Harvey. If you want it back, just let me know."

He set the pouch in her outstretched palm. "Be careful, Miss Cara."

"I will. Promise."

Harvey went back to muttering and started putting things away. We said goodbye but he didn't answer, so we let ourselves out and got in my SUV.

"I think I'm more confused than when we got here." I pulled my seat belt around and clicked it into place.

"So, Sarah Montgomery was Ernest's granddaughter. She was friends with Eliza Bailey and was supposed to marry John Haven. But we know they never got married. And Eliza and John both disappeared, but we don't know what happened to them. And someone was writing Eliza secret love letters. Then Sarah died before she could inherit her grandfather's estate and he supposedly hid his money."

"And somewhere along the line, the feud began. Maybe over his money, but that still doesn't quite make sense."

"And did it have anything to do with Eliza or John going missing?"

"I don't know, but apparently the squirrels have the answer." I gestured to the pouch with the pendant in it. "Is it weird that I think I've seen that before?"

She took it out and held it up. "Have you?"

"Maybe? I don't know. As soon as he said he found the same design on a chest, it made me think of the murder cabin."

"What's the murder cabin?"

"It's just this old cabin out by the hot springs. We filmed Bailey dancing out there and I helped Gav decorate it with Halloween shit to make it creepy for Skylar. She needed book inspiration or something. There was an old chest and it might have had this squirrel on it."

"Like the chest Harvey saw in the Haven House."

"I might be wrong," I said. "It just looks familiar."

"Harvey seemed excited that this was a clue, but even if there was a chest with a squirrel carving on it, I have no idea what that means."

"Fucking squirrels."

"I wonder who else in this town knows something." She tapped her lip. "People might be sitting on clues without even realizing it."

"Maybe."

"There's one way to find out."

"What's that?"

"I'll offer a reward."

I grinned at her. "Throw money at the problem?"

"It's very effective. And it wouldn't have to be much. Just enough to get people to dig out their old photo albums and family records to see if they have something that will give us a clue."

"I like where you're going with this," I said. "We'll probably have to sort through some bullshit, knowing this town, but maybe someone has another necklace with a squirrel engraved on it or something."

She put the pendant away. Then she reached over and tugged on my hat to adjust it. "Are you sure you like it?"

"Are you kidding? You made it for me. I love it."

She smiled, her green eyes lighting up. Damn, she was beautiful.

The craziest thing went through my mind.

Because I love you.

My heart beat hard. Because holy shit, it was true. I did love her.

And I almost said it. But for some reason, I couldn't quite get the words out.

35

CARA

*O*ffering a reward for information about Sarah Montgomery, Eliza Bailey, or John Haven had seemed like a good idea at the time. Harvey Johnston had known a lot about Tilikum's past. Someone had just needed to ask him about it. It stood to reason that there could be other long-time residents who might know things—information that might help put the pieces of this puzzle together. We just needed to find them.

I should have known better.

It wasn't that my reward offer went unnoticed. I wasn't offering a huge sum of money, but I got tons of calls. The problem was, everyone in town had a story, but none of them had any evidence. I'd spent the last week listening to an increasingly odd assortment of claims.

The ghost of Eliza Bailey haunted someone's house. Someone else said John Haven was their great-grandfather, but it turned out he didn't have any Havens in his family tree. There were stories about Eliza being abducted by Bigfoot or faking her own death to run away with a mountain man. About Sarah living in a tree house and John

Haven starting the Tilikum fire—years after he'd disappeared.

No one had anything useful. Not a single puzzle piece to be found.

But my curiosity hadn't just been tickled. I was hooked. I needed to know what had happened to these people and whether or not that treasure was real.

If I were being honest, it was also a nice distraction from my increasingly confusing personal life. Apparently having a baby and dating Logan Bailey weren't enough. My mother continued her attempts to persuade me to move to L.A. A part of me felt guilty for not flying down there to see her. Usually when she got this upset about something, I'd visit for a few days and calm her down. But I was getting too close to my due date to fly.

And I didn't really want to go down there anyway.

True to his word, my dad had come back to town for a visit. I'd met him for lunch, this time with Logan. I'd thanked him for the birthday cards, but other than that, we hadn't talked about the past. He'd spent the meal asking me questions about my life since leaving L.A. About college, and what my life was like living here in Tilikum. Logan and I even told him a little bit about our relationship—how we'd started out disliking each other, but the pregnancy had forced us to spend time together, and now here we were.

He told us more about his life. He was a welder and metalworker and owned his own business. I got the impression that my grandparents hadn't been his biggest fan when he'd started dating my mom. He'd been too blue collar for their taste.

I'd left that meeting feeling less antagonistic toward my father. Maybe not ready to forgive him for a childhood's worth of absence, but when he'd asked if we could get together again sometime, I'd said yes. And I'd meant it.

Saturday rolled around and Logan was on duty until the next morning. Gram had invited me for iced tea and snacks with her and the other girls. The late summer day was hot, so I was grateful for the relative coolness inside her house. I was due to have this baby in just over a month and my body was feeling the strain. My back ached, my feet were swollen, and I couldn't even remember what it was like to have actual ankles. Long skirts and slip-on shoes had become my best friends.

I sat at the big farmhouse table with Fiona, Skylar, Grace, and Gram, trying not to feel like the odd one out. Yes, I was having a Bailey baby. But the rest of them *were* Baileys, or would be soon. I wasn't and didn't have any reason to believe that I ever would be.

Hell, I didn't know if that was even what I wanted. I'd always insisted I wasn't wife material. I was too high maintenance for that. And I'd never expected Logan to marry me just because we were having a baby together. The idea of making an honest woman out of someone was some antiquated bullshit as far as I was concerned.

So why was I sitting here feeling out of place as the one not-Bailey at the table? Why did it matter?

I sipped my iced tea, letting the conversation drift past me. Baby Charlie was rolling over. Skylar was making wedding plans. Fiona had finished the restoration on her dream car. Everyone seemed to be avoiding the elephant in the room—Gram's financial issues.

Although I couldn't pay it all, I'd paid some of her debt. It wasn't enough to ensure she could keep her land, but it had bought them time. She didn't have to sell *now*. That was something at least. I'd helped find her a lawyer—he was a shark—

and contacted a private detective I'd worked with before. I was low on cash, but he owed me a few favors, so I didn't hesitate to call them in. I'd wanted to ruin people's lives before, but that Mike Phillips bastard had no idea what was coming for him.

"Well, we found a buyer for Logan's Chevelle not long ago, and now that my Belvedere is out of there, we have more space," Fiona said.

I'd been lost in my thoughts, so I didn't know the context of her comment, but she'd said something about Logan's Chevelle.

"Wait, wasn't that the car he only drove half the time because it barely ran? I thought it was in the garage at the Bailey bachelor pad."

"No, he was going to have Evan restore it, but when he found out about the baby, he asked me and Evan to find a buyer. He used the money he was going to spend on the restoration to buy his SUV."

I blinked a few times. "I didn't know that."

"It was so sweet," Fiona said. "That was a while ago. I'm surprised he didn't mention it."

"No, he just showed up one day in that SUV."

My heart squeezed in my chest. I'd been impressed at his decision to get a more kid-friendly vehicle, but I hadn't realized what he'd given up to get it.

I felt a pang of guilt. Not because it was more my fault than his. We'd gotten into this together. But Logan wouldn't have chosen me to be stuck with. Not in a million years. And I once again wondered how long this thing between us was going to last. And what our lives were going to look like when it was over.

"I love how excited he is to be a daddy," Fiona said.

"He is, isn't he," I said. "That's a good thing for me. The

way this kid is growing, I don't know how much longer I can keep him or her in here."

"You'd be surprised," Gram said. "A woman's body is an amazing thing."

"A woman's uterus can grow up to five hundred times its usual size during pregnancy," Skylar said.

I rubbed my belly. "Sounds about right."

"I miss it," Grace said. "But my pregnancy was so easy. I bet the next one won't be."

"You never know," Gram said. "You might be one of the lucky ones who has an easy time of it."

"The fact that you're willing to consider doing it again speaks volumes," I said. "And you've even been through the giving birth part."

"I've heard you forget the pain," Fiona said. "Otherwise no one would want to have more than one baby."

"I don't think you forget so much as you realize it's temporary and you can conquer it," Gram said. "And the end result is worth it."

"I'll be conquering the pain with the best cocktail of drugs they can give me," I said. "If I could do a few shots during early labor, I would."

Grace reached over and squeezed my hand. "You're one of the toughest women I know. You're going to be fine."

"Thanks, boo."

"Grace is right, Tiger," Gram said. "And you're going to be a great mother."

My breath caught in my throat. Had Gram just said I was going to be a great mother? Gram, the wisest, sweetest, most badass woman in the world? She thought I was going to be a great mom?

Blinking the tears back, I glanced away. "I don't know

about that. But if it takes a village, I have the best one. I suppose this kid has a chance."

"That's how it should be," Gram said. "None of us were meant to walk this path alone."

Fiona dabbed beneath her eyes. "I love this family so much. I don't know how I got so lucky."

"Me too," Skylar said.

"I guess I can admit I see the appeal in the Bailey men," I said, aiming for levity in an attempt to push aside the rush of emotion. "I thought you were all a little crazy. Although I'm just going to be a mom to a Bailey kid. It's not the same."

Gram met my eyes and there was gravity in her expression. But she didn't say anything—didn't argue with what I was implying.

"Really, *Tiger*?" Grace asked, emphasizing the word.

Gram's lips twitched in the hint of a smile.

"I have red hair. Tigers are orange." I shrugged. "Logan cycles through redhead nicknames like all his obnoxious versions of *bro*. Tiger isn't like Bear, or Sparrow, or Cricket."

Gram didn't comment. Just looked at me curiously.

"No?" Grace asked. Apparently she wasn't going to let this go. "You're the one who said Gram gives her grandsons' fated mates a nickname. She calls you Tiger. Don't you, Gram?"

I held up a finger before Gram could answer. "Only recently."

All eyes moved to Gram.

She took a sip of her iced tea—slowly, like we hadn't just put her on the spot. "These things aren't up to me."

What was that supposed to mean? A momentary hush settled over the table as if we were all waiting for her to explain. But apparently she'd decided to remain cryptic and mysterious.

Grace met my eyes. "I'm just going to say it. You and Logan are great together and he's totally in love with you."

In love with me? God, I wished.

Wait, did I?

I glanced away. "Now you're just being ridiculous."

"I'm not the one being ridiculous," she said. "But I'll give you a pass because you're pregnant and it's hard."

"She's right," Skylar said. "You guys are great together."

"And Logan is absolutely in love with you," Fiona added. "Just saying."

This conversation was starting to freak me out. It was treading too close to things my heart desperately wanted. Things I couldn't even think, because whenever I did, they made me ache with longing.

"Well, it turns out he's not all bad," I said, attempting to deflect. "I'm woman enough to admit when I'm wrong."

"That's very big of you," Grace said. I knew I wasn't fooling her. She could see right through me.

I could feel Gram's eyes on me, but a second later, she turned to Skylar. "How's the new book coming, Sparrow?"

I'd never been so grateful for a subject change.

Skylar's face lit up as she talked about her latest novel. Thankfully, the rest of the conversation stayed away from topics liable to make me have my millionth emotional breakdown of this pregnancy.

Eventually, our little get-together wound down. Grace needed to get home to Charlie, and Fiona and Skylar had things to do this afternoon.

We got up from our places at the table, but Gram put a hand on my arm.

"Wait here a minute, Tiger. I have something to show you."

Grace offered a little shrug, then gave me a big hug and

left. I hesitated near the table while the others left and Gram disappeared into another room.

She came back carrying a dark blue photo album and set it on the table. "I think this is the one."

I peered over her shoulder while she opened it and turned the pages. Most of the photos were of Logan and his brothers, around the time we'd all been in college. She flipped a few more pages and came to a spread with pictures of Grace's college graduation. I'd graduated at the same time, and Gram had a photo of me and Grace wearing our caps and gowns, standing in front of the Tilikum College sign.

She gently slipped the photo out of its place and handed it to me.

"Wow, look at us," I said.

"Beautiful girls."

Was this what she wanted to show me? I didn't understand. I flipped it over, not really sure what I was looking for. Gram's smooth cursive was on the back. The inscription read, *Tiger and Gracie Bear*.

I stared at it.

Tiger.

Questions ran through my mind, but I couldn't seem to get a single word out of my mouth. I just stared at the words on the back of the photo.

"I remember the first time we met," Gram said. "You were with Grace at her mom's house next door, and she brought you over here to introduce us. It was storming out that day and the two of you had raced across the grass to get out of the rain, but you still got soaked."

I felt a flash of remembrance. I could almost feel the water dripping from my hair. "You made us tea to warm up."

She nodded. "While you were still standing on the

porch, just after I opened the door, there was a flash of lightning off in the distance. It lit you up from behind. Then came the thunder, rolling across the sky with a low growl. And I thought, there's a tiger in our mountains now."

I looked up, meeting her eyes. "The first time you met me?"

"Indeed."

"That was so long ago. I've never heard you call me anything but Cara. Did I miss it?"

"No," she said, her tone matter-of-fact.

I handed the photo back to her and she tucked it in the photo album.

"But..." I trailed off.

"I can't show the bear where to make his den or tell the wolf who he should allow in his pack. The otter swims where he wants, and the raven soars as high as his wings will take him. Even a wise old owl can't force the world to bend to her will. But things usually happen as they're meant to, when the time is right. You just have to be patient." She patted my arm, then shut the photo album and picked it up. "Thanks for coming, Tiger. It was nice having you."

"Thanks for having me," I said, as if I were operating on autopilot.

Did this mean...

Were Logan and I...

Was it possible...

Fated mates. It was a fictional concept. I'd only used the term to make a point. And maybe *Tiger* just meant Gram was accepting me into the family as the mother of her great-grandchild.

But maybe it meant something else. And maybe I wanted it to.

36

LOGAN

*G*avin walked by and poked me in the side. "Hey, dad bod."

I shoved him away. "Shut up, jerk."

Mason and Levi stood nearby, snickering at me. The engine bay doors were wide open, letting in the warm evening air, and we'd just finished running gear checks.

"It's not an insult," Gavin said. "I bet Cara loves your dad bod."

"Do you give Asher this much shit?" I asked. "He's a dad."

"Hell no. Asher would kick my ass."

"And I won't?"

"You might try, but—"

I shut him up by throwing an arm around his neck and getting him in a solid headlock.

"Still think I won't kick your ass, baby bro?" I asked through gritted teeth, flexing hard to keep hold of him.

Gavin grunted, trying to break my grip.

I felt the distinct sensation of eyes on me. It reminded

me of being a kid, knowing I'd just gotten caught doing something that was going to get me into trouble.

Chief cleared his throat behind me.

I let Gavin go and tucked in my shirt where it had come loose.

"Boys," Chief said.

"Hey, Chief."

He just shook his head and walked on.

Gavin nudged me with his elbow. "Stop getting me in trouble with my future father-in-law."

"Stop calling me dad bod."

He put his hands up. "Fine, but body acceptance is healthy."

I laughed. "Oh my god, shut the fuck up."

Tones rang out and playtime was over. We sprang into action, hustling to gear up and move out. There'd been a car accident on the highway. The vehicle had struck a deer.

That wasn't good. A deer could total a car.

In minutes, we were on our way. Dispatch updated us as we headed out with an exact location and more details. Another driver had witnessed the accident and called 911. Vehicle passengers included an adult male, adult female, and a young child.

Fuck. A kid.

I stayed calm and focused as we drove, but a sick feeling rolled through my stomach.

Levi met my eyes and raised his eyebrows. *You gonna be okay?*

I nodded. *I can handle it.*

We got out onto the highway and drove to the scene with the ambulance just ahead of us. The unfortunate deer was still in the middle of the road. I felt bad for the poor thing, but my focus was the safety of the people. The front of the vehicle—a white, mid-sized SUV—was mangled. A second vehicle was parked nearby—the passersby who'd stopped to call 911.

The ambulance parked and the paramedics, Jenny and Derek, headed straight for the vehicle. Steve, the officer on duty, assigned tasks as we got off the engine. We got to work assessing the scene, checking for fluid or fuel leaks, and routing oncoming traffic around the accident site. Levi went to speak with the witnesses, who stood nearby.

The sound of crying caught my attention and I ran to the car. Jenny and Derek already had a gurney ready. The driver was awake and talking, but they'd clearly determined they needed to take him to the hospital.

"How's the kid?" I asked.

Jenny pulled him out of the backseat. He looked to be about a year and a half old, maybe two, with wispy blond hair. Although he was red-faced and crying, he didn't look injured.

"He was secure in his car seat," she said, handing the kid to me. "No injuries."

The little guy wailed louder and big tears ran down his round cheeks.

I held him close and rubbed gentle circles across his back. "It's okay, little brozinski. That must have been scary."

He let out another cry, but it wasn't quite as loud as the last one.

"I know." I eased him closer and he laid his head on my shoulder. "You're okay, buddy. You're okay."

I made sure we were out of the way of the rest of the crew and held him, rocking back and forth and rubbing his back. It only took a minute or two for him to calm down. I kept an eye on the parents. Both were responsive, which was a good sign, but both were being transferred to gurneys and bound for the emergency room.

When they loaded the mom into the ambulance, I followed, climbing in with them. The gurney fit on one side, leaving room for Jenny to maneuver and reach her equipment while she tended to her patient. I settled on the extra seat, holding the kid. Until someone higher up the continuum of care took charge of him, I was responsible. But as far as I was concerned, I was it for him until his parents or another family member could take him.

I wasn't letting him go.

"Is he okay?" the mom asked. Her face was drained of color, and although it was good to see her talking, my gut told me she was headed for emergency surgery.

"He's fine, ma'am," I said, holding him firmly against me. "I'll keep him safe."

Her eyes welled with tears. "Thank you."

"What's his name?"

"Brody."

I couldn't help but grin. "That's one of my favorite names."

That earned me a weak smile, although tears leaked from the corners of her eyes.

I rubbed Brody's back and let out a long breath. Adrenaline coursed through my veins and the fear in the mom's eyes didn't help. My kid hadn't even been born yet, but I understood that fear. She might have been afraid for herself, but more than anything, she was afraid for her child.

We arrived at the emergency department and I carried Brody out of the ambulance. The emergency crew was there to see to the mom. Fortunately, our little hospital was outstanding. She was in good hands.

Brody clung to me, his arms tight around my neck.

"Don't worry, little buddy. I've got you."

I took him inside and checked in with one of the nurses, letting them know I had charge of Brody. She took us back to a staff room. It was sparse but comfortable, with a couch, a few chairs, a TV on the wall with the sound turned off, and a vending machine.

Another nurse brought Brody's bag from the vehicle. Inside, I found a snack of crackers and juice. He let go of me long enough to sit in my lap and eat.

"There you go, Brody." I brushed his wispy hair off his forehead. "You've been a champion today."

His blue eyes met mine. He had cracker crumbs all over his face. Without saying a word—I didn't know if he was old enough to talk—he traced the TFD logo on my shirt.

"You like that?"

He nodded.

"Maybe you'll be a firefighter when you grow up, huh?"

He nodded again.

I liked this kid.

The hospital social worker came to check on him. His parents were both in surgery, but chances were good they'd pull through. They were visitors to the area—common this time of year. She'd contacted Brody's grandparents. They were on their way to get him, but lived several hours away. I assured her I had him. I didn't care how long I had to sit here with him; I was going to see this through.

After he finished his snack, I wiped up his face and changed his diaper. Asher had taught me how. Felt kind of proud that I managed it all on my own.

It helped that it was just wet.

His eyes looked heavy and I didn't blame him. It had been a rough day and it was probably past his bedtime. I settled in a chair and laid him on my chest with his head on my shoulder. I slowly rocked side to side and rubbed his back until I felt his breathing slow. I couldn't see his face, but it felt like he'd fallen asleep.

My heart beat in a normal rhythm, but I still felt amped. Something about holding this little guy during a moment of crisis was getting to me—stirring up feelings deep inside. My throat felt thick and my chest was heavy—and not from the weight of his little body resting on me.

I'd been through emotional calls before, but this was kind of messing me up.

Being Brody's safety net kept me focused. I wasn't the surgeon saving his mom's life or the nurses helping stitch his dad back together. But I could be his safe place tonight. Make sure he wasn't scared.

If it were my kid, I'd want someone to take care of him, too.

Brody slept like a rock for the next couple of hours. It felt like he was drooling on my shoulder, but I didn't care. I got the update that both parents were out of surgery and stable. I liked hearing that. Stable was good. Brody's grandparents were almost here. They were all going to be fine.

But the thrum of agitation inside me didn't ease up.

Finally, the social worker came back with Brody's grandparents. In a bit of a haze, I handed Brody off. Managed to acknowledge their thank yous and say goodbye to the sleepy-eyed little guy.

I felt the absence of his weight on my chest as I checked my phone. I had a message from Chief, telling me to call him when I transferred care of the child, no matter the time.

"Hey, Chief," I said when he answered the call.

"Are you still at the hospital?"

"Yeah."

"How's the little guy?"

"He's fine. I transferred him to his grandparents' care."

"Good. Do you need a ride home?"

"Back to the firehouse, yeah. I'm on until morning."

"No you're not," he said and I recognized his *don't argue with me* tone. "I'll come get you, but I'm taking you home. I need you to sleep this one off."

"Copy that, Chief."

I hung out for the few minutes it took Chief to get to the hospital. Normally I would have flirted with one of the night nurses, but that wasn't even on my radar anymore.

Chief didn't say much as he drove me home. Just asked me if I'd be okay before he dropped me off. I assured him I would. I just needed a good night's sleep.

Hopefully that was true. Because for some reason, I wasn't okay.

The porch lights were on, but the rest of the house was dark. Cara was probably asleep. I went in and shut the door quietly so I wouldn't wake her, then headed for the kitchen to get some water. I was both exhausted and amped, not sure if I'd be able to sleep, even though I needed it.

I didn't know what was wrong with me. This wasn't the first time I'd responded to a call where a child was involved. Brody was fine and so were his parents. We'd done our job —gotten them the medical attention they needed. He was so little, I doubted he'd even remember the night he slept on a firefighter's chest while his parents were in emergency surgery. He was with his family now. He'd be fine.

So why couldn't I stop shaking?

That had not been a worst-case scenario call. It was over, and all things considered, there had been a good outcome.

But I couldn't calm down.

"What are you doing, sneaking in here in the middle of the night?" Cara asked behind me. She flipped on the light.

Glancing over my shoulder, I blinked at the brightness.

"Did you think—" She stopped mid-sentence and her expression shifted to concern. "What's wrong? Why are you home early?"

I turned to face her. "Went on a call to a car accident on the highway. Family hit a deer." My voice sounded oddly monotone.

"Oh my god. That's my worst nightmare."

"The two adults needed emergency surgery but they were in stable condition when I left the hospital."

"Were there kids?"

I nodded. "One. Little boy. He was uninjured. Car seat."

She moved closer, approaching me slowly, and slid her hands up my chest. "So they're all okay?"

"They will be, yeah."

"Where's the little boy?"

"Grandparents arrived." I took a deep breath, trying to pull myself together. I didn't understand what was wrong with me. "I held him for a long time."

She moved her hands to the back of my neck and ran her fingers through my hair. "You were scared for him."

I didn't answer right away. Just let her massage my scalp.

"It was fucked-up," I said finally. "I got to the car and Jenny handed me this crying little boy. And I just kept thinking, holy shit, what would I do if it were our kid?"

The feel of her hands stroking the back of my head and neck started to take the edge off. But I still felt like a mess.

She brushed my hair off my forehead. "Come to bed."

I nodded. I was crashing hard, coming off hours of adrenaline. She took my hand and led me upstairs to her bedroom—our bedroom—and helped me undress.

We climbed into bed but instead of tucking herself against me, her back to my front, she laid on her side and cradled my head to her chest. My eyes closed and the tension in my body eased as she ran her fingers through my hair and kissed my head.

"Better?" she whispered.

"So much better."

And it was. Not just because I was nuzzled up against her tits, although that was one of my favorite places to be. Her soothing touch calmed my racing heart and eased my knotted muscles. The tension of that call—the fears that had bubbled to the surface—melted away. Within minutes, I relaxed.

I'd been on tough calls before, and in the past, I'd just slept them off. Maybe drank a little more than usual to blow off steam.

For whatever reason, this call had messed me up. But Cara's arms around me felt both soothing and secure. I didn't need anything else.

I only needed her.

That was some deep shit, but it didn't freak me out. I was smart enough to know she was good for me. I'd found a woman who could both challenge and take care of me. That had to be a rare thing.

And I never wanted to let her go.

37

LOGAN

*W*as there anything better than waking up with your girlfriend's boobs in your face? I couldn't think of anything. It was a great way to make a guy smile, especially after a rough day.

Cara was on her side, still cradling my head to her chest. One leg draped over mine, a substitute for the pillow she'd been sleeping with between her knees lately. Her tits were magnificent—pregnancy had done amazing things to her body—and I inhaled deeply, breathing her in. I could feel my brain light up, like I was an addict and she was my drug of choice.

Considering the state I'd been in when I'd come home last night, I felt great this morning. No adrenaline hangover. No lingering restlessness. I'd slept well, and now I was calm and refreshed.

It was her. She'd done that.

I'd always harbored some skepticism when my fellow firefighters talked about how much they loved going home to their wives. It wasn't that I didn't think they loved them. They probably did. But the thought of going home to the same woman after every shift for the rest of your life had seemed kind of boring. Where was the fun in that?

I got it now. I felt fucking amazing and it didn't have anything to do with sex. Yeah, her tits were nice—I nuzzled against them a little just to show how much I appreciated them—but that wasn't the point. That wasn't why I felt so good.

It was her.

Fortunately for me, I wasn't the most stubborn of the Bailey brothers, and I could admit I'd been wrong about her. I could also admit that Cara was good for me. Fucking crazy, but undeniably good for me.

What Gram had said when I'd told her Cara was having my kid came to mind. Something about how having a baby wasn't the worst thing that could happen to a man, even if it wasn't planned. And it might turn out to be the best thing.

Once again, Gram had called it.

Cara took a deep, slow breath. "What are you doing to my boobs?"

I kissed her right in the center of them. "Enjoying them."

She laughed softly, then shifted so she could stretch. "It's a miracle. I actually slept all night. Usually I have to get up to—ow."

I propped myself up on my elbow. "What's wrong?"

"The baby just kicked my bladder," she said, her voice straining.

She awkwardly rolled over and got up, then waddled into the bathroom, still wincing.

"If you pee in your underwear, just get naked," I called.

"Shut up, Logan."

"On second thought, get naked anyway."

She didn't reply.

I got up and used the other bathroom, then came back

to bed. I sent Chief a quick text to let him know I was fine and ready to come back to work on schedule—which wasn't for a couple of days, but I didn't want him to think he was down a guy.

Cara appeared in the doorway, still wearing her tank top and underwear.

"I thought I told you to get naked."

Heat flashed in her eyes and the corners of her lips turned up. "Are you trying to tell me what to do?"

"You bet your ass. Take your clothes off."

She hooked her thumbs under the waistband of her panties and slid them down, doing a good job of improvising when her belly got in the way of bending over. She finished by kicking them off.

"Naked," I said.

Her features betrayed a hint of self-consciousness as she glanced aside. "I know you like my boobs, but do you really want all this out in the open?" She gestured to her belly.

"Come here." I reached for her hand and drew her onto the bed. She curled up next to me, lying on her side, and I brushed her hair back from her face. "You're so beautiful. Your body is different, but you're still sexy as fuck. I love the way you look right now."

"Really?"

"Are you kidding? Even your pee waddle got me hard."

She smacked me gently. "I don't pee waddle."

"Yeah, you do. But it's adorable." I leaned in and kissed her.

"Thank you for not thinking I'm a disgusting blob. Because I feel like one."

I ran a hand over her belly and up to squeeze one of her tits. "You're a goddess. I can't get enough."

She moaned at my touch. "Careful. They said in the

baby class that nipple stimulation can induce labor. And it's too early to give this kid an eviction notice."

"Do you want me to stop?" I squeezed again.

"No."

"I didn't think so."

I helped her slip off her tank top so I could give her tits all the attention they deserved. I kneaded one side while I nuzzled and licked the other.

"God, that's not fair," she whimpered. "I'm so sensitive I could almost come like this."

Didn't I know it. I slid my hand between her thighs while I licked and sucked. She was swollen and wet.

"There's my beautiful pussy," I murmured as I stroked her. "This is mine. You hear me?"

"Yes."

I dipped two fingers inside her. "Whose pussy is this?"

"Yours."

"Tell me again, beautiful."

"It's yours, Logan. It's all yours."

My fingers went deeper and I sucked on her nipple. "Fuck yeah, it's mine."

Moaning, she leaned her head back as she rocked into my hand. I let her set the pace, fingering her in a steady rhythm while I nuzzled and licked her firm pink nipples.

It didn't take long before her walls pulsed around my fingers. Her body shuddered and her cries of pleasure were music to my ears.

I loved being the guy who got to make her do that.

Her orgasm subsided and I gently slid my fingers out.

"It's not fair that you're so good at that," she said, her voice still a little breathless.

"I think it works out pretty well for you."

"True." She grabbed my cock and gave me a firm stroke.

I groaned. Fuck, that felt good. "On your knees."

With a slight grin, she complied, getting on her hands and knees and arching her back while I positioned myself behind her. She glanced back at me, all that red hair draping over her shoulders. I had a flash of our first time; what we'd thought was a drunken mistake.

Turned out, it had been anything but.

I grabbed her hips and pressed my erection against her. She arched harder, needing more. One orgasm was never enough. My greedy girl needed me to make her come again.

I was happy to comply.

With a slow thrust, I slid inside her. I held there, wrapped in her heat, and groaned. When I told her I couldn't get enough, I meant it. This was everything.

She was everything.

Holding her hips, I drew out, then pushed in again. Watched my hard, glistening cock slide through her wetness. I moved slowly, savoring the feel of her. Growling with each long thrust.

"I love this pussy so much."

"Then fuck it harder."

With a grin, I readjusted my grip on her hips and drove in hard. Her answering moan amped me up, making my heartbeat quicken and my blood run hot. I gave her what she needed, fucking her harder. Faster. Heat and pressure built as my muscles flexed and my hips jerked.

"Is that what you need, baby?" I thrust in again. Hard. "You need to get fucked?"

"Yes," she breathed. "Harder."

"My pleasure," I growled, plunging in and out.

She clenched tight around me as I pounded her relentlessly. I groaned at the first pulse of her orgasm, my eyes rolling back. Holy shit. She felt so fucking good.

I rode the brink of climax while she came again, my thrusts hard and rough. She cried out in pleasure and it was all too much. I lost control, exploding inside her.

My cock throbbed, over and over, as I drove in and out. She looked over her shoulder, biting her lip while she watched me come.

I finished and slid out, breathing hard. Cara rolled off the bed and got up to use the bathroom again. But unlike the early days, when I'd been mostly a means to an orgasm to her, she came back to bed.

The difference wasn't lost on me.

Neither was the lack of fighting. Sometimes we still got off on riling each other up. I spanked her ass and pulled her hair and finished with fresh scratches on my chest and down my back.

But not always. Sometimes, it was like this. Hard and satisfying, but with a tenderness that went beyond fucking for pleasure.

It was amazing. I'd never known what I was missing.

Gathering her in my arms, I held her close. Kissed her forehead and inhaled her scent.

I loved her.

Did she love me back? Was this thing we'd built going to last? I didn't know.

But for now, she was mine.

38

CARA

The baby still loved the food at the Caboose. I didn't know what it was about this restaurant, but it was the one place in town that always smelled good. I'd gone through some serious ups and downs with food over the course of this pregnancy, but meatloaf from the Caboose had been a constant.

Logan and I walked in and I was immediately grateful that air conditioning existed. It was almost fall, but the weather was still full-on summer, which for this pregnant girl meant I was always too hot.

The bar was fairly busy with a few small groups of people talking and laughing. A couple played pool, the balls clacking together. We found a table on the restaurant side, which was quieter. A minute later, my dad arrived.

Since showing up in town on my birthday, he'd been back a few times to visit. This time, I'd reached out and invited him to have dinner. We'd offered to come to him, but he'd insisted on coming to Tilikum so I wouldn't have to make the drive. I still had a lot of mixed feelings about my father, but it did mean something that he was trying.

So was I.

He took a seat and we made small talk until the server came to take our orders. Logan had discovered he and my dad had a few things in common, including a love of classic cars. They chatted about their favorite models while we ate. I was content to let them talk while I enjoyed my meatloaf.

The meal wound down and I decided it was time for me to get some things out in the open.

"Can we talk about what this means? You coming here and spending time with us?" My questions were out of the blue, but I didn't see the point in beating around the bush. "Is this going to continue?"

Dad put his fork down. "Yes, I want it to continue. And I'd like to meet my grandchild. If you're willing."

That was the real question. Was I willing to let him meet my baby? Perhaps even be a part of his or her life? A part of me liked that idea. Growing up, I'd missed my father. Could I give my baby something I hadn't had?

But would he actually stick around?

I met his eyes. "I don't know if I'm willing. I'll give you credit where credit is due. You're here now. But I still don't know where you were when I was little. I get that my mother made things complicated. I know what she's like. But I can't let someone in this kid's life who's just going to disappear."

"Your mother didn't just make things complicated. She made things impossible."

"So impossible that the first time I remember meeting you is when I turned thirty?"

He watched me for a long moment. "You don't remember any of it, do you? No, I guess you wouldn't. You were so young."

"Remember what?"

"When you were three, I took you. After they got you back, I wasn't allowed anywhere near you."

"What?"

Logan put a hand on my leg, his touch reassuring.

"This is a lot to explain, especially if she never told you any of it." He took a deep breath. "Let me start at the beginning. Your mother and I met at a diner. I wasn't her type, and she wasn't mine, but there were sparks. We started dating but as I told you before, her parents disapproved. Strongly. And what happens when you tell two eighteen-year-olds they can't be together?"

"They sneak around and have sex in the backseat of his car?" Logan asked.

Dad's mouth hooked in a grin. "Something like that. Things got ugly when Layla found out she was pregnant. Her parents wanted me gone. So did she. I admit, I didn't know your mom well. We hadn't been together long and I was pretty blindsided when her true colors started to show."

Logan winced.

"Your grandparents had plenty of money, so they didn't want me to give your mom child support. They just wanted me out of the picture and they acted like I'd scored a get out of jail free card. But you were my daughter. I didn't want to walk away."

"Then why did you?" I asked.

"I stayed in your life as much as she'd let me. At first, I had to fight to see you, but she'd always give in and let me come over. Eventually we got into a routine. She wouldn't let me take you overnight, but I could come pick you up and spend time with you about once a week without it being a problem.

"But as time went on, I started to worry about you. Your mom carted you around to clubs and parties and would leave you with bartenders or the catering staff. Once I picked you up and you had an ear infection. Your mom hadn't taken you to the doctor because she thought you were just throwing a tantrum."

I swallowed hard. I'd flippantly told people that my childhood had been awful more times than I could count. But hearing about it from his perspective made my stomach turn over.

"After the ear infection incident, I couldn't stand aside and let you be neglected anymore. I filed for sole custody. Of course, your mom took that as a declaration of war. She stopped letting me see you, even for short visits at her place. One day I came over to try to visit, even though she'd been turning me away, and she'd moved. I didn't even know where you were."

"Oh my god," I said.

"I did everything I could to get custody of you legally. But in the end, your grandparents had so much money and so much influence, I couldn't beat them. My lawyer told me to consider myself lucky that in the end, I had any visitation with you at all. They'd tried their hardest to prevent me from ever seeing you again."

"But you still had some visitation?" I asked.

"I did." He paused for a moment and ran a hand over his beard. "And one day, instead of bringing you home, I left with you."

I gaped at him. How could I have no memory of this?

"It was just after your third birthday. I didn't exactly plan to kidnap my own daughter, but when it was time to take you home that evening, I found myself driving out of L.A."

"Where did you take me?"

"We headed east and stopped in a little town in Nevada. We lived there quite happily for several months before your grandparents tracked us down. And before you think I'm a complete monster, I sent your mom letters with pictures so she'd know you were okay. I'd mail them to my parents and they'd forward them to her. But in the end, the law caught up with me. It didn't matter that I had good reason to do it; it was still kidnapping."

"And you weren't allowed to see me after that."

He shook his head. "No. And to be fair, I didn't try. The custody case ruined me financially and losing you the way I did nearly broke me. Maybe I was wrong for taking you. All I wanted was to protect you. But if I'm being honest, my only regret is that I failed."

"Why didn't you ever tell me?"

"When you became an adult and I could finally reach out, I had no idea what you knew or what you thought of me. Our first interaction when you were eighteen didn't exactly go well."

He was right about that. The first time he'd called, I'd yelled at him and hung up. Dramatically. He'd tried again a few months later, and that time, we'd had an actual conversation. I'd agreed that we could stay in touch, but I'd still kept him at a distance.

"After that, I wasn't sure how to approach things with you," he continued.

"You knew how crazy my mother was and you thought I might be just like her."

"That's one way to put it. Like I told you before, I thought the best thing to do would be to let you come to me. If you wanted me in your life, you'd let me know. I tried to make sure you always knew I was available."

"Which is why you sent me birthday cards."

"Yeah. It wasn't enough. I realize that. But that leads me to today. That's why I'm here now."

"I wish I'd known," I said, and Logan squeezed my leg under the table. "She convinced me you didn't care."

"Cara, I'm so sorry you had to grow up the way you did. It's not enough for me to say I tried. I did try, but I should have done more. I should have come back and fought for you again, somehow. I'm sorry I didn't do enough and I'm sorry it took me this long to show up at your door."

My throat felt thick and my eyes misted over, but unlike earlier in my pregnancy, I didn't feel like I was going to burst into uncontrollable tears.

"I need to know that you'll be around," I said, doing my best to keep my voice steady. "That you'll show up for holidays and birthday parties and do whatever normal grandparents are supposed to do."

"I promise you I will. I'll be there as often as I'm welcome."

I turned to Logan. This wasn't just my decision. "What do you think? Should he be a grandpa to our kid?"

"Yes." He leaned in and kissed my forehead, then turned to my dad. "But let me be clear. I think you're a stand-up guy, but if I'm wrong and you hurt my girl or our kid, you're done."

Dad nodded. "That's fair."

I turned back to my father. "Thank you, Dad."

His eyes shone with unshed tears and he reached over to squeeze my hand. "Thank *you*, Cara. I won't let you down."

Maybe it was crazy, but I believed him.

We finished up and paid the bill. Logan seemed to realize without me saying a word that I needed to get out of there. I had a lot to process. We said goodbye to my dad and Logan led me outside.

"What do you need?" he asked, rubbing circles across my back.

"Ice cream," I said without hesitation.

"I like it. Do you want to walk or drive?"

The air had started to cool as the sun went down, and birds chirped. It was a nice evening.

"Let's walk."

He offered his arm and I tucked my hand in the crook of his elbow. The Zany Zebra wasn't far, and they had the best ice cream in town. Even my very pregnant self could make it.

I wondered if they still had huckleberry. The baby needed huckleberry ice cream.

Logan made a low noise in his throat and I glanced up the sidewalk. Josiah and Zachary Haven walked toward us. A flash of anger raced through my veins and I tightened my grip on Logan's arm.

Those assholes.

I thought they might cross the street to avoid us, but they kept coming and stopped, blocking the sidewalk.

"Bailey," Josiah said, and it was hard to tell if he meant it as a greeting or an insult.

"What the fuck do you want?" Logan asked.

"You should talk some sense into your gram," he said. "I'm not the bad guy here. We're trying to offer her a way out."

I tried to jerk forward, but Logan's arm flexed, hard as iron, holding me back.

"I want to claw his face off," I said. "Please let me claw his face off."

Josiah's eyes flicked to me, then back to Logan. Zachary just looked amused.

Dicks.

"You're not the bad guy?" Logan asked. "You're literally trying to take advantage of an old lady."

"We're not trying to take advantage of her."

"Seriously? Word gets out that she's having financial problems and you're right there to put pressure on her to sell. I'm sure you only have her best interests at heart."

"This could work out for everyone if your goddamn family would just listen."

"She's not selling," I said. "I don't give a fuck what we have to do or how many mountains we have to move. It's not going to happen. That's her home."

I glared at Josiah, wishing I could burn a hole through his head. Zachary crossed his arms casually, like he was bored by the whole thing. I turned my stare on him and he looked away.

I wanted to gouge out their eyes with my fingernails. But the tension in Logan's arm didn't release and I knew he wouldn't let me anywhere near them.

Josiah let out a heavy sigh, as if Logan was the one being unreasonable. "Look, she can sell to us or eventually her property will go to auction. At least this way, she'd have some control over the process."

"You're crazy if you think you'll ever get your hands on her land," Logan said.

"This isn't personal."

"Like hell it's not. Everything between us is personal, asshole."

For a second, it looked like Josiah might lunge at Logan. His hands clenched into fists and Logan took a subtle step, as if he were ready to put me behind him.

But Josiah's back straightened and his fists opened. "Do the smart thing, Bailey. Stay out of our way."

"Is that a threat?" Logan asked.

"Yeah," Zachary said. "It's a fucking threat."

Josiah glanced at his brother, then they turned around and went back the way they'd come.

"I'll ruin them both," I said between gritted teeth. "I want to take their whole family down."

"Easy, Tiger," Logan said. "Zachary Haven's full of shit. And they can put pressure on Gram all they want. We're not letting anything happen to her."

I glared at their backs. Damn right we weren't letting anything happen to Gram. Not if I had anything to say about it.

39

LOGAN

*A*nnoyance at the run-in with Josiah and Zachary stayed with me even after we got Cara's ice cream and came home. I was pissed that this was happening. Pissed that Gram was in trouble and we hadn't been able to fix it. And pissed that the fucking Havens were trying to take advantage of the situation.

Maybe I should have let Cara loose on them.

She sat on one end of the couch with her feet in my lap. I absently rubbed one of them, still brooding. I'd texted my brothers to tell them what Josiah and Zachary had said. They were all just as pissed as I was.

We needed a solution.

Maybe it was stupid, but I kept thinking about the Montgomery treasure. I wondered if there was anything else out at the murder cabin. I'd seen that squirrel carving somewhere.

The fact that the symbol was a squirrel made me wonder if it was all a big prank. Because seriously, a squirrel? What the fuck was that about?

But this was Tilikum.

I'd have to convince Levi to go out there with me to check it out. Cara would probably go if I asked her, but the road was bumpy as hell. She was uncomfortable enough as it was. I didn't want to put her through that.

I glanced over at her. The soft lamplight made her skin glow and her red hair shine. My badass tiger.

"What?" she asked.

"You're beautiful."

Her eyes moved away and she pulled her feet out of my lap.

"What's wrong?" I asked.

She didn't answer. Just shook her head.

"Thinking about your dad?"

"Yes, but..."

"But what?"

She got up and walked over to the window. "It wasn't exactly easy to hear what he told me today, but none of it surprised me. I knew she neglected me, and of course she'd make his life miserable."

"It's pretty crazy that he took you like that."

"My life would have been so different if he'd been able to keep me. I can't stop wondering, how much of who I am is because of her?"

"Your life would have been very different. Maybe it would have been better. Or maybe it would have been worse in ways you can't see. But who you are isn't all about your mom."

Crossing her arms, she shifted so her back was to me. It was a subtle movement, but it spoke louder than anything she was saying. Something was wrong.

"Talk to me, Tiger."

"I'm just trying to keep from going crazy Cara on you."

"Why? What's bothering you?"

"I don't know."

"Do you really not know, or is it just hard to talk about it?"

"Why do you do that?" She spun around. "How can you be the same Logan Bailey who drove me so crazy and yet you're so calm and fucking reasonable when I feel like I'm ready to burst apart for no reason?"

"What do you want me to do?"

"I don't know," she said, her voice rising. "Look at me. I'm weeks away from having a baby. Me, Logan. The daughter of a woman who wouldn't take her kid to the doctor because she thought an ear infection was a behavioral problem."

"You're not her."

"No, I'm not, but she raised me. My dad wasn't making stuff up. I really did grow up going to clubs and parties. My first babysitters were fucking bartenders. My mom has a picture of me sitting on some actor's lap, holding his cigarette for him. I was like five. But in a few weeks, they're going to hand me a baby and send me on my way, expecting me to raise it like a normal human?"

"Not just you. Us. You don't have to do this alone."

"But what if I do?"

"What the fuck is that supposed to mean?"

"How long do you really think this is going to last?"

My brow furrowed. "What? Us?"

"Yes, us."

My hackles rose and I clenched my fists in frustration. "What the fuck, Cara? What do I have to do to make you trust me?"

"We both know you're not the problem."

I stood. "Then what's the fucking problem?"

She didn't answer right away. Just turned back to the

window and swiped beneath her eyes, as if she could hide the fact that she was on the verge of crying. She said she was trying not to go crazy Cara on me, and here I was, poking at her. But I had to. She needed to know she couldn't push me away.

Hell, maybe I was the most stubborn of my brothers.

"I see what you're doing," I said. "It won't work."

"What am I doing?"

"Trying to push me out. Don't you get it? You can't. I'm already in."

She turned and met my eyes. Hers glistened with unshed tears, and the vulnerability in her expression almost undid me.

"I'm trying," she whispered. "I really am. And I do trust you. I just don't trust myself."

"Why?"

"When I tell you I'm too much, you always say I'm not. But how long will it be before I am? Before it's one argument, one outburst too many? And it won't even be your fault. It'll be my fault. Again."

"Again? What are you talking about?"

She was quiet for a moment. I wanted to gather her in my arms, but I knew better. There was something she needed to get out, and I needed to let her do it on her terms.

But I wasn't backing down. I'd meant what I said. I was in, and I wasn't going anywhere.

"It's my fault we hated each other," she said finally.

"What?"

"Do you remember the first time we met?"

"Of course I do. You'd just been hit by a drunk driver. How could I forget?"

I'd been a volunteer at the time—still in college. A guy had sideswiped her out on the highway and I'd been among the first to respond. They'd both gotten lucky. No injuries. But she'd been understandably shaken up.

"I saw you on campus a few days later," she said. "You invited me to lunch and you told me you'd been thinking about me. Wondering if I was okay."

"I was worried about you."

"You were just..." She trailed off. "You were so good. You were funny and hot and so goddamn heroic. I sat there talking to you and I thought, oh my god, this is the kind of guy I could actually..."

I stayed quiet, waiting for her to continue.

"It scared the shit out of me," she said. "*You* scared the shit out of me. Because at that point in my life, every time I thought I had something good, the bottom dropped out. Every guy I dated, every friendship I had, every time I thought my mom was getting better. And there you were, this hot firefighter who was just... everything. But I convinced myself you'd just screw me over like everyone else. I didn't want to wait for you to hurt me, so I sabotaged it before we even had a chance."

"Is that why you seemed like a different person the next time I saw you?"

She nodded. "I was a total bitch to you. In my defense, I was not in a good place at the time. I'd just moved here, it was before Grace and I became friends, and I've had a lot of therapy since then. That's not an excuse; it's just the truth. I was a lot more messed up than I am now. I thought what I was doing made perfect sense."

"You pushed me away so I couldn't hurt you."

"Exactly. I figured you'd just move on. But you didn't. You doubled down, and the next time we saw each other, you fired right back. So I just convinced myself I hated you anyway."

A part of me wanted to be angry at her. I remembered how she'd blown me off. It had been some serious Jekyll and Hyde shit. I'd thought she was crazy. But she was right: I'd retaliated by being a dick right back. I certainly hadn't given her any reasons to like me.

Except I wasn't angry. I understood her now. She was always waiting for the other shoe to drop. Because, for her, it always did.

Not this time.

I grabbed her shoulders and turned her so she was facing me, then slid my fingers into her hair, tilting her face up. "I need you to shut up and listen to me right now."

Her lips parted, but she didn't say anything.

"I love you. I love you in all your batshit crazy glory. I love you when you're pissed off and slamming shit around and I love you when you're massaging my head and letting me snuggle your tits. You don't have to push me away, because I'm not going to be the next person who fails you. I'll never hurt you and I'll never leave you because you're mine."

Her eyes widened and her mouth moved like she was about to reply, but I cut her off. I wasn't finished.

"I want to fucking marry you, Cara. Is that clear enough? I want to get married and raise this kid together. I want to wake up next to you every goddamn morning for the rest of my life."

"You want to marry me?"

"Yes, I want to marry you. I want to be a family."

My heart thumped furiously in my chest and a hint of fear swept through me. I'd just put it all on the line. Bared my soul to her. And I wasn't quite sure what she was going to say.

"I love you too," she said, her words tumbling out in a

rush. "I love you so much. I'm sorry I ruined everything when we first met. I never hated you."

I held her face and leaned down to kiss her. "I only hated that it wasn't me who was with you."

"I hated it when you dated someone else."

I kissed her again. "I hated knowing anyone else touched you."

"I love you." She kept trying to talk between kisses. "You drive me crazy, but I love you so much."

"You drive me crazy, too. I fucking love it. But you need to answer me."

"Answer what?"

I stopped kissing her and looked deep into her eyes. "Will you marry me? Don't tell me you're not wife material. I've heard you say that bullshit before. Let it go. This isn't about your shitty childhood or the sad parts of mine. This is you and me, right here, right now. I love you and I want to spend the rest of my life with you. That's all that matters to me."

"Yes, I'll marry you." Tears ran down her cheeks and she seemed to be having a hard time talking. "I'll be your wife and we'll have this baby and I'll try not to make you hate me ever again."

I kissed her, smiling against her mouth. "Tiger, I never hated you. And I never will."

That was the truth. We were a family. And Cara was mine.

40

CARA

*T*he baby's foot—or elbow or maybe knee; I really didn't know—poked me as I drove down the highway toward Echo Creek. I rubbed the spot absently. It didn't hurt so much as feel strange. Of course, the fact that there was an entire person inside me was weird.

Not for the first time, I wondered what he or she looked like. And whether it was a boy or a girl. My instincts had always said boy, although I had no idea if my instincts were reliable. I'd find out soon. I was less than three weeks from my due date.

But I wasn't anxious about it anymore. For the first time in a very long time, I wasn't anxious about anything. I was nervous at the prospect of giving birth—who could blame me—but even that didn't have me knotted up with tension.

Everything was going to be fine.

An unusual sense of serenity had overtaken me ever since Logan had asked me to marry him. I'd never thought I'd want to get married. I'd been rather against it, to be honest. But of course I was going to marry Logan, and not because we were having a baby together. He'd said it. I was his. And he was mine. It was as simple as that.

We were a family.

Logan and I were going to create the family neither of us had experienced as children. Knowing that—truly believing that he and I were as solid as two people could be—had eased every one of my fears. Parenting wasn't going to be easy. Marriage wouldn't be either. But I was no longer so afraid of failure—or betrayal—that I felt the need to push him away or avoid the attachments I'd always craved.

I could let him love me. And I could love him right back.

Even when he drove me crazy.

Maybe especially when he drove me crazy.

My back had been bothering me more than usual today. I shifted in my seat, trying to get comfortable. Rain beat against the windshield, so I turned on the wipers, then pressed the button to connect my phone's Bluetooth and started my playlist.

Logan had gone off somewhere with Levi today. Levi had picked him up, so I'd taken Logan's Explorer on my errand. I was getting a rocking chair for the nursery from a shop in Echo Creek, a town about thirty minutes outside Tilikum. I'd found a great deal on this one—look at me being responsible with money—and the people at the shop had assured me they could load it in the back. I wouldn't have to lift a finger. Logan and Levi would bring it inside and set it up in the nursery when they got back.

Grace had been planning to go with me—we would have made an afternoon out of it—but Charlie was teething and she hadn't slept much the previous night. I didn't wish a sleepless night on her, but it was a tiny bit reassuring to know Charlie was a real baby who actually cried sometimes.

He was always so happy, I figured he was setting me up for a shock when my kid was born.

I missed my boo, but I didn't mind. This was our life now. She was blissfully happy with a husband and a baby. And soon I would be, too.

Thinking about husbands made me think about weddings as I sped down the winding mountain highway. What kind of wedding did I want? Did I want a wedding at all? Logan had been ready to go down to city hall right then and there. He'd said we could do the legal part whenever we wanted and just throw a party with everyone to celebrate. But if I wanted a big wedding, he was down for that too.

I had to admit, I liked his idea. I didn't particularly want a wedding. I just wanted to marry Logan.

Plus, I wasn't stuffing myself into a wedding dress with this belly. Not that I was worried about getting married before the baby was born. Anyone who judged me for having a baby when I wasn't married could suck my dick.

My phone rang, so I hit the button on the steering wheel to answer through the Bluetooth. It was Grace.

"Hi, my fluffy little lamb. Is Charlie finally asleep?"

"Yes, thank God. Poor little guy was miserable."

"Shouldn't you be sleeping too?"

"I'm lying down but I can't sleep. Plus I miss you, so I figured I'd call."

"Aw, I miss you too."

"Are you on the road?"

"Yeah, I left a few minutes ago."

"You should stop by the winery when you get into town."

I adjusted my grip on the steering wheel. "Boo, I'm pregnant. I can't drink."

She laughed. "I know. But it's a great place for a wedding. Just saying."

"It is a beautiful place. But be honest. Would you be horribly disappointed if we didn't have a traditional wedding?"

"Not at all. You guys should do what makes you happy. I'm just excited that you stopped fighting it and you're together."

"Don't you mean you're excited we stopped fighting?"

"That too."

"God, Grace, am I really going to be a Bailey?"

"You really are."

"How did that happen?"

"It was always meant to be, sweetie."

"For both of us, apparently. Cara Bailey. Is it weird that I like that more than Miles? Because I really liked Cara Miles. I thought our platonic non-lesbian sexless marriage idea was pretty brilliant. But then these men got involved."

"Cara Bailey is the epitome of name perfection. Now you just have to figure out what to name the baby."

"Don't remind me. Logan's latest suggestion was Broseph if it's a boy. I don't even know if he was kidding."

"Probably not."

I did have an idea for a name if we had a boy, but I hadn't mentioned it to Logan yet. I was still letting it swirl around my mind, trying to decide how I felt about it.

"If it's a girl, we're in even more trouble. Neither of us can find a name we like, let alone one we both like."

"Have you asked Gram what she thinks you're having? Because she's usually right."

"You know, I haven't. Maybe I'll stop by her place on my way home."

"That's a great idea. I'm sure she'd love to see you anyway."

I didn't mention that I was close to exacting some

sweet revenge on the accountant who'd screwed Gram over. What my pretty peacock didn't know wouldn't hurt her.

And if she didn't know, she couldn't stop me.

"I'll call her after I pick up the rocking chair. By the way, do you need anything while I'm out there?"

"Thanks, but I don't think so. I'm going to visit my family at the winery next week. We're getting all the cousins together."

"Dinners with the Miles family must be chaos now with all those kids."

"There are so many kids," she said with a laugh. "But it's amazing. And just think, in a few years, that's how it's going to be at Gram's."

"You aren't wrong."

Evan and Fiona and Gavin and Skylar weren't having kids yet—*yet* being the operative word. We all knew they would. And if all four couples became parents, particularly of multiple kids, the Bailey clan was going to multiply quickly. And who knew, maybe Levi would settle down eventually and add to the Bailey baby boom.

It made me all the more determined to help Gram keep her land. I was still angry that I didn't have the funds to make this problem go away. But I was doing everything I could to help her.

"I should let you go," Grace said. "I'm going to close my eyes and hope Charlie takes a good nap."

"Get some rest. Love you."

"Love you, too."

I hit the button to end the call. Not two seconds later, Logan's number lit up the screen.

"Hi."

"Hi, beautiful. Are you on the road?"

The baby kicked again. I shifted in my seat, trying to get comfortable. My back was killing me. "Yep. What's up?"

"Nothing. I just wanted to hear your voice."

"Clingy much? Are we really turning into that couple?"

He laughed and the low rumble sent a pleasant tingle down my spine. "We're totally that couple. I predict a Christmas card with matching pajamas."

I gasped. "You take that back."

"The baby, too. And we'll have reindeer ears and red noses."

"You would never."

"Consider them ordered."

"Fine, but we have to pose out in the snow. My mother will hate it."

"Done. Listen, my phone doesn't have a great signal out here, but call me when you're on your way home."

"I'm fine. It's Echo Creek, not Mars."

"So? Tell Grace to make sure you call."

"Grace couldn't make it. She pulled an all-nighter with Charlie, so she's home getting some rest."

"You're by yourself?"

I laughed. "Don't sound so alarmed. I'm perfectly capable of driving one town away and finding my way home again."

"I know you are, but you're my girl and you're carrying my baby, and I worry about you when I'm not there."

That made me smile. I teased him about it, but I loved his protective streak. "Okay. I'll call you when I'm on my way home."

"Good. Love you, Tiger."

"Love you, too." I ended the call.

And couldn't stop smiling.

Just wanted to hear my voice. How dumb was that?

But I loved it.

A flash of movement across the road broke me out of my thoughts. It happened so fast, I barely had time to react. A deer leapt over the guardrail and stopped dead in front of me.

My hands tightened around the steering wheel as I hit the brakes.

But I didn't slow down.

Instinctively, I swerved to avoid the animal, pumping the brakes. It was like they weren't there.

The deer didn't move and I narrowly missed hitting it. The tires skidded on the rain-soaked pavement. I was going too fast, but I had no way to slow down, and the front of the SUV clipped the guardrail on the other side of the highway.

For a second, I didn't know what was happening. Everything spun in a sickening whirlwind. Metal crunched and scraped as the world whipped by and I was knocked around inside the cab.

And all I could think about was my baby.

Please, please don't let the baby get hurt. Please.

I finally came to a stop and silence rushed in. Where was I? I was shaky and disoriented, my heart racing. Had I gone over the embankment?

It took me a few seconds to make sense of what had just happened. The SUV had gone down a hill and the windshield was cracked. I didn't feel any pain, but the amount of adrenaline coursing through my veins meant I might not feel any injuries yet.

But that wasn't my biggest concern.

The baby.

I clutched my belly. The baby wasn't moving.

Oh no. No, no, please no.

My hands shook as I reached for my phone and dialed 911.

The dispatcher answered.

"I was just in an accident," I said, my voice trembling with fear. I held my belly, desperate to feel the baby move. "Please help me. I'm pregnant."

41

LOGAN

*L*evi's SUV bounced along the dirt road as we climbed the hill to the murder cabin. This was probably a waste of time, but after talking to Harvey, I'd kept thinking about that squirrel engraving. He'd found one that matched the necklace on an old chest in the Haven House. Unfortunately, that was gone. But I remembered there being an old chest in the cabin by the hot springs, and it might have had a squirrel design on it.

Or maybe I was just imagining things because we were running out of time to come up with the money to save Gram's land. Cara had bought us time—and god, I loved her for it—but we still needed to come up with a lot of damn money.

And even if there was a squirrel on the chest, I wasn't sure what that would mean. It wasn't much of a lead, but it was something. Seemed like it was worth a bumpy drive to figure out. Levi had agreed, so there we were.

We hit a particularly deep pothole and water splashed onto the window. I'd been hoping the rain would let up, but so far it looked like things were going to be soggy. Hopefully the cabin roof was still watertight.

All the jostling made me glad I hadn't brought Cara. The closer she got to her due date, the more her back and hips hurt. This drive would have been awful. I didn't love that she was going to Echo Creek by herself—I really wished Grace would have been able to go with her—but there wasn't anything I could do about it now. Besides, try telling her stubborn ass she couldn't do something. That never ended well.

But I still worried about her.

Although I hadn't put an actual ring on her finger, we'd made our engagement official by announcing it at Tuesday night dinner at Gram's. I hadn't been expecting the uproar, with my brothers giving me bear hugs and the girls getting all teary-eyed. Dinner had turned into an impromptu engagement party—which was to say, we built a bonfire in the back, toasted with a bottle of champagne Gram randomly had in her fridge, and ate pie for dessert.

It was happening. Logan Bailey was marrying Cara Goulding.

Sometimes life was fucking weird.

And awesome.

The cabin came into view and Levi stopped. The trees were thicker here, but the ground was muddy as shit. It was a hell of a lot more fun to come out here on a nice day for a dip in the hot spring. Or to film a prank movie. That had been a blast.

My feet squelched in the soft, wet ground and the misty rain beaded on my coat. "This weather sucks."

"No shit," Levi said. "I still don't know what you think you're going to find out here. Harvey's been looking for years. He knows about this place. Don't you think he would have found something?"

"Probably. But we don't exactly have any other leads. Maybe a fresh look will turn up something."

"Are you sure we aren't being pranked?"

"Nope. This could definitely be a prank."

He scowled. "Great."

"Hey brodentical, at least we're in this together."

He didn't look thrilled. But he was here, so that was something.

The cabin was in rough shape, with creaky stairs leading up to the front door. There were gaps in the weathered, graying boards and the covered porch sagged to one side. The murder cabin decor was gone, but the place was creepy even without the props I'd helped Gavin set up.

We went inside and surprisingly, it was completely dry. The roof was holding. A rickety table and chairs collected dust in the middle of the room and an old chest sat against one wall. But otherwise, it was empty.

"Is that the chest?" Levi asked.

I crouched in front of it and brushed dust off the lid. "No squirrel on the top."

"On the sides or back, maybe?"

"I don't see anything. Damn."

The latch was unlocked, so I lifted the lid. The skeleton arm we'd stuck in there to creep the place up was still inside. But otherwise, it was empty.

"Do you want to check the bottom?" Levi asked.

"Might as well."

We dragged the chest farther away from the wall and got a grip on the bottom to tip it backward. But a piece seemed loose on my side.

"Hold on." I ran my hand along the bottom on the side of the chest. "I think this piece might come off."

"Or it's broken."

I got a better grip, then wiggled it until it broke free. "It's a drawer."

"No shit?"

"It's like the whole thing has a false bottom."

I eased the drawer out carefully. It was almost as wide as the chest itself and about half as deep.

"You've got to be fucking kidding me," Levi said.

My thoughts exactly. Because carved on the bottom of the drawer was a motherfucking squirrel.

Unlike the main part of the chest, the drawer wasn't empty. Sitting toward the back was an antique key. It wasn't very big, just a few inches long, with a big ring at the top.

"What do you think this is for?" I picked up the key—it was surprisingly heavy—and held it up.

"The chest?"

"Looks too big."

The chest had an old lock, but I was right. The key didn't fit.

"So, not the chest," he said.

I stood, holding the key in the palm of my hand. "I guess this could mean something, but I have no idea how the fuck to figure out what this opens. If anything."

"I don't know, but let's take a picture of the drawer." He pulled his phone out of his pocket. "Why do I have like ten texts? Oh, shit. Logan, check your phone."

"What's wrong?" I pulled mine out, but I didn't have a signal. I stuffed the key in my pocket and went outside. As soon as my feet hit the porch, texts and voicemails flooded my phone.

Asher: *Where are you?*

Gavin: *Dude, answer your phone.*
Evan: *Did anyone get a hold of you yet?*
Grace: *They're taking Cara to the ER.*
Oh fuck.

Levi was already running for his SUV. I sprinted and climbed in the passenger seat, still scrolling through my messages, trying to figure out what was happening.

Cara had been in an accident. She'd called 911 and was being taken to the hospital.

I didn't say a word. Didn't have to. Levi peeled out through the mud, turning around as fast as he could, and we flew down the bumpy dirt road.

My heart was in my throat. I'd never been so fucking scared in my entire life.

I called Grace first.

"Oh my god, there you are," she said.

"What the fuck happened?"

"I don't know yet. I'm on my way to the hospital. Where are you?"

"On our way. Is she okay? Have you talked to her?"

"Not yet."

"Okay. I'll see you there."

I ended the call and let my phone drop into my lap. None of the messages were from Cara. My heart thumped hard in my chest and my body buzzed with adrenaline.

Was she okay? Was our baby okay?

Levi glanced at me. *I'll hurry.*

I dipped my chin. *Thanks.*

We whipped out onto the highway and Levi stomped on the gas. If he got a ticket, I'd pay it. I didn't fucking care. I just needed to get to her. Now.

I couldn't lose them. They had to be okay.

42

LOGAN

*D*espite Levi's total disregard for the speed limit, the drive to the hospital seemed to take forever. It felt like we were crawling across every inch of pavement, not racing down the highway. My heart seemed to echo in my ears and all I could think was *please*.

Please let them be okay.

We pulled up to the side entrance of the emergency department and I barely waited for Levi to stop. I flew out of the SUV and hit the ground running. Although I wasn't in uniform, I knew most of the staff.

"Cara Goulding," I said to the first nurse I saw. "Car accident. Where is she?"

"I think they just moved her," she said.

Moved her? Oh fuck. "Where? The OR?"

"Let me find out for sure."

I waited, helpless and desperate, while the nurse walked away. It felt like my heart was going to beat out of my chest. Where was she? I had to see her or I was going to lose my fucking mind.

"Logan." A hand touched my shoulder.

I whipped around. It was Gavin. In uniform.

"Breathe, man," he said. "They took her upstairs."

"Were you on the scene? Is she okay?"

"Yeah, I was there. She's okay. I stayed with her until they moved her like two minutes ago."

"Moved her where?"

"L&D. She's in labor."

Without another word, I bolted for the stairs.

Labor and delivery was on the fourth floor. We'd taken a tour as part of our baby class and my first-responder-trained brain had memorized the location. I flew up the stairs two at a time, adrenaline coursing through my veins.

I hit the fourth floor and practically crashed through the door into the L&D waiting room. The woman at the front desk stood.

"Can I—"

"Cara Goulding," I said between heaving breaths. "Brought in from the ER. She's my girl."

"Are you Logan?"

"Yes."

"Follow me."

It took all my self-control not to rush past her and start searching the floor for Cara. I walked behind the nurse, feeling like I was going to burst out of my own skin.

She led me into a room and pulled the blue curtain aside.

There she was.

My tiger.

The sight of her in that hospital bed nearly kicked the breath from my lungs. She wore a hospital gown and an IV had been started, placed in the back of her hand. The lights were dim and the blinds closed and a quick glance around the room told me she was alone.

I rushed to her side. A cut on her forehead had been taped closed, but otherwise, she looked fine.

"Oh my god, are you okay?" I gently cupped her cheeks and kissed her forehead. "What the fuck happened?"

"I almost hit a deer. I swerved but I couldn't stop."

"Why did they bring you up here? Are you really in labor? Is the baby okay?"

"I think so. They put me on a monitor downstairs and they said the baby's heartbeat is fine. I couldn't feel any movement at first. It was terrifying."

I lowered myself onto the edge of the bed and took her hand in mine.

"I was already having contractions; I just didn't realize it. I thought it was back pain. They've been coming really fast since I got here. Oh god, here's another one."

Closing her eyes, she squeezed my hand and started to breathe heavily.

I tried to remember what I was supposed to do. "You've got this, Tiger. Breathe."

The contraction lasted at least a minute. Finally, her grip on my hand loosened and she opened her eyes.

"Fuck," she said. "I keep telling them to give me drugs but no one is listening to me."

"Do you want me to get the nurse?"

"That's okay. They said Dr. Murthy is on her way."

"So you're all right?" I asked, stroking her hand. "Sorry I keep asking you questions. I just had a lot of worst-case scenarios going through my head on the way over here."

"I'm a little banged up, but I didn't break anything. I think your Explorer is fucked, though."

"I don't give a shit about that. Just you."

"I'm so glad you're here. When they told me I was in

labor, I was afraid you wouldn't make it. I would have called you but I don't know what happened to my phone."

"I'm here." I brushed her hair back from her face. "And I'm not going anywhere."

"Logan," she said, her voice uncharacteristically soft.

"Yeah?"

"I think we're going to have a baby today."

"Yeah we are."

"I don't know if I'm ready."

I brought her hand to my lips and kissed the back of her knuckles. "You're the most amazing woman I know. You can do this."

Her eyes brimmed with tears. "Not alone."

"Not alone. Never alone."

She let out a shaky breath and nodded. A second later, a spasm of pain crossed her features. "Here we go again."

I held her hand through the next several contractions, encouraging her with soft words. In between, I stroked her hands and got her a cold washcloth for her forehead. I texted Grace with an update and asked her to let everyone else know what was going on. The nurse came to check on her and said she was doing great. Her doctor would be there soon.

"Where are my fucking drugs?" she moaned, leaning her head back. "They're getting so much stronger."

Another contraction started. She'd barely recovered from the previous one. A sheen of sweat broke out on her forehead as she breathed through it.

"You're doing so great, honey. You're a badass. You can do this."

The contraction eased but in less than a minute, another one started. Where the fuck was her doctor? I stayed calm, encouraging her through each contraction. Letting her squeeze my hand and cooling her forehead in between.

Finally, Dr. Murthy came in. Cara was in the middle of yet another contraction, so she waited.

"Hi, Cara," she said in a soothing voice. "Looks like you had quite a scare, but I'm happy to see things are moving along just fine."

Still breathing heavily, Cara nodded. "Okay, but where are my drugs?"

Dr. Murthy smiled. "Let me just check and see how you're progressing, then I'll get an epidural ordered for you."

I moved to stand closer to the head of the bed while Dr. Murthy did her thing. She had to wait for Cara to have another contraction. Shit was getting serious.

"Well, Cara, the good news is your labor is progressing really well," she said, stepping back. "The bad news is you're almost ready to push, so I can't give you an epidural now."

"What?" Cara shrieked.

"You're nine centimeters dilated. Another contraction or two and it should be go time."

"Are you fucking kidding me?" Cara asked.

"I'm afraid not." Dr. Murthy's tone remained calm and soothing. "But transition is often the hardest part. You're almost there. You can do this."

Cara grabbed my hand and looked up at me. "What the fuck? I have to push this baby out and I don't know if I can do this."

I brushed a sweaty tendril of hair off her forehead and held her eyes. "Cara, you're a goddamn tiger. You can do this."

"I'm scared," she whispered.

"I know. But if anyone can handle this, it's you." I

squeezed her hand. "I'm right here. And you're strong enough. You've got this."

She moaned and closed her eyes, squeezing my hand hard as another contraction swept through her. The doctor and two nurses bustled around the room, getting things ready, but I ignored them. All my focus was on Cara.

My badass tiger.

"Oh god, I think I need to push," Cara said.

"Go ahead," Dr. Murthy said. "Your body knows what to do."

A nurse took one leg, giving her leverage against her foot, and I took the other. Cara gritted her teeth and pushed.

When the contraction ended, she dropped her head back and took deep breaths.

"That was perfect," Dr. Murthy said. "As soon as you feel that urge again, push."

I wiped the sweat off her forehead with a cold washcloth. "Great job, honey. You're doing so good."

She kept her eyes closed but the corners of her mouth twitched.

It couldn't have been more than ten seconds before she started pushing again. A few breaths later, another one hit. I watched her in awe, amazed at her strength. I'd known my girl was tough, but holy fuck. This was unbelievable.

For the next hour or so, her contractions came at regular intervals, and she pushed. And pushed. And pushed. It was incredible and terrifying and I was so fucking proud of her. I did whatever I could to help, holding her leg up, talking to her, telling her how awesome she was. I could see the energy drain out of her, but she didn't give up.

"Keep pushing," Dr. Murthy said. She seemed to have something in her hands. "You're almost there. Push, Cara. Push, push, push."

I had no idea how she could have anything left, but she kept going. She squeezed her eyes shut and groaned through the pain, pushing with everything she had.

"That's it, almost there."

"You can do it, Tiger," I said. "You're amazing. You're doing so good."

The world seemed to slow and the sound of my heart was loud in my ears. She let out another yell, then dropped her head back. I turned to look at the doctor.

"It's a boy," Dr. Murthy said.

She held a slimy, pink, squirming baby in her hands.

My baby.

My son.

Cara opened her eyes and held out her arms. Dr. Murthy placed him on her chest.

"Is he okay?" she asked, her voice shaking. "Isn't he supposed to cry?"

As if in answer, he let out a squawk. His tiny fingers opened and closed and his legs bent and flexed in little jerky motions.

One look and I was completely, totally, madly in love.

"There you are," Cara said. "Oh my god, Logan, look at him."

I was. I couldn't take my eyes off him. He had wet hair plastered to his head and he blinked his eyes open and closed a few times.

I reached out and touched his little fingers. "Hi, little man."

He cried again and a primal instinct flared to life inside me. This was my son. My boy. And I would do anything —*anything*—to keep him safe.

"Dad, do you want to cut the umbilical cord?" Dr. Murthy asked.

Dad. Holy shit. She meant me. "Yeah, I do."

The next several minutes went by in a haze. I cut the cord and a nurse took him off Cara's chest to get him cleaned up. I watched her like a hawk, ready to rush in and take him back, but stayed next to Cara. I held her hand while the doctor delivered the placenta and made sure everything was as it should be.

We got Cara cleaned up and comfortable, and the nurse handed her the baby. He was clean and wrapped in a little blanket with a knit hat on his head.

He was the most beautiful thing I'd ever seen.

Cara cradled our son in her arms, gazing at him. And really, that was the most beautiful thing I'd ever seen.

I pulled up a chair next to the bed and sat. "You were so amazing."

She glanced at me. "Thank you. I'm so glad it's over."

"I bet. But seriously, I'm in awe. You're a fucking badass."

"Thanks. I'm in awe of him. Look at the little meatloaf-loving intruder."

"He's perfect."

"He really is, isn't he?"

I couldn't think of any other way to describe him. He was perfect. Beautiful. Amazing.

Mine.

"You know what this means, don't you?" she asked.

"What?"

"Now we have to name him."

"After what I just witnessed, you can choose his name. That's the least I can do after that display of badassery."

She smiled. "Really?"

"Yeah. If you want to name him Cooper, or Leo, or what-ever... it's fine. I'll get used to it."

She laughed. "I don't really want to name him Cooper or Leo. Actually, there is a name I've been thinking about."

"Tell me."

"Broderick. It's my dad's last name. He didn't get the chance to give me his last name, so I thought maybe we could use it for this little guy."

"It's perfect. I love it."

"Are you sure? I know my relationship with my dad is kind of new, but this feels right to me."

"I'm positive. And look at him, he's totally a Broderick. Just promise me one thing."

"What?"

"Don't call him Ricky."

"Oh my god, no. I'll cut a bitch. Everyone is forbidden from calling him Ricky."

"Deal. What about a middle name?"

She leaned down and kissed his forehead. "I picked his first name. What do you think his middle name should be?"

"Can it be Levi? He's kind of like my other half, you know? I think it would be cool if my son had his name."

"Broderick Levi Bailey. I love it."

"Yeah? I love it too." I kissed her cheek, then placed a gentle kiss on Broderick's forehead. "And I love the two of you."

"Do you want to hold him?"

"Hell yeah. Gimme."

I scooped him into my arms and gently cradled him. He had soft, round cheeks and his eyes were closed. "It's been a rough day, hasn't it, little man?"

"Oh dear god," Cara said.

"What?"

"I don't know. The sight of you holding our baby is just... I can't even describe it."

It was a little bit hard to tear my eyes away from Broderick, but I looked at Cara. "I love you so much. Thank you for this. He's the most amazing thing."

She smiled. "Thank you for getting drunk and fucking me and accidentally knocking me up. I'm really glad it happened."

"Me too, Tiger. I'm glad it happened too."

And I was. Sitting here with my girl and holding our son in my arms, I knew beyond a shadow of a doubt that this was the best thing that had ever happened to me. They were my world, now.

My family.

43

CARA

*N*ew motherhood was no joke.

I sat on the couch with Broderick in my arms, surrounded by baby stuff. Somehow this tiny person had taken over the house. We had a nursing pillow, diapers, bouncy seats, a swing and a car seat, tiny little onesies and swaddling blankets, and at least a thousand burp rags. The only thing we might have had more of were takeout containers.

Food delivery had saved our lives.

Broderick had finally finished nursing. This kid liked my boobs more than his dad. Milk dribbled from the corner of his mouth and his eyes were closed. He was out. Logan called it a milk coma. I looked down at his sweet little face and smiled.

Somehow, Logan and I had survived ten days as parents. That first night was still something of a blur. After Broderick had been born, we'd been informed the waiting room was stuffed with family and friends, all anxious for news and to meet our new baby. Logan's brothers, Gram, the girls, even Grace's mom and stepdad had been there. When Charlie had been born, it hadn't surprised me in the least that everyone had parked in the hospital to wait for Grace to have her baby. Somehow, I hadn't realized they'd do it for me. So despite how exhausted I'd been, I'd loved that they'd filed into our room and gently passed Broderick around.

The next day, my dad had come to meet his grandson. When I'd told him Broderick's name, he'd gotten tears in his eyes. So had I.

A couple of days later, the hospital staff had made the highly questionable decision to let us walk out with our baby in a car seat. It had been one of the craziest experiences of my life. We'd loaded Broderick into my Jeep and looked around, both of us wondering if they were really going to let us take him. Were they nuts?

Apparently not. And we hadn't totally screwed him up yet, so we had that going for us.

I was tired, my boobs were sore, my lady temple was far from healed, and I was probably getting about half as much sleep as I really needed. But somehow, even with the madness of learning how to parent a newborn, I was happy.

Really, truly happy.

Neither of us had been prepared for how much we were going to love our son. From the moment I saw him, I was so in love, I didn't know what to do with myself. We'd spent a lot of our time in the hospital just staring at him in awe. Wondering how we'd gotten so lucky.

He was amazing. Beautiful. Perfect.

And yeah, he cried a lot. But he was our kid. We hadn't expected anything less.

Going home with a newborn while also banged up from a car accident hadn't been ideal. Fortunately, I hadn't sustained any major injuries—just some soreness and bruising. Logan's SUV, on the other hand, was totaled. But really, we were just glad the outcome had been good. It could have been so much worse.

I couldn't even think about how much worse it could have been.

Logan came downstairs in a t-shirt and shorts. His hair was a mess and his tube socks didn't match, but I didn't care. He was mine.

He'd taken Broderick for part of the night so I could get some sleep, then gone back to bed for a few hours this morning. I had to admit, he was handling the lack of sleep better than I was. He said he was used to it because of his job. I figured I was just high maintenance.

"Did you get some rest?" I asked.

He came around to sit next to me. "Yeah I slept like... well, like him."

"I hope he gets his days and nights figured out soon."

Logan rubbed his eyes. "Same. But like Asher and Grace said, this phase won't last forever."

I gazed at his sweet little face. We'd been arguing over who he looked like. All I could see was Bailey—his eye shape, his cheeks, his mouth; it was all Logan.

Of course, it looked like he was going to have red hair. That was all me.

"Want me to take him for a while?" Logan asked.

"I don't mind holding him."

"Don't hog our kid. I haven't held him in a few hours."

I laughed and passed him over, settling him in Logan's arms. That was another thing I hadn't been prepared for: how much I'd love seeing Logan holding our son.

It was magical.

My lady parts were totally out of commission, but even my traumatized body couldn't help but respond to the sight of Logan Bailey holding a newborn. Let's be honest: hot firefighter with a baby in his muscular arms? Any woman would swoon. Even my stubborn self.

"Don't move." I got up. "I want to take a picture of this."

I went to my office and got my camera. I'd taken approximately ten thousand pictures of Broderick already, but they were digital. You couldn't take too many. I brought it out to the living room and paused, just watching them. It wasn't just how cute Logan looked with his bedhead and tube socks while he held a tiny newborn in his arms. It was the way he looked at Broderick, gazing down at him. I knew that look—understood it—because I felt it too.

Sharing this with him made me love Logan even more.

I took a few pictures, wishing I could do them justice—capture the love I had for these two.

"You're so cute with him, it's disgusting," I said, taking another. "I'd post these on my Instagram, but I'd attract every thirsty woman on the planet."

He glanced up at me with a smirk. "They do say a baby is a great way to meet girls."

"Whatever. I'm not worried because you'll never do better than me."

His grin widened. "You've got that right."

My phone rang. I picked it up off the coffee table and my stomach turned over.

"Is it Layla?" he asked.

"How could you tell?"

"The instant look of dread on your face."

I'd called my mom to tell her Broderick had been born. I'd even texted her photos. But today was the first time she'd called me back.

Ten days. Ten fucking days.

I took a deep breath. "Hi, Mom."

"Hi, Cara. I hope I didn't wake you."

"No, I'm up."

"You need to be getting rest when you can."

I met Logan's eyes, my brow furrowing. Was she actually concerned about me? "Yeah, I'm getting as much sleep as I can. Logan and I are taking shifts at night."

"Well that's something. Lack of sleep isn't going to help your skin or the bags under your eyes. Especially at your age."

"I just had a baby and you're worried I have bags under my eyes? Of course I do. I'm a new mom. I think I'm allowed."

"Just make sure you aren't neglecting yourself in favor of the baby. Having a child isn't an excuse to let yourself go."

I rolled my eyes. "Lovely, Mom. Thanks."

"I was back to my pre-pregnancy weight in less than two weeks."

"Good for you."

"Do I see red hair in these photos?"

"Yeah, he has hair like mine. It might be darker though. More auburn."

Mom made a displeased noise.

"What's wrong with red hair?" I asked.

She sighed. "Nothing. It's just a shame you had to get so much of your father and pass it on."

I sank down on the couch next to Logan and leaned my head back. God, she was so frustrating. "Can we not talk shit about my dad, please? You don't have to like him, but I don't need to hear about it."

"I just don't understand how you could do this to me."

The hint of hysteria in her voice made my back tighten. "I didn't do anything to you."

"You named him Broderick. There are plenty of good,

strong names on my side of the family, and you decide to slap me in the face by using your father's name."

"Believe it or not, this isn't about you."

"I raised you. I sacrificed everything for you and this is the thanks I get. I'll have to teach my grandson to do better. Someone has to."

I was about to attempt to calm her down. Talk softly and soothe her so she wouldn't get upset. It was what I always did.

But I looked at my son. And a deep realization hit me. She was never going to stop. If I let her, she'd not only keep poisoning my life, she'd poison Logan and Broderick's too.

I couldn't let that happen. I had to protect my son from her, even though it was going to hurt.

As if he could read my mind, Logan reached over and put his hand on my leg. Our eyes met. His were full of sympathy, understanding, and most of all, support. He knew what I had to do, and he'd be there for me while I did it.

"Mom, I need you to listen to me carefully. I realize that you think having me ruined your life. You've been making me pay for it since I was little. I've put up with it because I felt like I had to—like I'd be disloyal to you if I didn't. But I can't do that anymore. I have a family of my own now, and I won't allow that toxicity into my son's life. I'd like to believe that deep down, you love me. And you're my mom; I'll always love you. But I have to protect my family. I can't have this kind of relationship with you anymore. If you get help someday—real help—maybe we can create a new, healthy relationship. But until then, I have to set a firm boundary to protect my child. I can't have you in my life anymore."

"You did ruin my life," she sobbed. "And now you're ruining it again."

Logan shook his head. "Don't let her do that to you."

I nodded. "Goodbye, Mom."

And I ended the call.

Logan shifted so he held Broderick with one arm and wrapped the other around me, pulling me against him. I sank into his warmth, leaning into him—literally—for support. But strangely, I didn't feel awful. I didn't want to throw my phone or cry or scream into a pillow, like I often did after talking to my mother.

I felt clear. Unburdened.

For the first time in my life, I felt free.

The weight of responsibility for my mother lifted from my shoulders. It wasn't my job to fix her, or bail her out, or solve her problems. It never really had been. I had a new responsibility now, one that required sacrifices. I didn't want to hurt my mother, but I knew without a doubt that I'd done the right thing. My family was my priority.

Logan kissed my head. "Are you okay?"

"Actually, I am. I didn't realize how much I needed to do that."

He hugged me tighter. "You're fucking amazing. I'm so proud of you."

I wound my arm around his waist and nestled against his chest while Broderick slept on, oblivious to the turning point his mom had just experienced. "Thank you."

I didn't have all the answers and I still wasn't sure I was cut out to be a mom. But maybe my experiences had prepared me more than I knew. Some people were doomed to repeat the mistakes of the past. Other people used them to do better. And I was determined to be the second type.

Broderick wasn't going to grow up like I did. I wasn't perfect—not even close. But I loved him, and Logan, with everything I had. And that had to count for something.

44

LOGAN

*B*eing a new dad was both harder and more amazing than I could have imagined. My little man was awesome. Handsome like his daddy, with a fierce spirit just like his mommy. Sure, he cried a lot, especially at night. Life with a newborn wasn't easy. But I loved him so much, nothing else mattered.

Skin to skin contact was his favorite—and mine. I sat in the beige upholstered rocking chair in the nursery with my shirt off and Broderick in nothing but a diaper. The light blue walls had a mountain silhouette behind the crib and Cara had found a sign that said *Little Man Cave*. The curtains were closed and a small bear lamp provided soft light.

Broderick slept soundly on my chest with just a blanket covering him. He'd been howling up a storm earlier. Feeding him hadn't helped. Changing his diaper hadn't helped. Walking around the house bouncing him hadn't helped. Finally, I'd brought him in here, stripped us both down, and rocked with him.

It had worked. He was zonked out, sleeping on me while I'd dozed for the last couple of hours.

I didn't mind. I loved holding him, and letting him sleep on me was the best.

Cara was in her office, taking a much-needed break. Last night had been the best night we'd had since he'd been born over a month ago. We'd both gotten some sleep, and at the same time, which felt like a miracle.

I'd known she'd rock the mommy thing, but she was incredible. Watching her give birth had been one of the most intense experiences of my life. And seeing her with our son made me love her so much, I thought I might explode.

The doorbell rang, waking me up from my semi-nap. Broderick was still sound asleep. I shifted so I could stand, and he didn't even move. I knew by now that when he was sleeping like this, he wouldn't wake up until he was hungry again. Which meant I could have put him in his crib and left him for a little while. But I didn't really want to.

Holding him against my chest, I went downstairs to see who was here.

Cara stood at the open front door, dressed in a t-shirt and yoga pants, her hair in a thick ponytail. I paused for a second to admire her ass. Because damn, that ass. But who was she talking to?

A guy the size of a fucking barn stood on the step outside. He wore aviator glasses and his tatted-up arms were so big, I didn't know how they weren't ripping out of his shirt.

He opened a large manila envelope. "He'd rented a luxury villa in Puerto Vallarta. Tried to pass himself off as a wealthy American tourist."

Wait, who were they talking about?

"We planted someone in his household staff. Primary objective was to flush him out of hiding and obtain proof of his real identity. Secondary objective, as you requested, was to make his life as miserable as possible in the process. I think you'll be pleased with the results."

I stepped closer and he acknowledged me with a chin tip as he pulled documents out of the folder and handed them to Cara.

"His villa suffered a flea infestation, intermittent losses of power and water, and our mark's intestines got a crash course in dealing with the microbes in the local water source. His attempts at bringing women home were met with obstructions as well. Toilets flooding sewage tend to be a mood-killer. And as requested, anyone involved in necessary clean-up efforts were generously compensated."

"Good. I wouldn't want anyone else to suffer," Cara said. "Just him."

"We were then able to get the documentation to prove his identity to the authorities and convinced him that his best course of action would be to return to the U.S. with us rather than rely on the Mexican legal system. Unfortunately for him, he ran into some trouble with Homeland Security when he attempted to reenter the country. Those body cavity searches aren't pleasant."

Cara thumbed through photos and paperwork. "Where is he now?"

"Being held in a federal facility."

"What about the money he stole?"

"That's the bad news. From what we can find, he already spent a lot of it. As for the rest, we haven't been able to locate it."

"Damn it," Cara said.

"He wasn't as smart as he thought he was," the giant

said. "And he was blowing a lot of money fast. Partying, drugs, that kind of thing. The villa and staff were running him ten grand U.S. a night."

Cara took the envelope and slid the papers back inside. "Well, at least he's thoroughly fucked."

"Indeed he is."

"Good work as usual," Cara said.

"Call us if you need anything else."

"I will."

The guy tipped his chin to me again, then turned and walked toward a black Range Rover in the driveway. It looked like it might be bulletproof.

"What was that about?" I asked as she shut the door.

"Just a little side project I had going," she said, her tone as casual as if she were talking about the scarf she was crocheting.

"Side project?" I followed her into the kitchen. Broderick was still out. "Who was in Mexico?"

"Mike Phillips."

I stopped dead in my tracks. Mike Phillips, the accountant who'd embezzled money from Gram. "Holy shit. You found him?"

"Mexico was so obvious," she said. "If he'd have been smart, he would have gone to a non-extradition country. Not that it matters. I knew they'd get him back across the border."

"How the fuck did you do that?"

She gave a cavalier shrug. "I have resources."

"Like captain muscles out there? Who the hell was that guy?"

"Roan."

"I was going to guess Ragnar or Brick or something, but Roan fits. But who is he?"

"He's a specialist with a particular set of skills and resources."

"And you hired him to go after Phillips?"

"In a manner of speaking. All I did was call in some favors. There wasn't even any money exchanged. This time."

I gaped at her, not quite sure what to say.

"Don't look at me like that. It isn't like I sent someone to murder him. He's in custody and the authorities can serve up justice."

"Tainted water and backed-up sewage? A little Cara karma?"

"Can you blame me for exacting petty revenge? Switching out his bottled water for tap water is hardly the stuff of an evil mastermind. Besides, I don't like to micromanage. They took what I asked for and ran with it."

I shook my head slowly. "I don't know whether to be impressed or terrified right now."

"Don't be too impressed. I didn't get Gram's money back."

"But maybe we will now. And if not, we'll still figure something out." I stepped closer and, holding Broderick against my chest with one arm, I slipped the other around her waist and drew her against me. "You're amazing. I love you."

"You're okay, I guess. I'll admit it's hard not to swoon when you're holding our baby shirtless like that."

I leaned down and pressed my lips to hers. "Just promise me something."

"What?"

"Don't ever send Roan after me."

Her lips turned up in a smile. "I'm sure you'd never give me a reason."

I laughed. "God, you're fucking scary. I love it."

"People should know not to mess with the ones I love."

"No shit."

"And I love you the most."

A big-ass smile stole over my face. "I love you the most, too. And I'm also glad you're on my side."

She looked me up and down. "As cute as you two are, we should probably get dressed to go to Gram's."

"Damn, does that mean I have to put on pants?" I passed Broderick to her and she settled him against her shoulder.

"Or shorts. It's still warm out there."

"Fine," I said, heading for the stairs. "I hate pants."

THE ONLY DOWNSIDE to spending time at Gram's was that everyone else wanted to hold my baby. Not that I was going to begrudge Gram time with her great-grandson. But after a couple of hours of not holding him, I wanted him back.

Levi and Gavin were on duty tonight, but everyone else had come over for dinner. The meal had been delicious, as usual. Despite the ongoing stress of Gram's financial situation, she looked happy. I had a feeling Charlie and Broderick had a lot to do with that. She'd spent most of the evening with one of them in her arms.

To the surprise of no one, she'd named Charlie Bear, like Asher. And the first time she'd held Broderick, when he'd been only hours old, she'd called him her little Bobcat. It fit him perfectly.

Because of course it did.

The girls had moved to the living room so Gram could hold Broderick on the couch while they chatted. Evan nodded to me and Asher, gesturing for us to follow him out onto the back porch.

We went outside and Evan made sure the door was shut. There was a seriousness to his expression—even for him— that made me wonder what was going on.

"I don't want to freak everyone out, so let's keep this quiet for now," Evan said. "But I think someone tampered with the brakes on your Explorer."

"What the fuck?"

"They towed it to Dusty's in town, so I went down there to look at it myself. Brakes on newer cars don't just fail like that. The brake line hadn't been cut completely, but there was a hole. Cara would have been losing brake fluid as she drove and when she tried to stop, nothing."

I stared at him in horror. It was one thing to know your pregnant fiancée had been in an accident. Wildlife on the highways was a fact of life out here. But the thought that someone had tampered with my car and put her in danger made my blood run hot with rage.

They could have fucking killed her.

"Are you serious?" Asher asked.

"Unfortunately," Evan said. "There's no way that was an accident."

"Who the fuck would do that?" I asked.

"My first thought is the Havens," Evan said. "But that's not a prank."

"No shit," I said. "That's attempted murder."

"But were they after you, or Cara?" Evan asked. "It was your rig."

"Hell if I know," I said. "This is fucked-up."

I didn't want to believe the Havens would take things this far. But I couldn't help but think about the last time I'd seen Josiah and Zachary. They'd basically threatened me. I'd figured it was just the usual taunting we always did. But had it been more? Were they willing to risk lives to get what they wanted?

"Don't get pissed at me for asking this question," Asher said. "But Cara doesn't have anyone out there who might want to hurt her, does she?"

I thought about Roan. She obviously knew people who could do some shady shit, but as far as I was aware, she didn't have enemies. It wasn't like she'd come from a background in crime. And her mom was crazy, but not the kind of crazy to try to have her daughter killed. Besides, her mom didn't have the money to pay for that kind of thing, even if she had been that evil.

"I don't think so. She hired someone to bring in that Mike Phillips asshole, but we just found out about that today. When the accident happened, he was still living it up in Mexico. Or maybe shitting his brains out by that point. But he doesn't know Cara had anything to do with that."

"So maybe the Havens did do it," Asher said.

"Those guys are dicks, but it's hard to believe they'd put someone's life in danger," I said. "But I don't know who else it could have been. I don't have any enemies. Everyone loves me."

"You sure you don't have a jealous ex out there?" Evan asked.

"I don't think so. I never really dated anyone long enough for them to go psycho on me. Plus Cara's the craziest girl I've ever been with."

"So what do we do?" I asked.

"Report it to the police," Asher said. "And watch each other's backs."

I nodded. Anger that someone would have done this mixed with a deep sense of disquiet. Our town felt different. Arson, tampered brakes. Those kinds of things didn't usually happen here. It was unnerving to think there were people out there—maybe people we knew and saw around town—who'd done this. Who might do something again.

Were they pranks gone wrong? Or were the Havens taking the feud to the next level?

This whole thing was fucked-up.

Cara opened the door to the porch. "We should probably get home. The witching hour is coming and we don't need to subject everyone to Broderick's nightly crying session."

"I'll take first shift if you're tired."

She smiled. "Thanks. I could use a few hours of sleep."

"You got it, Tiger. I'll be right there."

I said goodnight to my brothers. We'd have to let Levi and Gavin know about the brakes—and try to keep Gav from planning an all-out assault on the Timberbeast Tavern. Hopefully Skylar would help rein him in.

Then again, maybe it was Levi I needed to worry about. It was usually the quiet ones you had to watch out for.

I took my little family home. Changed Broderick's diaper and sat with Cara while she fed him. I'd tell her about the brakes later. I didn't want to disrupt the peace of our evening. I found myself living for these moments—the three of us on the couch. Maybe we'd start a wall of family photos like at Gram's house or the one at Asher's place. I played with Cara's hair while she nursed our son. And I knew this was where I'd always been meant to be. They were my family, and I loved them more than anything.

They were mine.

45

CARA

"Do we really need everything in the bag?" Logan scooted the bulging diaper bag across the backseat of the Jeep. "It weighs like fifty pounds."

I swayed back and forth, patting Broderick's bottom. We'd managed to wrangle him into the baby carrier, since he liked to be held, although I wasn't ruling out having Logan bring the stroller just in case. "Maybe I overpacked a little bit. But we've never gone anywhere with him except Gram's. I don't want to wish we had something."

Okay, so I'd definitely overpacked the diaper bag. We probably weren't going to need a dozen diapers, six changes of clothes, eight bottles, two extra packages of baby wipes, a stack of burp rags, bottled water, and teething toys he was too young to play with yet.

Still. This was our first big outing with him. I was nervous.

"Tell you what," Logan said, pulling things out of the bag and setting them on the backseat. "I'll thin this out a little and if we run out of anything, I'll come back for it."

"Okay. I guess."

"We're probably going to be out here for what, an hour? I think we'll be fine."

I glanced away. He was probably right. And he was using his calm voice. That meant I was starting to get dramatic.

We were in downtown Tilikum for the annual Art Walk. Businesses displayed the work of local artists outside their shops and people wandered around, enjoying the art, shopping, and sampling food from tents and food trucks. I'd always enjoyed it—Grace and I used to come together—but this year, I'd done something crazy. Maybe even crazier than having a baby with Logan Bailey.

I'd entered a display of my photos.

Maybe that was why I was so nervous.

Being vulnerable was not my favorite thing, and sharing something I considered, dare I say it, my art, made me feel raw and exposed. I felt like a fraud. I wasn't a photographer. I was a girl with an Instagram account, not an artist.

But Logan had encouraged me to have canvas prints made of my favorites and to show them at the Art Walk. In a moment of deluded weakness, I'd agreed.

Now I really didn't know how to feel about it.

He finished lightening the diaper bag load, and I hoped he was right and we wouldn't run out of diapers or burp rags. And Broderick didn't need that sixth outfit even though diaper blowouts and spit-up were a thing. He slung the strap over his shoulder, shut the door, and took my hand.

"Let's go."

My heart beat too fast as we wandered down the sidewalk. The fall air was still warm and it seemed like everyone in Tilikum was here. Doris Tilburn waved from her tent where she was selling baked goods. Amy Garrett handed out lollypops to her kids. Chief Stanley wandered arm in arm with Caroline, pausing to look at a ceramics display. I saw a dozen more faces I recognized—people I knew and, for the most part, liked.

I wasn't quite sure when it had happened, but somewhere along the way, Tilikum had become my home.

Logan and I wandered deeper into town, walking hand in hand. Broderick slept peacefully in the carrier. We nodded and waved and said hello to the people we knew, all the while making our way inexorably to the spot where my photos were displayed.

I kept my back straight, trying not to give in to the butterflies in my stomach. It was silly to be so nervous. I didn't want it to show.

Logan paused in front of Gerald McMillian's barber shop, the Art of Manliness, and met my eyes. "What are you so worried about?"

"Who says I'm worried? I'm fine."

"I don't know why you still think you can hide shit from me." He leaned close and brushed my lips with a kiss. "It's okay to be nervous. You're putting yourself out there. That takes courage."

I squeezed his hand. "Thank you."

We approached my display outside Happy Paws and my stomach did a belly flop. A little knot of people stood around the easels that displayed my photos.

Logan smiled. "See? This is awesome."

The people were smiling. They pointed at the photos, talking to each other about them. They actually seemed to like them.

I'd chosen photos that displayed my view of Tilikum. Different seasons, different aspects of the town. Some were images of nature. Tiny icicles hanging off a tree branch. A flower just starting to open in spring. The river outside my house.

But my favorites were the people. I'd taken one of Lacey Hanson's daughter as she blew dandelion seeds in Lumberjack Park. Another was Hank from the Caboose looking down as he mixed a drink at his bar. I was particularly proud of the lighting on that one. There were photos of Logan and Levi in TFD shirts, looking so much alike, it was almost hard to tell which one was which. Gavin and Skylar sitting on a bench outside the firehouse. A close-up of Charlie's big smile. Evan and Fiona trying to smear grease on each other in Evan's shop. Gram in her kitchen, the lines around her soft brown eyes crinkling with her smile.

I noticed Harvey Johnston standing in front of one of my canvases, his head tilted. It was one of the photos I'd taken of him.

"What do you think?" I asked.

"Is that me?" he asked.

"It's you."

It was a black and white image of him smiling, cropped close so you could see the light in his eyes.

"That's very nice, Miss Cara."

"Thank you. I told you, you have a nice face."

His expression darkened and he leaned closer. "Remember what I said, Miss Cara. Be careful."

An involuntary shiver ran down my spine. Logan had told me about the brakes on his Explorer. Someone had done that on purpose. I didn't know if they'd meant to hurt me or him, but it didn't matter. Either way, it was frightening. Especially because we didn't know who had done it, or why.

I wanted to ruin someone's life over it, but I didn't know who to go after.

"I'll be careful," I said. "Thanks, Harvey."

His concern seemed to disappear as quickly as it had come. He smiled and tipped his hat. "Have a nice day."

"Bye."

Logan sidled up next to me and put his hand on the small of my back. "See? People are enjoying them."

I nodded. Broderick shifted, so I swayed a little to soothe him back to sleep.

"Are you glad you did it?" he asked.

"Yeah, I think I am."

He kissed my temple. "I'm proud of you."

Before I could answer, a woman turned toward me. "Are you the artist?"

"The artist?" I asked. "Yes, I am. I'm Cara."

"I'm Jolene Livingston," she said. "These are absolutely beautiful. Can I get your business card? I work for a media company and we're always looking for good photography. I'd love to commission some work from you."

Business card? But I didn't—

"We're fresh out," Logan said. "But if I can get your email address, we'll get in touch."

"Absolutely." She took a business card out of her purse and handed it to Logan. "There's all my contact information. I look forward to hearing from you."

"Perfect." He slipped it in his back pocket. "It was nice to meet you."

"You too." She shook his hand, then mine. "And your baby is adorable."

I smiled. "Thank you."

She moved on down the sidewalk, and I turned to Logan, not quite sure what to say.

He winked at me. "Nice work, Tiger. I think you just landed a client."

A client? A giddy sense of happiness bubbled its way up from deep inside me. I'd never thought I'd be good enough at anything, let alone something I loved, to make a living with it. But maybe I could do something with my little photography hobby.

Maybe I had more to bring to the table than strong cocktails and sass.

"I guess I need to order some business cards," I said.

"You sure do. And you know what the best part is?"

"What?"

He slipped his hand around my waist and drew me close. "They're going to say Cara Bailey."

Oh my god, they were. In less than a week, I was going to do something I'd once thought unthinkable. I was marrying Logan Bailey.

MY WEDDING DAY had dawned clear and bright, not a cloud in the deep blue sky. Neither of us had been interested in what most people would consider a traditional wedding. A quickie marriage in Vegas would have been great, except for the traveling with a fussy baby part. So we'd decided to keep it simple. An afternoon ceremony at city hall followed by a low-key reception in Gram's backyard.

We didn't even particularly care if anyone, other than Grace and Asher who would be our witnesses, showed up for the wedding ceremony.

But this was Tilikum, and this town didn't let something like a wedding go down without a fuss.

Grace and I parked outside city hall. It was one of the original Tilikum buildings, made of red brick with old, paned glass windows. Wide concrete steps led to the double doors and a fountain sprayed a stream of water into the air.

I gaped at the crowd waiting on the steps and up and down the sidewalk in front of the building.

"What are all these people doing here?"

"They're here for the wedding," she said, her tone matter-of-fact.

"But we didn't even send out invitations."

"Did you really think word wouldn't get around?"

"Good point."

She reached over and took my hand. "Are you ready to become a Bailey?"

I narrowed my eyes. "Did you always know?"

"That you'd marry Logan?"

"Yeah. You teased me about being a Bailey for years. Are you like Gram? Did you know something I didn't?"

She shrugged. "I had a feeling. And I know you were really hoping we'd become platonic non-lesbian life partners. But I think being Bailey sisters is even better."

"Shut your beautiful face before you make me ruin my makeup."

"I love you, honey."

"I love you too, boo. Speaking of how much I love you, I need to tell you something."

"Yeah?"

"I get it now. Why you waited all those years for Asher. I don't know if I would have been as strong as you were, but I understand. I would have waited, too."

Tears welled in the corners of her eyes. "I guess you had different reasons to wait. But I'm so happy for you."

"Thank you, my lovely sunflower." I took a shaky breath and waved my hand to dry the moisture in my eyes before tears could make my mascara run. "Let's go before I come to my senses."

She laughed because she knew I was full of it. I loved Logan. I loved his stupid annoying ass so much and I was going to make him the best wife ever.

As soon as I opened the car door, cheers erupted from the gathered crowd. I adjusted my white strapless dress to make sure my boobs were properly contained. This dress did the job, but only just. Which was why I'd chosen it. I wasn't going to have these amazing boobs forever. I was going to take advantage of them.

I turned and waved at the crowd of family, friends, and neighbors. Grace came around the other side of the car and handed me my little bouquet. I'd been planning to do without, but Fiona had been horrified at the very thought of not having flowers for my wedding ceremony. She'd made me this sweet little bouquet of white flowers and honestly, I couldn't have loved it more.

Grace had done my hair and convinced me to hire a photographer. I could see him snapping photos on the other side of city hall as Logan got out of a car. He was dressed in a dress shirt with a vest and tie, and he probably had his stupid tube socks on under those slacks.

The thought of it made me smile. I loved those stupid tube socks.

His sleeves were cuffed. Knowing him, he was chafing at having to wear slacks, so he'd bared his forearms to balance things out. I wasn't complaining. The lack of formality fit. Nothing about our relationship had been traditional, so why pretend?

We were who we were, and we loved each other like crazy. That was enough. It was all that mattered.

I walked toward the center of the steps while Logan

approached from the other side. I caught sight of Fiona, holding Broderick. He was dressed in a little set of tuxedo footie pajamas Logan had found for him. Fiona looked absolutely adorable with a baby in her arms, and the way Evan was gazing at her made me wonder if he was thinking the same thing.

Maybe there'd be another baby Bailey soon.

My eyes swept over the rest of the crowd. Everyone I knew and loved was here. My dad. Gram. All of Logan's brothers. My girls. The Stitch and Bitch ladies. Even Marlene Haven stood near the edge of the crowd, although I had a feeling she wouldn't stay long. Tension between the two families was at an all-time high.

But for now, I wasn't going to worry about feuds or treasure or fires or brakes. I was here to get married.

Logan approached and licked his lips as he looked me up and down. "Goddamn, you look good enough to eat."

I smiled, feeling a pleasant tingle run down my spine. We hadn't attempted sex since Broderick had been born. But I'd been given the all-clear to try, and oh my god, did I want to try.

With birth control. I wasn't sure if another baby was in our future, but I had no interest in doing all that again any time soon.

But sex on my wedding night—even gentle sex with lots of patience and lube? Yes, please.

Logan took my hand and we walked up the steps to where Judge Deacon waited for us.

Our ceremony was short and to the point. And when he got to the part about pronouncing us man and wife, I lost it —laughing and crying happy tears that were undoubtedly ruining my mascara.

The judge said, "kiss the bride," and Logan surged in. He

gathered me in his arms, hauling me against him, and kissed me. It wasn't a wedding kiss. It was long and deep and totally inappropriate.

Which meant it was absolutely perfect for us.

I kissed him right back, delving my tongue in his mouth like the crazy harlot I was.

All those years I'd spent hating Logan Bailey, I hadn't hated him at all. It had taken a night of drunk sex and an unplanned pregnancy to open my eyes to what had been in front of me all along.

But things worth having aren't always easy.

Logan's protectiveness, care, and loyalty had been steadfast and strong. He'd taught me that it was safe to open up, to allow myself to be loved. And to love him in return.

Now, we were a family. An unlikely one, maybe. But a family nonetheless. I loved Logan, and our son, with everything I had.

And when I loved someone, I loved them fierce.

EPILOGUE: LEVI

Gerald's clippers buzzed across the back of my head. I'd been overdue for a haircut and starting to look like Logan. He'd always kept his hair a little longer —and messier—than me.

A college football game was on in the background—I could see the reflection of the TV in the mirror—and the scent of aftershave hung in the air. Gavin waited in a chair near the front door, looking at his phone. He had freshly cut hair, although he tended to keep his even longer than Logan. Every time we came in here, Gerald busted his balls about giving him a military buzz cut. And every time, Gavin would fly out of his chair and pretend he was going to leave.

I had no idea why they found that so funny but apparently it never got old.

"There you go, my friend." Gerald unsnapped the black cape and whipped it off me like he was doing a tablecloth trick. "What do you think?"

I gave myself a quick glance in the mirror. "Great. Thanks, man."

Gerald grabbed a broom and started sweeping around

the chair while I got up and tossed some money on the front counter—enough for my haircut and a tip.

"Anything else I can do for you boys?" he asked.

"I think we're good."

Gavin stood and pocketed his phone. "See you, Gerald."

He nodded to us and I followed Gavin outside. It was unusually warm for fall, although the breeze had a bite to it that hinted at the coming winter. The sky was a pale blue without a single cloud. Thankfully the wildfire season had been mild although we hadn't seen rain in months.

"I need to go pick up Sky," Gavin said as the door to Gerald's barber shop, the Art of Manliness, swung shut. "Want me to drop you off at home?"

"Sounds good."

The door to Tilikum's other barber shop, the Dame and Dapper, opened across the street and a knot of men filed out.

Havens.

It wasn't just one or two. Five Haven brothers—Josiah, Luke, Zachary, Theo, and Garrett—walked out and congregated on the sidewalk.

Five of them. Two of us. Not great odds.

Just seeing them sent a flash of anger searing through my veins. I was not usually the guy to start shit—I tended to operate in the background—but lately I wanted to pummel every one of those fuckers every time I saw them.

They'd been my family's rivals for generations, but this time they'd gone too far. They were putting pressure on Gram to sell her land to them, and it made me fucking furious.

The wind picked up and a flurry of brown leaves swirled in the air between us. They spread out in a line, all eyes on me and Gav. If this had been the Old West, we would have all had hands twitching next to the guns at our hips.

Shootout at the Dame and Dapper.

Maybe the odds weren't good, but if any one of those assholes said a fucking word—

"Let's go." Gavin put a hand on my shoulder.

Gav was normally the first to try to start trouble with the Havens, so if he was suggesting we walk away, it probably meant I should listen.

But fuck, those guys pissed me off. They hadn't said a word, but they didn't have to. I clenched my hands into fists, craving the feel of knuckles smashing against bone. Wishing there were something I could do to teach them a lesson.

My temper had a hair trigger these days, and that was probably why. There wasn't anything I could do.

I hated feeling backed into a corner.

But facing off when there were five of them and two of us would be stupid. Even Gavin knew that. So I let him turn me up the sidewalk and we headed toward his truck.

My phone buzzed in my back pocket. I pulled it out to check and almost laughed out loud.

Oh, the sweet fucking irony.

Juliet: *Hey, are you busy?*

I paused outside Gavin's truck and glanced back at the Haven brothers. They were standing in a knot on the sidewalk, talking.

The corner of my mouth hooked in a smug grin and I went back to my phone.

Me: *Nope. What's up?*

Juliet: *Not much. It's just been one of those days. And it's only two, so... yeah.*

I climbed in the passenger seat, shut the door, and put on my seat belt.

Me: *I hate it when that happens. Work stuff or family stuff?*

Juliet: *Both.*

Me: *That sucks.*

Juliet: *Thanks. It's not a big deal. But tell me something funny. I could use a good laugh.*

Gavin pulled out onto the street and I glanced at the Havens in the rearview mirror. If they only knew.

Because Juliet wasn't her real name. That was just how I had her in my phone so I didn't have to worry about nosy assholes—namely, my brothers—looking over my shoulder and seeing who I was talking to.

Annika Haven.

If the Haven brothers knew I was texting their sister, they'd be furious. And that thought made me happy.

Of course, if *my* brothers knew I was texting Annika Haven, they'd be furious too. We were just friends, but even that was forbidden according to the rules of the feud.

But fuck it. It wasn't any of their business.

Me: *Something funny, huh? I saw a drunk squirrel last night. He'd been eating a pear that must have fermented. Little bastard kept swaying like he was about to fall over but he wouldn't stop.*

Juliet: *Seriously?*

Me: *Yeah. And when he tried to scamper away, he fell flat on his face, just like a frat boy at a party.*

Juliet: *I'm cracking up. That's hilarious.*

Me: *Maybe that's the solution to the squirrel problem around here. Get them all drunk on fermented pear juice.*

Juliet: *Do you think he was hungover the next day?*

Me: *I bet he woke up and didn't know where the hell he was.*

Juliet: *And his squirrel buddies found him and dragged him home while he made bad jokes because he was still drunk.*

Me: *Or sang a squirrel drinking song and messed up the lyrics.*

Juliet: *I don't know why, but now I'm imagining pirate squirrels with tiny bottles of rum.*

Me: *Singing drunken sea shanties.*

Juliet: *Laughing. So. Hard.*

I chuckled as Gavin pulled up in front of our house.

"Who are you talking to?" he asked.

"No one."

"Bullshit. You're talking to a girl. Who is she?"

"It's not what you think."

"Dude, I'm your brother. You don't have to hide shit from me."

Actually, I do have to hide this from you. "There's nothing to hide. Just a girl I've been friends with for a long time. It's nothing."

"Did she friend zone you? What the fuck?"

"No, dickweed. She's a girl I'm friends with. That's not the same."

He narrowed his eyes like he wasn't satisfied with my answer.

I unfastened my seat belt and got out of the truck. "See ya, Gav."

"I'm going to find out who she is."

I slammed the door shut.

No the fuck you aren't.

I half expected Gavin to get out of the truck and follow me inside. When he wanted something, he could be pretty relentless. But apparently he decided finding out who I was texting wasn't interesting enough to be late picking up Skylar.

I went inside, toed off my shoes, and flopped down on the couch. Princess Squeaker jumped off the cat tree I'd built for her and stretched, arching her back.

Me: *I'm glad a drunk squirrel was enough to make you laugh.*

Juliet: *That was great. Next time I walk by a pear orchard, I'm going to see if I can spot a drunk squirrel.*

Me: *Here's hoping you get lucky.*

After I hit send, I realized I probably should have phrased that differently. The thought of Annika getting lucky with someone else made a coal of anger in my gut smolder.

Yeah, we were just friends. And not even friends who hung out together in person, although we lived about five minutes apart in a town small enough that we saw each other in public all the time.

I was not the Romeo to her Juliet.

But maybe I wished I was.

Juliet: *I'm not getting lucky any time soon.*

She finished her text with a string of laughing emojis. Making a joke. Because that was what we did. Joked around. Made each other laugh.

Just friends.

Me: *Me neither, unfortunately.*

Juliet: *I do have to go on a date this weekend, though.*

The word *date* was like tinder, flaring from the heat of the red-hot coal. I gritted my teeth together.

Me: *Have to? You don't sound thrilled.*

Juliet: *One of my brothers set me up. He's been bugging me about it forever. Finally wore me down.*

It took me a minute before I could reply. I kept staring at the word *date*. One of her fucking brothers had set her up, the asshole.

I'd known this would happen eventually. I hadn't dated anyone in a while, and neither had she, as far as I knew. But it had to come up at some point.

It wasn't like we could date each other.

Fuck.

I wanted to tell her not to go. That if she was ready to date, it should be me.

But that wasn't going to happen. It was one thing to text each other in secret. Just that would get both of us in trouble with our families, especially now. We couldn't have a conversation in public—and we never really had—let alone go on a date.

Disloyalty was a mortal sin in Tilikum. Dating the enemy would be unforgiveable.

Juliet: *Sorry if I just made things awkward.*

Me: *Not at all. Hopefully your date won't be too bad.*

That was a big-ass lie. I hoped her date sucked so whoever this guy was, he wouldn't get a second one.

Juliet: *Thanks. And thanks for the laugh. I needed it today.*

Me: *Anytime.*

Juliet: *I have to go but I'll talk to you later.*

Me: *Okay, bye.*

I stared at my phone for a long moment, scrolling back through our conversation. A date. Her goddamn brother had set her up on a fucking date.

The hair trigger on my temper fired. I flew to my feet and threw my phone across the room. Hard. It smashed against the opposite wall. I'd probably broken it, but I was too pissed to give a fuck.

I wasn't her Romeo, and it was stupid to think I ever could be.

～

DEAR READER

Dear reader,

For the record, it was always Cara.

Some of you knew that from the first time you saw them together back in Fighting for Us (book two). Leading up to the launch of this book, however, I was surprised at how many readers weren't sure if it would be Cara—and were quite enthusiastic in their vehemence that it HAD to be Cara.

As she would say: I got you, boo.

Fortunately for me, that was the plan all along. These two wouldn't have had it any other way.

The dynamic in this book was such a challenge in all the best ways. Very often, my heroes are the ones with a lot of growing to do. We're accustomed to that in our romance novels. A strong character arc for the hero is undoubtedly compelling and oh-so-satisfying. Who doesn't love seeing a big, strong (and maybe grumpy or asshole-ish) man brought to his knees by love?

But this book required something a little different. And I

think the result uncovered some unexpected layers in both Cara and Logan.

Cara loves to flippantly call herself a mess. Earlier in the series, she makes a few references to her "horrible childhood" and difficult relationship with her mother. But even I didn't see the depth of that toxicity coming. I love it when characters surprise me but my heart ached for poor Cara. She had so much love to give. She just needed to learn to trust Logan enough to fully give it, and allow herself to be loved in return.

I hope that you were happily surprised by Logan. I knew this book would revolve around a surprise pregnancy and I also knew the conflict would not be whether or not Logan would commit to being a father. Logan's perspective changes the minute he realizes Cara is having his baby. He grows up, steps up, and never wavers in his commitment to fatherhood.

I also knew their story was not going to be one of settling for each other simply because they were having a baby together. Rather than attempting to create a romantic relationship because of the baby (or maybe for the baby), the pregnancy serves as a "forced proximity" of sorts. It forces them to spend time together, to get to know each other, and learn to work together. Ultimately, that is why Logan and Cara fall in love. The pregnancy allows them to break through their previous pattern of behavior and create a new relationship based on love for each other and their child.

And can I just say, it's glorious when it finally happens.

I've had this story in my head for years and it's been such a creative pleasure to finally have the chance to tell it and share it with you. I hope their story met or exceeded your expectations—and I know expectations for this book were high!

Personally, I love this couple so much. I love their strength, their sass, their fire, and ultimately, their unfailing love for each other and their child.

I hope you love them as much as I do. Thanks again for coming on this journey with me.

Love,

CK

ACKNOWLEDGMENTS

Thank you so much to Team CK for all your help throughout the writing of this book. I literally couldn't do it without you.

Thank you to Nikki and Alex for your behind the scenes help, work, feedback, and support. And okay fine, you were right about adding chapter 29. Don't get too smug about it.

Thank you to Susan for another outstanding edit and for your flexible schedule (which saved this busy writer's butt!). And thank you to Erma for your eagle-eyed proofreading skills.

To Lori for the smoking hot cover! Thank you for sharing your talent with the romance world!

To Joseph Cannata for the beautiful cover photo.

To my awesome firefighter friend, David Woody, for answering my questions and being a fabulous human.

To my husband and family for always believing in me and for trying not to interrupt me too often. I love you with all my heart.

And to my readers. Thank you for being the majestic book dragons that you are. I love you!

ALSO BY CLAIRE KINGSLEY

For a full and up-to-date listing of Claire Kingsley books visit
www.clairekingsleybooks.com/books/

For comprehensive reading order, visit www.
clairekingsleybooks.com/reading-order/

The Haven Brothers

Small-town romantic suspense with CK's signature endearing
characters and heartwarming happily ever afters. Can be read as
stand-alones.

Obsession Falls (Josiah and Audrey)

The rest of the Haven brothers will be getting their own happily
ever afters!

How the Grump Saved Christmas (Elias and Isabelle)

A stand-alone, small-town Christmas romance.

The Bailey Brothers

Steamy, small-town family series with a dash of suspense. Five
unruly brothers. Epic pranks. A quirky, feuding town. Big HEAs.
Best read in order.

Protecting You (Asher and Grace part 1)

Fighting for Us (Asher and Grace part 2)

Unraveling Him (Evan and Fiona)

Rushing In (Gavin and Skylar)

Chasing Her Fire (Logan and Cara)

Rewriting the Stars (Levi and Annika)

The Miles Family

Sexy, sweet, funny, and heartfelt family series with a dash of suspense. Messy family. Epic bromance. Super romantic. Best read in order.

Broken Miles (Roland and Zoe)

Forbidden Miles (Brynn and Chase)

Reckless Miles (Cooper and Amelia)

Hidden Miles (Leo and Hannah)

Gaining Miles: A Miles Family Novella (Ben and Shannon)

Dirty Martini Running Club

Sexy, fun, feel-good romantic comedies with huge... hearts. Can be read as stand-alones.

Everly Dalton's Dating Disasters (Prequel with Everly, Hazel, and Nora)

Faking Ms. Right (Everly and Shepherd)

Falling for My Enemy (Hazel and Corban)

Marrying Mr. Wrong (Sophie and Cox)

Flirting with Forever (Nora and Dex)

Bluewater Billionaires

Hot romantic comedies. Lady billionaire BFFs and the badass heroes who love them. Can be read as stand-alones.

The Mogul and the Muscle (Cameron and Jude)

The Price of Scandal, Wild Open Hearts, and Crazy for Loving You

More Bluewater Billionaire shared-world romantic comedies by Lucy Score, Kathryn Nolan, and Pippa Grant

Bootleg Springs

by Claire Kingsley and Lucy Score

Hot and hilarious small-town romcom series with a dash of mystery and suspense. Best read in order.

Whiskey Chaser (Scarlett and Devlin)

Sidecar Crush (Jameson and Leah Mae)

Moonshine Kiss (Bowie and Cassidy)

Bourbon Bliss (June and George)

Gin Fling (Jonah and Shelby)

Highball Rush (Gibson and I can't tell you)

Book Boyfriends

Hot romcoms that will make you laugh and make you swoon. Can be read as stand-alones.

Book Boyfriend (Alex and Mia)

Cocky Roommate (Weston and Kendra)

Hot Single Dad (Caleb and Linnea)

~

Finding Ivy (William and Ivy)

A unique contemporary romance with a hint of mystery. Stand-alone.

~

His Heart (Sebastian and Brooke)

A poignant and emotionally intense story about grief, loss, and the transcendent power of love. Stand-alone.

~

The Always Series

Smoking hot, dirty talking bad boys with some angsty intensity. Can be read as stand-alones.

Always Have (Braxton and Kylie)

Always Will (Selene and Ronan)

Always Ever After (Braxton and Kylie)

~

The Jetty Beach Series

Sexy small-town romance series with swoony heroes, romantic HEAs, and lots of big feels. Can be read as stand-alones.

Behind His Eyes (Ryan and Nicole)

One Crazy Week (Melissa and Jackson)

Messy Perfect Love (Cody and Clover)

ABOUT THE AUTHOR

Claire Kingsley is a #1 Amazon bestselling author of sexy, heartfelt contemporary romance and romantic comedies. She writes sassy, quirky heroines, swoony heroes who love big, romantic happily ever afters, and all the big feels.

She can't imagine life without coffee, great books, and all the crazy characters who live in her imagination. She lives in the inland Pacific Northwest with her three kids.

www.clairekingsleybooks.com

Printed in Great Britain
by Amazon